Once Upon An Altar

by

Rhonda Hanson

Once Upon An Altar

by
Rhonda Hanson

ISBN 978-0-9703817-7-4

Copyright 2024

by

Grace Under Pressure Publishing
P.O. Box 337
Bell Buckle, TN 37020

graceunderpressure.com

Dedication

"Once Upon An Altar" is dedicated to my wonderful readers who so enthusiastically embraced "The Master Of Hawthorn Manor" and "Buying The Farm." You allowed me to deviate from the continuing lives of my characters that spanned across the Father Series, and the fanciful antics of my children's book "The Adventures Of Pahwoo And Her Friends", and explore completely new experiences and characters.

Your encouragement always makes me think I have one more story in me, and I thank you for that.

Rhonda Hanson

Once Upon An Altar

Grant Sellars stopped just inside his front door and let his gym bag and towel land at his feet, before reaching back out to grab the mail and nod at Lucy Wallace. She had called something out to him from across the street and he hadn't quite heard her, but he'd learned over the years to just smile and nod at Lucy Wallace and go on about his business. It was either that, or become attached to the losing end of a long and confusing narrative that was certain to qualify as all-out gossip.

He quickly stepped back inside and closed the door, silently congratulating himself for dodging that bullet and smiling with smug, but forgivable satisfaction.

He glanced over at the ringing parsonage phone with a sour expression and decided to just let whatever it was go to voicemail. He was in dire need of a shower after coming home straight from the gym, and that impromptu game of racquetball with Fred Buckley hadn't exactly made him smell like flowers.

Grant pitched the unopened mail onto his kitchen table and stopped by the fridge to uncap a bottle of water and down the entire thing before choosing to think about dinner after he cleaned up. He headed back to his room and wasted no time escaping into his shower and hiding out there until he ran out of hot water.

He grimaced over the tightness in his shoulder as he dried himself off and pulled on some pajama bottoms, snugging the drawstring around his waist.

"I thought I'd at least not be stiff until tomorrow morning," he muttered, with a frown. "I'm not even close to forty, for crying out loud."

1

The not even close to forty pastor of Grace Chapel padded barefoot back into the kitchen and revisited the fridge, considering whether the burrito he'd brought home earlier in the week had reached it's "go bad" date. He decided not to risk it and grabbed a carton of eggs instead, and was soon slow-frying them and waiting for a couple of English muffins to pop up out of the toaster.

Grant personally liked breakfast any time of the day but he grinned to himself, as he imagined the shock and dismay the ladies in his congregation would express if they knew that their poor, single, helpless pastor was eating eggs for dinner.

Fred had tried to insist that he join him and his fiancée Katie for dinner, but Grant reminded his buddy that Katie was coming over to cook for him because she wanted Fred's undivided attention to discuss wedding plans and, as happy as Grant was for his friend, he wanted nothing to do with weddings, other than reluctantly officiating at them, which he was often called upon to do in their small community. Weddings, funerals, and baby dedications... always expected to be administered by local clergy in any town and at any time. Apparently, those three functions ranked high in his chosen profession, although he wasn't necessarily keen to perform them.

Pastor Sellars took a moment to build little breakfast sandwiches with his eggs and English muffins, and grab some orange juice from the fridge before settling down to sort through the mail with his usual lack of enthusiasm.

Most of it consisted of advertising for what he called "church chaff" and while he knew he'd end up throwing it all in the trash, he still liked to amuse himself by flipping the pages and checking out the latest in reverend robes, biodegradable communion cups and what he referred to as "choke" collars.

Grant ran his hand through his dark blonde curls and allowed a sarcastic smirk to rest on his face as he encountered the many impressive pulpit stoles.

"Rich brocade, embroidered with golden thread," he read aloud, before laughing quietly to himself.

"And only fifteen hundred smackers. I'm sure I can get the elders to spring for that, no problem!"

He continued to separate the mail into junk, shred, and desk categories before getting up to toss the bulk of it, which was pretty much litter, but not before glancing down again at the church apparel magazine and shaking his head.

"Just jeans for me, I guess." He sighed dramatically. "My poor flock would be mortified if they could see how elite and successful ministers are fashionably attired, compared to their denim-clad, bearded, untidy pastor. I'd better not let that happen," he decided, shoving the images of rich brocade and golden threads into the kitchen trashcan.

It occurred to Grant to wonder if the earlier caller had left a voicemail. He took a leftover egg sandwich into his living room to crash with a bounce on the couch and grab the phone to check.

He narrowed his dark green eyes and hit the key to rewind, listening more closely this time.

Why was old Pastor James Morgan calling him? Grant was aware that the man hadn't been actively involved in the ministry for many years, and he must be upwards of seventy.

He only knew the retired pastor enough to recognize and greet him whenever their paths would cross, and he always found him to be a pleasant enough man, but the two of them had hardly formed a bond simply because they were both ministers.

He jotted down the number and hung up, stretching out his tall frame on the couch and dedicating himself to finishing his sandwich before returning the call. He hated to eat and talk at the same time and right now, eating was his priority.

Katie Allen aimed an impatient sigh at her fiancé and took the fabric swatches away from him, once she saw that his eyes had glazed over and he had begun to zone out.

"If you don't have any strong feelings about bridesmaids dresses, why don't I just pick the material, myself?" she asked.

Fred Buckley grinned over at her with a grateful expression. "If you want them to look halfway decent, that would probably be best."

He paused and thought about it. "Unless you *don't* want them to look halfway decent. When Abby got married, she made sure that none of her bridesmaids looked too good. She said no bride in her right mind would allow other women to outshine her, on her big day."

"Your sister was probably just messing with you," his girlfriend commented, flipping through the swatches absently. "She's not petty, Fred."

"You didn't grow up with her," he replied. "She was Princess Petty, if you must know."

"Stop," Katie laughed, giving him a light pop on the arm. "I might just tell her what you said."

"I'm not scared of her," he retorted, lifting a fist and trying to look menacing. "I can take her, any day!"

Katie laughed again and applied herself to inspecting fabric samples with the unparalled patience that only prospective brides can manage, before regarding her fiancé knowingly.

"I think you've been letting Grant Sellars coach you on how to be hostile toward women, but you better not try that on me, sweetie. I know how to nip that in the bud."

Fred leaned his head back on the couch and lifted his feet to rest them on the coffee table. "Grant's not hostile to women. He just doesn't go out of his way to be friendly to any of them. That's probably just as well, since he's a minister."

"Why should being a minister make him need to avoid being friendly to women?" Katie demanded, looking at him with a little frown. "Ministers aren't priests, you know."

"I think he got burned by a woman a long time ago, and he's decided to not touch that hot iron again," Fred speculated.

"What happened?"

He shrugged.

4

"I never asked him, but he made some comment once when I told him that I thought Rachel Doyle was interested in him. I can't remember exactly what he said, but it was pretty clear that he wasn't interested in dating. I think it was something along the lines of never giving another woman a clean shot to finish him off, next time. I took finishing him off and next time to mean that he had been pretty much riddled by someone. Anyway, it was a flat no for Rachel Doyle, or any other potential date I suggested."

Katie thought about it. "I believe Rachel Doyle ended up marrying that chef guy. Her name's not Doyle now, but I can't remember what it changed to. I think they moved to Denver, or somewhere out west."

Fred nodded, as he began to remember. "Grant did their wedding. I guess that's about as involved as he's willing to get with anything remotely related to marriage."

He watched Katie pause her chore to think about that, before surprising her and reaching down to tap a swatch.

"What about this?"

She gave him a deadpan look. "When we move into our new house and get ready to decorate, it'll make lovely drapes."

"Scarlett O'Hara wore drapes, and she was supposedly gorgeous enough to flag Rhett Butler's attention," Fred pointed out, fairly accurately.

Katie giggled at that. "If we find ourselves destitute and unable to afford any material, then I'll consider making my bridesmaids wear drapes. That way, they'll all quit and we can just elope."

"Fine by me!" he declared.

"Typical male response."

Katie put the fabric swatches to one side and leaned back to rest her head against Fred's, propping her feet up next to his.

"If men ruled the world, there would never be another wedding. All the grooms would just flag down a justice of the peace, say whatever they had to, choke down a hotdog to celebrate, and spend their wedding funds on a new bass boat."

5

"Yes!" He readied himself for a high five that she wasn't planning on giving him. "Come on, think about it! A new bass boat is nothing to sneer at."

"I'm sneering. Look at this face."

Fred studied Katie's pretty face with a little smile.

"Okay, you win. But you don't play fair."

She reached a finger to touch the slight cleft in his chin. "Playing fair is overrated."

"You'd better not let Pastor Sellars hear you say that," he warned, capturing her finger and the rest of her hand. "You might end up getting a sermon aimed at you."

"Grant doesn't do stuff like that," she said, wrinkling her brow. "But I've heard of some ministers who do. That's why my brother doesn't go to church, anymore. The pastor where he was going set out to publicly use him as an example in one of his loud 'thou shalt not' sermons. He decided that particular preacher was a little too vindictive for his tastes, not to mention high strung. He's pretty much done with church."

"We've got a good one," Fred informed her. "Grant's about as easygoing and good-natured as they come."

"Unless it involves a woman?"

"No, he still manages to be congenial," he replied. "But congeniality is as far as he's willing to go." Fred sighed and thought about it. "I actually tried to talk him into just being willing to date, but he shot me down like a skeet disc."

"I wonder why?" Katie mused. "I mean, regardless of what some woman may or may not have done to him, to just be done with all women, period, seems like an overreaction."

"Kinda like your brother," Fred pointed out, then muttered "Ow" when she frogged his arm. "I'm just saying, one pastor offended him and he bailed on church, altogether."

"I know," she sighed. "But he's my brother, so I have to take up for him."

Fred grinned at that, and leaned over to drop a kiss on her cheek. "I don't suppose there's any chance of leaving me out of the flower selection as well, is there?"

6

She fixed him with a pointed look. "What *are* you willing to be involved in, if I take on making things pretty?"

He thought about it. "Cake tasting."

"I might have known," his bride-to-be said dryly. "So, basically, you don't mind food-related decisions, but you'd like a pass on the aesthetics."

"Yes, please." He tried to look charming, when he admitted this, and Katie bought into it, with a condition.

"Only if you convince Grant to bring a plus one to the wedding. I want even seating at all the tables."

"But he's the minister," Fred argued, already sensing he was about to lose this round. "Ministers aren't expected to bring a plus one."

"He is, at *our* wedding," she informed him. "You take care of that, and you can be excused from picking out china patterns and invitations and save your opinions for things that are edible."

Fred exhaled and gave in, as she knew he would.

"Fine. But if Grant winds up bringing old Mrs. Fowler or even older Irving Lancaster, that counts as a plus one."

She shook her head slowly and held up the fabric swatches. "No deal."

"Alright! I'll see if I can talk him into it, but I can't very well force him."

"Tell him what's at stake. He'll feel sorry for you, if he's like most men." She took in her fiancé's cute scowl and raised herself up to convince him to kiss her.

He was glad to oblige her, although he somehow felt that chiffon versus organdy, and roses, as opposed to lilies, would be making a comeback to his list of responsibilities. Grant Sellars was the most stubborn friend he had, and would not easily be convinced to be seen in public in the company of a date, regardless of how platonic it might be.

7

The stubborn Grant Sellars hung up the phone and silently chided himself for calling Pastor Morgan back, but of course, he had to do it.

"That's me, old dependable Pastor Sellars," he muttered to himself, crossing his arms and eyeing the phone with dark resentment. "Weddings, funerals, and baby dedications; the big three, and wouldn't you just know that this would have to be a funeral, and for a total stranger?"

Grant sat mulling over his conversation with the elderly Pastor Morgan and of course, felt a stab of conviction over his attitude, and a decent amount of sympathy for the old man.

He'd been discharged from the hospital only the day before, after having undergone hip replacement surgery, and had just received a call from a family he'd known years ago, when he was still actively pastoring, asking him to officiate at the funeral for their son.

The parents hadn't been members of Pastor Morgan's congregation, but had been well known in the community and wanted their son laid to rest in the local cemetery, where they had long ago purchased plots.

The aged pastor asked if he might be allowed to send a replacement on his behalf, and was able to tell Grant that they didn't seem to mind at all, since there was no sentimental relationship between them and the retired minister. They simply wanted to ensure that their son had a dignified service and wanted clergy to oversee everything, rather than a representative from the funeral home.

Grant drew a hand across his beard stubble and allowed himself to mutely observe that having a minister at the helm, was most likely an attempt to put a spiritual spin on things, then instantly reproved his baseless accusation, since he didn't know anything about the deceased's parents. He might have been pastoring in this community for a number of years, but he wasn't originally from here and for all he knew, the family might turn out to be decent people.

He allowed a certain amount of compassion for any parent that outlived a child and told himself that if he would just get out of his own way, God might actually use him to share the gospel at the service, instead of simply eulogizing a man he had never met.

He began to feel better about agreeing to conduct the service and Pastor Morgan had thanked him profusely, before asking him how his church was faring and if he liked their little community. Of course, he always asked the young Pastor Sellars these same questions at all their chance meetings, but Grant knew he was simply trying to extend a gesture of friendly interest and gave him the same answers he'd given before.

He smiled now and admitted to himself that he actually liked the old man, which is why, as the current local pastor, Grant made an effort to be sure he wasn't trying to heal up all alone and that he had someone taking care of him. He'd even offered to have some of the ladies from the church bring meals to him and although Pastor Morgan declined, Grant could tell that the idea appealed to him and overruled his faint objections by promising him that he wouldn't have to worry about meals, while he was recovering.

Grant pulled himself up off the couch and made his way to his office to open up the church directory and see what he could do about lining up some food for the old clergyman which, as he wryly pointed out to himself, was considered as hospitality, which tied for fourth in the lineup of high ranking functions of his job description.

The other contender was visiting the sick. He had failed Pastor Morgan in that regard but since he was not a member of his flock, Grant simply opted for benevolence after the fact. He allowed a humorous grin to light up his handsome face as he facetiously wondered if this might cause the elders to award him a fifteen hundred dollar pulpit stole with rich brocade fabric and embroidered gold threads.

9

Chapter Two

Pastor Sellars chose to stop by and visit the recovering Pastor Morgan at a time when he knew home health workers were scheduled to be there, supposing that the old minister wouldn't be able to answer the door, himself.

The funeral for the man Pastor Morgan had called him about was scheduled later in the afternoon, but Grant realized that he knew absolutely nothing about either the deceased or his family, and felt it might help him do justice to the service, if he had a bit more information.

He was glad to learn that the woman who answered the door was the minister's sister and had arrived that morning to stay with him for a few weeks, while he recuperated. The widow introduced herself as Mrs. Ellen Abbott and led the young pastor back to her brother's room.

James Morgan was delighted to see him, so much so that Grant felt a sting of remorse as he decided that the man must normally lead a very lonely and quiet life. He did a quick, silent appraisal of the modest home's furnishings and saw nothing that indicated that a woman had ever had a hand in its sparse decoration. Grant had always assumed that old Pastor Morgan was a bachelor, and it seemed as if he'd been correct.

He took the chair that Mrs. Abbott had indicated and returned the smile the pastor gave him. "I hope it's okay to just drop by like this, Pastor Morgan. I'd thought you had told me that home health was supposed to be here, and I didn't want to interrupt, but I figured they could answer the door for you."

"No, when they called and found out Ellen was here with me, they asked if they could send someone out later this evening, so you're not interrupting a thing!"

11

He raised a thin, shaky hand and gestured toward what must have been the direction of the kitchen. "One of your very nice members came by this morning and brought something for our lunch later, and a nice cake. That sure was thoughtful of you to see to that."

Mrs. Abbott smiled and nodded. "I'm afraid James will tell you that I'm not much to brag about in the kitchen, so he would have been in bad shape if he had to rely on me to cook for him. It was a relief to see that nice Mrs. Payne at the door with a hot meal. Such a friendly lady!"

"Mrs. Payne loves to cook, and she was very enthusiastic about making something and bringing it over. She used to cook for a living and in fact, she owned a catering business, but she's retired now. She says she misses it."

Grant offered this bit of Mrs. Payne's biography as a means of reassuring both of them that not only was it no trouble for her to bring food, but that she actually enjoyed doing it, and he could see the glad look the pastor and his sister exchanged.

"Well, I may not be much of a cook, but I do know my way around a coffeepot, Pastor Sellars. I was just about to brew up a fresh pot."

Mrs. Abbott determined that their guest drank his coffee black, and headed off in the direction her brother had pointed toward, leaving the two men to visit.

Grant decided to get to the point of his mission, since the patient was looking a little tired.

"Pastor Morgan, would you mind very much if I ask you to tell me a bit about the family who wanted a minister for their son's funeral? I'm afraid I don't even know the name."

He nodded apologetically. "I thought about that after we talked, Pastor Sellars."

"Would you also be willing to just call me Grant?" he suggested with a grin. "That way, I'll know for sure you mean me. After several years in the ministry, I still don't recognize that people are talking about me, when they say pastor. I'm not sure I ever will."

"I know how you feel, and I'm happy to call you Grant. I almost phoned you back after we talked, when I realized that I hadn't told you anything about them, but then Ellen called to tell me that she was arriving this morning and I'm afraid I dropped off to sleep, after that."

"Oh, I understand completely. But it dawned on me this morning that I don't even know who to ask for, once I arrive at the funeral home. That's not good."

Grant grinned at the old minister's reaction to that, when he slapped his hand on the covers and broke into a chuckle.

"No, that's not good at all," he acknowledged, rubbing his eyes and smiling. "Well, the family name is Cullen. They lived here until probably fifteen years ago, maybe more. They were a well-to-do family, and I expect they still are, but they never were what you'd call church people.

"They were more of the country club set, and spent their Sundays out on the golf course, or riding their horses, but they were rarely inside a church, unless it was Christmas or Easter."

"Chreasters," Grant commented, with a nod.

"That's right, Chreasters," old Pastor Morgan agreed, with a little laugh. "That's what my professors at seminary always called the 'Christmas and Easter only' people, who slipped in and sat on the back row, and then took off like a shot as soon as they heard the benediction. Chreasters."

Grant sat smiling at the memory of his own professors using that term. "So, should I not hold out much hope for them being believers, then?"

"Well, I hate to say that, because with God, anything is possible, but it wasn't the impression I got, over the phone. Mr. William Cullen was just as blunt and arrogant as he ever was, so if he *is* a believer, it's probably only in himself."

Grant blew out a breath and took another deep one in.

"I bet I can guess what's troubling you," Pastor Morgan told him, with a knowing look. "I wish I could tell you that the son was a Christian, but from all indications, I don't think he was. It's a hard thing to preach a funeral if the deceased was not a believer.

13

"For one thing, the family typically expects the minister to just preach their loved one right on into Heaven, as if such a thing was possible and if you refuse to sugar coat things, they get downright indignant."

Grant nodded, having found himself in exactly that situation before, and not looking forward to being in it again.

"I've managed to upset a few family members for just that very reason," he admitted to the old minister. "But, at the end of the day, I'm not doing anyone any favors by simply trying to make them feel good about themselves."

"No, you sure are not," Pastor Morgan assured him.

"Will it just be the two parents, then?" Grant wondered. "Or do they have relatives living here that will attend?"

"I haven't seen any of that bunch around here in years," the pastor remarked. "But the father did say that his son was married, so I expect his widow will be there."

Grant looked up as Ellen Abbott came through the door with two cups of coffee, and received his with a word of thanks.

She sat a small lap tray up for her brother, and placed his coffee on it, giving his white hair a light ruffle, and heading off again to sit and have her own coffee.

He smiled after her and Grant was almost able to imagine the two of them as kids for a brief moment, from that simple interaction.

"She can't be very old."

Grant looked up with a confused expression, as he heard Pastor Morgan's remark.

"The widow, I mean," he explained, bringing the young minister back to their previous conversation. "I remember that son of theirs from when they lived here before and he was just a young fella. Barry was his name, although why I should remember that, I can't tell you. But it was Barry. I expect that at the time of his passing, he wasn't any older than you are, Grant, so I would think that his widow is a young woman."

He nodded, draining his coffee cup and rising from his chair, silently telling himself that he might as well get on with it.

"Are you going dressed like that?"

Grant saw a light of teasing in the old pastor's eyes.

"Don't get me wrong, I'm fine with you wearing blue jeans, and I almost wish you would. I'd love to be a fly on the wall, when William Cullen sees you show up at his son's funeral in anything other than a three-piece suit."

Pastor Morgan laughed at Grant's sour expression.

"If it were left up to me, I'd just stop by there on my way to the gym in my sweats," he informed Pastor Morgan, causing him to laugh again.

"But I suppose I'll at least wear some dress pants and a white shirt. I'll bring a jacket in the car, in case I'm asked to put one on, but I absolutely draw the line at wearing a tie."

"So you're not the collar-wearing variety of minister, then?" Pastor Morgan asked, enjoying the young preacher's fresh, casual demeanor.

"Choke collars?"

Again, the old pastor laughed and Grant grinned at him.

"I don't own a single one," he declared. "Although, there are some pretty tempting pulpit stoles on the market."

"I see you get the same quality junk mail that I do," Pastor Morgan observed, causing Grant to give way to an eruption of laughter that the old pastor's sister could hear, all the way out in the kitchen.

Grant shut the door of his truck and took a few strides across the parking lot before he rolled his eyes, and came back to retrieve the suit jacket from its hanger and slip it on with a decidedly bad attitude. He figured he'd probably be questioned about it by the blunt and arrogant William Cullen if he tried to go without it, and just wanted to avoid any unnecessary conflict, if he could.

He stepped inside the front entrance of the funeral home and was pleasantly greeted by the director, who knew the young minister well.

"Oh, it's you, Pastor Sellars," he declared with a smile and a handshake. "I didn't see your name on any programs. Are you overseeing one of our services, today?"

"Hello, Mark. I'm stepping in for Pastor Morgan," Grant explained. "I believe it's for the Cullen family."

"Oh, yes, the Cullen family," Mark Wynn repeated, nodding solemnly. "Yes, very sad, the whole thing."

Grant waited with a sense that more was coming and Mr. Wynn didn't disappoint him.

"Such a tragic way to die, and especially when he was so young! The woman who was with him is still in the hospital."

The man rubbed his hands together, as he said this, and Grant couldn't resist thinking that he was relishing the possibility of another funeral, but he quickly pushed that cynical thought to the back of his mind to be considered later, when he was in the privacy of his own home and would be free to laugh out loud.

For now, he simply drew his brows and regarded Mark Wynn with confusion. "I was under the impression that the widow would be present at the service today. Pastor Morgan must not have understood, if she's still in the hospital."

"Oh no, not his wife," the funeral director corrected, looking around before continuing in a confidential manner. "He was driving with another woman in his car and got in the wrong lane and ended up being hit by a dump truck. You know, Grant, those single frame dump trucks are bound to do a lot of damage. No plastic bumpers on those!"

Grant couldn't resist grinning at Mark Wynn's glowing endorsement of the rigid body vehicle.

"Is the woman in a local facility?" he asked and Mark shook his head. "All this happened out of state. But the Cullens had their son's body brought back here. They bought up several plots at Haven of Rest years ago, and they still have their large home here, although no one besides the caretakers have lived there for years. There's talk of them remaining here after the service. One hears things," he added, with a wink and a nod.

"I suppose I barely arrived in time," Grant apologized. "I would imagine the man's father is pacing back and forth."

16

"It's just through here," the director informed him, leading the way in his brisk, official manner, and indicating the room with an outstretched hand before hurrying back to the lobby to greet anyone else who might arrive.

Grant stood just outside the large double doors, and assessed the situation as well as he could, without actually entering. Apparently, recorded music was already playing softly and a few small clusters of individuals stood speaking in muted tones and looking around to determine who else was there. Grant couldn't find one face that he recognized.

He was finally able to signal the attention of a man who had glanced his way and then approached. Grant quietly introduced himself and asked if he would acquaint him with Mr. William Cullen. The man immediately looked relieved and led him over to a couple who seemed to be more interested in their phones than in their son's service.

"This is Pastor Sellars." Once William Cullen looked over at the minister, the man took himself away without further comment and rejoined his group.

"We had just about given up on you, young man!" the father of the deceased informed him gruffly.

If he was expecting an apology or an explanation from the minister, he was disappointed. Grant merely stood looking at him impassively.

"Louise, he's finally here," the man barked at his wife. She put her phone away and looked up at the pastor with surprised delight and carnal approval, slowly moving toward him as if she were stalking him.

Grant immediately decided he didn't like her any better than he did her husband, and turned his back on her, to address him directly.

"Do you have an order of service you prefer, or any special remarks to be made by yourself, or family or friends?"

"It was all I could do to get anyone to show up, let alone say a kind word about my son," his father said, loudly enough for all of them to hear.

17

"But you can bet they'll all belly up to the bar at the repast, or whatever that fool thing is called that Louise has brought in caterers for."

"Mr. Cullen, other than the eulogy and the brief sermon, is there anything else you had in mind for the service, itself? Will there be a singer, or a special song played at some point? Does your son's wife wish for anything special?"

"She probably wishes for him to be in Hell," he snapped, shooting a glance over in the direction of a dark haired, young woman who had apparently elected to sit over on the far side of the room alone. "I doubt seriously if she cares about anything, except getting this over with. Why don't you go ask her, yourself? We start in five minutes!"

If William Cullen added that last bit in the manner of a threat, Grant simply ignored it as he decided to approach the widow of the deceased to ask her if any of the details of her late husband's service mattered to her.

She didn't look up when he stopped in front of her and Grant quietly cleared his throat and attempted to get her attention.

"Excuse me, Mrs. Cullen? I'm Pastor Sellars and I'll be officiating at your husband's service today."

He heard her draw in a sharp breath. She moved as if she were about to lift her head and look up at him, but she seemed to be dreading it. A look of alarm shadowed her face and creased her brow with anxiety.

When she finally did raise her beautiful but pale face to look at him with soft brown eyes that were filled with remorse and dismay, Grant grabbed at his chest and took a step back, staring at her as if he were seeing a ghost.

18

Chapter Three

"*What's* eatin' you, Grant?"

Fred Buckley moved out from behind the freestanding punching bag and came around in front of it, staring at his friend with confusion. "Are you trying to take me out?"

Grant said nothing but stood waiting impatiently for Fred to either move out of the way, or get hit.

"You're punching like a crazy man," Fred said testily.

Again, Grant said nothing, but turned to pace back and forth, glaring down at the gym floor and causing his best friend to wonder who or what had set him off.

He watched him for a long moment, before coming toward him cautiously.

"You know it's just a matter of time before you tell me," he pointed out quietly.

Grant stopped pacing but looked off to one side of the gym at nothing, his eyes bright with emotion. "Drop it!"

"Or what? You're gonna punch me?"

Fred wasn't entirely sure that he wouldn't, but stood his ground in order to let him know that he was willing to risk it.

"Come on, buddy, beating a punching bag to death won't fix whatever's going on with you. Maybe you just need to talk about it. Sometimes, just hearing yourself say things can help."

"Leave me alone, Fred!"

Fred stood looking at his friend for a long, awkward moment before his own temper started to flare.

"You wanna be left alone? Fine! You got it, Preacher!"

He stormed off toward the lockers, and after Grant moved over to the bank of windows, he could see him speeding away in his pickup.

19

He stayed at the windows for a while, unable to dial back down as quickly as he was normally able to. He realized he was breathing hard and that his pulse was racing.

He leaned his head against the window and silently asked God to forgive him for not even trying to get past his anger after seeing Hazel's face. He had been devoted to stoking its heat and told himself that he deserved to be angry and that no one was going to take that away from him. He had so given himself over to his outrage, that he hadn't even taken the time to process the moment that triggered it.

"I'm not okay, God," he whispered, staring out at the parking lot and blinking back hot tears. "I'm not okay."

There was no reply, other than the sensation of a compassionate hand resting on him, but it served to slow his breathing and bring his heart rate into a more normal range.

After a few moments of simply resting against the window with his eyes closed, he straightened up and headed off to get his things and call it a workout.

When Grant came through the parsonage door, he knew there'd be unchecked voicemails on his phone, particularly from an angry William Cullen who was incensed that the young upstart of a preacher had dared to imply that his son wasn't in Heaven and had further insulted his family by informing them that they were just as likely to spend eternity in Hell, unless they repented of their sins.

When Grant had finished his terse remarks, he turned on his heels and simply walked out of the chapel, leaving the funeral home staff to have to deal with the interment portion of the service. He'd had enough.

Grant stood looking down at the phone, wondering if anyone else had left any messages but headed to take a shower, deciding that he didn't want to know.

He was just as surprised as old Pastor Morgan when he showed up at his house later. He wasn't sure why he'd come, but he didn't want to sit home listening to the phone ring.

When he got into his vehicle, he seemed to drive to the minister's residence automatically. He sat out in the driveway for a while before finally coming to knock on the door.

Mrs. Abbott showed him into her brother's room and discreetly left them alone, already having some idea of why the young man had come, after her brother's account of the angry phone call he'd received from William Cullen.

Pastor Morgan smiled kindly at the young minister and motioned toward a chair.

"Come sit down, Grant! It's good to see you."

"Are you sure about that?" he asked, before he could stop himself and the old man quietly laughed.

"Absolutely!" He lay looking at Grant with a bit of humor in his eyes. "I'm glad you're here, so I can hear *your* description of what it was that William Cullen said hit the fan."

Grant was still looking down at the floor, but he grinned at that, in spite of himself, visibly relieved that Pastor Morgan wasn't upset with him.

"Grant, what you said was the truth. I admit, you might have coated that pill with a little sugar, instead of shoving it down their throats sideways, but still... true is true."

"How do you know what I said?" he asked quietly.

"Because William Cullen thought it was bad enough just as you said it, and didn't feel the need to embellish it. He expected me to be as upset as he was, but every bit of it rang true. He was calling to demand an apology and I did apologize for being unable to conduct the service myself, but not for sending you. He hung up disgusted with the both of us."

Pastor Morgan chuckled to himself, seeming pleased to be included with Grant as burrs under William Cullen's saddle.

"He did make one claim that I wanted to clear up with you, though," the old minister remarked. "He said that when you stepped up to the podium, you were already angry, and that you more or less pronounced judgment on all of them and then just walked out and left them sitting." He watched Grant's face carefully. "Is that accurate?"

Grant let out a loud sigh and nodded. "I'm afraid it is."

Pastor Morgan seemed mildly surprised. Grant Sellars had always been regarded by the locals as a pleasant, patient, and kind man of God and what William Cullen claimed had seem farfetched and exaggerated.

"I didn't plan on saying any of that, Pastor Morgan," he said remorsefully. "It just came rushing out of me. The truth is that I did step up to the podium already angry, so I can't accuse the man of lying, regardless of how personally revolting I decided he was. He told you the truth."

"Were you angry because of how disagreeable you found him to be, Grant?"

He shook his head. "No, I've had to get along with obnoxious individuals before. That wasn't it."

Pastor Morgan waited a long moment, wondering if Grant was going to offer anything more, but he seemed content to just sit there, staring at the floor.

"Son, if you need someone to listen, that's about all I can do these days, but I'm pretty good at it."

Grant looked up at him, visibly fighting back strong emotions. The offer the pastor was making him was more than generous, particularly since Grant was supposed to have been representing him by agreeing to conduct the funeral for Barry Cullen in his place, and he did so by being rude and offensive.

"I'm sorry, Pastor Morgan," he offered quietly. "Whether what I said was true or not, it wasn't telling the truth in love. It was telling the truth in anger, but not even a righteous anger. It was completely selfish."

Pastor Morgan waited in patient silence and let him work through what he wanted to say.

"I was dealing with things fairly well," he continued, after a moment. "I admit, I wanted to just get it over with and get out of Dodge, especially when William Cullen's wife started acting like a cross between Potiphar's wife and Mae West."

He paused with a smile, when the old man laughed.

"I really can't say that I was particularly angry at anyone, until I asked Cullen if his son's widow had any preferences about the service and he told me to go ask her, myself."

"I saw her sitting away from everyone else, alone, and I walked over and introduced myself. When she looked up at me, that's when it all ended up hitting the fan."

Pastor Morgan drew his brows in confusion. "Why was she able to trigger anger in you, just by looking at you, Grant?"

"Because it wasn't a new anger," he responded, in a dull, tired voice. "It was a very old anger. I just didn't realize it was still there until it leaped up inside me, alive and well."

He could tell that he was confusing the minister even more and drew in a cleansing breath.

"Her name is Hazel Todd. Hazel Cullen now, I guess. We were engaged to be married. I haven't seen her or spoken to her in years, and I never felt the need to take any walks down memory lane. I just let her die, for lack of a better expression."

Pastor Morgan was more than a little surprised to learn how small the world had truly become. Grant Sellars wasn't from this small southern community and neither was the widow of Barry Cullen, yet here they both were, and while he couldn't speculate about the woman, it was apparent that time had done nothing to heal the young preacher.

"I can only guess that things must have gotten a little heated when the two of you broke off your engagement," the pastor speculated.

Grant flexed the muscles in his jaw, in an attempt to stop a sharp retort from escaping. His best friend Fred might be able to handle one of Grant's sarcastic outbursts, but the aged and very kind Pastor Morgan was going to be spared that sort of recklessness, if Grant could manage it.

When he finally did respond, his words were measured and without emotion.

"Perhaps, if we'd actually broken off our engagement, I might not have become so angry when I saw her again."

Pastor Morgan glanced over quickly at him, but held back any comment, simply waiting.

"I won't drag all this out, Pastor Morgan," Grant said with a tired sigh.

"I'll just cut to the chase and tell you that on the day of our wedding, I was there in plenty of time, dressed to the nines and ready to start our future.

"When the music began to play and no bride came down the aisle, it finally dawned on me that no bride was coming. She never bothered to show up."

The old preacher drew in his breath and felt an overwhelming amount of compassion for Pastor Sellars.

"You never heard from her again?" he finally asked in a voice that revealed his sadness for the young man.

"She actually invested in a stamp and mailed a letter to me. By then, she was long gone. I almost burned it without reading it but for whatever reason, I did read it.

"Apparently, the idea of being married to not only a minister but a pastor wasn't something she could handle. I'd told her well in advance of our wedding that I was clear about the calling on my life, and you would have thought she might have used the time between my sharing that with her and our actual wedding day to voice any objections or misgivings, but no. She just bailed on our wedding and left town."

"Grant, did she at least try to explain her reasons?"

He stared down at his hands, and wrestled with another swell of bitterness, but managed to get past it. "The long and short of it was that she had always longed to leave Mississippi to live in a big city and become an actress. I had no idea she was serious enough about it to just up and leave me, because she never really talked about it, but that was her excuse.

"I guess she might have had at least some success. Before I left to move to this county, her mother felt the need to inform me that she was living in New York and was an understudy for the lead in some play which, I guess, explains why she never returned."

He shrugged and Pastor Morgan peered over at him with a thoughtful air.

"That must be how she met Barry Cullen, then," he said quietly. He noted Grant's clueless expression and continued.

"That was something the Cullens always bragged about, that their son was an actor and was always appearing in some play or show. Of course, I always took everything the Cullens said with a grain of salt, but I suppose there might have been some level of accomplishment. It seems that my sister has actually heard of him, but then she keeps up with that sort of thing and she always has.

"According to Ellen, Barry Cullen was trying to maintain the stereotypical lifestyle of a celebrity and was something of a womanizer and an alcoholic. She reads those types of magazines, and visits those social pages on the computer.

"She tells me that the Cullen boy was riding through one of those curvy canyon roads in California with a lady companion, obviously not his wife, when his car veered into another vehicle's path and got knocked off the steep edge. Ellen said that woman has still not been identified, and that she was life-flighted."

Pastor Morgan gave Grant a remorseful grin. "And my telling you all of that makes me an old gossip, which I never thought I'd become. I don't know how much of it is accurate, Grant, but since your Hazel was involved in acting, as Barry Cullen was, and the two of them were married, there must be some strains of truth in it."

"She's not my Hazel." Grant was quick to correct him. "But I will say that your sister's account of how Cullen's son died seems to dovetail with Mark Wynn's version. He also said something about a woman who was with him and, as you pointed out, it was obviously not his wife."

The two men sat in silence for a moment, each following his own thoughts before Grant began to rise out of his chair.

"I really just wanted to apologize, Pastor Morgan, because I should have represented you much better than I did. For that, I'm truly sorry."

He waved it away and smiled at him. "I just wish I'd been there to see it," he confided, with a little laugh. "It's about time someone shot straight with William Cullen and it sounds like you hit the mark."

"I shouldn't have used buckshot, though," Grant observed, running a hand through his hair and grimacing. "I'm afraid that everyone got hit by the spray. That wasn't fair."

"I wouldn't beat myself up too badly over it, Grant," Pastor Morgan said kindly. "It was still truth, and we'll just pray that God will use it, somehow."

Grant wasn't willing to let himself off that easily, but he didn't belabor the point. "Thank you for the visit, Pastor, and for the ear. If nothing else, I think I'm much less ready to burst into flames, so that's at least something."

The minister laughed again. "Yes, it is!"

Grant paused by the door and looked back at him with a sheepish grin.

"I guess I'd better move on to the next stop on my apology tour. Maybe the more I do it, the better I'll get at it."

He gave Pastor Morgan a little wave and headed off to see if Fred was home and if so, if he'd even let him come in.

Louise Cullen strolled into her daughter-in-law's room without bothering to knock, something she was known for.

She flung herself into the nearest chair as dramatically as any director could hope for, being something of an actress herself, and rolled her eyes.

"I'm so sick of listening to William go on and on about that tiresome funeral," she complained, leaning her bleached head against the padded upholstery and resting the back of her hand on her forehead.

"And to make matters worse, the caretakers knew we were arriving, but do you think they thought to stock our bar? Oh, no! Not so much as a bottle of wine! If I have to listen to William keep bellowing at the top of his lungs about that pastor, I at least need something strong to wash it all down with!"

She let out a sigh of suffering before looking over at Hazel curiously. "What did you say to that minister, to get him so bent out of shape, anyway?"

26

Hazel looked up at her with genuine bewilderment. She hadn't said one word to Grant. All they did was painfully stare at each other and she quickly dropped her head down. When she dared to look back up, he had gone straight up to the podium and began to take his anger out on everyone there.

She had witnessed this in shock, certain that this was not the Grant Sellars she had known, and when he ended his sermon with, "Well, there it is! Deal with it!" and strolled out of the room, she could do nothing but sit frozen in disbelief.

She now became aware that her mother-in-law was waiting impatiently for an answer and shook her head.

"I never said one word to him," she denied honestly.

Louise raised her brows and began to inspect her nails in a bored fashion.

"Well, I can't exactly blame him for being a little put out with us. William was set on bullying him from the moment he walked in and when that hunk of a pastor didn't give him the satisfaction, he almost blew a gasket. I'm surprised he was as nice as he was, to be honest."

She smiled to herself. "Pastors sure didn't look like that when I was growing up. If they had, I might have chosen an entirely different kind of life. I wouldn't mind cozying up to a man of God who looks like that one!"

Hazel flushed with color that was more from anger than embarrassment. She was used to Louise Cullen's careless mouth and her lack of tact and was usually able to either laugh it off, or just ignore her, but when she heard her speak of Grant Sellars in that vulgar manner, something inside her rose up.

"If he could tell you were thinking of him that way, that might explain some of his anger," she replied quietly.

Louise looked up at Hazel with her lips pressed tightly together and a flash of anger in her heavily made up eyes.

"You must be forgetting that Barry's not around to protect you, if you think you can speak to me with such disrespect, young lady!"

"Is that how you remember Barry, then?"

27

Hazel dared to ask the question, not sure where this rash bravery was coming from, but giving into it. "You think he protected me? Is that what he was doing, when he was out running around with Brandy Hillstead and got himself killed? Protecting me? That's rich!"

Louise stood up to look down at Hazel with growing fury. "I've got news for you, Missy! If you can't keep a civil tongue in your head, you can pack your things and go! Your only connection to this family is six feet deep at Haven of Rest, and you're only here now, because of our benevolence. We owe you nothing!"

Hazel smiled to herself, thinking that if Louise Cullen knew how good moving out sounded to her, she'd try another tactic, rather than threaten her with something she'd very much love to be able to do. In fact, she had been thinking it through and wondering how to proceed, when her mother-in-law had burst into the room.

Hazel had her own home, of course, and there was nothing stopping her from heading back to California, but she knew their place would be crawling with reporters. Besides, it didn't feel any more like home than her old college dorm in New York had. She had never truly felt she had a home since she was a young girl.

Louise Cullen watched the conflicting expressions on Hazel's face and took her silence as admitting defeat. She stood to give her a condescending smirk.

"You just think about that, young lady," she advised, before sweeping out of the room as quickly as she had swept in.

"That's all I *can* think about," Hazel said in a tired murmur, after the woman had gone.

She got up from sitting on her bed and walked over to the large floor to ceiling windows to stare out at the trees with a vacant look in her pretty, brown eyes. Those eyes were filled with uncertainty and leftover tears that had been brewing in them once she had looked up and rested them on Grant Sellars' handsome, angry face.

She wasn't feeling sorry for herself. She knew she deserved all of the past few years and she had especially deserved the look of disgust that Grant had planted on her before he turned and walked away from her. It wasn't that Hazel felt she should have just ignored what she wanted to do with her life, but she should have talked to Grant about it.

True, he hadn't told her about his calling to the ministry until after she had accepted his proposal, but there had been plenty of time for her to voice her objections. Even if they ended up arguing and broke off their engagement, as she knew they would have, she could at least have given him the respect of telling him how she felt. But she didn't even try.

She had just kept putting it off, as their wedding day loomed closer and closer, as if she thought the issue would just magically resolve. It did no good to remind herself that she was barely eighteen, at the time. She told herself that she still knew the difference between right and wrong, and being eighteen was no excuse.

Even though she was a Christian, she hadn't even prayed and asked God what to do, because she had been afraid that He would want her to let go of her dream and stay behind in that nothing little town, living out the drudgery of an existence as the mousey little wife of a preacher.

The kind of wisdom that always seems late in arriving caused her to realize now that she might have been far better off if that had been her fate, but she couldn't unring that bell, so she brushed the notion aside impatiently.

Her thoughts returned to the funeral service for her late husband, a term she used loosely, and try as she might, she couldn't stop the little smile of amusement that came to rest around her lips as she remembered the way the once charming, polite, and disarming Grant Sellars stood behind the pulpit and gripped its sides as if they were the steering levers of an army tank and proceeded to plow through the room, and inform everyone that if Barry Cullen hadn't received Jesus as his savior, he was now burning in Hell and if the rest of them followed his pathetic example, they would suffer the same fate.

He then hopped off his tank and strode out of the funeral home's chapel as if he were shaking the dust off his feet, leaving everyone wondering if the service was over, until a visibly shaken and effusive Mark Wynn reluctantly came in and advised them to please exit out the side entrance to their vehicles in order to proceed to the cemetery.

Hazel had half-expected a still angry and unapologetic Grant Sellars to boldly be waiting for them at the graveside, but it was a member of the funeral home staff who very meekly and correctly offered a brief interment ceremony.

She reached her hands to embrace her slim arms in a self-comforting hug and tried to pull her thoughts back onto a more practical path. She needed to determine where home was, now. It didn't take a shrieking Louise Cullen for her to realize that it certainly wasn't as a member of this family.

She had never fully become a Cullen, particularly since her marriage to Barry had been arranged for publicity. He didn't suddenly become blind to other women and in fact, opted to double down on his playboy reputation, spending long periods away from home with whomever he pleased, and doing whatever gave him enjoyment.

He was a gossip magazine's dream and he seemed to take an adolescent delight in pandering to them. Hazel was surely the only one at the funeral who knew that Grant Sellars was simply stating the facts and she respected him for that, even though he hardly desired her respect or any other consideration from her.

She swept a fingertip across her cheek to catch another one of those persistent tears that was looking for a means of escape before alerting the rest of them that it had found a way out and inviting them to follow.

She couldn't give into them. She needed to think clearly. She tried to determine how she could discreetly find out what her financial situation was. For the most part, she and Barry maintained separate accounts, although they used the same bank.

Hazel was a star in her own right however, and she generated her own income.

The problem was that Barry blew through his money. She knew that the business manager they both used would be able to help her figure things out.

Hazel didn't dare try to reach him while she was in this house, not trusting her intrusive mother-in-law to mind her own business. She decided that she needed to take a drive and clear her head.

She was glad she'd chosen to drive her car here, rather than fly with Barry's parents, since it left her with a means of escape which she had instinctively known she would need, once the funeral was over and done.

The trip had taken her several days, but she had used the time to prepare herself to return to the southern state she had grown up in, although to a different and unfamiliar part of it.

She had been nervous about it, but reminded herself that she would be in a small town north of where she had lived before that she had never been to, and wouldn't run into anyone from her past.

She had already decided that she wouldn't attempt driving another few hours to her hometown, after the funeral. There was nothing there for her anymore, and no one there who wanted to see her. Her mother might be the exception, but it wasn't her daughter she wanted to see, it was the actress.

She had told herself during her long drive from California that by not returning to her hometown, she would be able to avoid any chance of running into Grant Sellars. The last thing she could have expected was that he would be the minister officiating at the funeral of her late husband.

Hazel pushed the thought of their encounter away and quietly picked up her bag and keys. She slipped down the back stairs to get to her vehicle unnoticed, then pulled away from the impressive but ostentatious Cullen residence with a feeling of relief.

Chapter Four

Hazel was unfamiliar with this little community, which she had to admit was appealing, despite the Cullen's association with it, and drove through the downtown area slowly, looking for a place to sit and think. She spotted a lovely little park just off the square where she imagined that the locals probably frequented during their lunch breaks, and stopped there to find a nice little bench under a beautiful spreading oak.

She calculated the time difference and decided that she might be able to reach their business manager now, and tried phoning him. He must have looked at his caller ID, since he answered right away, seeming to have expected her call.

"Hazel, dear!" The dutiful and hard-working Charles Finley greeted her warmly. "I've been thinking about you over the past few days. I almost called you, but I knew that you were in the middle of dealing with a funeral, so I decided to hold off. How are you coping?"

She wasn't surprised by his caring response to her call. Charles Finley was the business manager for many of the people in her profession. He was held in high regard by those who had the sense to appreciate his integrity and dedication to his clients.

"I guess I'm good, Charles, all things considered," she responded. "I'm a little lost, though."

"I can just imagine!" he observed with genuine sympathy. "I'm sure I don't have to ask how I can help. I've been anticipating our conversation and looking into things so that I could give you an idea of where you stand now."

"Charles, I can't tell you what a relief it is to know you're looking out for me," she sighed.

"Well, someone has to, if you'll pardon a bit of candor," he returned dryly. "Of course, my responsibility has been to represent both of you fairly. But I've been able to keep track of what Barry was doing with his money, and from time to time, I was able to move funds into that savings account we opened."

"I remember," Hazel said softly. "At least, I do, now. But I'd honestly forgotten that you and I set that up."

"Well, you've certainly had other things on your mind, the past few years. But you pay me not to forget, so I kept track of it. Do you still use that private email address?"

"I do, but I've not checked it in a long time," she admitted.

"Well, I've not sent anything to it, but I'd like to send you a link to some secure documents of what your financial package looks like. When you click on it, you'll have a code sent to your phone and you'll need to enter it to be able to access them and then there'll be instructions, once you're logged in, to let you know what's needed. When would you want to deal with it? Don't feel rushed."

"I'm not sure how long I can be away today, without creating even more animosity with Barry's parents, but if you're ready to send them, I expect I can find a library or a coffee shop nearby with a computer."

"Well, you could try using your phone, but the documents might be hard to read on a small screen and tedious to download. Once you view them, you wouldn't be able to log back in without my sending you a new link. It's a security thing.

"The link will keep in your inbox, if you can't manage it today. I have everything ready on this end. I'll send you the email and you can go from there. Call me back if you have any problems, Hazel, and if you don't mind, once you've gotten the documents and read through them, I'd appreciate it if you simply reply to the email I send, to let me know."

"I will. Thank you so much, Charles. I hope you know how much I appreciate everything you do for me."

"I'm glad to do what I can. I hope it helps. Take care, Hazel, and let me know how you are."

She thanked him again and ended the call, sitting quietly for a moment, wondering if she should look for a computer, or head on back to the Cullen's residence, before they noted her absence. Of course, she wasn't a prisoner, she could come and go. But the last thing she felt she was up to was an interrogation by Louise Cullen.

She finally determined that if her financial situation turned out to be adequate, she could go ahead and inform them that she would be moving into her own place, although she wasn't sure where that might be.

Hazel was almost embarrassed to admit it to herself, as she sat looking around at the idyllic park and breathing in the clean, crisp air, but this town felt strangely like home. She knew that, even if he hated her, it was because Grant was here. Despite their estrangement, he represented a more innocent, and happy time in her life and there was something safe about his presence, even if it would anger him to know she felt that way.

Hazel swallowed a lump in her throat and wiped impatiently at a tear. She decided she really needed some time to move slowly, and she wondered if there was a bed and breakfast or an inn nearby that would give her a temporary reprieve from William and Louise Cullen and enough time to think in order to figure out what her next move should be.

Hazel pulled up a browser on her phone and searched the town for public computer access. She managed to find both a library and an internet cafe. The cafe turned out to be on the main street she'd just driven down to get to the park, so she drove back and parked close, hoping that the internet cafe was also a coffee house.

The door gave out a soft chime when she opened it and a pretty girl with blonde curls and slight dimples smiled at her from behind the counter.

"Well, hello there," she offered. Hazel was so thankful for a friendly face that she smiled back and returned the greeting.

"You just might be my good luck," the girl confided confidentially. She gestured around at the empty shop.

"I was hoping that this was just a lull, but it's a new venture and I guess the word hasn't really gotten out about it, yet. In fact, I was thinking of closing up early, which is probably not the smartest thing I could do with a new business."

Hazel breathed in deeply, with a look of quiet joy. "Oh, it's coffee!"

"Hey, that would be a great name for this place. 'Oh, It's Coffee!' I like the sound of that," the girl behind the counter laughed. "It is, and it's very good coffee! How do you like it?"

"Black, please," Hazel answered. "I think that's true," she added hesitantly, speaking from the years she had spent in a coffee shop while she was working her way through college. "You sort of have to hit the ground running with new businesses and have consistent hours, even when there doesn't seem to be a good reason for being open. Do you have a lot of competition, as far as coffee shops?"

"Actually no, so you would think the masses would be beating down my door. Maybe if I offered something else with coffee besides sweet pastries?"

The girl behind the counter found it surprisingly easy to chat away with this newcomer, as if they were the best friends in the world.

Hazel glanced down at the Danishes behind the glass and nodded. "They look wonderful, and sometimes people want a little sugar rush along with their caffeine, but I do know that when people come in on their lunch break, they may be hoping for something a little more savory."

"Savory." The friendly girl seemed to be considering that concept. She grinned. "That means I need to learn how to cook. But hey, I'm up for a challenge."

Hazel smiled at her. "I was wondering, please, if the search engine was right about this being an internet cafe? I just need to check my email."

The girl pointed over to a small seating area. "There's a computer over there you're welcome to use and the coffee's coming right up."

36

Hazel was so glad she'd chosen this place, instead of the library. She'd never had good experiences at libraries, mainly because she'd usually been asked to leave.

She smiled at those memories and reminded herself that her bad behavior had been during her freshman and sophomore high school years and she doubted if anyone would have asked her to leave, today. Still, the library didn't serve coffee, so all in all, she'd chosen well.

She settled down at a small desk and woke up the sleeping computer then checked for a browser.

"Just some friendly advice," the shop's employee offered, as she brought a hot cup of coffee over to the beautiful stranger. "I'd either use a private browser window or dump the browsing history and data, when you're done. That's one downside to using public computers."

"Oh, I hadn't even thought of that," Hazel admitted, lifting a hand to her cheek and widening her expressive eyes.

The girl laughed. "Well, my fiancé tells me that I have a suspicious mind, so I'm probably too cautious, but I think it's good advice. Are you just passing through? It's a small town, so I know most faces that belong here."

"I am. But I thought about staying for a couple of weeks, while I decide where to go from here, if I can find a place. I'm sort of just now beginning to make a plan."

"That sounds like a mystery," the girl teased. She held out a friendly hand. "I'm Katie Allen. I guess this dump is mine." She gestured around the shop with her other hand.

Hazel took her hand gladly. "I'm Hazel," she offered. "And your shop is wonderful."

"That's because you love coffee. I can tell," Katie replied, looking up as the door chimed again and laughing.

"I knew you were good luck! Let me know if you need anything else. I'll just be behind the counter."

She gave her a grateful smile and launched the browser, as Katie headed off to check on her customer.

Hazel sat staring blankly at the computer.

37

It took her a moment to remember her log in details for her email, but she thought back to how many years ago she'd set it up, and that suggested to her what it might be. She was able to access it fairly quickly and was happy to see Charles Finley's email sitting in her inbox.

Surprisingly, there was something else, which Hazel hadn't expected, since she'd never told anyone but Charles about the email address, but she shrugged and told herself that spammers could find anybody, then proceeded to navigate to the documents Charles had sent her.

As she focused her attention on the screen, a slow smile indicated that she found herself in much better circumstances than she had dared to hope for. She knew that she owed it to Charles Finley, who had a reputation for looking out for his clients and making an effort to keep them solvent.

The documents listed the bank where her funds were being held and the account numbers as well. Hazel glanced around behind her, then held up her phone to take some photos of a few particulars.

She made sure she had seen everything before logging out, remembering Charles warning her that he'd have to send a fresh link, if she needed to get back in. She was about to close out the browser when she noticed the other email in her inbox and studied it thoughtfully.

Hazel read the subject to herself. "You Should Know..." She let out an impatient sigh. "I should know this is junk mail," she muttered quietly. She clicked on the link anyway and narrowed her eyes, trying to decipher the message.

She felt a cold, clammy sensation when she realized that the email was from her late husband and it had only been sent a day or two before he was killed.

It wasn't too hard to believe that Barry Cullen would have been digging around in her personal things, during one of his drunken periods of boredom and would have come across her email address.

Hazel's look of concentration was so pronounced that Katie noticed from across the room but stayed behind her counter, trying to busy herself.

Hazel absently lifted a hand to push her shoulder-length, brunette hair back and wondered why Barry felt the need to put all this in an email when he could have just called her and told her, especially since he knew she would have been fine with it.

Dear Hazel,

You should know that as soon as my run in 'Silver Lining' is done, I'll be removing my things from our place and moving in with Brandy.

Of course, this certainly won't be a surprise to you. That's one thing you have to admit about me, I've never tried to sneak around and hide things from you. Brandy and I have decided to take a condo together in Dana Point, so you should be receiving divorce papers shortly after. It'll be the basic irreconcilable differences thing. Pretty standard stuff.

I'll only be taking my own things from the house, so please don't worry that Brandy and I are out to steal anything from you. You'll be fine, as far as all that goes.

If nothing else, at least our marriage was good for publicity and that was the plan. People were calling us a "power couple" but I think that's more fitting for Brandy and me, to be honest.

You're a beautiful woman, Hazel, but you've always been just a little too moral for your own good. You don't need to stay married to a guy like me, who likes to enjoy life and have a good time, anyway. Honestly, you'd be better off if you marry a preacher or someone like that, next time.

You'll hear from my attorney soon, but again, not until after 'Silver Lining' wraps. You can hire your own, but there's really no need. It's pretty cut and dried. Take care.

Barry

Hazel wasn't necessarily surprised, as Barry pointed out, and certainly not disappointed.

She did draw in her breath though, when she read his opinion that she should marry a preacher, next time. How ironic could life get, she asked herself, blinking back tears of regret.

She almost logged out then remembered that Charles had asked her to reply to his message. Acting purely on instinct, she forwarded Barry's email to him, instead.

She typed a quick note to Charles at the top of it, letting him know that she had read the documents and might need to contact him again when she had her own laptop around, so that she could download them. She added a quick note: *"I don't expect this will change anything, but it was in my inbox when I logged in today. Thank you again, Charles."*

Hazel sent it then logged out, remembering what Katie had advised and clearing out the cache and cookies before closing the browser.

She sat staring down at her hands for a moment, with a frown resting on her pretty face, wondering what to do next.

She looked up when Katie appeared by her side with a fresh cup of coffee.

"I can't have you drinking warm coffee," she chided, taking Hazel's original cup and replacing it with the hot one.

"I'm sorry," Hazel offered, realizing that she'd forgotten she even had coffee.

"You were concentrating," Katie excused her, with a wave of her hand.

She pulled up a chair and took a seat, since things were quiet in the shop.

"You mentioned earlier that you were looking for a place to stay, while you worked out your plans, Hazel. Did you already have a place in mind?"

"I'm afraid not," she admitted, sipping the coffee and raising her brows as she realized how good it was. "I don't know the first thing about this town, but I had to come for personal reasons and it just seems like a good place to make decisions."

"I love it here!" Katie declared, happy to endorse it. "I thought I might have an idea about where you could stay."

40

She laughed at Hazel's curious expression. "Of course, you might not feel too excited about it, and I guess I wouldn't blame you, since I'm as much a stranger to you, as you are to me.

"I'm getting married in a few weeks," she explained, and stopped to acknowledge Hazel's congratulations with a grin.

"Not even three! I wish it was three months, to be honest. My fiancé has been dragging his feet, as far as helping me plan the wedding, but I guess that may be why I'm probably more prepared than I think I am."

Hazel laughed at that. "If you find a man who's actually excited about planning a wedding, he's typically not the type you'd be marrying," she pointed out and Katie giggled.

"I should be grateful that Fred's balking at fabric and flowers then, I guess," she conceded. "The thing is that I've been so focused on the wedding, that I've completely dropped the ball on subletting my apartment. The landlord has been very nice about allowing me to do that, but I just forgot to advertise. But, if you're looking for a place to stay, you'd be welcome to move on in. It's a two-bedroom.

"And if you liked it enough, you could pick up the sublet after I move out. Of course, there would still be three months left on it but if you like it, you could always pick up the lease, later. You'd like the landlord, he's a member of our church and he's a very sweet old man."

Hazel sat staring at Katie without even realizing it. She felt a slight acceleration in her heartbeat at just the thought that she might be able to return to the Cullen's house and simply get her things and leave.

"But would having someone there in the weeks leading up to your wedding put extra stress on you?" she wondered, laying a hand on her throat, almost afraid to hope this might be a solution for her.

"It'd be the opposite of stress, to be honest. Whenever I did manage to remember the sublet issue, it just reminded me that there was something else I hadn't taken care of. Of course, there's a cat, so if you're allergic, that might be an issue."

Hazel smiled at that. She used to have a cat and she had loved him ferociously. Grant had always laughed at the way Grover would slowly move his heavy self across his lap on the couch and then wedge himself down amid the two of them, and complain to Hazel that "something has come between us".

Grover had ended up staying with her mother when she left and had lived out his life expectancy, fat and spoiled.

She lingered around one of her better memories, before realizing that she was keeping Katie waiting.

"Oh, no, I'm not allergic at all. I love cats!"

Katie looked relieved. "Her name is Dolly Madison, and I have no idea why, but that's the name she came from the rescue shelter with. So, Dolly, for short. She's a ragdoll. Oh!"

Katie face-palmed herself. "Dolly. Ragdoll. Duh! I just now got it!"

Hazel's eyes lit up. Grover had been a ragdoll. She was absolutely beaming, without knowing it.

"Listen," Katie said, reaching over to touch her arm lightly. "You should see how happy you look right now. That should tell you that this is a good idea. I mean, sometimes, you just have to live in the moment, right?"

Hazel liked the sound of that.

Something about the whole plan was trying to bother her though, and she knew what it was but she deliberately pushed it back and promised herself that she could deal with it.

"Could I do anything for you, to help with your wedding or keep laundry done and the place cleaned? I like to cook." Hazel was trying to find a way to make this a good thing for Katie as well, and she laughed.

"You don't have to do a thing. I can tell, just by looking at you, that you don't leave messes or throw wild parties, so we're good. Plus, Dolly will love having you around. She spends way too much time alone."

Katie pulled her phone out of her pocket. "Want me to text you the address?"

Hazel looked slightly dazed. "Are we really doing this?"

"Why not? You need a place to stay and I need someone to take over the sublet, so it's a win-win. Unless..."

Katie stopped and pursed her lips thoughtfully.

"Those three months left on the lease... It'll be three more months, *after* the wedding. I don't want you to feel forced to have to stay that long, if that wasn't your plan. You did say something about a couple of weeks. Is my offering you the apartment messing up your plans?"

Hazel look relieved that this was Katie's only drawback. "Not at all. I have the time to spend and I'll put it to good use." She tapped on her phone until she found her number in the settings and held it up to Katie, who put it in her own and sent a text with the apartment address.

"Oh, hang on!" The petite, blonde bride-to-be hopped up and rushed over to the counter to dig around in her purse, then sprinted back, obviously excited. "You'll need keys! One to the apartment and one to the mailbox."

She dropped them in Hazel's hand and she stared down at them, suddenly becoming emotional. When she looked back up at Katie, there were tears puddling in her eyes.

"Thank you for trusting me, this way, Katie. I mean, you don't even know me."

"I have good instincts," Katie assured her with a little pat on the arm. "You're good people, I can tell."

The door chimed and Katie hopped up again to get back to the counter.

"Again, with the good luck! Just head over there anytime you want, Hazel. Today is fine, no worries. Just let me know."

Hazel picked up her bag and gave Katie a little wave and mouthed a silent "thank you" to her, as she passed by the customer at the counter and let herself out the door.

Chapter Five

Fred took the sweaty towel from around his neck and popped it at Grant with a grin.

"So that was Workout, The Sequel, but without the punching bag. Not nearly as exciting."

Grant stepped neatly out of the towel's aim and gave his buddy a guilty smile.

"I'm never gonna hear the end of that, am I?"

"Oh, at some point, when I get enough mileage out of it, I may let up," Fred loosely promised.

"I told old Pastor James Morgan that I was going on my apology tour," Grant informed him. "You're stop number two."

"Who was number one?" Fred wondered if he should be offended at not being Pastor Sellars' top priority.

"The good Pastor Morgan, himself," Grant admitted. "I kinda had to start with him, since I blew that whole funeral gig he asked me to take on for him."

"How do you blow a funeral gig?" Fred demanded. "I mean there's the eulogy and a song about pie in the sky, in the sweet by and by, and then you throw some dirt on it."

Grant shook with silent laughter that ended in a little cough. "You're bad for me. I need to find new friends."

"I'm just sayin' a funeral is pretty much a dud, right out of the box," Fred insisted. "How're ya gonna blow that?"

Grant tried his own towel pop and connected.

"Out of the box. Nice one, Fred." He put his towel back around his neck and grabbed his gym bag, feeling around in it for his keys.

"What are you and Katie doing this evening?" he asked, mostly from habit. It was usually something wedding related and he lost interest quickly, but he felt he should at least ask.

"She's got a new friend."

Grant narrowed his eyes at him. "The wedding's still on though, right?"

"Not that kind of friend," Fred said, with an exaggerated eye roll. "No, I mean she found someone to sublet to, and had her go ahead and move in. So, a new roomie."

Grant continued to look concerned. "She at least knew the person, already?"

"Nope. Just met her yesterday and had her move right in. It was all very copasetic."

"Someone read a dictionary."

"Katie. It's her big word. Anyway, she really likes her new roomie and it turns out that she's a cat person, so I think copasetic is the word of the day."

Grant just looked at him for a moment, then shook his head in wonder.

"Maybe you'd better drop by over there and check that situation out, since your fiancée is going to be sleeping there at night with a complete stranger in the house."

"I'm actually heading over there after I go clean up. Turns out that Roomie can cook, and tonight's special is braised short ribs."

Grant frowned, as an unwelcomed memory of Hazel cooking him braised short ribs came rushing at him.

"You should come," Fred suggested. "Man can't live on take out alone, you know."

"I've managed it, so far," Grant retorted. "Anyway, I'm not done with my tour. I still have one more offended party I have to placate."

"Can't it wait?"

"I'd better keep at it." Grant pushed open the glass doors and Fred followed him out into the parking lot.

"If you change your mind, swing by," he insisted. "You can use that gift of discernment to read the new girl."

46

Grant grinned at him and tossed him a wave. "Maybe some other time."

He drove to the parsonage to grab a shower, and almost took Fred's advice to let stop number three wait, but decided that Mark Wynn deserved some sort of apology, even if he wasn't yet up to an actual explanation.

After all, Grant was a highly visible pastor in their little community and he had to deal with the funeral home regularly enough to be on a first name basis with the man. The least he could do was apologize for creating a disturbance and causing the funeral home's clients to leave angry.

He decided to not put it off and arrived just in time to see Mark leading a small group of people down the hallway. Grant remained in the lobby, waiting for him to return and when he did, he appeared startled to find the pastor who had made such a stir simply standing there with his arms crossed, as if nothing out of the ordinary had happened.

"Why, Pastor Sellers," he exclaimed. "You're not doing another service today, are you?"

Grant laughed at the look of dread on the man's face.

"No, you can relax, Mark." He lifted his arms slightly and glanced down at his jeans and baseball tee, to further convince the funeral home director that he wasn't there in any sort of official capacity.

"Actually, I came to apologize," he said, watching relief wash over Mark Wynn's face.

"Oh, Grant, you don't need to do that," he protested, but Grant raised a hand to insist.

"Oh, I think I do. I don't really have an acceptable reason for losing my temper the way I did, Mark, but I shouldn't have allowed myself to give in to the temptation to light William Cullen's fuse, the way I did."

Mark Wynn waved his words away. "Oh, that man! When it's his time to go, they can pack him in ice and ship him to Siberia, for all I care."

Grant was taken aback by the normally polite and gracious man's low opinion of the disagreeable William Cullen, but he had to smile at his way of expressing it.

Mark Wynn was more than a little put out, but not with the pastor who had left the Cullen service in such a state of disarray, a few days before.

"Talk about entitled and petty! Those people made so many changes and last minute demands that, of course, there was a balance due and, do you know, that man absolutely refused to pay one penny!

"He claimed that he and that psychotic wife of his were emotionally damaged by the service and that I should just be glad they haven't decided to sue us!"

Grant looked as aggravated as Mark did, hearing this.

"I had hoped they'd just leave town, as soon as the funeral was over," Mark continued. "But, oh no! They've decided to rule and reign again, over in their pretentious home. It looks like they're socked in, although I can't imagine why, unless it's simply to annoy everyone."

Grant was about to offer to pay the balance, since he was responsible for upsetting the Cullens, but Mark wasn't finished.

"I will say, however, that the beautiful young widow of Barry Cullen seems to be completely the opposite of those obnoxious people. Apparently, she heard the two of them bragging about refusing to settle their account and she came by and very sweetly asked me to send any balance to her. I assumed she meant to her address in California but she gave me a local address. I suppose that means she'll be staying in town for a while, but not in that gaudy Cullen house."

Grant stared at the man, appearing to be listening, but completely stunned. What did Hazel mean by deciding to remain here? Was she just being spiteful, now?

He was only slightly aware that Mark was continuing to speak, but he just stood there, trying to work through what he'd just heard.

He lifted a hand and quietly interrupted. "Excuse me, Mark. Did you say she gave you a local address?"

48

"Why, yes. Over at the Glendale apartments. I think a man from your church owns those."

Grant drew in his breath sharply. He had to get out of here. He reached and gave Mark Wynn a light clasp on his arm.

"I'm really sorry, Mark, for my part in upsetting the Cullens. I'll try to be better disciplined, in the future."

Mark smiled and repeated waving away his words. "It's fine, believe me, Grant. He had it coming to him!"

Grant gave him a weak smile and murmured something about needing to be somewhere before heading out to his vehicle and just sitting quietly in it, in order to process.

His mind was racing but to nowhere in particular. He couldn't seem to string two cohesive thoughts together. He finally took a deep breath and began to slowly put the pieces into place. As impossible as it seemed, Katie Allen's new roommate had to be Hazel Todd, or Cullen, or whatever she ended up calling herself. For all he knew, she'd changed her entire name when she began acting.

Fred obviously hadn't known who Katie's friend was, but then Fred didn't know anything about Hazel anyway, so even if he'd known her name, it wouldn't have meant anything to him.

Grant was so tempted to drive right over, on the fringes of Fred's invitation, but he admitted to himself that the dormant rage that Hazel had awakened in him at the funeral had already done enough damage. The last thing he wanted to do was to create an even bigger disturbance by storming over to Katie's apartment to make things worse by loudly demanding that Hazel explain herself and leave town.

He decided to just go back home and try to talk to God about it, not that he didn't already know what He was going to tell him. Grant knew that it wasn't okay with God for him to continue to be this angry with Hazel, but he didn't seem able to just put it away.

His mind ruthlessly took him back to that moment when he stood waiting in breathless anticipation for the woman he loved to appear in the doorway of the church.

49

He had readied himself for that moment when she would meet his eyes as she came moving toward him in stately beauty and grace, to join her life with his.

He could still remember every quickening of his pulse, every rapid heartbeat, as the music began to play softly and all the guests turned around to look for the bride, but none more eagerly than the groom.

He closed his eyes tightly now, with the still vivid memory of that first pause in his breath and of the quiet whispers that began to be heard, and then that final, humiliating moment when all gazes eventually focused on Grant Sellars, as he became the object of pity when the undeniable truth was revealed, and everyone knew that no bride would be coming to meet the young groom.

He had stood frozen, with a shrill ringing in his ears and it was only the compassionate grip on his arm by the minister that somehow compelled him to be led into a private, back room. His eyes had begun to burn with an angry shame, as he tore his wedding garments off and returned to his faded jeans and sweatshirt, furiously leaving the church without responding to anything or anyone. He was done.

Grant was embarrassed, even now, alone in the privacy of his vehicle, to realize that tears were beginning to blur his vision. He wiped his eyes impatiently and started the engine. He just needed to go home and be alone.

Fred greeted Hazel pleasantly after Katie introduced them and wasted no time letting her know how amazing the kitchen smelled.

Katie happily agreed. "She didn't even use a cookbook. She just started whipping up stuff, like a magic act."

Hazel smiled and continued to finish up a side dish of cheese grits, having decided that polenta would challenge her time constraints for putting dinner on the table soon.

"It's been literally cooking for hours," Katie sighed. "I can't remember this apartment ever smelling this good, before."

"Red wine and pancetta," Fred observed, impressed. "Of course, you know who is gonna be hating himself for turning me down to come for dinner."

"More for us," Katie comforted him, reaching around his waist and giving him a little squeeze. "I'm glad you two made up, sweetie. You were looking a little bummed, the past couple of days."

She grinned over at Hazel. "Fred and his bestie had a falling out. Apparently, Fred took issue with the way the poor punching bag at the gym was being bullied."

Hazel turned the heat off under the grits and shook her head, with a little laugh. "Well, if you can't stick up for a poor, defenseless punching bag, then why even go to the gym?"

"Exactly!" Fred dropped a kiss on Katie's forehead and continued to keep his arms wrapped loosely around her. "And believe me, it needed defending. The last time we were there, he hit it so hard when I was behind it, that I got pushed back a couple of feet right into the wall. The guy should be in training."

"What was he so upset about?" Katie wondered, looking up at him and brushing a bit of hair off his forehead.

"He never would say. He just kept telling me to leave him alone, so I finally did just that. Today, he was being his normal, easygoing self again, so I didn't ask any questions. I was just glad to have him back."

"This has been resting long enough, I think," Hazel said, lifting the lid on the Dutch oven and allowing even more aroma to flood the apartment.

"Is it soup, yet?" Fred demanded.

"Oh no! I didn't make soup!" Hazel pretended to be dismayed before finally relaxing her face into a smile and making Katie giggle.

"I told you she fits right in," she informed Fred.

"But, does she fit over here?" he asked, pulling a couple of chairs out from the table. "Because this is where I need her to be and she needs to bring them vittles with her."

51

"He's so fancy," Katie muttered to Hazel, while batting her eyelashes at her intended. "And to think he's all mine! How did I get so lucky?"

Hazel laughed and grabbed a couple of potholders to carry the Dutch oven over to the table, while Katie handed Fred the plates and silverware.

Hazel began feeling nostalgic and a little sentimental when Fred reached for their hands and asked a blessing over their meal. She couldn't remember the last time she'd seen anyone do that, then silently told herself it was probably Grant, so a long time ago.

Most of the conversation centered around Hazel's cooking ability and the meal itself, before Fred innocently speculated that Katie should hire Hazel as a chef and add a little punch to her cafe's menu.

Hazel laughed but Katie's eyes sparkled and she looked at Fred with a big grin. "That's brilliant!"

He shrugged carelessly. "Of course it is. Wait'll I get going, honey, I have all kinds of brilliance going on up here." He tapped the side of his head, and tried to look humble.

Katie looked over at Hazel with her eyes wide and excited. "Have you ever thought of cooking professionally, or is it more of a hobby, and not what you really care about?"

Hazel seemed to be thinking about it. "I guess I did what I always wanted to do professionally for several years, but it seemed to just leave me empty, even though I paid a big price for pursuing it. Cooking is a sort of therapy for me."

"I think you could use more therapy," Fred quipped, grinning at Katie's light pop on his arm. "Hey, listen, I'm just saying, if you feel the need for more therapy, we're here for you, Hazel. Say, this same time, tomorrow night?"

Hazel broke into unexpected laughter. "Yep, you sure are lucky, Katie! I've never seen such selfless sacrifice on my behalf. I just don't know what to say."

"Say yes, and let's discuss tomorrow night's menu," Fred replied, laughing quietly at his Katie's harmless little attempts to pound on his arm.

52

"Well, I know you're trying to work out your plans, so I won't pester you about it," Katie said seriously, after they had finished eating. She reached over to touch Hazel's hand lightly.

"But if you ever feel like you might be interested in trying some dishes at the cafe, you don't even have to ask. Just show up and tell me how much you want to be paid and you can just have at it, Sister!"

"I'll think about it," she said quietly, smiling at their attempts to make her feel wanted, but not at all feeling confident that she could continue to stay here as long as she'd hoped to.

She had been rethinking things all day. It was only a matter of time before Grant found out she was in town. Sooner or later, someone was sure to innocently mention her presence here, and he'd probably become angry and tell her to leave.

It was his town, she told herself, a shadow of sadness resting on her face.

Fred noticed and nodded for Katie to look, and she stared back at him with concern.

"Are you okay, honey?" she asked Hazel gently. "I hope Fred and I haven't upset you. I'm sure we could have found a more tactful way to tell you how much we enjoyed this meal, without making you feel uncomfortable."

Fred glanced down as his phone vibrated and stared at the text with a bit of confusion, then lifted his brows as he continued to read Grant's message.

He quickly tapped back that he'd call him as soon as he could leave, and raised his eyes to find Katie watching him then looking down at his phone pointedly.

"Oh I'm sorry, I didn't mean to be rude," he said to Hazel. "Katie's right, we enjoy teasing our friends, and I'm probably way over the top in that regard, but I hope we haven't upset you. We meant every compliment we paid you."

Katie nodded in approval and looked back over at her new friend. "We're sorry, honey."

"Oh, no!" Hazel protested, shaking herself out of her solemn thoughts and giving them both a bright smile. "I'm really fine, I promise. I appreciate every kind thing you said."

She pushed back her chair and stood up. "Please leave everything and I'll clear it up in just a bit. If you don't mind, I'm starting a little bit of a headache, maybe a sinus thing, and I just need to go find something to take for it."

She smiled at Fred. "I hope you're still here when I come back, but if not, thank you for making me feel welcome and for your kind words. It was so nice to meet you."

She slipped out as quickly as she could, leaving Katie staring after her in deep thought. She turned her attention back to Fred when he nudged her, then looked down at his phone that he was holding up for her to see.

She focused on the screen and her confused expression slowly morphed into shock.

She raised her eyes to Fred's, then glanced back toward Hazel's room before leaning closer to him.

"Is Grant angry with us because of this?" she asked, as quietly as she could.

He shook his head. "I don't think so. I can usually tell when he is. But I can see that he's restless and he needs to talk about it. Do you mind, honey, if I head over there?"

She shook her head slowly, then got up when he did and walked with him over to the door.

Fred rested his eyes on hers then pulled her into his arms, giving her a gentle kiss and brushing her hair back.

"Don't be upset. It'll work itself out. I don't know how, but it will. It wouldn't hurt to pray about it though. Maybe you'd better go see about Hazel."

He gave her another kiss and a light squeeze, then left to go check on his friend.

Chapter Six

Katie looked up as the shop door chimed and relief immediately washed over her, when she saw Fred giving her a soft smile. He came around the counter to embrace her and drop a kiss on her lips.

"I tried to come during the lull," he said, glancing around the coffee shop and thinking that he'd managed it.

"I wish I could claim that it's between the morning rush and the noon rush. Anyway, we should be able to relax a little."

Katie led the way over to the seating area and dropped down onto the small sofa, waiting for him to join her.

He settled down beside her and took her hand, giving her a little smile. "Who goes first?"

She let out a sigh. "Fred, honestly, even if I had known who Hazel really was and all the back story, I still think I would have asked her to move in. She's just really a wonderful person, in spite of what I know you're going to tell me, especially after talking to Grant last night."

Fred sat in quiet thought for a moment. "No, I can tell that she's what we call 'good people' and I'm not gonna let Grant affect my opinion of her. To be honest, he didn't even try. He didn't ask me to come over so that he could rant or make wild accusations or even any demands. He just wanted to talk. Mark Wynn told him that Hazel gave him a local address and when it turned out to be the apartments, he figured out the rest."

He glanced over at Katie curiously. "You mentioned a back story. Do you know the back story, then?"

She shook her head. "We didn't really talk. I could see that she'd been crying but she blamed it on a headache. She

55

tried to insist on coming back in to clean up the kitchen, but I finally got her to agree to let me get the big pieces soaking and rake off the plates, and I'd leave it until this morning. That's the only way I could get her to lie down and get some sleep."

She looked at Fred with a sad face.

"Hazel's a very sweet, conscientious girl, honey, so it's hard for me to understand what Grant meant by texting *'I was once engaged to the girl living with Katie. She's the reason I was so angry at the gym.'* I can't understand how she could make anyone that angry. I didn't mention the text to her, though."

He nodded, and drew in a deep breath. "Well, Kate, Grant and Hazel were engaged years ago. She was eighteen, so Grant must have been somewhere around twenty-three. He said something like that. Both of them were really young, anyway. "

He stopped and exhaled. "Do you want me to just bottom-line this, and then go back and fill in the blanks?"

She nodded. "Just in case someone does come in, before you can finish."

"Okay, the bottom line is that Grant stood waiting at the altar in a church that was packed with wedding guests and Hazel bailed on him. Pulled a runner."

Katie put her hands over her mouth and tears immediately sprang into her eyes, some for Katie, but most of them for their close friend and pastor.

Fred saw her tears and thought about the ones he'd seen in Grant's eyes the night before.

"He was humiliated, of course, especially with everyone staring at him and beginning to whisper but more than that, he was devastated. He had no idea that Hazel was having doubts about marrying him. She'd never said one word to him about being unhappy.

"Then, on top of skipping out on their wedding, she skipped out of town. A few weeks later, she sent a letter but it raised more questions than it answered for Grant. By then, he'd gone from hurt to angry and didn't care what her reasons were.

"The sad thing is that if she had immediately gone to him and talked to him, it might have helped.

"But by leaving and taking as long as she did to contact him, it seemed to Grant that she was just trying to make herself feel better about what she'd done to him by finally offering an explanation."

"But that doesn't even sound like her," Katie breathed. She looked at Fred with troubled blue eyes.

"I realize that I've only just met her, Fred, I get that. But I don't have a check in my spirit at all about Hazel, when I'm praying. I really believe that she's not the same girl who jilted Grant. It's more than just being older and wiser, I believe she's a Godly woman."

He nodded. "I'm inclined to agree, sweetie. Same thing, I get no check at all about her, even after talking to Grant about it. The reason he was angry at the gym was because he had just seen her and all the rage that he thought had burned out immediately fired up again and he was still feeling it."

"He saw her? How did he know she was here?"

"Hazel is a widow," he told her, seeing her surprise. "She was married to that actor guy, Barry Cullen. You know, stage stuff, plays? Always in the news for drunk driving and drugs? Playboy type?"

She didn't seem to connect with the name, and shook her head before Fred continued.

"Hazel is also involved in theater and she's an actress. Barry Cullen was in a car crash in California and killed, and his parents wanted him buried here, since they're from here. That's why Hazel is here. But, in a big twist of fate, the minister who was supposed to conduct the funeral service was unable to do it and Grant agreed to step in for him."

Katie gave him a wide-eyed look. "So he saw her at her husband's funeral, then?"

Fred nodded. "He went over to someone who was pointed out to him as being Mrs. Cullen to ask her if there was anything special she wanted put into the service, and when she raised her head and looked up at him, it sent him into a tailspin. Anyway, he took his anger out on everyone there, and basically told them all they were going to Hell, and stormed out."

Katie gasped. "Grant wouldn't do something like that!"

"I guess you never know what a person would or wouldn't do, unless you've been exactly where he is. He did do it, and when he got to the gym, he was still boiling over, which is why we had our little run-in."

The door chimed and Katie stood up to give a little wave to a customer.

"Don't leave, please, Fred?" she asked, laying a soft hand on his cheek.

She hurried to the counter to pour up a coffee to go, and finished the transaction by seeing the man to the door, before coming back over to sit down with her fiancé.

"I hope it starts picking up," she told him. "Once Ed Crockett comes in, it seems like it does, a little."

She took his hands in hers. "Fred, don't you think I should let Hazel know that I'm aware of her past with Grant? I mean, she doesn't even know that we're friends. It hardly seems fair to keep that from her."

"I think you should. In fact, you're the only one I can imagine being able to talk to her, just now."

She nodded then let him pull her to her feet as he stood up to head back to his office.

"I'm hoping that letting Grant get it all out in the open last night will begin to take the edge off his anger, Katie, because he really does love God and he's genuinely committed to serving Him. He's no less a pastor just because he has the ability to be hurt. I wouldn't be much of a friend to him, if I didn't allow him to feel what he feels."

"I know. You're right," she agreed quietly. "I just hope I can be that kind of a friend to Hazel, without damaging my friendship with Grant."

❦

Hazel looked up as Katie let herself in the apartment and gave her a nervous smile.

Katie could immediately tell that she should just wait, instead of talking to her about Grant Sellars right away.

She could sense that Hazel had something that she wanted to say herself, so she came over and dropped onto the couch, making some comical remark about her day, and then asked Hazel if she was feeling better.

"Not entirely," she answered, glancing down at her hands, as she laced her fingers together. She looked back up at Katie with her sad, brown eyes and made herself say what she had been wanting to say, since the day she moved in.

"I need to tell you something, Katie. It may not be important to you, if you don't know this person, but after I got here, I found out that someone from my past lives here. It's not a past I'm proud of.

"I realize this is a small town, so I expect you actually do know him. Practically everyone here does, from what Mark Wynn told me." She breathed a sigh and looked back down at her hands.

Katie remembered her surprise to learn that Hazel was a recent widow. "The guy from the funeral home."

Hazel nodded. "I met him right after I arrived here, and I had to see him again a couple of days ago on some business."

She stopped and realized that she was starting at the middle of her story, instead of the beginning.

"I'm messing all this up," she confessed, with a sad little smile. "I guess I've already confused you."

Katie just shook her head and waited, glancing down at Dolly, as the big ragdoll cat began to stare up at her, silently suggesting that Katie pick her up. She lifted her onto her lap, and continued to give Hazel whatever time she needed, wondering when the right moment would be for her to admit that she already knew most of what she wanted to tell her.

"I was married. The reason I came here is because my husband was killed in an accident in California, and his family insisted that he be brought here. They have a home here and already own plots in the cemetery.

"His funeral was last week." Hazel stopped when she saw Katie lift her hand.

Katie saw no reason to let this hurting young woman rehash all this. "It's okay, Hazel. The fact is that I already know about that. I actually know about most of your story."

Hazel hung her head, and a few tears got past her lashes.

"I'm sorry, Katie," she whispered.

Katie put Dolly back down on the floor and came over to sit beside Hazel and put her arm around her.

"Don't be sorry, honey," she said gently. "I was a total stranger. Why should I have expected you to share something so personal, when you weren't even sure if you'd want to stay here or that you could even trust me? I'm not upset."

She gave Hazel a light pat on her back. "I tell you what," she proposed, with a little smile. "Let's make this easier on the both of us by me telling you what I do know, which isn't a lot, and then you can tell me whatever you feel I should know, but you don't have to even do that, honey, if you're not up to it."

Hazel smiled faintly and nodded.

"Remember last night, when I said that Fred and his bestie had a falling out?" Katie waited for her to nod before she continued. "Fred's best friend is Grant Sellars."

Hazel drew in her breath and her cheeks flooded with color. She didn't know what to say.

"We didn't know about your husband, or the funeral, Hazel, or that Grant turned out to be the one speaking at it. Fred and I were ignorant of all that. That's why Fred couldn't understand the way Grant was acting at the gym, the next day.

"He was angry, and tearing into that punching bag and Fred said he thought he'd be next. Anyway, Fred got mad too, and ended up leaving and then Grant showed up at his place later, to apologize. Those two really are more like brothers, so I knew it wouldn't last long."

She watched Hazel carefully to make sure she was okay. "Fred told me that Grant put on quite a show. I guess they'll be talking about that funeral for a long time, around here."

Hazel couldn't stop the reluctant smile that finally made it to her eyes. "I was shocked," she admitted. "I never thought he would turn out to be that kind of a preacher."

60

"Oh, he's not!" Katie hurried to reassure her. "That's why Fred got such a kick out of it!"

Hazel still had a trace of the smile on her face. "He just stood up there and said that if we didn't repent, we were all going to burn in Hell, then stormed out of there and it was like you could hear the air roll up and leave with him. No one moved or spoke, until Mark Wynn came in and asked for everyone to exit to their cars to go to the cemetery."

She wiped a leftover tear off her cheek. "He managed to make my father-in-law so mad that I thought he was going to have a heart attack."

She lifted her eyes to Katie's with an embarrassed grin. "I was sort of proud of him," she admitted, in a little whisper.

Katie laughed at that. "Well, just so you know, Hazel, that was completely out of character for Grant. He's not one of those shouting preachers at all. He's one of the most liked, kindest people around. Fred says that even the old retired pastor who asked Grant to fill in for him thought it was funny."

Hazel smiled again, then immediately began to blink as more tears kept trying to come.

"He hates me," she said in a low voice.

"He doesn't mean to," Katie told her, giving her another pat. "He doesn't want to. Fred would tell you the same thing, Hazel. I guess you might have figured it out by now, but when Fred got that text on his phone last night, it was Grant."

She shook her head. "I didn't know who it was."

"Well, there was no reason why you'd make that leap," Katie admitted. "But when Fred saw it, he texted him back and told him that he'd stop by there later. Mark Wynn innocently mentioned that you were staying at these apartments, which is why Grant sent the text and Fred knew that he just needed to talk about it."

"Can I ask what the text said, or would you rather not tell me?" Hazel asked uneasily.

"It said, *'I was once engaged to the girl living with Katie. She's the reason I was so angry at the gym.'* But honey, Grant doesn't want to keep feeding that anger. That's why he reached out to Fred.

61

"He just needed to talk to him about it. Fred said he wasn't yelling anymore, and he wasn't trying to change Fred's opinion of you, or anything like that. He just needed for his best friend to know he was hurting."

She nodded, but remained silent.

Katie watched her continuing to lace and unlace her fingers, and could see that she was struggling to keep from crying. She rested her arm around her shoulder.

"What is it that you need for me to know, Hazel?"

"So many things that I'm ashamed of," she said in a broken voice. "Things I'm embarrassed to admit."

"Then, instead of so many things, how about just one thing, and we'll deal with that first?" Katie suggested kindly.

Hazel closed her eyes for a moment before she looked back up at Katie. "I've never stopped loving Grant."

"Even when you married your husband?" Katie asked, after getting over her initial shock at Hazel's confession.

"I didn't marry him because I loved him. I knew that Grant was done with me, so I gave up any hope of his forgiveness and just let Barry's agent and his public relations team talk me into marrying him. The wedding was a huge, lavish publicity stunt that was supposed to boost both our careers. That part worked. We were considered to be a power couple.

"Of course, we weren't really a couple, in any sense of the word. Barry continued to sleep around the entire time and didn't try to hide it. I guess my own career took off because I became an object of public sympathy. If I felt anything when he died, it was probably relief just to be free from all of that."

Hazel couldn't look at Katie when she said this. She knew how horrible it sounded.

"After Barry died, I found an email from him, saying that he was divorcing me, as soon as his current play wrapped. He was moving in with another actress. He was with her when he was in the car crash. She was airlifted to the hospital but I don't know what happened to her, after that. She might have died too, but I haven't been told anything. I haven't been answering my phone, unless I'm expecting the call."

"You've been looking as if you've been crying, Hazel, and I assumed that it was because your husband died, but you're telling me that you've been crying because of Grant?"

She nodded miserably.

Katie sat processing everything and could pretty much accept what Hazel was telling her, but she kept returning to her admission that she never stopped loving Grant. There was no way she couldn't challenge that.

"Hazel," she began hesitantly, then paused to decide if she could ask the question.

Finally she gave her a direct look and pushed past it.

"If you say that you never stopped loving Grant, then you're asking me to believe that you loved him when you left him alone at the altar. I'll have to take your word for that. But if I'm struggling with it, surely you can see how Grant, of all people, has struggled with it?"

"I do see, and as far as I'm concerned, Grant should be allowed to feel anything he wants to feel about me, or believe anything he wants to believe. I would never say that his anger is unjustified. I don't deserve his forgiveness.

"I try to think back to that day, Katie, but it all seems like a bad dream, now. A lot of it is hard for me to even remember, as shameful as that sounds. It's like I don't know that girl, but I refuse to play the 'I was only eighteen' card. That's no excuse for what I did."

"Why is that no excuse?" Katie objected. "Most of the eighteen-year-olds I know aren't anywhere near capable enough to handle their daily little social media dramas, let alone deal with something as serious as getting married. If your parents were around, I'm surprised they didn't try to stop you from getting married that young, in the first place."

Hazel's eyes flickered with surprise at Katie's words. No one had ever said anything like that to her, and she found herself having to decide if it felt right to her because it was the truth, or because it absolved her.

Katie saw her struggle.

"As much as I love and respect Grant, honey, he wasn't much more than a kid himself, back then. I think he's let himself stay trapped in that moment, so he's still feeling what that kid felt and thinking the way that kid thinks, because he can't leave that place. But it's years later, and it's time he did. It's time you did, as well.

"Yes, when a bride leaves her groom at the altar, it's a really bad thing to do, but since the bride and groom were both just kids, maybe you should spend more time remembering that very important fact and less time camping out around the embarrassment and the guilt of the whole thing."

Katie had decided to just speak her mind and be done with it, but she found herself hoping she hadn't gone too far.

She was relieved when Hazel suddenly gave her a tight hug and a tearful "thank you".

She pulled back and examined Hazel closely. "You're a Christian," Katie stated simply, and she nodded and waited.

"Then, sweetie, why haven't you been talking to God about this, all these years? He would have told you this, and so much more, if you had just asked Him."

She nodded sadly. "I know. I've always loved God, but I got so caught up in wanting to be an actress that I didn't want to pray about it. I was afraid He would tell me to just settle down and be a pastor's wife, and stop chasing that dream. I wish now that He had and that I would have listened, but it's too late for wishing, now.

"The more I advanced in my career, the more I began to spend less and less time trying to stay spiritually grounded, until I was so embarrassed at how long I'd gone without talking to God, that I just stayed away. I guess I knew He was probably upset with me."

"I'm pretty sure He just missed you. Why should He have been upset? He knows we're just dust. We don't surprise Him when we act like the little dirt bags we are.

"He knew all that about us way head of time, and sent His Son for us, anyway. 'While we were still sinners.'

64

"That alone is reason enough for us to stay up in there, under His wings, and talk over everything with Him. You think He doesn't have to listen to me going on and on about every little detail about my wedding?"

Katie grinned and drew a little smile from her roommate.

"He already knows, Hazel, that you wish things could have been different, but He also knows whether or not you and Grant were rushing things back then. You can't let your opinion of yourself pass for God's opinion of you. He doesn't think like us, and that's a good thing."

Hazel sat staring at the floor for a long while, just taking in everything Katie had been telling her and feeling the embers of truth beginning to burn in her.

For years, she would absolutely not allow herself to even consider any excuse that might pardon her for what she had done to Grant, but she now began to remember that pardon was what God had in mind, when He sent His Son.

She also began to see that she didn't have to deserve pardon. In fact, the very notion that any human deserved forgiveness was completely unscriptural.

As this began to unfold to her, Hazel could tell that the Holy Spirit had put it in her heart and was breathing on it. She somehow sensed that wanting to be out from under the burden of all that guilt wasn't a selfish thing. It was what God wanted for her all along, whether she deserved it or not.

She hoped that Grant would forgive her and she was willing to ask him to but at the same time, he might not. God's forgiveness had to be enough for her.

Hazel silently told herself that in the future, when she prayed for Grant to no longer be angry with her and to forgive her, it wouldn't be so that she could feel better, but it would be so that Grant could be free from the humiliation of the public way she had hurt him, that he was still wearing like chains.

They might never cross paths in this life again, and if Grant were to truly become free, it might mean that his heart would heal enough to allow him to open it to someone else that God might send to him to build a future with.

If that was God's will, Hazel had to accept it and make peace with it. A sense of resolve began to stir inside her spirit.

She lifted her eyes to find Katie watching her processing.

"It looks like you're getting it," she commented, with a little wink.

"I got it," Hazel confirmed, reaching to give her a hug. "It took me long enough, but I finally got it. Thank you, Katie."

She laughed and reached over to muss up Hazel's hair.

"You can thank me by teaching me how to make braised short ribs before I get married. And since the wedding's only a couple of weeks away, we'd better get up and get started right now. This is gonna take a while."

Chapter Seven

Grant looked up with mild surprise, as someone tapped on his office door. He'd assumed he was all alone at the church today, and he hadn't heard anyone come in.

He waited, and when the knock sounded again, he called out for whoever it was to come in.

He made no effort to hide either the irritation or disgust on his face as Louise Cullen came in with a coy smile.

"Oh good, this is the right church, then," she purred, with a look of satisfaction.

Grant immediately stood up after she slipped into a chair and walked past her to his door, stopping just outside in the hallway, very obviously waiting for her to come out, as well.

"I don't see women alone in my office, Mrs. Cullen. That's my policy and I don't see it changing anytime soon, so if you feel we have business, I'm afraid we'll have to take it out into the courtyard."

She raised her arched brows with surprise and laughed. She stood and moved toward him, deliberately slowing down and smirking up at him, taking her time and brushing up against him as she passed into the hall.

He moved back, then led the way through the front doors of the church and out to a side area that was clearly visible to anyone passing by who chose to look that way.

She seemed to be thinking of defying him and remaining inside the church but when he continued walking away from her, rather than waiting for her, she rolled her eyes and followed him out to some benches.

"Are you deliberately trying to be insulting, Pastor Sellars?" she asked, slowly seating herself on a bench and crossing her legs.

"Are you deliberately trying to be pathetic, Mrs. Cullen?" he returned.

Again, she raised her brows. "You know, for a man of God, you are decidedly lacking in social graces. Perhaps you should consider being a bit more pleasant."

"Perhaps you should seek your pleasure elsewhere," he returned smoothly, as he remained standing with his arms crossed, waiting impatiently for the aggravating woman to get on with whatever it was she had come for.

"I wouldn't be so quick to alienate me, if I were you, Pastor Sellars. I may be the only friend you have left after your little stunt at my son's funeral."

"And how do you arrive at that conclusion?"

"I'm not the one who's thinking of suing you."

She watched him to see what sort of effect her words would have on him, but his face was unreadable. He simply continued to wait for her to elaborate.

"My husband has been considering it, you know," she informed him, glancing down at her nails in a bored fashion.

"You might try asking your husband if he is aware of the futility of attempting to extract blood from a turnip, Mrs. Cullen," he advised her coolly.

She smiled to herself. "Fortunately for you, William knows that you little country preachers barely make enough money to keep the lights on. It wouldn't be worth his time. But he did find your theatrics to be abusive, especially considering the fact that our son was lying in the coffin you stood behind to damn us all to Hell."

"If you and your husband have no fear of spending eternity in Hell, then one has to question why neither of you are able to simply shrug off my remarks and go on about your business. Apparently, I struck a nerve."

She seemed to react ever so slightly to his comment and took a moment to compose herself.

68

"I don't think it was very appropriate for you to take advantage of our being in an emotional state and imply that our Barry is in Hell," she informed him in a tight voice.

"I'd hardly qualify the two of you standing next to your son's casket, while surfing social media and the stock market on your phones as being in an emotional state." Grant looked pointedly down at his watch. "I suggest we cut to the chase."

She sized him up indecently and began to approach him, wondering how close she could stand next to him before his aloof attitude was betrayed by his masculine inclinations.

"I see now why you were so upset by my reference to Hell," Grant commented calmly. "The demon inside you knows that's his fate, but he doesn't want you to realize that it's yours. But now, you know."

She stopped and stared at him, wide-eyed and shaken.

"You obviously have no real business here, Mrs. Cullen, and I feel no obligation to allow you to take up any more of my time. I'm sure you can find your car from here."

Grant turned and retraced his steps back into the church, locking the door to discourage any further attempts on her part to engage him.

Louise Cullen stood frozen for a long moment, before her eyes narrowed and a streak of anger contorted her features. She vowed to herself that this insignificant minister would regret speaking to her with such disrespect.

She continued to bore her gaze into the door that had been so firmly closed behind Grant Sellars as he left her where she stood, and thought back to the funeral.

Louise Cullen would be accused by some to be so vain and self-indulgent that she rarely noticed what was going on with anyone else around her, but she had been alert enough to watch the handsome preacher when he walked over to Hazel to ask her about the service.

She had been quick to notice how rapidly Hazel's face drained of color and the way she tried to keep her head down and not respond, before finally looking up at him.

She also hadn't missed the immediate rush of anger that darkened the minister's countenance the moment she did, and the way he turned away from Hazel and made his way to the podium to very coldly and deliberately notify them all of not only Barry Cullen's eternal fate, but the fact that they all were likely to share it.

Of course, when she asked Hazel later what it was she had said to upset the preacher, she insisted that she hadn't spoken to him at all, and perhaps she hadn't. Apparently, all it took was her looking up at him to upset him. Louise Cullen silently asked herself exactly why that was the case.

She had been annoyed with Hazel for being insolent with her after her observation about the pastor's attractive physical attributes, and had intended to return to her room later to once again make sure that she understood that she would not be permitted to speak to her again in that manner, or she would be evicted from their home. She was aggravated to find that Hazel had quietly left the house and was even more enraged when she later returned and began packing her clothes and informed her that she was leaving.

Louise had enlisted her husband to demand that Hazel tell them where she was going, but he seemed relieved to learn that his son's widow was moving out, saying that it was her business and that they didn't need to know the particulars.

The truth was that after William Cullen had spent some time brooding and blustering about the remarks the pastor made at their son's service, he had privately begun to wonder if there was any truth in what the man said.

He hated thinking about it, because if it was true, then he had to resign himself to considering that his only child was more than likely trapped in an eternity too horrible to imagine and he was forced to feel that he was responsible to some degree.

He made a strong effort to push the pastor's words aside but they troubled him during the day and robbed him of his sleep at night.

He'd waved aside his wife's indignant insistence that he find out where Hazel was going, and seemed to find humor in the fact that Louise had threatened Hazel with eviction, only to have Hazel turn the tables on her and simply move out, taking the wind out of her sails. He dryly informed his wife that Hazel was a grown woman and told her to leave her alone, but Louise wasn't done with her just yet.

Grant had been so upset by the Cullen woman showing up at the church that the more he sat and fumed over it, the angrier he got. He finally decided that what he needed was a good run, and headed over to the parsonage to change into his sweats before starting out with a light pace to help him clear his head and talk to God. Grant did a lot of his praying when he jogged, or mowed the lawn, or anything outdoors, and a good, long talk with God was overdue.

He began his run, of course, by acknowledging Lucy Wallace's wave with his own, then grinned as she wrestled her old dog back away from the gate. She seemed to want others to believe that Buck was a threat to anyone passing by, but the old retriever never attempted any adventure further than the yard, and his bark sounded more like he was coughing up a lung.

Grant did a mental calculation of the day's calendar and remembered that he had a counseling appointment in the late afternoon. He frowned, as he realized that it was pre-marital counseling for a young, starry-eyed couple that he had already determined were living in a fantasy world.

The very young, prospective groom talked confidently about all the practical plans he had for ensuring their future and the even younger bride-to-be hung on to his every word with her adoring gaze, as if her future husband had hung his own moon.

Grant wore a grim expression, as he told himself that the best counsel he could give them would be to postpone any thought of marriage until they were much older.

At the very least, he should warn the young man to make sure that his fiancée wasn't hiding some secret longing to be a fashion model or desire some other exotic career that would require her running away to achieve.

Of course, Grant knew that such counsel was biased, and arrived at by way of his own disappointments, and confessed as much to God as he maintained a consistent speed through town.

He ran along the sidewalks of the downtown square and made his way to the little memorial park that began where the main street ended. Its gates invited anyone who just needed to sit and think, stroll around water features, or take a walk or jog along the asphalt trails.

Grant continued in, veering to the right and following the trail through young trees that had been planted in memory by the families of others who had passed away. Again, Grant struggled with his cynicism as he asked himself if William Cullen would choose to memorialize his son by planting a money tree.

Grant sent up silent remorse to God and tried to move his thoughts away from anything to do with those people and devote them to more divine purposes.

He felt he had succeeded until he followed the trail around a curve and moved over to accommodate a woman who was out for a walk, before becoming aware that it was Hazel.

Grant stopped just before he reached her and took in a measured deep breath to slow his heart rate. He saw her stunned reaction to his suddenly appearing in front of her, as she paused, unsure of whether to keep walking or to wait.

Hazel dropped her eyes and hung her head as he stepped closer. There was a humility in her attitude that was genuine and unaffected and Grant was surprised by it, since he would have expected her to either be defensive or ashamed. She was neither of those, but she was meek.

Other than that quick moment of recognition at Barry Cullen's funeral, Grant hadn't been willing to really look at Hazel and now found himself to be unprepared for how the years had matured her and enhanced her beauty.

This Hazel wasn't the thoughtless eighteen-year-old who had remained trapped in his memory, the one he had been so angry with. He was forced to admit that he didn't know this woman standing in front of him, even though she was someone that he had loved... someone he had kissed.

As she silently submitted to his scrutiny, Hazel was also dealing with the realization that the twelve years since they were to have married had defined Grant's handsome features and removed any trace of adolescence. His physique displayed the results of regular exercise and she only now realized that he had a beard. It suited him. He was no longer the young, impulsive lad who eagerly desired for her to join him in his mission. She regarded him as a disciplined man, although not in the inappropriate and vulgar way that Louise Cullen had, but with respectful appreciation.

After the long moment of stillness began to reverberate, Hazel lifted her eyes to his and he was quietly amazed at the gentle peace and kindness in them.

She softly spoke. "I'm so sorry."

It was little more than a whisper, and he watched those eyes brim with unshed tears.

Grant had imagined such an encounter, over the years, and had even rehearsed his curt response to the apology he knew she would eventually offer if he ever saw her again, but now that the moment had come, he was thrown by the authenticity behind her words.

He wasn't ready for this rush of emotion and didn't trust himself to respond. He ran an impatient hand through his hair, then continued forward, to pass by her on the trail.

Hazel remained still, looking down at the ground, struggling not to cry, and acknowledging that she had done this to herself and that no matter how she regretted her actions, she couldn't undo anything or make Grant accept her apology.

"Hazel."

She lifted her head at the sound of him speaking her name. He had stopped on the trail, but hadn't turned around. His back was to her and his head was bowed.

She approached him timidly and came around to look up at him, not expecting to see tears crowding his own eyes, as hers finally spilled over.

"I'm just so sorry, Grant," she whispered again.

They exchanged a long look before Grant folded his arms and stared beyond her into the trees, drawing in a deep breath. After a moment, he returned his gaze to hers and felt something that had been tightly gripping him for years begin to release him.

"Thank you, Hazel."

It was all he could manage but for Hazel, it was a gift. She gave him a trembling smile and he faintly responded with a similar one, before moving away and continuing down the trail, leaving her softly crying tears of gratitude and quietly thanking God for this moment.

She didn't try to send it out into the future or make more of it than it was. She just accepted it as God's way of telling her that He loved her and was listening to her prayers.

Chapter Eight

William Cullen hung up the phone with a look of distaste on his face which failed to improve at the sight of his disagreeable wife, who was dragging down the stairs in a slightly disheveled state, after drinking until the wee hours of the morning. He pushed the phone to one side and observed her with a sour expression.

"What?" she demanded irritably, making her way across the floor to crumple into the nearest chair.

"You took it upon yourself to call Mavis Dunning," he said flatly. "And before you start lying, let me inform you that I just got off the phone with her."

Louise Cullen waved the accusation to one side and closed her eyes as the hangover she woke up with began to make her head pound.

"So what if I did?"

Her husband continued to assess her with both anger and aversion. "No one authorized you to do that!"

"I don't need you or anyone else to authorize me! I'm a grown woman!" she declared, quickly gripping her forehead before it split apart.

"It's my name on those contracts, not yours," he reminded her darkly, "and I made sure that Mavis remembers that. Barry's post-mortem affairs are for me to deal with, not his binge-drinking mother, who has no legal leg to stand on, or any other legs, from the way things look."

His wife shot him a grimace and closed her eyes, again waving a hand toward him as if it were the remote to a television she wished to turn off.

William Cullen had managed Barry Cullen's career from his earliest days on the stage, dating back to his teen years. He had been instrumental in securing roles for his son and for negotiating his contracts. He was less than enthusiastic when both Barry's newly acquired agent and his public relations team seemed to partner up and concoct their wild scheme for Barry and Hazel Todd to marry and be presented as a sort of overnight Broadway power couple.

Hazel had shown no enthusiasm over Barry's sudden proposal, so William Cullen was more than a little surprised when she accepted.

There was much made over the romantic aspect of the arrangement, although it was clear to William that romance could hardly have been considered as a factor, either in the beginning, or at the end of their marriage.

When the wedding planners pounced to present the young couple with a well-publicized, lavish and costly ceremony, Hazel Todd apparently had little to say about it, or anything else. Her personality onstage was misleading, because she seemed to leave it there. She had the unusual ability to become whoever the director had in mind but as soon as she heard "cut", she immediately morphed back into a listless, apathetic wallflower, who never bothered to question anything, but simply did as she was asked. She seemed to be resigned to her fate.

It was her striking beauty and her instinctive acting ability that made Barry's team so eager to introduce her as his fiancée. Barry was more than ready to sign whatever was put in front of him. It was obvious that Hazel didn't care, one way or another. This made her even more desirable to obtain, but Barry soon tired of the challenge and returned to his usual pursuits, once it was clear that Hazel fully understood just how scripted their marriage was and had no intention of pretending to be emotionally or physically invested, just to satisfy Barry's ego.

William Cullen grudgingly had to admire her for that.

Mavis Dunning was the owner of the theater where Barry's play, "Silver Lining" was playing to sold out audiences.

Of course, following the shocking news of her leading actor's untimely death, Mavis had been left reeling, as ticket sales plummeted and refunds were demanded. Rather than try to push forward with the understudy, Mavis felt she had no choice but to close the show.

Louise Cullen couldn't have picked a more opportune time to call the theater's owner and suggest that if Barry Cullen's widow, Hazel Todd, were to be cast as the lead in "Wayward", it would bring the deceased star's fans streaming back into the theater and save Mavis Todd from losing a great deal of money.

William Cullen scowled darkly as he rubbed his temples and thought about the phone call he'd just had with Mavis Dunning. She told him that Louise had initially called her to ask if cast insurance had been taken out on her son and, if so, who was listed as his beneficiary.

That had made the man angry enough, since he alone was the executor of his son's affairs, but when Mavis mentioned Louise's suggestion regarding their son's widow, seeming to regard it as a serious one, he caustically reminded her that "Wayward" required an actress who was willing to do nude scenes and that Hazel Todd wouldn't even consider it.

Mavis actually attempted to persuade William Cullen to try to convince Hazel to take the role as a way of honoring Barry Cullen's memory. When he scoffed at the idea, Mavis advised that she had already put in a call to Hazel's agent and he responded by slamming the phone down in her ear.

It was at that moment that he had the unpleasant experience of seeing his meddlesome, alcoholic wife come staggering down the stairs.

He stood up now, and glared angrily at her, pointing a finger in her face and speaking through clenched teeth.

"If you ever meddle in affairs that don't concern you again, it'll be the last time. Do you hear me, Louise?"

She merely grunted and tried to find a more comfortable position on the chair before placing a pillow over her head and gesturing for him to go away.

"You're so obsessed with going after Hazel," he said in a cold tone. "You've always been jealous of her. Continue trying to set her up, and you'll be the one evicted from this house!"

He continued to regard her with contempt before reaching for his car keys, intent on being anywhere but there.

Katie stood staring at her reflection, while Hazel approved the bride-to-be's lovely gown with a little gasp.

"Katie, it's like this dress was designed just for you," she breathed and Katie turned to look back at her with happy eyes.

"Does it seem to fit alright?" she demanded, already knowing what Hazel would say, and that was simply because the dress fit her to perfection.

That is exactly what Hazel told her, and Katie hugged herself in excited anticipation.

"Can you believe we're only a few days away from our wedding?" she asked, almost whispering. "It seemed like it was taking forever, and then, all of a sudden, here it comes!"

"But you're happy about that, right?" Hazel flashed her a teasing smile.

"I really am, Hazie!"

Hazel wrinkled her brow and looked at Katie in confusion. "Why did you call me that?"

Katie continued to inspect herself and absently asked what she meant.

"Hazie."

She stopped turning this way and that, and gave Hazel her attention. "I'm sorry. I come up with nicknames for all my friends, and you've certainly become a friend to me. But I didn't mean to offend you."

"No, you didn't," Hazel hurried to assure her. She gave her a little smile. "Grant used to call me Hazie. Either that, or Hay. I just wondered if you knew that."

"I didn't, and I'm sorry, sweetie." Katie lifted the skirts of her gown and stood regarding Hazel sadly.

"No, no!" Hazel rushed to put a stop to that. "No, I'm not upset. No sad face! You stop that, Katie Buckley!"

Katie had to laugh at that.

"When I first met Fred, I told myself that I would never fall in love with him, just because his name was Fred, but of course I did, and pretty much right away. Then I told my mom not to keep hinting about us getting married because there was no way I'd change my name to Buckley. She's probably going to stand up at the reception and tell everyone that too, knowing my mom! Fred's family is just gonna love me for that!"

Hazel smiled, relieved to see Katie return to her happy mindset, only to have Katie stand still and look at her with big, blue, serious eyes.

"I have a favor to ask you, and I don't know how."

"Just ask, silly," Hazel suggested. "You've been so good to me, so whatever I can do, just let me know."

"Do you mean that?"

Katie carefully pulled her long skirt to one side and sat down slowly on the edge of the sofa, before looking back up at her with that same serious look.

Hazel moved the garment bag over to one side and sat down to wait for her to get on with whatever it was that seemed so difficult for her to ask.

"Would you come to my wedding?" she finally asked, almost wincing as she prepared herself for Hazel to decline.

Hazel looked down at her hands, sadly. "I wish I could."

"But, Hazel, why can't you?"

She lifted her eyes to Katie's. "I don't have to remind you that Grant is the one marrying the two of you. I wouldn't do that to him. It would be like a slap in the face."

"But you said that the two of you talked."

Katie had so been hoping that this meant she could ask Hazel to come, not just to even out her tables, and not just because Grant had done as Fred predicted, and solidly refused to bring a date, but because she genuinely liked Hazel and hated the idea of her sitting alone at the apartment while everyone else was having a good time at the wedding.

"No, it wasn't like that. I wouldn't call it talking." Hazel drew in a deep breath and let it out in a sigh. "I just told him I was sorry."

Katie sat regarding her with a sober expression. "But, he wasn't mean to you, or anything like that, was he?"

"Not at all. We ran into each other on the trail in the park. We just stood there, kind of awkwardly, and I told him that I was sorry. At first, he didn't respond, and started walking away, and then he stopped and said my name, but he didn't turn around or add anything else. So I told him again that I was sorry and he finally looked at me and thanked me and then walked away. That was all."

Katie reached over and rested a hand on Hazel's arm. "But that sounds like a lot, Hazel!"

She just shook her head and gave Katie a faint smile. "Thank you for wanting me to be there, Katie, and I appreciate it so much, but I have plenty to keep me busy and I don't want anything to mar your special day. You're sweet for asking me."

Katie couldn't seem to let it go. "But what if Grant was okay with you coming?"

"That would take a miracle," Hazel said with a melancholy smile. "And I wouldn't want him to feel pressured. It's not important for me to be there."

"It is to me!" Katie almost managed a scowl, which was completely foreign to her optimistic, sunny demeanor. "What about this? What if Fred just asks him if it would upset him and if he says that it would, then we'll just drop it, once and for all? We won't try to talk him into it."

"Hazel, Grant can say that it's okay, but that won't be the truth. He would claim it's okay, in order to not disappoint you and Fred on your wedding day, but he wouldn't be happy about it. That would just be one more thing for him to resent me for."

Katie looked down at the floor and she seemed to be more than a little disappointed, but she didn't say anything more. After a moment, she got up and told Hazel that she needed to get out of her gown before Fred showed up, and Hazel picked up the garment bag and followed her to her room.

Katie took one more look at herself in her mirror before saying a temporary goodbye to her beautiful gown and letting Hazel help her step out of it and return it to its protective bag.

Fred's sharp knock sounded and Katie let out a giggle. "We timed that perfectly!"

"Not quite," Hazel replied. "Maybe you'd better actually put your jeans back on while I let Mr. Buckley in."

She tossed a smile at her and pulled the door to behind her, before heading over to let Fred in.

"Hello, Roomie!" he greeted. "What's cookin'?"

"All the pots are cold," she informed him. "Sorry about that, but maybe I can make up for it, later. Katie's been trying on her dress, so she's just getting back into her clothes."

"I hate I missed that," he said, moving into the room and grabbing a barstool next to the kitchen counter, "but Katie swore that if I ever caught a peek at her dress before the wedding, she'd send it back and start all over, so I haven't even tried. No one wants to start this process all over again."

Katie came padding barefoot into the kitchen and stopped to give her future husband a loud smack on his cheek. "I said it, and I meant it," she confirmed. "One little peek, and you'll be up to your ears in fabric swatches."

Fred sent a laughing glance over to Hazel. "You can see why my curiosity has limits."

Katie came around to stand behind him and rested her chin on his shoulder, giving him a dramatic sigh that caused him to turn his head to see her better.

"What's that about, Kate?"

"My roomie won't come to the wedding."

Fred looked back at Hazel with a grin. "Well, just so you know, Hazel, Grant would be fine with it, if that's what's stopping you."

"Oh, I doubt that," she said, with a faint smile.

"I actually mentioned it to him," Fred persisted. "And he said that it would have been much worse if the wedding would be the first time the two of you saw each other but that you've had two encounters now, so he's over the shock."

Katie fastened her wide "I told you so" eyes on Hazel with a pleased grin.

"He's just being nice because it's your big day," Hazel objected quietly. "He wants you to be happy. But he wouldn't be able to enjoy himself with me there. Honestly, Katie, I wouldn't know anyone there, so I'd just be sitting, shaking my head at waiters and checking my phone."

"I hate the sound of that," Fred muttered, knowing how awkward things could get at social functions when you didn't know anyone.

Katie thumped his arm.

"I'm just sayin', what Hazel's describing is a nightmare! Ow!" he added, when she whacked him again.

"I agree with Fred," Hazel said, wrapping her hands protectively over her own arms and moving back out of harm's way. "But while we're all three here, I did want to ask you about your cafe, Katie."

Katie came from behind Fred to lean on the counter next to him and looked up at her curiously. "What about it?"

"You mentioned having to close it while you two are on your honeymoon. Is that something you want to do, considering that it's a new business, and you're just starting out?"

"I don't have anyone who can run it while I'm gone," she admitted with a little frown.

"Would you like me to keep it open for you?"

Katie stared at her with a slow smile beginning to light up her eyes. "I mean... wow, Hazel. But, I'd have to give you a crash course in brewing the coffee and how things run."

"I did a little barista work when I was getting my degree in New York," she admitted. "I'm not a professional, by any stretch, but as long as the orders don't get too fancy, I can manage an espresso or a cappuccino."

Hazel paused and pursed her lips thoughtfully. "I wouldn't think you'd have any sort of important deliveries scheduled to arrive while you're gone?"

"Nope, I did make sure of that." Katie was still smiling. "That's very tempting. Are you sure, though? I mean, you have your own plans and things to tend to."

"Nothing that has to be dealt with all at once. I've got the time, if it would help. I know that when businesses have to close their doors for any real length of time, it can be hard to get customers back in, especially if you're new, and I think you said your honeymoon is for a couple of weeks."

Katie nodded. "How about this? Why don't you open with me in the morning and let's just spend the day making a few brews and learning how to take payments and stuff, and then if you feel you still want to, then that would be awesome."

Hazel nodded. "Let's move in that direction, and while your wedding is in full swing, I'll actually be somewhere that I enjoy, keeping busy and trying to get better at the whole coffee shop experience. It's a win-win."

Katie gave her a knowing look. "I walked right into that! This is the ace up your sleeve for getting out of coming to the wedding."

"Well played, Roomie!" Fred offered her a fist bump.

Hazel connected with it, with a little laugh. "I mean, it works out well for me to have something to do, but I was going to offer, anyway, when I heard you say that you'd have to close up shop for a couple of weeks."

"Well, tomorrow I'll let you make me a Venti Mocha Frappuccino, light, half-caf, low foam, no sugar, stirred exactly ten times counter-clockwise, and then we'll see if you've managed to get out of going to the wedding, after all," Katie threatened with a grin.

"In my sleep!" Hazel claimed, flexing her arm and inviting Katie to check it out.

Fred shook his head and laughed at both of them. "I am so gonna be there when it goes down."

Chapter Nine

Hazel ran a dishcloth across the counter before draping it over a drying rack and looking around with a pleased sense of accomplishment. It hadn't taken her long to get back into the zone of coffee shop management, which was her job when she was attending college and getting her degree.

She'd already learned some of the local's names and had exchanged pleasantries with them, letting them know what news she was hearing from Mr. and Mrs. Fred Buckley, who were finally enjoying being on their honeymoon, once Katie was convinced that her cafe would still be there, when they returned.

A comforting, warm aroma began to permeate the air, and Hazel reached for an oven mitt to check the tray of individual quiches she had decided to bake. She'd made some the day before and when Ed Crockett had come in on his coffee break, he was delighted and claimed that the shop smelled like his grandmother's kitchen.

Hazel had decided that when he returned to work, Ed must have sounded the alarm that there was fresh quiche at the cafe because everyone who had come in afterward seemed to be asking about them. She made extra this morning, just in case Ed Crockett was still a fan, counting on his endorsement to sell them to his co-workers.

Hazel took a deep sniff and smiled to herself, as she pulled the tray out of the oven and sat it on a folded towel. She took a moment to arrange the quiches in the front glass display and was so intent on making sure she hadn't mixed up the different varieties that she was only faintly aware of the door chime ringing.

"I hope this is just a little method acting."

Hazel recognized her agent's voice immediately, but restrained herself from looking up or appearing surprised. She finished sorting the quiches, then closed the sliding door behind them before finally putting the tray away and turning to rest her eyes on Clayton Ballard's amused ones.

"I'm helping out a friend," she replied simply, offering no further explanation.

"Then it's only temporary, and not an indication of your new choice of career," he returned, unable to ignore the fragrant smell of Hazel's baking efforts. "Are those for sale, then?"

"That's the intention."

She waited for her agent to either order something or tell her what he was after. He seemed to want to do both, but opted to get down to business.

"Why are you still here, Hazel?"

"Have I failed to show up for a play I wasn't aware I was cast in, Clayton?"

"No, but if you want to be in one, you need to get back to where plays are actually being performed, not hiding out in some backwoods cafe."

She crossed her arms and eyed him with a bit of resentment. "If I didn't want to be here, I wouldn't be. So you may conclude that I'm exactly where I wish to be."

"Easy, now!" Her agent lifted a hand to ward off Hazel's willingness to send him packing.

Hazel Todd had always been a source of frustration to both her manager and agent because, unlike others who craved the applause and attention generated by being in the spotlight, she had never seemed to especially care. Their frustration stemmed mainly from the fact that Hazel was a rare talent and could make anyone in the audience believe her but hardly went out of her way to secure a particular role.

As a result, Clayton Ballard was faced with the difficulty of convincing his star actress to accept a role that he already knew had little chance of success when he presented it, but one that he knew she would shine in.

"I'm here to offer you the role of a lifetime, Hazel."

"I wasn't aware that you own a theater."

"Offer, in the sense that you are the only actress that the theater is asking for, so it's yours if you want it."

"Well, that's a red flag, right there," she muttered, turning her back on him and reaching for the dishcloth to busy herself.

She stopped, as something occurred to her, and turned back to look at Clayton Ballard with narrowed eyes.

"Who told you where to find me?"

"Are you kidding?" he asked rhetorically. "As small as this town is, there will always be at least one fan of the arts."

"I want a name." She crossed her arms again to wait.

Her agent let out a sigh and decided to just shoot straight with Hazel.

"Alright, Mavis Dunning thought I might find you here."

"Here," she repeated flatly, gesturing around at the shop.

"In this town. This cafe was just one of the places I stopped in, to ask if anyone knew where I could find you."

Hazel continued to regard him with nothing in her eyes to give away her thoughts about that. A long moment passed while she processed the fact that the owner of the theater where her late husband's play had been running had suggested to her agent where she might be found.

"Who initiated the contact between you and Mavis?" she asked pointedly.

He saw no sense in hedging and admitted to her that Mavis Dunning had called him, looking for Hazel Todd.

"She wants you for the lead in Wayward. Now, Hazel, a lot of actresses would jump at the chance for that role, but she wants you specifically."

Hazel wasn't sure why she was sensing so strongly that Louise Cullen had something to do with this, and she wondered if it might be God warning her. In any event, it wasn't difficult for her to realize what this was about. She owed nothing to Mavis Dunning or to Louise Cullen.

"I have no interest in propping up Barry's legacy, or helping Mavis recoup her losses, Clayton." she informed him coolly.

"If she's had to close a show, I'm sure it's not the first time. I won't be stepping in to bring her audience back."

Her eyes let him know that she meant exactly that, and she turned her back to him to reach for a bowl, in order to add some scones to the day's menu.

Clayton watched her, a sense of both disappointment and aggravation washing over him.

"You can't be serious!" He was incredulous.

Hazel smiled to herself, as she recognized a sense of peace settling over her and quietly thanked God for it.

"I'm sorry you drove all the way out to this little backwoods cafe, Clayton. Maybe next time, just call."

"You know good and well that I've been calling you!"

That was true, she admitted to herself. He had been calling and she had been ignoring him. She turned now to look at him calmly.

"Yes, you have. I'm sorry that I didn't take any of your calls. I was dealing with the funeral and the aftermath of that, but I did see that you called as recently as yesterday and I didn't call you back. That was rude, and I apologize.

"The thing is, Clayton, that I'm not entirely sure I'll be taking any more calls from either you or Morris, in the future."

Her agent continued to be astounded, particularly now, as she included her manager, Morris Trent, in the list of people she had chosen to ignore.

"Exactly what does that mean, Hazel?" He felt a small bit of panic. "You do remember that you have contracts with both your manager and your agent."

"I'll be having those looked at by my attorney," she said with a little shrug. "I seem to remember a phrase suggesting that you both would be acting with integrity in my best interest.

"You both know that those contracts acknowledge the fact that I categorically refuse to do nude scenes and yet, here you are. I don't consider that to be in my best interest. I do, however, consider it to be a breach of contract."

The door chimed and Hazel looked up with a smile as Ed Crockett immediately smelled the warm quiche and made a beeline for the counter.

Clayton Ballard moved to go find a chair and sit down in an effort to mull over the best way to proceed, in light of the fact that Hazel seemed completely fine with cutting all her ties with the theater and with her representation.

He half heard Ed Crockett's praise of the quiche and Hazel's laughing response to his remarks and was still sitting there, staring down at the table after the man took his coffee and lunch and left with a happy wave.

Hazel glanced over at him but left him to his despondent thoughts as she began mixing the batter for both her savory and dessert scones.

"You do realize, Hazel, that all I did was relay a theater owner's message to you. I haven't tried to convince you to take the part. I simply told you about it, which is an agent's job."

She turned around at the sound of Clayton's quiet comment and regarded him thoughtfully.

"I do realize that, Clayton. If that's where it ends, then I'm willing to try not to overreact, by bringing my attorney into things, but please don't contact me with any future requests for parts that you already know I won't accept."

He breathed a sigh of relief, still not looking forward to having to tell Mavis Dunning that Hazel Todd was turning down the role, but knowing that continuing to try to persuade her was the worst possible route he could take.

He enjoyed having Hazel Todd listed on the roster of talent that his agency represented and if she were removed from that list, it would seem like a strike against him in the industry. He knew that his best course of action was to keep his actress onboard and to not make waves.

"Well," he offered, a bit deflated, "if that's your last word, then that's just how it is. I'll let Mavis know to look elsewhere. In the meantime, are you open to hearing about any new roles, or are you taking time off?"

Hazel rested her forearms on the counter and studied him pensively.

"I haven't actually thought that far ahead, Clayton. I've just been resting and clearing my head. So, yes, I guess that means I'm taking some time off. I'm in no hurry."

"So don't even tell you about any roles at all, then? I just want to be sure," he added quickly, not wanting Hazel to return to her former remarks about not taking calls from her agent or manager in the future.

"If I don't answer, leave a voicemail and I do promise that I will actually listen to the message. If I have any questions, I'll call you back."

He stood up with a smile. "I don't suppose I can walk out of here with what the last customer ordered?"

Hazel laughed and reached for a small box to send him on his way with something he might consider to have been worth his trouble.

Grant Sellars leaned back in his chair and looked around the big table in the church's library with a feeling of being outnumbered by the Christmas play committee, and he was.

On some days, Grant could simply vote no on an issue and all the other votes would swing his way, but today was not one of those days.

No matter how taken some of the ladies were with their young, handsome pastor, when they dug their heels in on something, he wasn't young enough, or handsome enough to persuade them, and the committee's heels were firmly dug in on the idea of approaching Hazel Todd to direct this year's play.

Apparently, some of the women who had taken food to Pastor Morgan's house had become friends with his sister, Ellen Abbott and their small talk led to the fact that an important actress was right here, in their small town.

Once word had made its way to the committee, today's meeting had taken a decidedly prejudicial bent in favor of securing the celebrity to direct their annual Christmas play.

The play was their big fundraiser and relied on ticket sales. They were sure that having Hazel Todd at the helm of this year's production would make it their best fundraiser ever, and said as much, over and over, to their weary pastor.

It was when Ivy Parker crossed her arms and demanded to know if Pastor Sellars could give them one good reason why they shouldn't ask Hazel Todd to direct their play, that he expelled a loud breath and gave up. He couldn't very well tell them that he'd rather not have to interact with the woman who had accepted his marriage proposal and then left him at the altar.

He did suggest that something this important should be brought before the board, but that notion was immediately shot down when the committee reminded him, rightfully so, that they had never had to bring their Christmas play ideas before the board and saw no reason why they had to start now.

"I'd like to make a motion to nominate Pastor Sellars as our contact to convince Miss Todd to direct this year's play," Ivy Parker announced, and a clamor of seconds was rapidly laid down, immediately leading to a unanimous vote in favor of the nomination, all while Grant was still trying to follow what was happening. The committee moved and seconded to adjourn as he desperately tried to remember the last thing he'd just heard.

Ladies were pushing back from the table in varying degrees of satisfaction and excited chatter, some to head home to cook lunch, some to take care of grocery shopping, some to meet up with friends on the square, but all with a sense of accomplishment.

Their pastor was left sitting alone with a dazed look on his face. He closed his eyes and leaned forward to rest his head in his hands, clutching his hair in his fingers in frustration, and frowning at the realization that Fred was on his honeymoon, so he couldn't just pass this off for him and Katie to deal with.

He considered being upset with Hazel over the whole thing but knew fully well that she was completely in the dark about the Christmas committee's plans and had no involvement in the way things were beginning to take shape.

Although he couldn't understand why she was still here, she had come for a funeral. She could hardly be held responsible for where her late husband's parents had purchased their plots years before, and after meeting them, Grant knew that Hazel would have just agreed to the arrangements, in order to keep the peace. Besides, how could she have possibly known that her former fiancé was now a pastor in that small town that neither of them had ever heard of before?

Grant leaned back in his chair and rested his legs on the edge of the table, crossing his arms and closing his eyes. He needed to process all of this. The Christmas committee represented most of the women in the church and he could hardly afford to cross them solely because of his own desire for self-preservation.

Of course, it wasn't as though he expected Hazel to agree to the church's request. He had reluctantly checked online, once he discovered she was in town, and knew that Hazel Todd was a big name in the world of stage and theater. She probably felt some obligation to do what she could to help Katie, since the two of them had become friends, but once Katie returned, she would more than likely be ready to return to her career and to California, if that was where she lived.

Grant rubbed his eyes and absently fingered the little cross that hung on a chain around his neck. It was a habit he had when he was deep in thought, so the patina was pretty well pronounced on its surface.

He had been surprised when he realized that Hazel wasn't attending Katie and Fred's wedding. All the quiet fretting and feelings of unrest that he had engaged in had been for nothing. Katie had made no secret of the fact that she had begged Hazel to come and she told Grant this defiantly, just to make sure he knew that she had wanted her there.

Fred had waited until Katie was claimed by her mother before he confided to Grant that Hazel had turned Katie down, saying that she wouldn't do that to him. He said that she'd told them it would be like a slap in the face to him and that she wanted him to be able to enjoy himself.

Fred said that Hazel asked if she could be allowed to keep Katie's shop open while they were gone for two weeks, reminding Katie that it was a new business and could really suffer by immediately having to be closed for so long. According to Fred, her offer turned out to be a gift to Katie, since Hazel used her time to add a few things to the menu to keep the locals coming in, hoping to establish them as regulars.

Grant drew in a deep breath now, and wondered which Hazel this was. The eighteen-year-old Hazel was a very nice girl, but she didn't necessarily go out of her way to put someone else's interests ahead of her own. It wasn't that she was selfish. She was just a teenager.

When Grant took the time to study her closely on the walking trail, he was forced to admit that she was a woman he didn't know, regardless of how much he had once loved her.

He hadn't loved that woman, he reminded himself dryly. He had loved an eighteen-year-old girl, and he wasn't exactly an example of wisdom and maturity back then, being only five years older than Hazel.

He wanted to mutter under his breath that it had been nothing but puppy love, but he hesitated, even now, to call it that. If he did, then he would have to deal with the fact that he had spent the past twelve years hurting over something as insignificant as infatuation, rather than real love which he felt involved commitment, passion and intimacy, none of which he and Hazel had shared together.

Grant knew he had to face the fact that the kind of love he had once thought was the foundation he was ready to build a marriage on was immature at best, and that if he wasn't willing to admit that to himself, he was living a lie and being rebellious. He felt a sting of conviction.

He knew he could be a more effective minister for this church and less prone to carnal emotions, such as the ones he gave into at Barry Cullen's funeral, or at the gym with Fred, if he would just let the Holy Spirit change his mindset regarding the wounds he had been nursing for so long.

93

He had spent all those years grimly telling himself that his anger was justified, that he had a right to feel what he felt and that no man would blame him for resenting the woman who had inflicted that kind of pain and public humiliation on him.

It wasn't that he hadn't been genuinely hurt, but he had to find a way to walk away from it. He realized that by keeping his pain alive, he had built a memorial to it and it had become an idol that he kept sacrificing to.

It was exactly the sort of counsel a responsible minister should give to any young man who found himself in the same situation, and Grant silently prayed now for God to help him accept what he knew the Holy Spirit was telling him and to yield to it. He knew that holding on to his pain was pride, and he also knew that God resisted the proud, but gave grace to the humble.

He pushed up from his chair and breathed out a sigh, as he told himself that one sure way to deliver a blow to his pride would be to humble himself enough to do what the Christmas committee had nominated him to do, and ask Hazel Todd to direct their Christmas play.

Chapter Ten

Hazel stood staring around the cafe with a vacant look on her face. She knew there had to be more flour, because when she let Katie know that she hadn't seen any and had picked up a small bag, Katie apologized and told her that there was actually plenty "up on the shelf" but so far, no bag of flour was leaping out at her from any of the shelves, and she was completely out.

She pursed her lips and continued to train her gaze slowly, thinking that maybe it was in a canister then, instead of a paper bag. She told herself that she would definitely keep flour in a sealed container instead of just in a bag, so she tried to repeat her search with that in mind and finally stopped to consider a round, blue bucket-looking thing up on the top shelf.

Hazel drew her brows and frowned. Why, in the world, would Katie keep the flour way up on the top shelf? Katie was just a little, petite thing and even though Hazel was considered to be tall, she was certainly not tall enough to reach that.

She looked around for something to stand on, after first determining that there was no ladder in the store room. She finally decided that all she needed was a lift to the countertop, and that she could reach the bucket by standing on that, so she pulled a barstool over and took off her shoes, then carefully planted herself on it, slowly rising and wondering why all the barstools were padded.

She was a bit wobbly, but took her time and finally made it onto the top of the counter. She could tell that the blue bucket was heavy, so whatever was in it, it was full.

She heard the door chime and called out over her shoulder that she would be right there, then attempted to grasp the bucket by both hands to see how hard it would be to move.

"Get down, Hazel."

The low, quiet command came from Grant. She drew in her breath and almost fell, as soon as she heard it. She moved to obey, but her legs suddenly began shaking.

"I'm trying to," Hazel said, with a nervous little laugh.

"Wait," he instructed, coming around behind the front counter to stand by the barstool and hold a hand up to her. "All you have to do is just sit down."

She grasped his hand so that she was steady enough to be able to lower herself down to sit on the countertop, before looking up at him with soft, brown eyes and an embarrassed, self-conscious smile.

"Thank you."

She figured she could get down now, but she'd have to wait for him to move, to be able to do it. She was flustered, but she at least had the presence of mind to let go of his hand.

"What are you after?" Grant questioned, glancing up at the bucket on the shelf.

"I'm trying to find the flour, and I wondered if that might be it, since it doesn't seem to be anywhere else. I wanted to look really good, before I gave up and bothered Katie."

Grant nodded, then slipped his thumbs into his jeans pockets and let his eyes travel around the shop. He was a good deal taller than Hazel, so he wouldn't need to stand on the countertop, but he did need at least an extra foot of height to manage the weight of the bucket.

He finally spotted a little plastic folding footstool under the sink and pulled it out and positioned it on the floor, next to the counter.

"Hop down, Hay," he said absently, still estimating the height of the stool against his own height and not realizing he had just called her an old nickname.

She noticed and smiled faintly, as she used her arms to boost herself from where she was sitting on the edge of the counter to the floor, and nailed the landing.

"Ta da!" she cheered quietly and saw a quick flash of amusement hurry across Grant's face, as he heard her.

He managed to reach the bucket, and suspected that it might contain flour after all, since it was heavy. He brought it down and placed it on the countertop, reaching to unsnap the lid and take a look.

"Well, it's either flour or Katie's little shop is a front for manufacturing explosives," he observed, wetting the end of his pinkie and dipping it in to taste.

"It appears to be flour after all, so maybe she's managed to rehabilitate herself," Grant commented, replacing the lid before turning to look at Hazel who quickly stopped studying him and dropped her gaze with a flush of color.

Grant glanced back up at the shelf, then around the kitchen area. "There has to be somewhere more sensible to keep the flour, one would think."

Hazel joined him in considering it, then pointed to an area between the corner of the wall and the microwave.

"Is it too big around to fit in that space?"

"Not once you realize that a freestanding microwave can be moved."

He lifted the large bucket and when it needed a couple of inches more to slide in, he demonstrated the portability of the microwave oven.

Hazel gave herself a little facepalm. "That's impressive. If you work cheap, you're hired."

"How cheap is cheap?" Grant asked, noticing that the lid on the bucket hadn't snapped down completely, and fixing it.

"I'll give you twice what I'm making," she offered.

She suddenly frowned, then crossed her arms and let out a big sigh. "Well, that's just great. Now, I can't remember why I needed flour," she confessed, twisting her lips into a little scowl when Grant seemed to roll his eyes.

"So you want the flour back up there?"

"Don't you dare," she warned. "But seriously, thank you, Grant. I'm pretty sure I'd be lying on my broken back, buried under a pile of white flour by now, if you hadn't stopped by. Especially since it's not self-rising flour."

They both winced at her lame joke, then she looked up at him with curious wonder on her beautiful face. "Were you just walking by and saw me through the window, or something?"

"I'm actually here intentionally, although I don't want to be," he replied and immediately noticed the sadness in her eyes.

"No, that's not... I mean, it's true that I don't want to be, so I won't lie, but it's not because of what you're thinking. I've actually been sent."

She seemed relieved but still confused.

"By a committee," he added.

"Are they running me out of town?" she asked, with a little grin. "Are you their enforcer?"

"Hardly. Just the opposite, in fact."

He looked around and Hazel easily interpreted the question in his eyes.

"I just brewed some," she said, reaching for a mug and warming it up with some hot water before pouring his coffee.

He took it from her with a word of thanks and led the way over to a little table, pulling out a couple of chairs.

Hazel felt a little rush of adrenaline as she realized that this would be the first real conversation with Grant in years. He seemed to recognize that fact as well, and sat looking at his mug quietly, an odd hint of a smile resting around his mouth.

"You seem to be trying to determine if it's really me," he observed, glancing up at her.

"It's just that I never saw you with a beard, before. It's really nice."

Hazel wondered if that sounded as lame to him as it did to her, but decided to not make it worse by changing it.

"I suppose we're both different. You cut your hair," he pointed out.

Hazel's hair had once been long. She had worn it either in braids or a ponytail, but only loose for bed. She reached for the ends of it that just brushed the top of her shoulder.

"I guess it's been like this for several years. Easier to manage and I'm a lot less likely to wake up and find gum in it."

Grant grinned at the memory of being told that she had stayed home from school once, not because she was sick, but because she had a huge wad of gum in her hair.

"Do you still fall asleep reading at night, with gum in your mouth?" he wondered.

"I fall asleep reading but I'm not the big gum chewer I used to be. I saw myself in a video once, chewing gum, and I was disgusted. Why didn't you ever tell me what I looked like?"

He shook his head, and lifted his coffee to take a sip. He didn't want to focus on what she looked like then, or especially now, since it made it hard for him to concentrate.

When he set his mug back down, he continued to stare at it for a moment before looking back up at her.

"One of the aggravations a pastor has to contend with is anything that involves a committee. They're invariably made up of women, if you'll pardon that sexist observation, who have a lot of time on their hands and assume that I do, as well."

"Have you just come from a committee, then?" she asked, unable to hide her smile.

"What gave it away? The heel marks on my chest they left, when they adjourned and rushed out, leaving me for dead?"

Hazel actually rippled out a laugh at that image and he quietly joined her.

"It's that time of year," he began with a grimace, "and the annual Christmas play is upon us. I'm just going to tell you plainly the favor that I've been sent to ask you for, and then let you refuse, and I can go back and truthfully tell the committee that I tried, although I hope they don't ask me how hard I tried."

Hazel had picked up on the word "play" and had an inkling of where this was going but waited to let Grant say what he wanted to say.

He leaned back to cross his arms, something very much in keeping with his character, and fixed Hazel with a direct look.

"They want you to direct their Christmas play. One, two, three, go."

He waited but she didn't just shake her head and say no, as he'd expected her to. Instead, she seemed to think about it.

99

"You were the only one who voted no," she said, raising her eyes to his with the hint of teasing in them.

"If we're being honest," he admitted, wondering what she thought about that.

"Well, Grant..." Hazel stopped herself, and tried to work out if they would be better off clearing the air, or if they should just leave it all unsaid.

He watched her work through conflicting thoughts, silently noting her soft sculpted jawline and how flawless her complexion was, and immediately pulled himself back in line and tried to focus on why he was here.

She rested her eyes on his and spoke softly. "When I saw you on the walking trail, and told you that I was sorry, I never meant anything more in my life. In fact, I don't think I'll ever stop being sorry, even though the scriptures seem to want to lead me away from staying in that place."

Grant raised a brow in surprise when he heard her reference the scriptures. He assumed that she had moved on to the kind of life that made no room for spiritual things.

"Right now, though, I'm still there, in that place of being more sorry than I can say. I've been there a long time."

She had been looking down at her hands, but raised her eyes again to meet his. "Grant, I would love to help your church, but if you don't want me there, I won't do that to you."

He was uncertain about that.

"Are you saying that I'm the reason you wouldn't want to be involved with the play?"

"I'm saying that if I were to help with the church's play, we'd probably end up spending time together more often than you would want, and I can't blame you for feeling that way. I wouldn't want to make you uncomfortable."

"Would *you* be uncomfortable, Hazel?" Grant waited.

"I don't know what you want my answer to be," she began slowly, "but I'm not uncomfortable right now. Are you?"

He held her gaze and shook his head.

"You won't be upset with me, if I agree to help them?"

100

He was surprised to realize that he wouldn't be. Again, he simply shook his head.

"I'm subletting Katie's place and there's something like three months left on it, so that would keep me here anyway, until after Christmas. I'm still uncertain about what to do after that," she confessed, "but it gives me time to pray about it."

Grant was once again unprepared to hear Hazel speak about something spiritual like prayer, but asked no questions. He simply sat looking at her quietly and she returned his look, while they took a moment to read each other.

"What's the name of it?" she asked, after a long silence.

He furrowed his brow. "Pardon?"

"The play?"

Grant closed his eyes, trying to think, before looking at her again with a grin. "I have absolutely no idea."

"Is it an adult cast or..."

Again, he sat shaking his head.

"Children, or..."

Grant saw no reason to stop shaking his head, so he continued, until Hazel erupted into beautiful laughter.

"Maybe I'd better meet with your committee," she suggested, and he lifted a finger to touch the side of his head.

"There's a good idea," he said, a wry grin lighting up his eyes and causing Hazel to think about how handsome he was.

"Do I come to your church, or... do they want to come here?" She looked around the shop. "Of course, it's the lull here right now, so if they did, it would need to be this time of day. But I can just come there, if it can wait until Sunday or Monday? That's when the shop is closed."

Hazel was obviously working through her mental calendar, unaware that Grant was again studying her face closely and marveling at how beautifully she had grown from a young girl into a woman. She finally stopped looking into the air, where she seemed to be watching her thoughts, and rested her expressive eyes on his again.

"Isn't Monday like a pastor's day off? I've always thought that, for some reason, but I'm not sure why."

"It's supposed to be. It rarely works out that way, though. I'm pretty much on call, especially since I live in the parsonage, next to the church," he explained. "If you need to meet on a Monday, that's not a problem. I just need to let the ladies know in time for them to plan for it."

"Actually, if it could be this Monday, that would be good because, believe it or not, when you're talking about something like putting on a play, they've almost left it too late, as it is."

Grant raised a brow at her words. "That's unfortunate, seeing that their annual play is a ticket-selling event and their biggest fundraiser of the year."

Hazel looked alarmed. "Oh, Grant, it really needs to be this Monday, then."

He nodded, and seemed to be about to stand, then stopped himself.

"Hazel," he began, after she gave him the time to think through what he wanted to say. "I'm sorry for what I said at your husband's funeral, especially with you already grieving..."

She raised a hand to stop him.

"No. I won't go into it, but no. I wasn't grieving, but if he really is in hell, of course I'm sad for that, and I guess I never saw anything to indicate that he wouldn't be. But I wasn't grieving, as cold as that sounds, so I won't pretend I was."

Grant looked up at her sharply, stunned by her words. He almost asked her if she would reconsider and explain, but he forced himself to let it go.

"Still, I'm sorry I said it, Hazel," he repeated.

"Don't be sorry for that, Grant. It was the truth."

He met her eyes in order to determine if she really meant what she'd just said.

"It was hardly the right time or place to deliver such an assault on everyone, regardless of whether or not it was the truth," he pointed out quietly.

"You'd just had a shock," she offered, almost speaking in a whisper. "And my face was the last one you ever wanted to see again. Under the circumstances, I think you showed a great deal of restraint, especially with how the Cullens were behaving."

"I'm sure I did more harm than good, though," Grant decided, unwilling to simply write his behavior off to a fit of bad temper. "For that, I'm sorry."

Hazel had run out of protests and now simply rested a sweet smile on him that made him catch his breath.

"We'll just have to pray that God uses what you said," she replied.

"You've maintained your relationship with God, even with your career?" Grant couldn't resist asking the question and Hazel was truthful.

"Not so much maintaining, as discovering. I'm only recently coming to a place of repentance over the unloving way I treated God, for so many years. I had been avoiding talking to Him because I was afraid of what He would say to me, but He seems to not be angry with me, like I thought He would be. So, I guess the simple answer, without overcomplicating it, is that I do have a relationship with God. Which is very comforting," she added, with a little smile. "I rely heavily on Him."

Grant continued to weigh Hazel's words and discern her spirit and was able to see that the young girl he had convinced to share his future and his calling, but who impulsively ran away when she became overwhelmed by it all, was forever gone and so was the target of his anger.

Hazel saw him struggling with something else he wanted to say and waited, uncertain of what emotions might rise to the surface, now that the years had finally brought them to this moment, but believing that God was watching over the both of them. She regarded him with tender eyes.

"It was wrong of me to expect you to just sacrifice your future and join me in mine," he finally said in a low, soft voice.

"For years, I wouldn't admit that, because I was proud and I wanted to be angry. I wanted to think that you were in rebellion, but that was evidence of my lack of spiritual maturity.

"It was never that I doubted that God was calling me to the ministry, Hazel. But maybe He wasn't calling me right that moment, without my having been taught or growing into that calling. And even if He was, He wasn't necessarily calling you.

103

"I acted as if you and I were a package deal, and that was wrong. I shouldn't have expected you to just drop everything and join me in something that neither of us really knew anything at all about.

"The Ministry," he said, emphasizing the mysterious nature of it with raised brows and a little grin. "I have to admit, that probably sounded a little scary to a young teenaged girl.

"Not showing up at the church might not have been the best way to let me know that you couldn't marry me."

Instead of being angry, Grant seemed to be teasing her.

"I do wish we could have talked about it privately, but I'm sure you wish that too, now."

"I do wish that," she confessed, unable to stop a stray tear from finding its way down her face. "I've wished so many times that I really had been the adult I tried to pretend I was. What I did to you was so mean. I've longed for years to beg you to forgive me, but it's unforgivable."

Grant reached a finger to wipe her tear away, then rested his hands on hers, not in a romantic way, but as one lifelong friend comforting another.

"It's not unforgivable. So, let's forgive each other."

He pulled a napkin from the table's dispenser and tucked it into her hand as fresh tears began to gather in her pretty eyes.

"We move on," he said quietly. "It's time we left the grave of all that behind us, Hazie, and stop bringing it flowers."

He gave her hands the slightest squeeze. "Yes?"

She nodded and gave him a trembling smile.

"Yes, please."

Chapter Eleven

Mrs. Ivy Parker pounded the bottom of a jar of cold cream she'd found in her purse on the table, in lieu of an actual gavel, and stood waiting patiently for the chatter to die down, so that the committee meeting could begin.

Grant almost interrupted to caution her about the possibility of breaking it, but paused to consider the way she had run roughshod over him at the last meeting and decided that if she broke it, she broke it, and that she could clean it up.

She started to speak, then stopped and turned to look at her pastor almost accusingly. "Where is she?"

"She'll be here," he assured her, with a little wave of his hand that Ivy seemed to take issue with.

"But she *is* coming?" she persisted, as all the other women quieted down and stared at him in unison.

If she had asked Grant Sellars that question a week ago, he might have suggested that perhaps Hazel had pulled a runner and skipped out on them, but the thought hadn't even occurred to him now, especially since Hazel had gone to great lengths to convince him that she was coming. Of course, the talk they had at the shop went a long way toward reassuring him, as well.

"Again, she'll be here, Ivy. Perhaps you should have a reading of the minutes or take care of any outstanding business that she wouldn't need to concern herself with, so that when she does get here, you can move right into the actual play."

Hazel had texted Grant, during the pounding of Ivy's cold cream jar, to tell him that just as she was opening the door to leave, she walked right into Fred and Katie, who were back from their honeymoon and were eager to check on things.

She told them that she was on her way out and promised to catch up with them later in the day, but all that was now going to cause her to be a few minutes late. She added a wide-eyed surprised emoji to her text and Grant responded with an angry face and fist, which caused her to send a laughing one.

Of course, Grant could have just said as much to his nemesis, Ivy Parker, but he was enjoying watching her fret, and sat smugly confident, smiling quietly to himself.

Ivy called for the tiresome reading of the minutes and Geraldine Fowler tried to oblige, despite the fact that she had sat on her glasses in the car, and could only look through one lens, now. As a result, Ivy's patience finally reached its limit and she dispensed with the minutes, in an effort to keep them on track.

"That's quite alright, Geraldine, we were all here, we remember what we said."

She stared down at her notes, then looked back up to steadily regard each individual member.

"Points for drama," Grant mused silently to himself.

Whatever Ivy had been about to scold them for was forgotten as the door opened and Hazel slipped in hesitantly, to the enthusiastic applause of the Christmas play committee.

She seemed surprised and a little embarrassed, despite her career depending heavily on applause, and smiled graciously at the ladies, while hurrying over to the chair Grant had apparently saved for her.

He lifted his notebook and phone off the chair and flashed Ivy Parker a triumphant smile.

She flashed him one of her own and gestured toward Hazel. "Pastor Sellars, won't you introduce our guest?"

"I'm so sorry," Hazel whispered, covering her mouth with her hand. Her dancing eyes suggested that she was not at all sorry and was enjoying his predicament.

Grant gave her a slow smile that let her know that he wasn't afraid of her or Ivy Parker, and rose to his full height, indicating their local celebrity by resting a hand lightly on her shoulder.

"Ladies, we are indeed fortunate to have with us, in our small town and modest church, an undisputed star of the stage. She is not only a multiple award-winning thespian, but an experienced director and a published playwright."

Hazel was staring up at Grant with her eyes beginning to mist over, as she realized that he had researched her career. She lifted a hand to rest against her throat and drew in a deep breath to steady herself.

He seemed to sense her emotion and looked down at her with less teasing and more kindness in his eyes.

"Yet, for all her acclaim, she is truthfully one of the most humble and generous people it has been my privilege to know. You are all well-acquainted with our own newly wedded couple, Fred Buckley and Katie Allen Buckley."

As the women nodded their assent, Grant continued to rest his eyes and his smile on Hazel.

"While she could have simply left town to continue what is clearly a successful career, she put the needs of her friend Katie first, and single-handedly kept her coffee shop open for the entire two weeks that Katie was on her honeymoon, and she did it completely free of charge. It was an act of love."

He saw that Hazel was in danger of needing a tissue and showed her mercy by wrapping up his introduction. "Ladies, please welcome Hazel Todd."

He gently added his applause to the standing ovation his words generated, before taking his seat and grinning at the whispered threat she leaned over to breathe into his ear.

"Remind me to kill you later."

Ivy Parker was effusive with her thanks for Hazel's willingness to be involved in their fundraising effort and took a moment to tell her what they had done for their Christmas play in previous years, and that they sadly fell short of their goal.

Ivy seemed to be waiting for Hazel to comment, and she reached over to touch Grant's notebook with a question in her eyes. He flipped a few pages back, then folded it over and handed it to her, along with his pen.

"I expect you to come to class prepared," he muttered, causing her to have to suppress a giggle.

He glanced down with a faint smile as he watched her jot down the date and purpose of the meeting, noting that her handwriting was exactly the same as he remembered, but failing to associate it with the letter she had written him. Healing was slowly and compassionately fading those memories for him.

"What play do you intend to perform this year?" Hazel tucked a strand of her dark hair behind one ear and glanced up at Ivy Parker and then around at the group.

They all seemed to be looking at each other for the answer, then back up at Ivy Parker.

"Well, we thought it might just be easier to do 'A Christmas Carol' again, since most of us are familiar with the script," she said, as the other ladies nodded in agreement.

"But..." Hazel looked over at Grant and he gave her a grin that playfully dared her to cross Ivy Parker. She impressed him by rising to the challenge.

"Since you've done 'A Christmas Carol' several years in a row, and you're telling me that your fundraising has failed to meet your goal, have you considered that this may be one of the reasons? It may be that the townspeople are unable to feel any enthusiasm for something that holds no surprises for them.

"I expect many of them decide to simply purchase tickets but not attend, and after enough time passes, they may also never get around to actually buying the tickets."

A rippling of alarm made its way through the committee before Ivy Parker appealed to Hazel for a solution.

"There really isn't nearly the amount of time you might think, before the Christmas play is actually performed. A lot of front work goes into a successful show.

"I've adapted the historical account of the penning of Henry Wadsworth Longfellow's 'Christmas Bells' into a script that doesn't involve a large cast, and has a minimal amount of set change. I've not allowed it to be performed before, but I would allow it to play here, and direct it for you."

There was an immediate ripple of excitement among the ladies of the committee. Even though many of them might not be aware of the circumstances behind the words, they knew and loved the beautiful Christmas hymn and were eager to be able to claim to be the first to perform the play.

Grant quietly processed the fact that Hazel had undertaken the task of scripting the documented account of the nineteenth century poet's beautiful composition, written in the face of tragic loss; a reluctant admission of the truth of what the Christmas bells were telling him, despite his own personal despair. It made Grant think of the scriptural reference to a "sacrifice of praise".

She seemed to be anxiously hoping for his approval and he smiled faintly to himself and gave her a slight nod, not missing the relief it gave her.

Rather than ask Ivy Parker for permission to change the play, Hazel simply continued as if the decision had been made. She was satisfied with the pastor's approval.

"Do you have any seasoned actors, or any who have shown promise in previous performances?"

She directed this question as a general one, and several of the ladies began to suggest names. One name was that of an elderly gentleman who had begun attending the little church only a couple of years ago, but who had impressed the congregation with his brilliant portrayal of Ebenezer Scrooge.

Hazel looked up quickly when she heard the name and her face registered shock.

"Excuse me," she said, when the chatter continued to grow more animated.

"Ladies!" Grant broke in, causing them to give him their attention. He gestured for Hazel to continue.

"Excuse me, ladies, but did one of you say the name Irving Lancaster?" She waited breathlessly, searching each face and drawing in her breath when they nodded.

"He attends this church?" Hazel looked at Grant so intently that it took a moment for him to collect himself.

109

"He does, but he's still considered to be a newcomer, compared to most of our congregation. He moved here a couple of years ago from the east coast."

Hazel laid a hand on his arm and explored his face with childlike eyes. "Can you tell me how to find him?"

He drew his brow and tried to understand her sudden urgency, but told her he'd get the information from his office, after the meeting.

She stared down at the notebook for a moment, unable to hide the emotional state she was in. She made herself look up and advise the group that she would be posting a list of characters and audition times in Katie's shop, aware that this would bring traffic there, and that she'd also have Pastor Sellars announce the information, once they had the details worked out.

There was some discussion between Ivy Parker and the ladies about concessions and organizing a food committee, but Hazel sat hugging Grant's notebook tightly, unable to focus. He could see that she was struggling for composure.

"Ladies," Grant interrupted, "Miss Todd has a busy day ahead of her, so if there is no more discussion about the play, I'll let her get on with that and leave you to finish these other details."

The ladies all joined in to thank Hazel as she responded to Grant's hand on her elbow and stood to their applause. She gave them a smile as she let him lead her out of the library and to his office.

"Have a seat, Hay," he invited, reaching for the directory he kept on his desk, having not gotten around to transferring the information to his computer, although he knew he needed to.

She sank onto the chair that faced his desk, and he came around to rest on the front edge of it, flipping through the pages in search of the information she had asked for.

He stopped to look at her and when she became aware of his gaze, she raised her eyes to his and gave him a smile.

"Do I get to know?" he asked quietly.

"He's a close friend," Hazel said, slightly clearing her throat. "He was a mentor to me and we lost touch after I went to California. I had no idea where he was.

"I tried finding him, but he'd moved as well, and no one seemed to know where he'd gone. He was said to have retired, but that was all I could find out. He doesn't involve himself in any sort of social media."

"I don't have to ask if he's an actor," Grant commented, "because I saw his performance in last year's play and that was clearly evident. But he seemed reluctant to receive any accolades or divulge much information about himself. I haven't persisted to ply him with questions."

Hazel smiled at Grant's description of her friend. "He's not just an actor. He's one of the greats."

He reached down to coax her to release his notebook that she was still clinging to and she gave it to him with a look of apology.

He opened it to a fresh page and copied what he found in the directory, then tore it out to give to her. "Did you want the rest of your notes?"

She stared down at the address he had given her and he had to repeat his question.

"Yes, I'm sorry. Yes, please," she answered, making an effort to pull herself together.

Grant carefully tore the perforated pages from the notebook, then stretched behind him for a folder to put them in. He handed them back for her to take and waited silently for her to realize that, and reach for them.

"I suppose I don't have to ask what the rest of your day is like," he ventured, and she smiled up at him.

"I'm supposed to meet up with Katie and Fred at the shop in a bit." She stood up and dropped her eyes to the folder in her hands, since standing put her in a much closer proximity to Grant, as he rested against the edge of his desk, than when she was seated.

"You have me trapped, or I'd move for you," he pointed out with a quiet laugh.

111

She grinned at him, and stepped to one side.

"What are your big day off plans?" she asked, as he moved away from his desk and stood in front of her.

"I may actually end up over near the shop, since I generally take a run in the afternoon, even though it's closed, today. If I see Frederick and his bride through the window, I may toss them a wave."

Grant stopped and studied her. "I'm actually surprised that you haven't run into Irving in the park, Hazie. I see him there quite often. He takes walks there, or more accurately, strolls. He seems to take his time and notice things."

She brightened up at that. "Does he seem to be in good health, then?"

"He does. He's rather spry and always up for a good chat when I run into him. I quite like him."

She flashed him a bright smile. "I'm glad."

"I'm sure you'll be able to connect with him."

Something seemed to occur to Grant and he hesitated, before asking.

"Your late husband's obituary was in the paper and online, Hazel. I'm surprised that I didn't see Irving at the service since he had to have known he'd be able to see you."

She looked down at the floor and frowned, shaking her head. "He wouldn't have come anywhere that William and Louise would be, if he could avoid it. Particularly Louise. He would expect me to understand that."

"If you'll pardon my saying so, I can also understand that. When she showed up here, it was all I could do to not physically throw her out the door."

Hazel drew in her breath and stared up at him. "She came here? Why, Grant?"

"She never got around to telling me that. She just breezed in, since the main door was unlocked and took a seat. I immediately made her go outside to the courtyard.

"I don't see women alone in my office. You're the exception today, because, as you can hear from the loud discussion going on in the library, we aren't alone."

Hazel continued to look up at him, unaware of the effect her steady gaze was having on him.

"I'm sorry that she did that, Grant. I imagine she was probably amusing herself. She does that when she gets bored, or when she's been drinking. Of the two of them, believe it or not, William is the least bothersome."

"Oh, I can believe that," he muttered. "I'm still unclear as to why she came, but she did let me know that she took issue with my remarks about Hell. If she expected me to take them back, she was disappointed. Instead, I doubled down."

Hazel stood trying to figure out what Louise's angle was. She still felt that she had something to do with her agent showing up on behalf of Mavis Dunning, but hadn't tried to pursue finding out what it was.

Grant noted her sober expression and wondered what it was about.

"Hazie?"

She smile happily to herself to discover how easily Grant had resumed using his nicknames for her.

"As time permits while you're here, you and I need to have more intentional conversations."

That sounded good to her. She had always loved talking to Grant and they had been able to talk about all sorts of things. She was relieved that he seemed to still want to, and nodded.

"So, we'll make that happen, then," he said. "You bring all your questions and I'll bring mine."

She laughed. "Do we get to approve each other's lists?"

"We never had to, before," he reminded her. "Let's just wing it, and see how it goes."

"Say when," she agreed, leaving him smiling as she waved her fingers at him on her way out.

Chapter Twelve

"Hazel!" Irving Lancaster's tearful smile and warm embrace immediately drew the same response from the beautiful young actress and she closed her eyes and gave him a tight hug, before standing back to look at him.

"Come in, come in!" He stood back to allow her to enter his rustic but lovely cottage and motioned toward an array of chairs and a sofa.

Hazel hesitated to sit down, just taking a moment to continue to look at her friend, taking in his beautiful white hair and distinguished beard and the sparkle of his blue eyes, still vibrant, despite his advanced years.

"Irving, when I found out you were here, I was sitting in a room full of people and couldn't afford to break down in tears, but I wanted to. My goodness, Irving! I've been looking for you, but you left no trail and I thought I'd never see you again. Where have you been?"

He gave her a tender pat on the shoulder and again suggested with a gesture that she be seated. She lowered herself onto a chair, as he did the same, and waited for him to explain.

"To begin with, dear, I owe you an apology," he began, in his careful way. "I saw the notice of Barry's funeral service, and I wanted so badly to see you, but I selfishly resisted and spent the day just walking around the park, thinking about you."

Hazel lifted her hand.

"Irving, you and I both know that nothing good could have come from your having to interact with William and Louise. I had no idea that you were here, so of course, I wasn't upset about your not coming, but if I had known, I wouldn't have wanted you to put yourself through that."

He nodded and gave her an appreciative smile.

"I knew that you would understand, my dear. As to the loss of your husband, I suppose the decent thing for me to do now is to offer you condolences, but I despise hypocrisy, so I ask you to pardon me for not insulting you by doing so."

Hazel twisted her lips into a grin and shook her head. "I have missed you so much, Irving! Real friends are a premium for me because they are so scarce in my life. I can count them on one hand.

"Barry Cullen was as much a stranger to me as the people in the back row of any theater. I didn't really know him, but what I did know, I didn't respect, so I couldn't very well grieve his passing."

She raised her eyes to his and let out a sigh. "No one tried harder than you to stop me from agreeing to that ridiculous marriage, and all I can say now is that my biggest regret is that I didn't take your advice, if that's any consolation."

"I can hardly be consoled by that, Hazel. It brings me little joy to celebrate how right I was, while realizing the price you paid for your decision." He glanced down at the floor with a bittersweet smile before looking back up at her.

"Where have I been, you ask?" He reached over to pick up his glasses, just to have something in his hands, and wondered where to begin.

"Did you know, Hazel, that this charming little town once had one of the most beautiful little theaters you could ever imagine?" He saw her look of surprise.

"My, yes. It was just off the square. I've been tempted to visit that location since I've been back, but I can't seem to make myself. I'm sure that the building is either gone, or has become something perfectly horrible and there are some things I simply cannot know. In this case, ignorance truly is bliss.

"I guess I was quite a bit younger than you are now, when I acted in my first play there."

Hazel continued to look stunned but waited in silence, just listening to her friend.

116

"Back then, I was an understudy for a lad named Walter Tibbett. You wouldn't know that name, of course, but he was quite the draw and was the lead in Hamlet, before he unwisely set out to entertain a couple of fine ladies, and ended up being rather badly beaten by their husbands, who objected.

"I was thrust into the lead, nervous but excited and completely immersed myself in the part. It was well that I did, because it opened the door for the next role and the next, until I had established myself as a lead actor."

He paused and noted how completely she was hanging to his every word and it seemed to touch him.

"Of course, now you know why I constantly insisted on advising you in your moments of indecision, by invoking my first role and declaring 'The play's the thing!' as if that was the basis for every decision. Well, for me, it was."

Hazel looked down at her hands and smiled at the memory of Irving Lancaster's impulsive declaration nearly every time she balked at auditioning for a role of any importance.

"Yes," she said softly. "The play's the thing."

They sat in silence for a brief moment, while Irving collected his thoughts, returning to her question.

"Where have I been?" he repeated, with a faraway look. "I've been to Chicago, I've been to Boston, I've been to New York, I've been to San Francisco, I've been to Paris, I've been to Stockholm, I've been to Tokyo, I've been to Rome. I've been to London, to see the queen."

He had articulated a few of the stages and travels of his life as a celebrated actor, before stopping to smile faintly at the memories and rest his eyes on hers.

"And now I'm home. This sleepy little southern hamlet is my birthplace. I'm done seeing the world and I wish to spend my remaining years here, resting on my laurels."

Hazel thought about how wonderful coming home sounded and a wistful expression washed over her lovely face.

He seemed to interpret it and wondered what it was that made his decision so appealing to her, but at the same time, he thought he knew.

"I had supposed, Hazel, that once the funeral was over and done, you would have simply returned to California. Had I known that you were still here, in my home town, of all places, I certainly would have made the effort to locate you."

He regarded her as if trying to read her mind. "What is it that keeps you here?"

She thought about his question, since she had asked herself the same one but had no real answer, other than she believed that God had a hand in orchestrating the healing between Grant Sellars and herself, if nothing else. She hadn't allowed herself to think beyond that, to a day when she might wear out her welcome or have to leave in order for their friendship to end on a healthy note.

While she was sorting out her answer, her friend decided to embellish his question.

"I have learned, to my dismay, that the Cullens have ensconced themselves in the home that they swindled an old friend of mine out of, but she is thankfully living in her eternal home now, and has no need or desire for what has become a pretentious monstrosity."

Hazel looked up quickly as he said this, and he shifted his position in his chair and continued.

"It was tempting to just pack my things and leave, once I learned that they were here and seemed bent on staying, but I thought it over and told myself that I was born here, and that I will not allow the presence of insignificant, ambitious frauds to challenge my decision to remain here.

"But of course, you are well aware of their taking up residence here, my dear, and yet, here you remain, despite the fact that there is no love lost between the Cullens and yourself, although the origin of that phrase once meant the exact opposite of how it is used today."

She nodded, continuing to stare vacantly at nothing, mulling over his words before speaking.

"I drove here, from California. It took a few days but I wanted to just be alone and think.

118

"The plan was to only stay long enough for the service, and then maybe take my time working my way back there. But something happened at the funeral that I hadn't expected to be faced with."

Hazel leveled her gaze at her dear friend.

"Do you remember when we first met, Irving, in New York, and I told you how I had done something so horrible to someone I loved very much, and that I would have to live with it for the rest of my life?"

"You failed to walk down the aisle to meet your groom, who was waiting for you," he said, without bothering to water it down. "He wanted to answer the call to the ministry, and you wanted to answer the call to tread the boards. Had you not done so, we never would have met, so I resist passing judgment."

"You and I have a mutual friend, here," she said, after a moment. She saw him wrinkle his brow, as he wondered who it might possibly be.

"Since you have just reminded me of the man you might have married, I can only assume you have found him to be here, but I can't imagine how I have come to share him with you as a mutual friend."

"He's your pastor," Hazel said softly, not missing his raised brows as she surprised him.

"The good Pastor Sellars was to have been your groom?"

She simply nodded and Irving pressed his fingertips together and brought them to his mouth, as he pondered this. After a moment, he glanced over at her.

"Am I failing in my loyalties to you as a friend, if I confess that I find the young minister to be quite likeable and enjoy running into him, from time to time?"

Hazel laughed gently at that. "Not at all. In fact, that's what he has to say about you."

Irving sat up straight in his chair and studied her closely. "Is he still angry with you?"

She shook her head. "He's forgiven me, and he's actually very kind to me."

119

"This doesn't surprise me," he said lightly. "I don't find that young man of God to be particularly religious, but I do find him to be authentic which, I must say, I prefer over piety."

He continued to regard his young friend knowingly. "He is the reason that you are still here?"

"Not at first," she said. "At first, I agreed to sublet an apartment of a girl I met here, because I wasn't sure what I wanted to do and I thought if I could just stop here for a bit and pray about it, then I could make better decisions than I've made in the past. Of course, I didn't know, at the time, that the Cullens were going to stay as long as they seem to be staying."

He expelled an exaggerated sigh and gave her a nod of sympathy. "Clearly."

"I have a purpose for staying here now, Irving, at least temporarily, which is why I'm here. To ask a favor."

The venerable, renowned actor leaned back in his chair and simply waited, always reluctant to deny a request made by his young friend, although he had done so, from time to time.

"I've been asked to direct the church's Christmas play."

He laughed softly. "Is this your young man's revenge?"

Hazel laughed with him. "He was the victim of a committee and they nominated him to ask me."

"A committee of women, I've no doubt," he speculated, with another laugh. "Our poor pastor was railroaded."

She nodded. "I met with the committee today and it turns out that their annual play is their biggest fundraising effort but it hasn't been very successful, the past few years."

"Ah, yes. 'A Christmas Carol', ad nauseam. I was their Ebenezer last year, you know," he added. "I was rather good, if I do say so."

"That goes without saying," Hazel declared, rolling her eyes. "But, as you seem to already know, they've been doing the same play over and over, for several years. Actually, that's how I found out you were here. I asked if there was anyone who particularly shined in a performance in the past, and your name was the first one I heard."

"How gratifying," he mused softly. "But I do hope, my dear Hazel, that you aren't asking me to once again don a nightcap and storm about in a dressing gown, declaring Bah! Humbug! at every opportunity. The Latin phrase 'ad nauseam' has never been so full of meaning as when applied to 'A Christmas Carol'."

"I agree. I've managed to steer them in another direction this year."

"What strange powers of persuasion do you possess, that you can bend Ivy Parker to your will?"

Hazel laughed and he smiled at the imagery.

"I'm allowing them to perform a script from an adaptation I wrote."

"You're allowing them to feel exclusive," he accused, with a grin.

"It sounds really bad, when you say it," she observed.

"Not at all! All methods of persuasion are permissible in the effort to stop the seasonal madness that is personified in the embodiment of Ebenezer Scrooge."

He paused and considered the young actress, having read some of her adaptations. She had managed to impress him with her unexpected treatments of dull subject matter.

"Have I read the adaptation of the play you have in mind?" he wondered.

"No, I've never shown it to anyone, but the script reads well. I know it'll play, Irving. I have a feeling about it."

"What is it that you have adapted, since you force me to ask, having already warned me that some sort of favor is attached to it?" He smiled at her flush of color.

"I wrote a script based on the circumstances and events that led Henry Wadsworth Longfellow to write 'Christmas Bells'. I brought a copy for you."

Irving Lancaster ceased teasing his young friend and drew in his breath before asking in a hushed voice, "And the favor would be?"

"That you would be my lead."

121

He grew quiet for a long moment, but a soft smile rested on his face and reached his eyes.

"Of course, Longfellow was twenty years my junior when he penned his beautiful poem, but that is for makeup to be concerned with. He was forced to grow his beard after the burns to his face made shaving painful and difficult and it is his beard that is most associated with his image. I have that down."

He brushed the back of his fingers across his own beard and looked over at her, still pondering. "Even with the magic of stage makeup, I can't be expected to manage that portion of his life that takes place in his younger, clean shaven years. You would have to cast a young Longfellow and then leave it to me to bring the latter portion of the narrative to its conclusion."

"You'll do it?" Hazel held her breath.

He regarded her with a challenging gaze, as a slow smile began to light up his countenance.

"Try and stop me."

Chapter Thirteen

Katie looked up as the door chimed and smiled at the man who stopped to look around the cafe.

"Hello!" She gestured toward the menu board behind her. "These are our brews and food items. If you need a moment to look, just let me know how I can help you. Feel free to have a seat."

The man nodded with a faint smile and continued to scan the board before asking for a cappuccino and a cheese danish, then gestured toward a nearby table.

Katie extracted the espresso and then began frothing the milk, as she saw the man glance over and notice a flyer he hadn't seen on his way in. She watched him stare at it curiously.

He got up to approach it and after he read it, he took his phone out and snapped a picture of it. He studied the photo as he made his way slowly back to his table and then tapped it in a way that made Katie think he was texting the image to someone or uploading it to a social media page.

She shrugged and continued preparing the cappuccino, deciding that he was obviously from out of town and found the Christmas play interesting.

She finished preparing his coffee and plated the danish before bringing it over to his table.

"Let me know if you need anything else," she said and he lifted a hand to interrupt.

"Excuse me, but how can I contact the director of this play?" He pointed toward the flyer he had just taken a picture of and Katie glanced at it before looking back at him.

"I'm pretty sure the web site on it has an email address, once you view it. At least, that's what I'm told."

"And that's the only way you know of? No phone number or address?"

Katie looked at him in the same direct way that her husband had come to know meant business.

"Is there some reason why you can't simply visit the web site? If no other method of contact was put on the flyer, then I'm sure that was intentional."

"Do you know the director?" he persisted.

"Do you?" Katie crossed her arms and waited.

"I'm her manager. Morris Trent."

He reached into his lapel pocket and laid his card on the table for her to inspect.

Rather than pick it up, Katie continued to regard him in a manner that was openly challenging.

"You're her manager," she said flatly. "And yet, you're asking me how to contact her."

"She not answering her phone," he said gruffly, picking his card back up.

"Well, that might mean something."

Katie returned to her place behind the counter as the door chimed again and another stranger came into the shop.

She was a woman in her fifties, expensively dressed and completely out of her element, standing in a small town coffee shop. Katie sized her up and nodded toward Morris Trent.

"He's over there," she said shortly and the woman smiled tightly before making her way over to his table.

Katie shot them both a dark look, then pulled her phone out of her pocket and sent a quick text to Hazel.

'Don't come in the coffee shop until I say it's okay. I'll explain when I can.'

A response came back almost immediately.

'Okay. Walking in the park. Say when.'

Katie snapped a photo and sent back a reply for her to stay in the park until she heard back from her and then pocketed her phone.

Her heads up to Hazel seemed to have gone unnoticed by the strangers, since they were obviously in a deep discussion.

124

Katie didn't particularly want to, but she approached the table to ask if the woman would like anything and, of course, she wanted a cup of tea. She simply nodded and made her way back to the counter, rolling her eyes, but starting the tea to brew while she readied the tray.

The two strangers continued to talk in a muffled but animated fashion, and when Katie brought the tea to the table, she was hardly noticed.

It was quite some time before they finished their conversation and walked out, but not before the man threw a wad of whatever bills he had in his pocket on the table, for Katie to sort out.

She started to text Hazel that the coast was clear but hesitated. She had the oddest feeling that it wasn't. Instead, she told her to avoid downtown because a man and a woman were looking for her and they didn't seem like people she would want to talk to.

Hazel sent back a thumbs up, then put her phone back in her pocket.

She looked up at Grant with a sigh. She had run into him in the park. Almost exactly as before, Grant had rounded a curve and saw Hazel walking toward him.

Unlike their first encounter which created shock and dread, this time their faces both lit up with something happy and welcoming. Grant changed his course, and they naturally started walking together without even thinking about it.

Now he bumped her shoulder with his and looked at her closely. "Is something wrong?"

"I'm not sure," she admitted. "Katie seems to think I need to stay in the park until she says the coast is clear."

Grant slowed their pace to a stroll and looked down at her carefully. "What's that about, Hay?"

"I think I'm being set up," she answered truthfully. "It could be the Cullens. Katie doesn't know them. But it also sounds like either my manager or my agent, and the owner of a theater who could be working together."

This didn't go very far to enlighten Grant. She realized it and gave him a smile of apology.

"Maybe this should be one of those intentional conversations you said we need to have."

Grant brought them to a stop and glanced around, before locating a bench off the trail, under some low-spreading limbs. He steered Hazel toward it by resting a hand on her back and moving her in that direction.

He reached down to brush some beautiful fallen leaves off the seat and a couple of twigs then patted the back of the bench for her to sit. Grant settled down next to her, close enough to occasionally brush against her, as he rested an ankle on one knee and folded his arms.

"Whatcha got, Hazie?"

"Maybe nothing, but right after Katie and Fred's wedding, I was working in the shop and my agent just showed up out of nowhere. I haven't been taking calls, so maybe that's on me. I probably should have, but I really don't want to talk to any of those people, to be honest."

Grant raised a brow, surprised that she felt that way, but continued to listen.

"He brought a message that the owner of a theater in California was looking for me. Her name is Mavis Dunning and it's her theater that Barry's play was running in when..."

She stopped and looked down as her phone dinged. Katie had texted her a picture and she tapped it and then showed it to Grant with a frown darkening her sad eyes.

"I guess the signal's not great out here. This pic must have been downloading."

Grant studied the image closely. He'd never seen either the man or the woman in it.

"It's my manager, Morris Trent and that's Mavis. I guess they met up at the shop. Katie's right, I don't want to talk to them." Hazel looked troubled and Grant studied her quietly.

"Who's making you, then? Why do you feel the need to hide from these people?"

"It's more about avoiding, than hiding. I don't want to be involved with what they're after. I can't explain why, but I have the weirdest feeling that Louise in tied up in it, somehow."

"That's reason enough to not want anything to do with it," Grant replied, with a scowl of disapproval resting on his face.

Hazel nodded and put her phone away.

"Mavis's theater is where Barry's show was running when he was killed. Of course, I don't know this for sure, but I'm pretty certain that Mavis had to close the show, since the understudy was an unknown. Barry was her draw.

"When something like that happens, a lot of times, people will immediately lose interest in the play or demand refunds, so she would be likely to lose a lot of her investment. It could be that she had cast insurance on him, but I wouldn't know. I'd only be guessing. Not all theaters invest in it."

She let her gaze wander out in front of them and noted to herself that more leaves were falling, even as they sat there. It sent her a silent reminder that she needed to stay focused on the Christmas play, since autumn was definitely in full swing.

Grant gave her another slight bump with his shoulder.

"Are we done, then? I feel that we've not achieved full chat. I require full chat."

She laughed at him. "I do know that about you!"

Grant smiled to himself and waited.

"I think that they're making a push for me to return and take the lead role in a play at Mavis's theater to entice Barry's fans to come back. In fact, I know they are, and I told my agent a flat no and that I was having my attorney go over my contracts, since I feel that both he and my manager are no longer acting in my best interests. They both know I would never be in the kind of play that Mavis is suggesting, and yet both of them are trying to strong arm me."

She sighed and thought about that.

"Well, I don't know about Clayton. He's my agent. He seemed to accept my decision and I haven't heard from him again, so he might have just let it drop.

"Or it could be his fault that both Morris and Mavis are in town. Bringing in the big guns."

She folded her arms and seemed to lean against Grant without realizing it. It was something she had always done whenever she was troubled or needed comfort. He noticed and glanced down at her with a soft smile.

"How long have we known each other, Hay?"

"Third grade, for me. You were the guy I kept praying would stop aging and let me catch up."

"I tried." He seemed to be in some far off place.

She wondered where he was, then drew in a sharp breath, as an alarming thought presented itself.

"They were in the cafe. That means they saw the flyer for the Christmas play."

Hazel's eyes began to glisten with emotion. "They're going to ruin everything! I just know it," she whispered.

Grant lifted his arm to lay it behind Hazel and gave her shoulder the slightest squeeze before resting his hand there.

"Tell me how you see that playing out, Hazel," he suggested quietly.

"My name is listed as the director and Irving is on the flyer as the lead." Hazel looked at Grant with tears continuing to threaten. "My name will generate ticket sales, but Irving's name, alone, is enough to pack the house, and force extra shows. He's always been very sought after as a lead actor and after he dropped off the radar for a couple of years and sparked all kinds of rumors, now that he's suddenly resurfaced, it's going to generate a huge response."

Hazel anticipated Grant's obvious question.

"That would be great for the fundraiser, but horrible for the play if all the tickets get bought up in bulk, but the seats remain deliberately empty. I wouldn't put it past Louise and Mavis to do something like that just for spite. Louise has done it before," she added miserably.

Grant sat mulling all this over for a moment before asking Hazel if her adaptation of a public domain work was protected in any way.

"Everything original that I brought to it is. But it's not any sort of copyright challenge that I'm worried about. It's having Irving finish his amazing career with bad reviews because of low attendance, which would be interpreted as no interest. That is just the kind of thing Mavis and Louise would try to pull, to intentionally hurt someone that I really care about."

"Are you considered to be the producer, or is that our church? Can't one of us control whether or not entire blocks of tickets are allowed to be sold?" he asked.

He felt her looking directly at him and rested his eyes on hers to interpret her thoughts.

"I could kiss you right now!" she declared impulsively, not thinking of how Grant might or might not take that.

"I'm a man of God. Get away from me, Jezebel," he commanded with a grin, after his initial shock. He brought his hand back from resting it on her shoulder, and crossed his arms in an exaggerated manner to emphasize his intent to block her from compromising him.

Hazel laughed her first real laugh in years and happily settled back against him.

"The tickets haven't gone on sale yet! You're brilliant!"

"It says that on my résumé," he informed her loftily.

Hazel was too excited to buy into his cavalier teasing.

"No, Grant, I'm saying there's still time. We're using the senior center's stage for our play, which is their contribution to the fundraising effort. The ticket sales can either be handled by your church or I can have my attorney set me up as my own production company and the sales will have to go through me.

"I'm sure Mavis expects us to just use one of the online third party sites, but we won't do that. We'll force the tickets sales to be controlled by us and we won't allow bulk sales or reselling until the last day of the show and not until within an hour of the last performance.

"That way, we will have already had a successful run and the last performance won't suffer any real defeat, especially if we all know what to expect.

"If it appears that we'll have an empty house, we can advertise that we're offering free seats during the last thirty minutes before the last performance, to ensure that we fill them and have Irving perform to a packed house."

Hazel was practically glowing as she gazed at Grant. Her eyes were filled with excitement and he was mesmerized.

He had to put some effort into not continuing to look into them and simply reached to tap the end of her nose.

"Back to full chat," he began and she giggled at that.

"What is it about the play Mavis has in mind, that you object to? You said that your agent and manager both know that you would never be in the kind of show she's talking about. One has to ask."

"There's a clause in my contract, as well as my rider, that venues get well in advance, that states very clearly that I will never do a nude scene," she admitted, glancing away from him in embarrassment. "That's what it is. It's a play called Wayward. I guess the name says it all."

"I guess it does," Grant agreed, training his gaze toward the trees across the way and expelling a slight sigh. "I'm proud of you, Hay, for staying true to your convictions."

She smiled down at the ground when he said that.

"Have you completed assigning roles, then?" Grant asked in order to fill a long moment of silence that seemed to hang in the air between them.

"Would you like to try out for one?" she teased.

He shook his head decidedly. "Not my thing. I have enough trouble being myself, without deliberately trying to be someone else."

He glanced around the park with a smile. "I'd love to know how you managed to get Fred Buckley to play the role of the younger Longfellow, though."

"Oh, Fred was easy. All I had to do was roll out my secret weapon."

Grant had to laugh at that.

"Yeah, Fred's pretty much done for, now. That little bride of his is the very definition of bringing in the big guns."

Hazel lifted her phone. "She's the entire cavalry."

They sat appreciating the warm autumn sun and golden wash of color around them, each with private thoughts, before she looked at him, deliberately reading him.

"You know, good and well, how long we've known each other. Was that a trick question?"

"I just wondered if you remembered."

She let the ghost of a smile rest around her mouth.

"I remember like it was yesterday. I was ushered onto the school bus and instructed to sit by you. I thought the bus driver didn't like me, but then I found out it was an alphabetical thing to keep the peace. You big guys were making trouble."

Grant gazed out at the path across from them and again seemed to be staring into their past.

"Of course, the next day, Patty Strickland was back on the bus, and I thought your little heart was gonna break in two," he reminded her with a grin.

She folded her arms and affected a petulant scowl.

"The older woman! I wanted to tear her hair out. I had already staked out my claim and she was in my way."

"Literally," he laughed.

"That's okay. She only rode as far as the mill, so by the time I was good and mad, it was time for her to get off."

"And you slid right over by me, a stickler for the rules."

She pursed her lips with a little pout.

"If that's how you want to remember it."

"That *is* how I want to remember it." He laughed quietly. "I did the math and waited forever for you to grow up. I couldn't even legally date you, until you turned eighteen and when you finally did, that's the year it all fell apart."

The little moments of silence between them began to feel less awkward and more comforting, so neither of them tried to rush things. At length though, Grant gave Hazel the usual little nudge with his shoulder.

"So, I have a question."

"I'm sure you do," she replied with a little smile.

131

He indulged in a lazy grin that faded into a more serious expression and then looked down at her.

"At Katie's shop, you told me you weren't grieving."

They were going to talk about it then, she realized. She looked up at him and nervously waited.

"Was there ever a time when you would have been?"

Hazel let her gaze drop and flushed with color, knowing how her answer was going to sound, but wanting to be honest.

"No." She raised her eyes to his and let him read them. "It was an arranged marriage."

Grant appeared to be startled and didn't try to hide it.

"What are you telling me?"

Hazel felt the sudden rush of dread, thinking that there was no way he was going to understand it, let alone accept it.

"Please don't hate me," she pleaded, in a whisper.

"I don't hate you, I just don't..." He was stunned. "I'm feeling the impulse to say something that's going to be hurtful, and I don't want to do that. It's probably better if we just back off of this. I'm sorry I even asked."

Hazel reached for his hand and held onto it.

"You're thinking that I was willing to marry anybody else, as long as it wasn't you, but you're wrong. That's not what it was, Grant."

She made no effort to blink back her tears.

He looked down at her hand on his and closed his eyes, in a effort to control emotions that were suddenly all over the place, suggesting to him that he wasn't nearly as healed as he had begun to think he was.

"What was it, then, Hazel?"

She gently squeezed his hand to get him to look at her.

"It was how much I hated myself. By the time I got my degree and started gaining some recognition on stage, I didn't care about it, anymore. I couldn't get away from what I had done to you. I knew I had messed up, and couldn't repent. I killed anything you ever felt for me, and it was too late. I didn't want to be happy. I wanted to hurt."

He continued to study her intently, trying to determine what she meant by saying she messed up and couldn't repent.

"Barry's agent and his PR people came up with the stupid plan to have us portrayed as some kind of Broadway darlings. They wanted us to get married and become what's known as a power couple. A lot of actor marriages are nothing more than that.

"Irving was so angry at me, that it almost cost me our friendship. He was livid and tried every way that he could to stop me from agreeing to it, but I was so apathetic and unfeeling by then, Grant. I was dead inside.

"I just signed whatever they put in front of me. The whole thing became some big media event and it had the effect that his people had hoped for. Neither of us could keep up with the offers for roles. All we had to do was pretend to be happy."

Grant drew in a breath and made himself ask her the one thing that he had to know.

"Was it ever a real marriage?"

She shook her head.

"Are you telling me the truth?" He fixed her with a look that let her know not to waste his time with anything else.

"I promise I am, Grant. We had a place in California but we were rarely there at the same time and even when we were, he had his quarters and I had mine. To be honest, we didn't even like each other. In fact, once we signed the license, Barry grabbed a bag and celebrated by spending the night with whoever his current squeeze was. I can't even remember her name, now."

Grant held her gaze and deliberately searched her eyes. "And you were fine with living the rest of your life that way, married to someone you didn't even like?"

Hazel looked down at her phone and turned it on, to pull up her recently added email account, then found the message Barry had sent her just before he was killed.

She looked up at Grant and silently offered it to him.

He took the phone but continued to hold her eyes with his for a long moment before finally looking at the email.

133

His face was grim as he read it. He gave the phone back to her. "He was the one filing for a divorce, not you, so I guess that's a yes, then."

Hazel's heart began to break. She had wanted him to read the email to see for himself that it wasn't a real marriage, but all he saw was that Barry had been the one to file for the divorce, instead of her.

"Grant, did you read all of it?" She held the phone up again. "Barry said, himself, that it was for publicity. If I'd hadn't known that I'd lost you forever, I wouldn't have married him or anyone else, not as long as there was a chance for you and me.

"I didn't think about filing for a divorce because I didn't care, one way or the other. The only reason he filed was because he wanted to get out of our contract to marry Brandy, the girl who was in the car with him."

"If it wasn't a real marriage, why wasn't it an annulment, instead of a divorce?" Grant's tone was cool.

"The public wasn't supposed to know that."

"Twelve years," he muttered under his breath. "And the only reason you've asked me to forgive you now, is because we've been unexpectedly thrown together."

"No, that's not true, Grant! I did go back home to ask you to forgive me, but you weren't there anymore, and your family was still angry with me. They wouldn't tell me where you were and my mother claimed she didn't know, but I didn't believe her. She only cared about her daughter being an actress, so she could brag about it. I went back to New York and that's when they began pushing the whole marriage thing. I just signed it, to be left alone. I didn't care anymore about anything. "

He looked away from her. Hazel watched him anxiously and laid her hand on his arm. Her words were broken by grief.

"Grant, are you taking it back? I'm not forgiven?"

He heard her, but waited to respond. He heard a faint gasp and when he did look at her, she had dropped her head and was sobbing.

Grant instinctively reached around her and pulled her close. "You're not playing fair," he whispered, looking around vacantly with troubled eyes.

Hazel buried her face in his jacket and continued to cry softly. She was clearly devastated.

Grant lifted his hand from her shoulder to reach up and caress the back of her head with his fingers, closing his eyes and silently asking God to protect him from getting lost in this woman again. He spoke softly, trying to soothe her.

"Stop it, Hazie, we're okay. We can have hard talks without breaking anything. It's okay, we're good."

She lifted her beautiful, damp face to his, silently begging him to mean it. He rested his eyes on her, wondering if he could be the kind of friend to her that he had been for so long, without making himself a target.

There was a calm, silent moment of lingering together on the bench, wordlessly checking each other for damage.

"All done?"

She wiped her face and nodded.

Grant gave her a slow smile.

"Good. Now, let's talk about why you gave Fred my braised short ribs."

Chapter Fourteen

William Cullen came out of his study as he heard the voices of a man and woman who had just been admitted into the house by Louise. He stood regarding Morris Trent and Mavis Dunning with disapproval before turning a more blatant look of disgust onto his wife.

"You were warned, Louise!"

"I'm so scared," she mocked, having apparently already imbibed enough to achieve a false sense of bravado. "What are you going to do?"

Morris Trent and Mavis Dunning looked at each other with uncertainty.

"Hello, William," Morris offered tentatively. "I hope we're not intruding."

"Do you?" He lowered his brows and moved over to the seating area, wanting them to say what they had to say, and then leave. He motioned impatiently to some chairs.

"Of course, Mavis, I know exactly why *you're* here," he said dourly before eyeing Morris Trent with suspicion.

"What I can't figure out, Morris, is why you appear to be a party to it. Does your star client have any idea that the two of you are working in tandem to convince her to step into my dead son's place to save Mavis's reputation? You do realize that this will only get you fired?"

"No one intends to try to force Hazel to do anything that she doesn't want to do, William," her manager denied. "We just want to explain the benefits of her taking on such a coveted role at an opportune time, when fans and patrons are sure to respond with enthusiasm."

137

"Opportune time," he retorted, with a scowl. "Meaning before Barry's body is even cold?"

He sat glowering at them darkly.

"I must say, William," Mavis ventured, after an awkward silence, "I'm a bit surprised at your appearing to be protective of Hazel. I was never given the impression that either you or Louise actually held any regard or affection for her."

"That's a fact, if I ever heard one!" Louise stated, coming over to sit on the arm of her husband's chair. He promptly pushed her away and she staggered a little to regain her footing, finding a nearby chair more to her liking.

"You'll pardon me, Mavis, if I find your motives to be self-serving, at best. You had an insurance policy that should have more than covered your losses in the event of Barry's being unable to complete his obligation. Is there suddenly a problem with that policy?"

"No, and that should tell you that this isn't about money," she began.

"Oh, please!" William held up a silencing hand. "It's always about money, Mavis, so don't waste my time trying to make me believe that this is some sort of posthumous homage to my son. You're just trying to capitalize on his death by presenting the widow of Barry Cullen on your stage to generate buzz for your theater."

"Theater patrons loved your son, William," Morris interjected. "So, of course, they would feel a connection to Hazel, as the grieving wife he left behind."

"Grieving!" William sat up straight and made no effort to take the edge off his anger. "Hardly! And why should she be grieving? She should be celebrating, as far as I'm concerned!"

Mavis and Morris stared at him in surprise.

"Don't try to convince me that you believe anything different! That marriage was nothing more than a stunt, and we all know it! I wanted nothing to do with it, but I wasn't able to stop Barry and his agent from pushing it through.

"And speaking of his agent, am I the only one who has noticed that she didn't even bother to send flowers, let alone actually attend the funeral of her star?"

"Cheryl copes with things her own way," Mavis said, with a wave of her hand.

"I'm sure we all know how Cheryl copes," William returned dryly. What I *don't* know is why she isn't here, saying her lines? Is she not on board with your little scheme?"

"We stay in touch," Morris admitted reluctantly.

"Oh, I'm sure!" William continued to maintain an attitude of offense and impatience.

"You do realize, Mavis, that when Louise called you to manipulate you into this insanity, she was drunk, as usual? Not exactly her best moment, or yours."

Mavis looked at Morris to appeal to him for support.

"William, as I said before, no one is here to try to force Hazel into anything."

"That's just as well, Morris, because I can tell you now that not only are you going to fail, but I wouldn't be surprised if every one of us doesn't find ourselves named in a lawsuit, if she begins to feel ganged up on. Her attorney is already involved."

"Whatever for?" Mavis demanded. "We're only offering her a role in a play. It's done all the time! Why should that be grounds for a lawsuit?"

"You already know that the role you're offering her is in direct conflict with her contract, and yet you offer it, anyway, and not only offer it, but seem to be willing to push for it.

"If Hazel begins to feel harassed, this could turn legal in a heartbeat and, lawsuit or not, the negative publicity from it will do some real damage and the truth about that so-called marriage will come out! Why are you trying to proceed with something that you already know is going to end badly? It just shows that none of you really gave a crap about my son!"

William stopped to regard Morris Trent with cynicism. "How much is Mavis cutting you in for, Trent, for delivering Hazel to her?"

He seemed to be examining him thoroughly. "It would have to be a great deal, to entice you to risk being fired by your top client, which you will be, so don't act surprised when she gives you your walking papers."

Morris had no intention of disclosing a partial ownership in the very successful venue that Mavis was offering him, and simply smiled in a way that most of his clients found disarming, but that reminded William Cullen of a Cheshire cat.

"William, one has to wonder why you wouldn't desire to be a part of what could only be a touching and inspiring tribute to your son's memory, by having his young widow approach the stage in an effort to stir everyone's memory of his contribution to theater."

William directed a stare at Mavis that made her regret her flowery words.

"By having his young widow approach the stage with no clothes on, to stir something else, you mean! Barry's memory, that's a laugh! I hope she drags us all into court, after all!"

"This from a man who hated his son!" Louise wailed out with exaggerated anguish, as if she had actually loved him.

"That's enough from you," her husband muttered, flashing a look at her that stopped her from saying anything else.

"Not that it's the business of anyone here, but I hardly hated my son," William Cullen coldly informed the two that he clearly regarded as intruders. "But I hated the stupid way he died, charging around in that blasted sports car with that little porn star girlfriend of his!

"I hated his refusal to grow up and take responsibility for his actions, instead of running around drinking like his boozer mother and smoking whatever he could get his hands on!

"I hated his stupid playboy reputation and I hated the public way he rubbed Hazel's nose in it. I hated it all! He owes his death to it, and I will never forgive him for that!

"But what I hate even more is the hypocrisy that has arrived, uninvited, into my home! How dare either of you try to convince me that you had any regard at all for my son? You're jackals, the both of you!"

140

The father of the late Barry Cullen walked swiftly to the door and angrily threw it open for them to leave.

"You have gained nothing by coming here today, so get out of my house!"

Pastor James Morgan smiled with delight as his sister brought Grant Sellars into the kitchen where he sat resting, after having moved carefully around the house in what Ellen Abbott informed him was known as "gentle exercise".

"Pastor Sellars! I've been wondering about you, and here you are! Come have a seat, Grant," he added, indicating the chairs around the table. "There's coffee."

Grant grinned at his welcome and reached to lay an affectionate hand on the old minister's shoulder.

"I was hoping there would be," he admitted, seeing that Ellen had already poured a cup for him.

He took it with thanks and fixed his eyes fondly on Pastor Morgan. "Look at you, up and at 'em! The last time I saw you, you were decidedly bedfast."

"Oh, Ellen won't put up with that," he declared, telling on his sister and making her laugh.

"Doctor's orders," she replied. "No pneumonia for you, so you might as well stop complaining!"

She headed off to put fresh linens on her brother's bed, while he enjoyed a visit with his young friend.

"Well, I hear there are exciting things brewing for this year's Christmas play," Pastor Morgan declared. "Mrs. Payne and some of the other wonderful ladies from your church come by fairly regularly, and they've been keeping Ellen and me informed. They're all very excited."

He couldn't resist giving Grant a knowing look. "I can only guess that you were a committee casualty."

"That's fairly accurate," Grant admitted, with a grin. "The chairwoman is Ivy Parker."

"I heard!" Pastor Morgan laughed. "My goodness, you are made of tougher stuff than I, my young friend!"

141

Grant laughed quietly at that, as the pastor continued.

"It would take an Ivy Parker, I would imagine, to make you agree to allow the young lady who caused you such heartache to now be the one directing your play."

"It actually turns out to be a good thing," Grant replied. "Because of Hazel, we won't be doing 'A Christmas Carol' again, as we have for I don't know how many years in a row. She pointed out to the committee that this was why their fundraising was suffering and, of course, she had their attention after that."

"Mrs. Payne tells me that the play is to be from an adaptation of the life of Henry Wadsworth Longfellow. I must say, I intend to see it, hip surgery or no. It sounds wonderful."

The elderly pastor smiled to himself.

"I also hear that she's managed to convince Irving Lancaster to take the lead role. Irving and I are childhood friends, you know."

"Are you?" Grant was surprised. "He's only been here a couple of years."

"But he's from here, originally. That's why he's back, he's come home to roost. We were young lads in this town, back in the day, and very good friends, although I knew nothing about acting and the theater. We managed to be pals in spite of such things, rather than because of them. I'm very eager to see him in your play. He's a legend, you know."

"I've heard," Grant replied quietly.

Pastor Morgan could see thoughts racing around in Grant's head and allowed a lull in the conversation to see if he would offer any insight.

"You've obviously spoken with her." He decided that Grant needed a little help getting started.

"I have." He raised his eyes to Pastor Morgan's with a wry look. "It was rapidly moved, seconded, and unanimously voted for, that I be the one to ask Hazel to direct our play."

The minister laughed in his kind way. "Oh, my!"

Grant grinned. "Actually, we'd already had a brief encounter when I was jogging in the park. I rounded a curve and literally ran right up to her.

142

"She was out for a walk and we both just stood there, being stunned. She told me that she was sorry and I said 'thank you' and that was it."

"I'm encouraged that you're telling me you thanked her, Grant. That's actually a lot."

"It's hard to explain why I did. But when I heard her say the words, I could hear the truth in them and I felt some sort of tightness in my chest begin to ease up. When I thanked her, it felt right. I meant it."

Pastor Morgan sat thinking about it and nodded. "Some people go their entire lives with that sort of tightness in their chests and don't even realize it's there. Some are aware of it, but assume that it's some sort of medical issue. So often, it's simply an indication of the need to forgive someone.

"It's fortunate that you made the decision to forgive her, Grant, or both you and Hazel might have carried the weight and scars of all that to the end of your days, and that would be such a tragedy."

He studied Grant's faint reaction. "Is it going to be okay then, your having to work with her for the play?"

"Some days I wonder if we can manage it, so I'll be honest," he confessed. "At times, it feels as if we're just as close as we ever were and at other times, we're dangerously close to thinking that it's too late to be friends again. I am, I mean." Grant corrected himself, with a sigh.

"Hazel is completely willing to work through any issue or misunderstanding and keeps displaying this childlike confidence in me that I don't deserve. We've had some conversations that came very close to toppling everything to the ground, but she just keeps trusting us to ride it out. She behaves much more like a pastor than I, if I'm being honest."

"That's because she loves you."

Grant looked up quickly at Pastor Morgan's words, surprised at first, and then relaxing as he decided that he was referring to their friendship.

"I guess you're right. I mean, we've known each other since she was a little third-grader on the school bus.

143

"She was only eighteen when the whole wedding fiasco happened. She's a thirty-year-old woman now. That's a lot of shared history."

"Well, I'm sure the third-grader loved you in her own sweet way, as did the confused eighteen-year-old." Pastor Morgan reached over to a pile of magazines and papers and picked up the flyer for the play, laying it down in front of Grant.

The photo of beautiful Hazel immediately drew his gaze, as he heard Pastor Morgan speaking.

"But this is the woman who keeps trusting in the two of you to work through things. That's because *she* loves you," he repeated with a smile.

Grant ran his hand through his hair and leaned back into the chair, resting a worried look on the seasoned minister.

"Pastor Morgan, I'm not sure I can afford for her to love me. I know she was only an eighteen-year-old girl. I've said as much to her, myself. I get that, and it's largely due to that fact that I can forgive her. But it doesn't change what happened. I can't see ever trusting in her love again."

"You think she has to earn your trust."

"Yes."

"And when will she have done that?"

Grant looked steadily at him, wondering what he meant.

"That's a very popular saying, Grant. 'Trust has to be earned.' I'm sure someone, somewhere, has it stitched on a pillow. Some might call it a cliché, while others see it as a platitude. I'm not sure where it originated, but it wasn't in the scriptures. Can you imagine, if we had to earn God's trust? We might as well all give up now, and go back to the dirt.

"Only God can truly be trusted, and no other. We, ourselves, are often untrustworthy and yet we demand that others be. You may not realize it now, but when you've made as many trips around the sun as I have, you will come to know that telling someone they have to earn your trust is to place an unrealistic and unbearable burden on them. They can never satisfy that requirement."

"Then how do you get past betrayal?" Grant asked, with a sort of quiet urgency. "How do you just start over, as if it never happened?"

"God does that with you, every morning," Pastor Morgan replied with a peaceful smile. "In fact, He arranged for His mercies to be new every morning, for that very reason. If we are to love others as God loves us, we are commanded to forgive others, as Christ has forgiven us.

"Forgiveness has to do with choosing to get beyond a particular transgression that is then allowed to be swallowed up into the past and not be brought up again. It deals with an isolated offense, whether one offends us seven times, or seventy times seven. All of those are separate offenses and are put away by the act of forgiveness.

"Trust, however, does not focus on isolated offenses, but insists on a virtue of character and the impossible guarantee that one will never fail us in a particular area. No human can earn such a thing as trust. Only God can be trusted because He never changes. We humans are constantly changing. Our vessels are much too leaky to carry around something as precious as trust. Yes, Grant, we are commanded to forgive others. But we are not commanded to trust others. It is God *in* a person who can be trusted, not that person."

Pastor Morgan studied Grant intently and breathed a silent prayer for God to do a work in him, regardless of how things did or did not work out with Hazel. It was this young man he was burdened for.

"You said that Hazel keeps trusting the two of you to ride things out. It's God in both of you who she's trusting."

Grant sat in silence for a while, trying to listen to the Holy Spirit and when he finally lifted his eyes to look at Pastor Morgan, the old man was grinning broadly at him.

"I bet you leave our little visits so put out with me, Pastor Sellars," he declared. "Here, you come to just sit and chat and I shove a sermon in your face."

He wiped his old eyes, as he laughed quietly. "You are the very model of patience and endurance!"

145

Grant stood and gave his friend a light pat. "Thank you. No matter what sort of issue I manage to bring with me when I come here, you always seem to say just the right thing."

He promised to visit again soon and Pastor Morgan's sister showed him to the door.

Grant hesitated before leaving.

"It's interesting how your brother seems to know so much about things like love and relationships. I wouldn't expect a bachelor to be that full of insight."

Ellen Abbott narrowed her eyes and gave Grant a confused smile. "Why do you think James is a bachelor?"

"I guess I just assumed. He's always lived alone."

"Since you've known him. But, not always," she said quietly. She glanced back toward the kitchen before reaching to open the front door and stepping out, waiting for Grant to follow her.

She moved away from the door and toward Grant's vehicle, intending that he walk with her.

"When James was a young man, he started his ministry by pastoring just over the state line, up in Tennessee. That's where he met Martha. Marty, we called her. They were married for only one very brief year, so you see, he wasn't always a bachelor. She was the love of his life. She was a pretty flower of a woman and everyone loved her, but of course, no one loved her more than my brother.

"They were married after a whirlwind of a romance, and Mother and Father decided, early on, that she was family. She fit right in, and brought a lot of laughter with her."

Ellen pressed her lips together tightly and wiped the corner of her eye, as she thought about her sister-in-law, who had been more like a sister and a best friend.

"Marty had an accident out in their yard one winter evening, right after it got dark. She slipped on a sheet of ice and her head struck the large root of a tree.

"She somehow managed to get up and when she came back in the house, she told James about it, laughing of course, and joking about the headache she was going to have.

146

"He was upset, but she insisted she was fine. She went to bed that night, and never woke up. James was inconsolable."

Ellen was reliving it with the telling of it, and touched the hem of her apron to her cheeks.

"I thought he might actually leave the ministry, but when he moved back home here, he accepted the offer to pastor. I honestly think that's what helped to heal him."

Grant listened to what Pastor Morgan's sister was telling him in shocked disbelief and his heart broke for his friend, who still steadfastly believed in the trustworthiness of God.

Chapter Fifteen

Katie propped her chin on her hand and leaned on the counter, staring down at her script with a frown.

"This is my worst nightmare," she informed Hazel with a scowl. "Well, second only to public speaking, but this is the same thing, so wait, I'm right. This is my worst nightmare."

Hazel glanced up from where she was sitting at one of the cafe's tables and rested her pen on top of her notes. She gave Katie an apologetic smile, but her mind was made up.

"First of all, when you read me your lines, you were better than anyone else who tried for that part, and second, the younger Henry Longfellow is going to kiss his wife. Since that's Fred, then the part of Fanny automatically goes to you."

Katie raised her eyes and gave Hazel a knowing look. "I didn't even have to read lines. As soon as you cast Fred for his part, you had me in your sights."

"Do you want your husband to kiss another woman, Kate?" Hazel grinned down at the list she was making.

"I wouldn't have thought so before this, but now I'm not so sure," she said blandly. "Instead of kissing her, why can't he just give her twenty dollars and tell her to go buy herself something pretty?"

"Oh, stop." Hazel waved her over to the table. "Come help me with this."

Katie opened the drawer in front of her and laid the script out of sight. "Hang on. The owner of the coffee shop hasn't had any coffee, herself, this morning."

"Maybe that's why you're so gloomy, then," Hazel speculated. "Since you're pouring, though, I wouldn't turn down a little mood enhancer, myself."

Katie obliged her and brought their coffee over to settle down beside her friend. "What's all this?"

"I need to know who's who in the zoo," Hazel replied. "For instance, costumes. Who has been involved with that sort of thing in the past?"

"Marjorie Crain," Katie supplied. "She's the go-to for any kind of deal around here that needs costumes."

"Does she volunteer, or does she expect to be paid?" Hazel paused before writing down her name. "I mean, of course all the materials she would need would be furnished, if not by the church, then I can take care of it. But is she typically hired?"

"Not typically. It'd be nice though, if she could receive something for her time. When she takes on a job, she stays at it pretty much around the clock, and her work is beautiful."

"I won't ask the church to pay her, because I don't want that kind of thing to get hung up in their committee, and end up having the women get in a tizzy with each other over it. I'll just take care of it, myself."

Hazel continued looking at her list. "Set design."

"Well, if you need something built, then Charlie Fulton is your guy. He owns the hardware store and he's always built things for the church anytime they call him. He's good at what he does. For design and painting and all that, usually the kids at the high school's art and drama classes volunteer."

Hazel glanced up at her thoughtfully. "I've not met any of them. I wonder if I should approach their teachers first, then? Or maybe their parents, but the teachers could talk to the parents, I guess."

"You know one of their teachers," Katie informed her. "Barbara Sykes. She's one of the art teachers."

Hazel thought about it. "Isn't she on the church committee? Is she the one who never says anything and then, just before they adjourn, reads off her comments from a list that she's been sitting there making?"

"That's her. Her lists are legendary."

"Oh, I like her!" Hazel said with a little smile. "She's the only one who can take on Ivy Parker and make a decent showing. Not even Grant can do that."

Katie laughed at that. "Ivy Parker is Grant's kryptonite."

Hazel shrugged and wrote down Barbara Syke's name. "Well, somebody has to be, I guess. That cape has to come off, sooner or later."

"Speaking of the man of steel, has he been maintaining that tough exterior around you, or has he softened up a bit?"

Hazel glanced up from her list and gave Katie an accusing look. "Like you and Fred haven't already decided."

"Actually, we haven't. Fred says Grant doesn't seem too willing to talk about it at the gym, so he tries to give him his space. That's what guys do, apparently." She rolled her eyes.

"Well, I don't blame him," Hazel said quietly. "I've dropped a few bombshells on him, without meaning to."

"Better now than later," Katie reasoned.

"I guess."

Hazel made an effort to steer the conversation back to the play. "Okay, props and, believe it or not, props is huge. I need a good prop master and someone to help with prop prep."

"Prop prep, prop prep, prop..."

"Stop it!" Hazel threatened her silly friend with the point of her pen. "Seriously, who has always handled that?"

"It depends. What is it?" Katie wondered.

"Once the sets are designed, we'll need to furnish them. Things like lamps, furniture, pillows. Period pieces so, for this play, nothing modern, no phones or electronics. Someone who's knowledgeable about the mid to late eighteen hundreds and has a good eye.

"Jarvis."

Hazel drew her brow and gave Katie a puzzled look. "What's that?"

"Who, not what. Jarvis." Katie thought about it. "I don't even know his last name but he has that antique store just as you drive south of here and he's a big Civil War buff."

"That's actually just the right period, so that's perfect." Hazel wrote down the name. "Just start driving south until I see an antique store?"

"I'll get you an address before you leave."

"You're a pal," Hazel said lightly. "Okay, the guys from church say they usually handle light and sound for the church plays. They seem to know what they're doing, as long as we don't get way out into gels and spotlights and that kind of thing. Hopefully, they can also handle Foley work, but we'll try to have as little of that as possible."

"I don't know what that is, but I agree." Katie's coffee was kicking in.

Hazel smiled down at her list. "Sound effects. Horse hooves, bells, that sort of thing."

"And Foley was some guy's name?"

"It was. You're a quick study."

"I feel so much smarter than I did before I sat down." Katie looked over as the door chimed.

"Stranger danger," she muttered under her breath to Hazel, who continued to look down at her list, wondering if there were even enough people in the little town to help behind the scenes, let alone perform a play.

"Hi, how can I help you?" Katie asked the man who seemed to be looking around to get his bearings.

He glanced up at the menu and asked for her darkest house coffee.

"Good choice," Katie commented. "Room for cream?"

"Just black." He generated a look of approval from Katie, then motioned toward the tables. "Anywhere?"

"Sure, I'll bring it to you."

He heard his phone make a noise and glanced at the screen impatiently then saw Hazel across the room as he was putting it back in his pocket.

"May I?"

Hazel looked up from her list and was unable to hide her startled expression. "I guess so," she said quietly, reaching to move her things over to one side.

152

"It looks as if I'm interrupting."

"Nothing I can't get back to," she said, resting her eyes on him steadily and simply waiting.

"I'm the last person you expected to ask to share your table, I'm sure," William Cullen observed.

"You're were at the top of my list."

He smiled at that and looked up as Katie set his coffee down in front of him, curious as to why he seemed to have gravitated over to Hazel.

She looked at her with the silent question.

"Katie, this is William Cullen. Barry's father. William, Katie is my very good friend, and the shop owner."

"It's very nice."

Since Hazel wasn't sending her any signals that she was upset, Katie simply murmured her thanks and moved back to busy herself behind the counter and keep a watchful eye.

Hazel closed her notebook and rested her hands on top of it, again waiting for him to begin.

"I'm not sure if you're aware, Hazel, but it seems that Louise and I are not the only visitors from California who have descended on this little town, as of late."

"I'm aware of two more," she replied. "They came here looking for me but so far, I've managed to avoid them."

"I wish I had been so lucky," he said dryly. "Louise had them come to the house."

"You weren't glad to see them?" She tilted her head and studied him.

"I was not." He sat with his hands wrapped around his warm mug and stared down into it. "In fact, I threw them out of the house."

She couldn't hide her reaction.

"Just because I was Barry's father, Hazel, doesn't mean that I've been onboard with every stupid idea that has come out of his camp. I never made it a secret that I opposed that farce of a marriage."

"You're not the only one," she admitted. "Irving Lancaster didn't speak to me for months."

153

"I hear he's back," William said lightly. "Retired. Well, that's probably a good decision for him. I'll be following his example as soon as I can manage it."

She was surprised, but made no reply.

"I didn't come here looking for you," he said, watching her discomfort and deciding to put her at ease. "I was downtown and the thought of coffee appealed to me. But since I saw you sitting here, I wanted to take this opportunity to speak to you, since it seems meant to be."

Hazel looked down at her hands and drew in a breath. "I don't know anything else I can do, at this point, William."

He looked confused. "What is it you think I'm asking you to do?"

"I'm hoping that since we did go ahead with that marriage, that I'm not expected to now continue to present myself publically as something that's not authentic. I don't wish to be unkind, I really don't. But I'm not a grieving widow, William. I'm just a widow, and even that isn't accurate."

He waved her words away. "No, that nonsense needs to be over. In fact, in keeping with what you've just said, I'm here to ask you to *not* do something."

She leaned back and looked at him questioningly.

"You're being double teamed by your manager and Mavis Dunning."

She glanced away and a frown washed over her face. "I didn't want to believe that Morris was actually working with her, but they're the ones who were here recently and they were obviously together, which I never would have expected."

"I don't know what Mavis is dangling in front of Trent to get him to put his job in jeopardy, but let me suggest that just the idea that he is even willing to be a part of what she has in mind, should be enough for you to kick him to the curb. You ought to be able to trust your manager, Hazel. That's why I never allowed anyone else to be Barry's manager. I couldn't always get him to listen to me, but at least I had his best interests at heart. I can't say the same for Trent."

154

"You're obviously right," she admitted, with a troubled look in her eyes. "I don't know if my agent is part of the deal or not. He came here first, but when I told him that I wasn't interested, he didn't pressure me, not to any real degree. In fact, I've not heard from him since."

"I doubt Clayton Ballard would persist in persuasion, once he knew that it would cost him his artist. No, I suspect this is all Mavis and Morris. And Louise. Let's not understate the role she's obviously had in all this, since she's the one who initiated it."

Hazel knew her mother-in-law despised her, but even that didn't do much to keep her from looking disappointed.

"It's not so much Louise at the end of the day, Hazel, as it is that monkey she carries around on her back. Her drinking has progressively gotten worse and if she doesn't get help... well, that's a discussion I guess I need to have with her, rather than with you."

William gave his former daughter-in-law a searching look. "So you already knew what those two wanted?"

"Clayton told me. I should have been surprised, but I guess I wasn't. Mavis doesn't exactly stand on principle."

"Hardly!" He made a scoffing sound and shook his head. "The most preposterous thing about all this is that the woman had the nerve to try and convince me that all this was being done in an attempt to pay some sort of tribute to Barry's memory and that you, as his grieving widow, would be the one all his fans rallied around to commemorate him."

His expression grew hard and angry. "Liars, the both of them! That's exactly why they're trying to force a script on you that they both know you would categorically refuse to perform. This is all about striking while the iron is hot and making a bundle off my son's death. Not only will I not be a participant, but I intend to pull out all the stops, if they proceed with this, and create enough bad publicity to make them wish they'd never started it."

Hazel understood how he felt and simply nodded. He looked at her.

"They're willing to throw you to the wolves to do it, Hazel. I guess I should have already known that you would want no part of it, but I just wanted to tell you what they're up to. Of course, you already know, so it was hardly needed."

"But it's appreciated, William," she said softly.

He smiled ironically to himself and stood to leave. "Well, this is probably not the smartest thing I've ever said, but if you begin to feel cornered and you and your attorney decide to come out swinging and file a lawsuit, I won't be upset if I'm listed as one of the defendants. It may just be the price I need to pay for ever allowing my son to get messed up in what I thought was going to be his brilliant career. Maybe I'd still have a son, if that hadn't happened."

He was surprised to look at Hazel and see tears glistening in her eyes. She reached over and touched his hand.

"I think we've all been through enough, William. I agree with you. This nonsense needs to be over." She gave him a sad smile. "Thank you for taking the time."

He blinked rapidly and gave her a little wave before he stopped by the counter to lay some money there for his coffee. He turned at the door and gave Hazel another long look.

"You're a good kid," he offered, as he left.

Grant reached for both his plate and Hazel's and carried them over to the sink.

"You know, I was just teasing you when I asked why you gave Fred my braised short ribs." He flashed her a grin and began to rinse the plates before handing them to her.

"I think you were just trying to cover up your frustration with humor," Hazel accused him, taking the plates from him and setting them in place on the dishwasher rack.

"That's not too big of a stretch," he admitted lightly. "But it did get me invited for dinner. I will tell you that I never thought your ribs recipe could be even better, but you seem to have been perfecting it just to show me what I've been missing."

156

Hazel laughed. "It hasn't changed at all. It's the exact same thing I cooked for you way back when."

He looked over at her curiously. "How does a teenaged girl achieve something like braised short ribs, when all her young friends are barely able to master grilled cheese?"

She smiled to herself, and closed the dishwasher door with a little shrug.

He continued to examine her. "I think I know."

"You do know," she admitted, moving past him out of the little galley kitchen and back to the dining table.

Grant leaned against the frame of the kitchen door and crossed his arms, regarding her with the light of teasing in his eyes. "So if I had innocently happened to mention that I liked venison, back then?"

"I'd have become a deer hunter," she replied, keeping a straight face and settling back down in her chair.

He laughed at that, and reached for a drying towel to come wipe down the table.

"Look at you, all domestic," Hazel observed.

"I have to be, to keep the women at church from feeling sorry for me, and coming in shifts to clean my house."

"Oh, I'm sure they'd be thrilled to do it," Hazel replied. "Especially Frieda Gathright."

"What?" Grant drew his brows, surprised that Hazel even knew who the granddaughter of Ivy Parker was.

He pulled out the chair next to her and lowered himself to sit and question her. "Do you know Frieda Gathright?"

"We've met," she informed him, leaning toward him provocatively and returning his probing gaze.

"You've met."

"We've met," she insisted, her inner actress taking over and keeping her beautiful face solemn and serene.

Grant continued to look bewildered. "When was this?"

"What difference does that make?"

"You can't say, because you've not met. Nice try."

157

"Then how do I know her name? I certainly didn't ask the universe to randomly send me someone named Frieda Gathright. Blonde? Red lipstick? Not even twenty, by the way!"

"How *do* you know her name?"

"You seem upset that I do."

"I'm not upset, I'm just surprised."

"So, has Frieda Gathright ever offered to come over and clean your house?"

Grant deliberately goaded her. "Oh, many times."

She twisted her lips into a scowl.

"That didn't go the way you planned, did it?" he asked.

"I guess not."

He laughed quietly at her and brushed her chin with a light fist. "Don't start something you can't finish."

"I'm not done," she informed him.

"No? Should I be worried?"

"Maybe, since we *have* met."

Hazel leaned back in her chair, crossing her arms and fixing him with a challenging look. "She came to see me."

She watched him grapple with that.

"Frieda Gathright?"

She nodded slowly.

"She came here?"

"She stopped by the coffee shop, looking for me."

Grant tried to determine if she was just messing with him, but her face was composed.

He persisted. "Frieda Gathright."

Hazel rolled her eyes and let out a loud sigh. "Yes! Do we have to keep saying her name?"

"I didn't start this," he reminded her.

"She asked if you and I were dating."

Grant grew quiet and waited for Hazel to say that she was kidding but she didn't.

"Hazie, I need you to be serious, right now."

"I'm being serious."

Suddenly, she wished she wasn't. Not only was Grant not smiling, he was obviously disturbed.

"What did you tell her?"

Hazel wrinkled her brow, torn between simply answering the question and being annoyed that it mattered to Grant what she told Frieda Gathright, one way or the other.

"Are you afraid she's mad at you, now?"

She pushed up from the table and went into the kitchen, opening the fridge door and staring into it as if she were looking for something.

Grant immediately got up and followed her. "What did you tell her, Hazel?"

She slammed the fridge door and shot him an angry look. "Why? Are you worried about her reaction?"

"I might be."

She held his gaze, little flecks of emotion doing amazing things to her beautiful eyes.

"If I'd known you had something going on with Frieda Gathright, I wouldn't have said anything," she informed him in a tight voice.

She moved to get past him but he gripped her arms and blocked her.

"I didn't say I had anything going on with her!"

"Then why do you give a flying crap what I told her?"

"Because when you talk to Frieda Gathright, you're really talking to her grandmother!"

They exchanged heated looks before Hazel slowly began to understand what he was saying.

"Ivy Parker told her to come ask me that?"

"I'd bet on it. What did you tell her?"

Hazel was still upset with him. "I told her that we're just friends, if even that, and that's all we ever *will* be!" she snapped.

She pressed her hands against his chest to push out of his grip, and began looking around the kitchen for anything else that needed to go into the dishwasher.

"Stop."

He took the spoon she found out of her hand and laid it back into the sink.

159

Hazel folded her arms and stood looking down at the spoon, breathing unevenly, but refusing to cry.

Grant moved close and coaxed her to turn around, then caught her shoulders lightly in his hands.

"I'm sorry, Hay. I shouldn't have kept asking you that over and over, until I upset you. I should have told you right away what my concern was."

She looked down and gave him nothing.

Grant waited then lifted her chin when she insisted on rebuffing him. "I'm sorry."

Hazel gazed up at him, then put her hands behind his neck and leaned into him. She rested her head on his shoulder, as he wrapped his arms around her and held her tightly, closing his eyes and feeling a rush come over him, not unlike the first time he ever held her.

After a long moment, she lifted her face to his and her eyes seemed to be pleading with him.

He traced the curve of her face with a fingertip and then outlined the shape of her lips.

"We can't kiss," he whispered.

"I know," she whispered back.

She closed her eyes and took in a deep breath, then looked back up at him with a sad smile, gently stepping out of his embrace.

"I told her that we weren't dating, and that we were just friends, Grant. I'm sorry that I didn't realize that she wasn't acting on her own, but that's all I told her. Nothing that should upset Ivy Parker.

"I won't be answering anyone else's questions about me and the local pastor. It's a small town. I get that."

Grant reached and caught her hand, caressing it and studying it with a strange expression on his face.

"You thought I cared about Frieda's reaction." He lifted his eyes to look closely at her. "Just so you know, Hazel, if I ever did allow myself to care about what a woman thought, it would be you."

160

"Was I right?" she asked him softly, looking down at the way he cradled her hand, stroking it slowly, as the familiar way it felt to him came stealing back to awaken his senses.

"Right about what?"

"That friends is all we'll ever be?"

She faltered then tried to continue.

"I don't want to keep hoping for something you've already decided can't happen. If I do, you'll be uncomfortable around me, and then even our friendship will be over."

Hazel struggled and made herself finish.

"If what I told her was right, and friends is all you can manage, then I'll take it. It's more than I was hoping for. I already know that I'll never earn your trust. I get that."

Grant reached for her other hand and brought them up to his lips, raising his eyes and looking deeply into hers.

"Maybe trust is overrated. Let's just see what happens."

Chapter Sixteen

Grant looked up and indicated a chair with his hand.

"Come in, Ivy. Since we're not the only ones here today, please close the door."

She looked surprised but complied and came around to take a seat. During all the years she had been here, Pastor Sellars had never specifically asked to meet with her.

"Is there a problem with the play?" she wondered.

"Potentially," he replied. "If our director becomes upset enough to walk out then yes, I'd call that a problem."

She widened her eyes. "Would she do that?"

"If anyone else takes it upon themselves to approach her in a public establishment and boldly ask her if she and the pastor are dating, then yes, she might, and I would encourage it. Why should she have to put up with that?"

"You mean Frieda."

"I mean Frieda. What possessed her to do such a thing, if I even need to ask?"

"I can tell that you think I put her up to it, Pastor, but you're wrong about that."

"Am I?" he asked evenly. "So you're categorically stating, right here in a house of God, that you did not either send, suggest, have foreknowledge of, or approve Frieda asking Hazel about whether the two of us are dating?"

"I didn't, but I'm not surprised to hear it," she said, convincingly. "I'm sorry, and I'll talk to her about it. I don't expect it to happen again."

"Again, Ivy, I have to ask. What possessed her to do such a thing? What difference could it possibly make to her, one way or another?"

163

"I suspect she has a crush on you."

"All of a sudden." He was skeptical.

"Well, maybe she just realized it, all of a sudden. I mean, a beautiful woman like Hazel Todd has come to town and there's an obvious connection between the two of you. We can all see that there is. Frieda, more than likely, became jealous."

He was dumbfounded. "I've never given your granddaughter a single moment of any more attention than I've given anyone else in my congregation. Actually, much less attention, since I make it a practice not to spend any time alone with any woman at church, and certainly not a single one."

"Oh, Pastor Sellars, no one is suggesting that. You wouldn't have had to give her any attention. Young girls are just young girls. They feel everything on a much more exaggerated and passionate level.

"No one is more likely to make rash decisions based on emotions than a young girl. I'm afraid that's what Frieda did when she approached Miss Todd."

"Hazel told Frieda that we aren't dating. Do you anticipate that will create any sort of false hope for Frieda? If so, that needs to be dealt with sooner, rather than later."

"Well, I agree, Pastor, but let me deal with it, please. I know it's hard to believe, looking at me, but this old woman was once a young girl. I know what it's like. My goodness, I was so sure I wanted to be a tightrope walker when I was in high school that I literally climbed out of my bedroom window in the middle of the night, when the circus finally made it to our town, and tried to convince them to let me go on the road with them!"

Grant stared at Ivy Parker as if she'd suddenly grown another head.

"It's true!" She had to laugh at his open mouth. "If you don't mind, Pastor, I'll have a talk with her. I promise, if I can't sort things out, I'll bring her in here to talk with you, myself, but let's not embarrass her if we can avoid it, please."

Grant was still trying to picture Ivy Parker, not only as a young girl, but making her way across a tightrope.

"Pastor?"

164

He shook himself.

"Alright, Ivy. I won't say anything to her. I'll let you deal with it."

"Would you like for me to apologize to Miss Todd?" she offered, again surprising him.

"No, we talked about it. I'll check with her again, just to be sure things are good, but I feel that they are. We're still on track with our play.

"In fact, Hazel needs to meet with everyone who is involved with backstage activity and anything that just generally falls under production, but not the actors, just yet. That will be a separate meeting."

He was relieved to be able to move the conversation back into normal parameters.

"So we need to get the calendar out and check with the people on the list she gave me. Did you get a copy of that?"

"I did. Do you want me to get them all to commit to a meeting time, then?"

"Please, Ivy, I would appreciate it. Whatever date and time you can make work, then Hazel and I will just have to adjust to it. It's hard to get so many people to agree on the same time, so we'll definitely adapt to them."

She rose to leave.

"Ivy."

She turned to look back and was surprised to see him smiling at her.

"Thank you."

She looked puzzled. "Well... you're welcome."

She let herself out, still wearing her confused expression.

Grant took in a deep breath and deliberately played back the very helpful and liberating conversation he had just had with, of all people, Ivy Parker.

She had no idea of the revelation she had just given him, simply by speaking so frankly of not only the impulsiveness of young girls, but of her own urgent attempt, as an impetuous teenager, to leave home and join the circus.

165

Between what she said to him and what Pastor Morgan had offered him from his own deep well, Grant began to look at eighteen-year-old Hazel Todd in a different way. He suspected that yet another layer of bitterness was beginning to release him and fall away. He closed his eyes and breathed in deeply, silently thanking God for His mercies that were new every morning.

He glanced down at his phone and checked the text that just came in with a slow grin.

'Jarvis is amazing! You should see all this stuff!'

He shot back his response.

'Is that an invitation?'

'Yes, please. And bring your pretty, pretty truck.'

He laughed out loud.

'Oh, so it's my truck you love. Fine, I see how it is.'

Hazel widened her eyes at the way he was teasing her but simply sent back a profusion of hearts, kissy faces, and all the silly, flirty emoticons she could quickly find.

'Be there soon.'

Hazel and Grant both put away their phones with the same little smiles on their faces. He pushed back from his desk and headed over to the parsonage to change and grab his keys.

When he walked into Jarvis Petrie's antique shop, which was more like a warehouse, he found Hazel at the top of a tall ladder, trying to reach behind some hat boxes for whatever it was she had spied.

"Get down, Hazel."

She frowned to herself and muttered, "Déjà vu!"

Grant laid his hands on the ladder and looked up at her.

"What is this thing with you and climbing up on stuff, for as long as I've known you? You already know how it ends."

"I just want to get this lantern."

"Come down. I'll get it."

She looked down at him with a nervous little laugh.

"Why do my legs always shake when I try to get down from something?"

"Eccentric muscle contraction," he said shortly.

He climbed halfway up the ladder.

166

"Or, in your case, guilt. Either way, the effect is the same. Come down a rung. I've got you."

Hazel obediently lowered her foot, then hastily brought it back up when she began to tremble.

"You know how we do this," Grant reminded her.

He moved up higher. "Come down one, Hazie. I'm right below you. Come on, I've got you."

"Can't I just stay right here?"

He could actually feel her shaking the ladder.

"Sure, if this is the new location for the play, and you plan on directing it from up there."

She took a deep breath and nodded. "Okay."

"One and done," Grant said softly, just as he'd said when a young and scared Hazel climbed up a hackberry tree in his parent's backyard to rescue a feral kitty. It showed its gratitude by hissing at her and jumping down without her help, leaving Hazel to get down the same way she'd gone up, which is when Grant first became aware of her issue with not being able to climb down.

He'd felt as if it took forever to get her out of the tree because she shook uncontrollably when it was time to make her descent, and he ended up climbing to her and slowly bringing her back to solid ground.

"One and done, Hay. Come on."

She felt Grant's hand on the small of her back and slowly brought one foot down until she heard him say it was safe to rest it on the rung.

"Good girl. Again. One and done."

They repeated this until she could see that she was only a couple of feet off the floor and Grant stepped off the ladder and let her take her last couple of steps.

She turned around to offer him a look of contrition.

"I know what you're gonna say."

"I bet you do." He gave her a disapproving scowl. "You knew I was on my way. The lantern couldn't wait?"

167

He glanced up at the top of the ladder and back down at her with bewilderment. "How did you even know there was a lantern up there, anyway?"

"Jarvis told me."

She continued to look up at him with a blend of remorse and relief.

"One of these days, I'm just gonna leave you at the top of wherever you've managed to get to."

"That's what you always say."

She stroked her fingertip across the frown lines on his brow and gave him a soft smile.

"One of these days, I'm gonna mean it."

He reached up to capture her hand.

"Thank you," Hazel said quietly.

Grant looked at her intently for a long moment before letting out a sigh.

"Stop with the brown eyes, and let's get to work."

She moved back and watched him scale up the ladder and reach behind the boxes. He brought the lantern down without the drama and held it out to her.

"Here, you stinker."

Hazel laughed and took the lantern over to put it in a carton, while Grant glanced around, wondering what she had in mind for the play.

"Hazel, the senior center doesn't usually let us begin storing things there until after the Fall Festival. The only reason they let us use it at Christmas is because after October, they're pretty much done with it until spring."

She came back toward him, fussing with a strap on her overalls, that wouldn't stay hooked. He watched her frustration then moved her hand out of the way.

"It keeps sliding off my shoulders and coming undone," she complained.

Grant pulled the slider and the strap until it rested snugly on her shoulder, then stepped back and gave her a deadpan look.

"What did you do?"

"You must have someone in California who dresses you," he muttered, rolling his eyes.

Hazel stood staring at the slide on her strap, trying to see how Grant managed to fix it. When she looked up, he was gone.

She blinked around with a worried look that immediately faded when she heard him call her.

"I thought you got mad and left," she admitted, when she located him around the corner.

"Don't give me any ideas," he replied. "Did you hear what I said about the senior center not letting us store things for the play until after the festival?"

"They said I could." She set her carton down.

"How did you get Marvin Washer to agree to that?"

"I asked him."

Grant looked up from inspecting what he thought might be a crack on a hat tree and saw her regarding him with childlike innocence.

"Never mind," he said. "I see how you did it."

She wrinkled her brow, wondering what he meant by that, but he ignored her and indicated the hat rack.

"Wrong period?"

"I'm afraid so. It's probably from the thirties. But if we don't find another one, we can cover it with a coat and hat and it might work from a distance."

Grant glanced over as Jarvis Petrie came toward them with a spiral bound tablet.

"Hello, Pastor!" the old man called out and Grant reached a hand to clasp his shoulder.

"How are you, Jarvis?"

"Just a little stiff, but not enough to call Mark Wynn."

Hazel belted out a loud laugh, and Jarvis grinned.

"Let's keep this pretty lady around. She's hasn't heard all my jokes before, so I have a fresh audience."

"She's all yours," Grant returned, flashing a little wink at Hazel's pout. "How are we handling this, Jarvis?"

"Well, it's all on loan, unless someone sees something they like, so I'll list each item and put the price off to the side.

169

"Just bring it back after you're done with it and if it's on the list but not on the truck, then just give me the money for what's missing and we'll be good."

"Works for me," Grant approved, watching Jarvis lift the top sheet and slip some carbon paper under it with a shaking hand, before pulling the top sheet back over it.

"Old school," the old man laughed, and Grant grinned at him and nodded.

"Nothing wrong with old school."

"No, indeed," the shop owner agreed. "You young people just put whatever you need over there by that roller door, where Miss Todd has already started a pile. I put a hold sign in front of it and I'll just write things down as you take it 'em out to the truck. Holler at me before you leave."

He made his way slowly back around to the front entrance to rest behind his counter and chuckle to himself about his clever little Mark Wynn joke.

Tom Pollard stood as Hazel Todd was shown into his office and came around his desk to enthusiastically greet the award-winning, beautiful stage actress.

"Miss Todd! It's an honor."

He offered his hand and Hazel took it graciously.

"Thank you for seeing me, Mayor Pollard."

"Tom, please!! He moved back around to reclaim his own chair after asking her to sit.

"My goodness, my wife has been after me to make your acquaintance ever since the first whispers that you were in our small town. She's been afraid that you would return to California before that could happen."

Hazel smiled at that. "I'm in no hurry to return, and I'd love to meet your wife, whenever that might work out."

"Her name's Lynn and she's such a fan. We saw you in 'Day Trip' when it played in New York."

"Wow, that's going back a bit," Hazel laughed.

"It was wonderful! I didn't know you could sing!"

"Well, you do what you have to, I suppose."

"Oh, you have a lovely voice!"

"Thank you, Tom." She hurried to get to the reason for her visit, partly because she had never mastered the art of how to respond to overly effusive fans.

"I have some questions regarding something that I've been very curious about and you seem like the right man to come to for answers."

"I do hope so. How can I help?"

"One of my very closest friends is actually from this town, although most of his years were spent here when he was young. He's recently returned from where he was living back east. He's a stage actor."

The mayor nodded. "Irving Lancaster, I'm sure you mean. Yes, he's wonderful, isn't he?"

"He is," Hazel agreed, with a smile. "He told me that this town once had a very beautiful playhouse. Would you know anything about it or where it was located? He just said it was off the square, but I drove around it a bit, and I didn't see anything that looked as if it could have once been a theater."

"It was called 'The Boards'. Mr. Lancaster was right when he told you that it was off the square, but he meant the square that he would have been familiar with, when he began his career here. When the courthouse burned, it was rebuilt a couple of blocks from its original site and the square reformed to surround the courthouse, as town squares generally do. Of course, all this was before my time."

Hazel raised her brows in surprise. It never would have occurred to her that the current town square wasn't the original one. It looked so established, as if it had been there forever.

"There's a lovely picture of it in the library," Tom Pollard continued. "That is, if you want to see how it looked in all its glory. I'm afraid it looks nothing like that now."

Hazel moved forward to the edge of her chair. "It's still standing, then?"

"It is, although it has been mentioned at various town meetings that it needs to be torn down."

"But why would anyone do that?" Hazel gasped. "It's part of the town's history."

"I suppose no one has had the vision or the bankroll to restore it and, even if someone did, I'm not sure what they would do with it. It was flooded, you know. In fact, that entire portion of town was, after the river crested, which was the reason that the courthouse and the square migrated to higher ground. The theater had already been sitting there empty when that happened, so no effort was made to repair the damage. No insurance claim was filed against it."

"Who owns the building, Tom?"

"Originally, a non-profit foundation that folded. After that, it sat on the market with no offers. When the flood happened, that was the end of that. The town acquired it eventually, more or less, by default."

Hazel drew in a breath and considered what he was telling her with a bit of disappointment but she wasn't ready to completely abandon her quest.

"Is there any access at all to see the building?"

The mayor looked startled. "I don't even know if that's safe, Miss Todd."

"Hazel," she insisted with a smile.

He looked pleased and repeated himself. "I don't know if it's safe, Hazel, to go into that building."

"Is there anyone who would know? The sheriff's department or an inspector, or someone like that?"

He thought about it. "Well, I'm sure that the Portmanns might know. The Portmann brothers own a construction and restoration company. Of course, we have a codes office, but the Portmanns have actually been inside that building and could tell you more about it than anyone, I expect.

He paused and rested his chin on his hands and regarded Hazel curiously.

"It almost sounds as if you have more than a passing interest in the old theater, Hazel."

172

"I'm very interested in knowing if it's beyond all hope. I have to admit, it's beginning to sound that way."

"Well, the most I can offer at this point, is the contact information for Larry and Marshall Portmann.

"They will either be able to help you or they'll refer you to codes. I agree, it doesn't look too promising, which is why the question of demolition comes up, from time to time."

Mayor Pollard retrieved the information from his secretary and gave it to Hazel. He did have a few questions about the Christmas play and she was asked to let him know if the town could help in any way.

Hazel thanked the mayor and promised to hold tickets to the Christmas play for him and his wife, then headed in the direction of a good cup of coffee.

Chapter Seventeen

Hazel rolled over and reached out a hand in the general direction of her phone, and finally located it. She raised up and turned on the lamp, before opening her eyes and checking the screen to see who was calling her so late.

She frowned and hurried to answer.

"Grant?"

"Hazel, are you awake? I need you to be awake."

She sat straight up.

"I'm awake. What is it?"

"I want you to call William Cullen and tell him to come get his wife!"

"What?" Hazel put Grant on speaker and began pulling on a pair of jeans. "She's at your house?"

"She started out trying to get into my house. Now she's out there, between the parsonage and the churchyard and about to wake up the entire street."

"I'll call him right now."

"Thank you."

Hazel called William Cullen's number, continuing to get dressed and looking around for her keys.

He answered quickly and somehow seemed to know why she was calling.

"Hazel, is Louise there?"

"She's at the church, William."

"The church! Where is it, what street?"

She quickly gave him the address and hurried to her car.

When she pulled up in front of the parsonage, Grant was keeping a watch, in case a drunken Louise Cullen wandered off.

"William's on his way," Hazel said, hurrying over to stand next to Grant and look toward where he was indicating the woman was.

It wasn't too difficult to tell, since she was alternately yelling and sobbing incoherently at the top of her lungs.

It was cold outside and Louise was hardly dressed for it. She had apparently left the house in her robe and little else.

Hazel looked up at Grant, not surprised to see an angry set to his jaw. She wondered how in the world Louise Cullen had managed to get there, especially wearing nothing but a robe, but didn't ask any questions, since he was clearly not in the mood to answer any.

She reached over to touch Grant's arm when William Cullen whipped his car up against the curb. His headlights had revealed exactly where his wife was and he threw his door open and strode quickly across the grass to get her, not even looking their way.

"He's fired up," Hazel whispered to herself.

Grant heard her. "Who could blame him?"

They watched while William steered the hysterical and disoriented woman to the car, with a grim stiffness on his face.

He forced her around to the passenger seat and harnessed her in, not bothering to respond to any of her bizarre ramblings. After he had her secured, he slammed her door and then just stood resting his weight against it, with his head down and his hands running through his hair.

"You know the man," Grant said quietly to Hazel. "Do we approach him, or do we let him be?"

"I'll go," she answered, giving his hand a squeeze before walking through the grass out to the street.

William Cullen looked up at her without really seeing her at first, then his expression became less dazed.

"I thought she was just roaming around the house, when I couldn't find her," he explained, still breathing unevenly from his distress. "I don't know how she got here, unless she called a cab, but what cab driver would pick her up in this state?"

176

He looked off down the street and shook his head with a grimace.

"I guess if you wave enough cash in the air, it wouldn't be an issue."

He moved to one side so that Hazel could see the crumpled bills stuffed in his wife's robe pockets and spilling out onto the floor of the car.

Louise had her eyes closed and her mouth open, apparently feeling that the car was some sort of refuge, ceasing her rants, and giving in to the alcohol's sedation.

"She's been using a cab service here because I took her car keys, so I imagine she has it saved in her contacts."

He leaned back against the car and crossed his arms, looking around the dark neighborhood with defeat clearly in his stance and attitude.

"I'm so sorry, William," Hazel offered softly. "She seems to have gotten worse, but I guess you're the only one who would know that for sure."

"She's absolutely worse," he confirmed.

After a moment, he turned to look toward Grant, who stood quietly waiting to determine if his presence was either needed or wanted.

"Tell the pastor that I appreciate his not getting the police involved."

Hazel looked back at Grant as well. "No, he only wanted you to know."

He nodded. "Of course, one of the neighbors may have called them. I can see some of them are awake."

Hazel looked around at the normally quiet neighborhood and wondered. If anyone had, they'd know soon enough.

She stood in thought beside William Cullen, before deciding to tell him what she'd recently learned.

"She's come here before, William, but not like this. She came one day a few weeks ago, and showed up at the pastor's office. She was still angry with him over his remarks at Barry's service, or at least that seemed to be why she was upset."

William smiled down at the ground ironically. "Well, who knows? Maybe the man's right. Maybe we're all headed to Hell. One never knows."

"You can know," she replied hesitantly. "It doesn't have to be like that."

He seemed to be turning her words over in his mind, and the street light caught the unmistakable glint of unshed tears.

"Well," he said, straightening up and giving her a light pat on her arm. "Maybe it doesn't."

He gave her an apologetic smile. "I'm sorry for the disturbance. I do see a few house lights being turned off now though, so I guess the excitement's over. Hopefully, they'll all go on back to bed."

She looked around and nodded.

"Please apologize to the pastor for me, Hazel. I think I'm in no condition to be caught between expressing regrets and defending Louise, right now. I just need to get her back to the house and figure out what happens next."

"I will, William. Call me though, if there's anything any of us can do."

She stepped back to allow him to move around and get into his car in order to take his wife back home and felt a pang of sympathy for him, as she watched him drive away.

Grant silently came to stand beside her and looked at the departing vehicle with a solemn expression, sighing to himself and supposing that William Cullen was much less obnoxious than he'd first believed, and much more desperate.

He rested a hand on Hazel's back that suggested she should return to her own car.

"It's cold, Hazie. You need to get back to bed."

She let him steer her in that direction but waited before opening the door and having the car lights come on.

"William asked me to apologize, Grant, and to thank you for not calling the police."

He clenched the muscles in his jaw and looked out in the direction he had driven, and Hazel could see that he was silently processing everything.

"I hope no one else has," he finally replied. "I think if someone had, there'd be a cruiser here, by now."

"I'm sorry, Grant."

He seemed surprised by her soft apology.

"Why?"

"It's because of me that all these people have descended on your town. It's like I can never seem to stop messing up your life, and I'm really sorry for that."

"Stop," he fussed, giving her a tender smile and stroking her chin lightly. "You know I don't blame you for any of this."

"You should."

"Well, I'll keep that in mind, the next time I find you stranded up in the air, unable to get down."

He rested against her car, seeming to forget that he had just finished telling her that she needed to go home. She settled against the door next to him, and he bumped her shoulder.

"So, here's a thought to take home with you, that will guarantee that you're awake for the rest of the night."

He could hear her softly laughing and grinned.

"Would you ever have thought that Ivy Parker had aspirations, as a young teenage girl, to run off with the circus and be a tightrope walker?"

Hazel looked up at him with disbelief, unsure if he was being serious or trying to make her laugh.

"That's probably how my face looked when she shared that bit of her personal history," he said lightly.

"She really told you that?"

"She did." He moved slightly to be closer and she leaned against him.

"I was put out with her over her granddaughter approaching you at Katie's place, but Ivy promises me that she absolutely did not put her up to that stunt. Her explanation is that Frieda has a crush on me and, in her words, someone as beautiful as Hazel Todd coming to town made her jealous."

"Beautiful!" Hazel scoffed. "Yeah, look at me now, at two in the morning, fresh out of bed. I bet I'm gorgeous."

179

"You'd win that bet," Grant informed her, looking at her in a way that raced her pulse.

They lingered for a reflective moment before Hazel murmured to herself. "A tightrope walker!"

Grant looked out across the dark churchyard with a grin.

"That's what the woman said."

He reached an arm around Hazel and brought his other arm around to complete the circle of his embrace. She snuggled into it without even being aware of doing so.

"And so I was thinking," he continued softly, "that when you and I were teenagers, I doubt if either of us was so mature that we wouldn't have climbed out of our bedroom windows in the middle of the night, to try to run away with the circus, if that was our dream."

"That's what she did?" Hazel gazed up at him stunned, her face only inches from his.

"It is." Grant rested his eyes on her face, studying the line of her cheek in a way that she could almost feel.

"I'm sorry, Hazel," he whispered.

She looked at him with a question in her eyes.

"The young, idealistic version of me has always insisted on his right to be angry with eighteen-year-old Hazel Todd, but this grown man is ashamed of that. I'm so sorry."

She continued looking up at him, then turned in his arms to wrap hers around his neck and harbor there.

He lifted her chin and let his eyes search hers.

"We can't kiss," Hazel whispered.

"I know," he whispered back. "But only because Lucy Walker's light is on."

Hazel giggled as the spell was broken, and she pulled her car keys out of her jacket pocket.

"Tell Lucy Walker to go to bed!" she exclaimed, with a pretend scowl.

"Oh, she will, as soon as you drive off."

Grant opened her car door and waited for her to get her seatbelt on.

"Thank you, Hazie, for helping with all this."

"The understatement of the year is me telling you that it's the very least I could do," she replied, with a smile.

"Tomorrow is the meeting with the backstage crew," Grant thought to remind her. "Or rather this evening. Get some sleep. I'm sure we'll both need it."

"Okay, maybe *that* is the understatement of the year," she decided. "Goodnight, Grant."

"Goodnight, sweet girl."

He closed her door and watched her drive away, then noted Lucy Walker's intent to also turn in, with a sarcastic grin.

"At least she didn't sic old Buck on us."

Katie had been smiling to herself all day and her husband laughed when he came into the shop and saw the same pleased expression on her face that had been there that morning.

"Has she been by?" he asked.

"No, but I just texted her. She said that she and Grant are actually a couple of blocks away and that they'll stop by when they're done."

"When they're done with what?" Fred came around the counter and claimed a light kiss. "Are they at the park?"

"She didn't say." Katie looked down at the strings on her apron that kept coming untied and cinched them tighter before trying to tie them again.

"How's that whole Grant and Hazel thing going, anyway?" He gently turned his wife around and took over the bow tying.

"You've been doing this upside down and backward."

He finished and inspected his work. "Is this the same apron you normally wear?"

"No, and that's why I can't get it to stay tied. The ones I usually wear just have little Velcro side closures, but I took them home to wash them and forgot to get them out of the dryer. I had this one in the store room."

181

She stopped and thought about his question. "I think it must be going really well. She certainly does look a lot happier, for one thing."

"Ditto for Grant," Fred added. "The punching bags are no longer in danger."

Katie laughed at him. "Well, from what I've been able to get out of Hazel, they're just enjoying being friends and getting to know each other again."

"Boring!" her husband declared. He reached into the glass display and brought out an oatmeal raisin cookie.

"I know, right?" Katie snapped off half the cookie and popped it into her mouth.

"Does she have any idea at all that you had a new sign put up today?"

"She hasn't said anything and she would have. She would have called me or come in here right away, if she had seen it. I wish, whatever they're doing, they would be done already."

"Me, too. I was hoping to be here when she comes in, but I have a property closing in an hour. I'll have to leave about a half hour before, to do some paper shuffling."

"I'm usually glad that you're a real estate attorney, but not today." Katie affected a convincing pout.

"I'll quit right now. Anything for you, babe."

"Wait 'til this place takes off first, and then we'll talk about it." She looked down at her phone.

"They're headed this way! Don't leave, Fred!"

"Are you kidding? You couldn't blast me out of here."

Katie looked down at her apron, and smoothed it with her hands. "I'm so nervous!"

"Oh, stop, she's gonna love it."

"She will, right?"

"Breathe." Fred looked down at his cute little wife and gave her blonde curls a little tug. "What's the worst that can happen?"

He stepped over to the main display window and peered both ways. "Oh, they were driving. They're in Grant's truck."

"Come back! Come over here, honey!"

"No, let's watch her see it."

"Oh, right!" Katie ran around the counter and joined him in watching Hazel and Grant get out of his truck and begin walking toward the shop.

As they neared the door, Grant grabbed Hazel's elbow and stopped her, then nodded for her to look up over her head at the new swinging sign.

Katie was about to jump out of her skin, but when she saw the happy look on Hazel's face, she exhaled a deep breath of relief. "She likes it!"

She and Fred turned to see them come through the door and Hazel stopped in her tracks and fastened Katie with a big grin. Katie jumped up and down in place, with a little clap.

"What did you do?" Hazel demanded.

"Well, for one thing, they changed the name of this place," Grant observed, looking almost as pleased as Hazel.

"I can't believe you remembered that!" Hazel suddenly had little happy tears crowding her eyes, and made her way over to give her friend a big hug.

Grant looked over at Fred, completely clueless. "Fill me in, buddy."

"It's something Hazel said, the first day she came in this place and met Katie."

Grant turned to look back at Hazel. "You said 'Oh, It's Coffee!' and Katie remembered that?"

"Yes!" Katie sang out. "And I said it would make a great name for this place, and it just never would get out of my head, after that."

"The sign's really nice," Grant told her. "It pops. Well, for the normal person walking down the sidewalk, it pops. Hazel is in her own little world right now, so I had to stop her and get her to look up."

"I saw that!" Fred laughed. "If she'd come in here without even seeing it, Katie would have burst into tears."

Hazel had come back over to stand next to Grant and he reached his hands to capture the sides of her head. "It's not her fault. She's got big things going on in here."

"What kinds of things?" Katie demanded.

"Big, big things," Grant informed her solemnly. "Things that most people dare not even dream of. All right up in here."

"Stop squeezing my head!" Hazel smacked his chest.

Katie and Fred exchanged wide-eyed stares, then aimed them at the couple smiling at each other in front of them.

"You're not gonna tell us?" Katie was incredulous. "But I made you a sign!"

"That's right, she made you a sign," her husband chimed in. "That outta be worth something."

"How about this?" Hazel suggested. "How about when I think it's safe to talk about it, you and Fred will be the very first ones to know?"

"Are you getting married?" Katie blurted out, getting ready to start jumping and clapping again.

Hazel and Grant both looked startled.

"Why, what have you heard?"

Hazel smacked Grant again. "Don't say that, you'll make her think she's right!"

He grinned and caught her hand, in order to keep her from hitting him again.

"No, honey, it's nothing like that," Hazel replied to Katie, after giving Grant a playfully fierce look. "It's just a project I'm hoping to take on but I still have a lot of hurdles to clear, so I'm not wanting to say much about it just yet."

"Oh." Katie's disappointment was obvious. "Then, that's okay. You can just start with Fred and me, when you're ready. In the meantime, come and tell me what I did wrong on these turnovers."

William Cullen stood in his doorway and regarded the woman out on the front stoop with both surprise and aversion.

"I can tell you're thrilled to see me," Cheryl Jamison said with mild sarcasm.

"Try another word," he suggested.

"I know I'm not your favorite person, William, but I've come all this way. Won't you at least let me come in?"

He grudgingly stood to one side as the auburn-haired, attractive woman breezed past him and paused to appraise the large house appreciatively.

"The question is *why* have you come all this way? It seems to me that entire state of California is closing in on this little town, one opportunist after another."

"Would you not include yourself as one of those?"

"I am the one with the dead son, in case you need to be reminded." His aversion was becoming contempt.

His son's agent smiled insolently at that, before turning around to focus on him.

"Of course, Barry's death was devastating to us all, but you and Louise would surely have been shattered."

"We noticed how devastated you were," he returned blandly, returning to his chair and leaving her to sit or stand, as she wished.

"Oh, William, it's not that I wasn't grieving, but once a person is gone, what good does it do to dive into the depths of despair and take little walks down memory lane, which is always a disappointing trip? Barry would be the first one to agree with me, and you know it."

"It's called respect, Cheryl. I'm not exactly disappointed, since no one in their right mind would expect that from you."

She checked her glib response, not wishing to antagonize the father of her late star, since it wasn't in her best interest. "I apologize, William, it was thoughtless of me to not reach out in some manner. I can see how hurtful my oversight was to you and Louise."

He narrowed his eyes and inspected her closely.

"What do you want?"

She smiled smugly and took a pointless stroll around the lavishly furnished room.

"So, how's Hazel?" she asked, seemingly out of nowhere, but William Cullen had always had a keen sense of discernment where Cheryl Jamison was concerned. It wasn't out of nowhere.

185

"You can't be serious."

He fixed a look on her that let her know that he expected her to knock off the chit chat.

"I merely asked how the dear child is, William."

"She's hardly dear to you, Cheryl, and she's nobody's child. I don't remember you concerning yourself with Hazel's welfare, in the past."

"You're allowing your resentment over the marriage between Barry and Hazel to influence your impression of me, but I assure you, William, if either of them had been opposed to it, it wouldn't have happened."

"My impression of you was formed long before your asinine little PR stunt. State your business and leave, Cheryl."

She drew in her breath, unprepared to have him give her this ultimatum so soon after her arrival. She took a seat across from him and decided that she would do as he suggested.

"My commission from Barry, which was always deducted after his earnings went into our Client Trust Account is still owed to me. Apparently, someone took it upon himself to stop my check authorization and the account is now inaccessible."

"Perhaps your *client* didn't *trust* your *account*," William said with stressed sarcasm. "Why come crying to me?"

She rolled her eyes. "You were his manager and you handled his contracts. Who else would I come crying to?"

He shrugged. "Perhaps my son began to get wise to your skimming off the top. Why don't you ask Brandy? I heard his glitzy girlfriend escaped any real injury and I happen to know the two of them were setting up house together."

She frowned at that.

"I expect his widow might be more privy to his financial affairs, since they shared the same business manager."

"If you came here intending to ask her about it, you'll leave disappointed. She doesn't live here."

"I would hardly expect her to, but you do know where she is, so why don't you save us both a lot of time and just tell me, William?"

"To begin with, I don't know where she is, because I haven't asked, since she's a grown woman and it's none of my business. If she wanted me to know, she'd tell me.

"If I did know, I would hardly share that information with you, just as I wouldn't share it with your two partners in crime who were also here recently, trying to locate her."

William stood up and crossed over to the door, resting his hand on the handle and implying that she was finished.

She came over with an angry flush of color.

"By the way, Cheryl, in case you get any ideas, Hazel already has an agent. And it's not you."

He opened the door and his turbulent demeanor clearly suggested that she'd better go out the same way she came in, and not be all day about it.

Chapter Eighteen

Irving Lancaster paused and looked up, in order to read the attractive sign that was suspended by chains from the overhead awning that ran the length of the downtown row of shops, allowing it to be viewed from either direction.

"Delightful!" he chuckled.

He proceeded into the cafe to be happily welcomed by the owner, who came around the counter to clasp his hand.

"Mr. Lancaster! This is your first visit," Katie observed.

"I've been remiss, my dear, but I'm here to remedy that."

He smiled at her with a twinkle in his blue eyes and gave her the slightest bow.

"What's your pleasure, sir?" she asked, adapting to the dashing, elderly gentleman's formal manner by offering him a curtsey and a smile.

"I'm to meet with our Miss Todd and, since I have a later appointment in town, she suggested this very nice establishment. I see that I have preceded her arrival."

He glanced around and she nodded, reaching over for a paper menu.

"Let me show you to a table," she suggested and he acquiesced with a little nod, then followed her over to what she considered to be the one with the most comfortable chairs.

Katie assisted him by accepting the bowler hat he offered and helping him remove his soft, Tartan plaid scarf and his salt and pepper overcoat. She placed the items on the seat of a chair and he hooked his cane on the back of it, before taking the chair beside it and graciously thanking his hostess.

Katie couldn't help noticing the beautiful mahogany cane with its ebony handle, carved into an exquisite raven.

189

Irving Lancaster noticed her appreciation with a pleased smile. "Shades of Poe. One must attempt the obligatory deference, in my profession."

"It's absolutely wonderful," she breathed.

"Why, thank you, charming Katie."

She was fascinated as she watched him smooth his beautiful white beard. She had always been intrigued by the refined actor, fancying him to be a time traveler.

She moved the menu over to him. "Can I get you started with something to drink?"

"I wonder, my dear, if you brew tea in your lovely shop, that I am aware does *not* feature a sign bearing the exclamation 'Oh, It's Tea!'? I hope my request is not an insult."

"Not at all!" She laughed at his mention of her new sign. "Earl Grey?"

"The horror!" he responded, lifting his brows. "The one tea that I will not tolerate. It tastes of old woolen socks. That's not a criticism of your ability to brew tea, my dear," he added, with a light pat of her hand. "No, the blame fully lies with Charles Grey, who falsely believed that adding oil of bergamot was a thing to be desired. He was quite mistaken."

Katie had no idea that this was what gave that particular type of tea its strange smell, but she had already decided that she didn't like it.

"A Scottish breakfast tea, if you have it, please. I prefer its woody oaken flavor over that of moldy footwear." He smiled at her engagingly. "However, an English or Irish breakfast tea is also acceptable."

"I'll get that right away," she said, glancing up as Hazel came into the shop. "I see your meeting is about to begin," she added confidentially to him, as she left to begin preparing his tea.

Hazel stopped to give her friend a light hug before joining Irving Lancaster at their table.

"Oh, please don't get up, Irving," she protested, as he attempted to rise.

She rested a hand on his shoulder and smiled down at him before sitting.

190

"And how are you faring, lovely Hazel?"

He reached a hand to give hers an affectionate clasp.

"All things considered, very well, actually. I'm so sorry I'm late. I stopped by the church to deliver the scripts, that are being passed out tonight and there seemed to be some confusion over which of two auditions was the one I actually approved."

"Oh, my," her friend sympathized. "I hope you were able to settle the dispute."

"Actually, it was a bigger effort to convince either one of them to do it. Each was afraid of hurting the other's feelings, to such a degree that I began to panic, thinking we'd have no Edith at all, by the time we were done."

"Oh, that can't be," Irving insisted. "Why, 'Edith with golden hair' must make an appearance, otherwise the narrative of The Children's Hour will raise more questions than it answers."

"I'm happy to report that it was resolved," Hazel said, and the elderly actor smiled complacently.

"All's well." His comment was made with light humor.

She widened her eyes in exaggerated relief.

"Your lovely friend, Katie, is brewing me a cup of tea," he informed her.

Hazel tapped the menu in front of him. "But you need to have something to eat with your tea, Irving."

"If I were having my tea at home, I wouldn't bother, but the aromas of this worthy cafe are seducing me."

"I recommend the savory scones or the chicken salad croissant, since you aren't a fan of many sweet things."

"Nonsense. I am your greatest fan!"

He chuckled at the crickets stare he got, and slid the menu back to her. "The croissant sounds very nice, thank you."

Katie approached them with a loaded tray and Hazel got up to rescue her coffee from the side of it, so that Katie could set up the teapot and china for Irving Lancaster's tea.

"I heard chicken salad croissants," she said. "Two?"

"Thanks, Kate. Big tip for you." Hazel settled back into her chair with a grin, while Irving inspected his tea setting with a pleased smile.

"Thank you, my dear." He reached a hand to give Katie's arm a little touch. "It all looks wonderful."

"You're so welcome! And you're right," she confided in a stage whisper, close to his ear, "I opened the Earl Grey and took a sniff. It does smell like moldy socks!"

He laughed with delight, as Katie headed back to plate their lunch.

"Your little friend is a pure joy," Irving said. "I've seen her in church on occasion and around town, but I've never had the pleasure of simply chatting with her. She's quite fun."

"She sometimes feels like a sister to me," Hazel told him, glancing toward her with a smile.

Irving took a moment to pour hot water into his cup before placing a bag of tea in to steep for exactly three minutes, actually placing his pocket watch on the table to monitor the process, as Hazel knew he would do.

"Tell me, dear friend," he began, as he glanced up from his efforts. "Are you any closer to resurrecting the grand old Boards, or is it beyond all hope?"

"Honestly, Irving, it isn't as bad as I thought it would be, but I admit, I began with assuming the worst case scenario. I'm hoping that if I can succeed in having The Boards declared a national historical landmark, that I can secure a grant or some other type of funding to help with the restoration.

"Grant and I met with the Portmann brothers there last week to talk to them about the feasibility of all this."

"Our fine pastor! You've managed to enlist his aid."

"He's been urging the mayor and the city council to accept my offer, instead of demolishing it, so fingers crossed."

Hazel reached inside her bag and brought out an envelope. "They wouldn't allow me to go up into the balcony area, but they did let me take some photos of the places they felt were safe enough for me to be in."

"I'm afraid to ask if you could even breathe inside, after it sat for so long, closed up and having been deluged with nasty river water," Irving admitted, reaching for the envelope she offered him.

192

"I honestly didn't think it was nearly as bad as I was told to expect, but Grant said I was smelling with my heart."

Irving laughed faintly at that, and pulled the photos out of the envelope after putting his wire-rimmed spectacles on.

Hazel sat still, watching his face as he slowly moved one photograph behind another in his hands, that were shaking more from excitement than from age.

"What a lovely, lovely old girl," he murmured to himself, looking at each image of the still beautiful theater as if he were gazing into the past. "I would certainly hope you succeed in obtaining the national declaration, even if no funds are allotted for its restoration. That is something that can be discussed at a later time," he added with an air of mystery.

"Their criteria states 'a property must retain the essential physical features or characteristics that enable it to convey its historic identity' and I think that is easily satisfied."

Hazel reached for the photos that Irving held out to her.

"From these photos and what you remember, Irving, is it too far gone? The library's picture was just of the outside of it and it was taken before the flood."

"Not at all. Of course, I can only attest to the aesthetics. I know nothing of structural compromises or the dreaded black mold. I certainly hope that won't be an issue but I wouldn't be surprised at your having to clear either that hurdle or anything dealing with asbestos. I'm sorry," he added, glancing up with a smile, as Katie brought their lunch to the table. "I only wish to give you as honest a review as I can."

Katie moved to look over Hazel's shoulder at the top photo. "Oh, this is what you told Fred and me you were doing. Does it look like this now?" She waited for Hazel's nod.

"It's beautiful. Can you imagine, if this is what it looks like after the flood, what it used to look like?"

She glanced over at Irving. "I'm so jealous that you got to see it, back then. I wish I was a time traveler, like you." She gave the old man a conspiratorial wink of teasing.

He returned the wink with a straight face and touched the side of his nose, before she laughed and went back to the counter to start a fresh pot of coffee.

Irving had noted Hazel's pressed lips when he mentioned mold and asbestos, and gave a sigh of regret.

"It's indeed a shame that the foundation that owned the theater didn't attempt selling it while it was at the peak of its stellar reputation and before they ended up dissolving. But they continued to put off the inevitable and once that happened, its fate was more or less sealed," he stated, in a way that revealed his personal disappointment.

Hazel began to comment, but looked up when the door chimed in response to a woman's arrival. The expression that immediately swept across her face alerted Irving to the fact that she was more than a little displeased.

"Cheryl Jamison," she muttered to Irving.

He drew his brows in alarm. "And we were having such a pleasant time. Is she approaching, then?"

Hazel leaned back in her chair and crossed her arms. "Unfortunately."

Cheryl Jamison waved aside Katie's greeting and made her way straight back to where Hazel and Irving were seated.

"Finding you has been like looking for the Holy Grail," she began, focusing an accusing look at Hazel.

"You ignored the shop owner's greeting when you came in," Hazel pointed out quietly.

"Did I? I'm sure I didn't hear her."

"Is that why you waved her off so rudely? Because you didn't hear her?"

Katie could hear just fine and she smiled to herself as Hazel was offended on her behalf.

"Would you like for me to go out and come back in and say something trite and meaningless, just to satisfy you, Hazel?" She gestured toward the entrance.

"Start by going out, and we'll see how that goes," she replied in clipped tones, while Irving lifted the teapot and refreshed his cup with a look of satisfaction.

"Oh my, you're upset with me," Cheryl observed, almost as if she cared. "I suppose you're still on uneven footing, though, with Barry's service having been not so long ago."

"The service you didn't bother to attend?"

Cheryl Jamison rolled her eyes. "Not you too! My goodness, between you and William Cullen, I'm being batted about like a cat toy."

Irving allowed a slow smile to spread across his face and into his eyes, as the image that conjured up seemed to amuse him. He glanced up to see Hazel reading him like a script and allowed himself to laugh quietly.

The late Barry Cullen's disreputable agent turned to flash a scornful look at him.

"Irving Lancaster! I see the reports of your demise have been greatly exaggerated. What a shame," she added with a scowl, causing Hazel to stand to her feet and glare at her with a blaze of anger in her beautiful eyes.

"I'm sure you're here for your own purposes, Cheryl, which fails to surprise anyone who knows you, but let me tell you here and now, that if there's any sort of request you plan on making of me, the way to assure yourself of the swiftest and most fervent refusal is to let another stupid remark like that be spoken to my friend!

"Irving Lancaster happens to be one of the greatest talents the stage has ever witnessed! He's of the caliber that you will never have the privilege of working with, which I would imagine you know, thus the bitter, fatuous commentary.

"And if I may suggest, the next time you try to plagiarize Mark Twain, you might at least quote him correctly!"

Hazel was so incensed and focused on the object of her disgust that she failed to become aware that Grant had entered the cafe. He frowned and looked over at Katie, who simply drew in a breath and shook her head.

Rather than insert himself in what he could clearly see Hazel was more than capable of handling, he stood quietly, monitoring the situation in case it began to upset her beyond what he knew she could deal with.

195

Cheryl Jamison lifted a hand to ward off the effects of her own making.

"Alright, alright! I'm sorry!"

"Is that a character reference?" Hazel's hostile question brought another smile to Irving's face, while she continued to bore her brown eyes into the woman with cold precision.

"I admit it, Hazel, I do speak off the cuff and I say things that I later have to take myself to task for, but it's not intentional." She was making a big effort to placate the highly praised, much sought after actress, who was having none of it.

"How is your saying that Irving Lancaster's not being dead is a shame, *not* intentional?"

Hazel narrowed her eyes and took a step toward Barry Cullen's agent, causing her to retreat back.

Grant folded his arms and Katie couldn't help but notice the proud look in his eyes, as he watched Hazel champion her longtime friend, Irving Lancaster.

Cheryl waved her hand, clearly done with being put in her place by Hazel Todd, which had not been her plan, at all. She reached into her wallet and brought out her business card, slamming it down on the table and tapping it with her finger.

"I suggest, Hazel, that when you stop being so easily angered, you take the time to call me to find out why I'm here. If you don't, you might find yourself the target of a law suit."

Hazel picked up the card and slowly ripped it cleanly in half. "If you point a lawsuit at me, sister, you'd better not be shooting blanks. Because I can guarantee you I won't be."

The two women stood facing each other for a long moment before Cheryl Jamison turned and stormed out of the shop, realizing that she had just awakened a part of Hazel Todd she had never seen or even knew existed.

Hazel was fixated on her exit, ready to make sure she didn't come back in, and had still not noticed Grant's presence even though she had slowly made her way forward toward the door and was practically standing next to him.

"You okay then, Hazie?" he asked quietly.

She looked over at him with startled eyes and suddenly revealed herself to be embarrassed.

"I'm sorry. I guess that wasn't very Christ-like behavior."

Grant raised his brows. "Did I miss the part where you called her a brood of vipers and suggested that she was of her father, the devil?"

Irving seemed to find great comic relief in his young pastor's facetious question and turned in his chair to rest his evocative eyes on him.

"Join us, my good Pastor Sellars," he invited, with a welcoming smile. "The very hospitable Katie makes a delightful chicken salad croissant."

"This, coming from one of the greatest talents the stage has ever witnessed." Katie said, commending both Irving and herself, and motioning Grant toward the table.

"He's right, I do. Go sit down and I'll hook you up."

"Twist my arm," Grant replied, reaching to rest his hand on Hazel's back and persuade her to return to her chair.

"And now that we are met, Sir Lancaster," Grant began, pausing to laugh at Katie's wide-open stare, her waving arms, and her repetitive pointing in Irving's direction.

"Yes, Katie, on top of all his other achievements, our esteemed thespian has also been knighted," he informed her, and Irving turned to look in her direction with a grin.

"Ah, but that was in *another* world," he informed her, again touching the side of his nose and favoring her with a cunning wink.

"If I keep getting this caliber of clientele, I may have to raise my prices," she announced, reaching for a fresh croissant.

"Now that we are met," Grant repeated, "please favor us with a few lines of your selected Longfellow verse."

The distinguished man rose slowly from his chair, causing Katie to pause and join the others in waiting expectantly.

He placed one hand on the table to steady himself, and laid the other on his chest, closing his eyes and silently allowing himself to become immersed in becoming Henry Wadsworth Longfellow, choosing words of gratitude for their kindness.

197

When he spoke, it was with a voice that Hazel had always described as a rich, dark brown. Irving Lancaster knew of her tendency to associate both sounds and scents with color and regarded rich, dark brown as one of the highest compliments anyone had ever paid him.

> "If any thought of mine, or sung or told,
> Has ever given delight or consolation,
> Ye have repaid me back a thousand-fold,
> By every friendly sign and salutation.
> Thanks for the sympathies that ye have shown!
> Thanks for each kindly word, each silent token,
> That teaches me, when seeming most alone,
> Friends are around us, though no word be spoken."

Hazel immediately sprang up from her seat and tearfully embraced her dear friend, while Katie and Grant vigorously applauded his emotionally delivered performance.

Hazel began laughing at herself for spontaneously bursting into tears, but Irving had been missing from her life for a long time and it was the first occasion for her to witness his gift in many years.

She fanned her eyes with both hands, powerless to stop. "Help, I'm leaking!"

Irving leaned toward her and patted her cheek in fatherly delight and a pleased chuckle.

"Ticket sales just went up," Grant predicted, as Hazel returned to sit next to him.

Irving carefully lowered himself into his chair, as Grant reached into his leather jacket's inside pocket and pulled out a folded document, merely handing it to Hazel without a word.

She opened it and looked at with a wrinkled brow, then stared at Grant, once again giving way to tears.

"Here we go," he laughed quietly, reaching for a napkin and tucking it into her hand.

He took the paper and offered it to Irving, who reached for his spectacles and read it with a smile lighting up his face.

"Okay, somebody better tell me what all that's about, or I'm cutting you all off," Katie threatened, coming around with Grant's croissant and a fresh pot of coffee.

"They accepted my offer!" Hazel breathed, almost afraid to say it out loud.

"Wait..." Katie looked around for a safe place to set her coffee pot, in case this was what she thought it was. "The city, you mean? For the theater?"

She nodded and Katie was glad she'd put the pot down, so that she could jump up and down without making a mess.

Irving sat studying Hazel with a quiet look of pride, watching her joy become contagious.

"Congratulations, my dear," he offered when she had managed to compose herself and things quieted to a sweet calm.

He reached to lay a hand on hers and met her eyes with a knowing look that spoke volumes.

"And now, it begins."

Chapter Nineteen

Vincent Albright, known as Vince to most of his clients, rested his briefcase on the desk and sat back to view this particular client with an amused look, before deciding to open it and pull several folders out, then search for his glasses.

"Good grief, Hazel Todd, you're certainly increased my workload literally overnight."

The attorney looked down at his notes. "I'm going to be helping to set you up as a production company, helping to set you up as a nonprofit and, if that isn't enough, I'm expected to throw down, legally speaking, and take aim at a few wolves. Have I covered it, or do you have any more surprises for me?"

She laughed and clasped her upper arms in a manner she had of hugging herself, then exhaled a deep cleansing breath.

"I can't tell you how much I appreciate your actually being willing to physically show up on my behalf, Vince. That carries so much more weight than my own threats."

"Well, that's why you pay me the big bucks," he joked. "I feel bad, running the pastor out of his office today, though. He insisted that we use it as long as we need to, but he might not be aware of how long my Hazel Todd list of things to do actually is. Maybe I should have warned him."

Hazel gave him a hand swipe though the air. "No, he's perfectly fine with us being here. Believe me, if he had a problem with it, I'd be the first one to know. We go way back to when I was an eight-year-old girl."

"Is that right?" Her lawyer looked up from flipping through some papers.

"That might explain why he's not in your legal crosshairs, then. It seems that all the ones who are, didn't appear on the scene until after you made a name for yourself."

"That, alone, should tell you something," she replied.

"Oh, it tells me plenty," he laughed. He continued to look through the notes he'd made when Hazel called him, and glanced up curiously.

"Are any of these people still in town or have they gone back to California? Or do you know?"

"I doubt that Cheryl Jamison has gone back, yet. If she has, it would have been within the last twenty-four hours, and I didn't get the impression that she was leaving town." Hazel's eyes darkened as she thought about their recent encounter.

"I'm not sure at all about Morris Trent and Mavis Dunning. I did have a courier deliver my letter to Morris, advising him that his services are no longer required and I have his signature. It was delivered to him at his hotel, a couple of days ago. So, he was still here, then.

"Of course, I have no idea if he's simply going to fold his hand and walk away, or not. He and Mavis Dunning both seem to behave as though I'm under some obligation to them, and Mavis is the most outrageous of them all. She acts as if she doesn't realize that she's being consistently told no."

Vince nodded and made a face. "Well, that will become painfully clear in short order. They're both being sent 'cease and desist' letters. I'll check first to determine their whereabouts, but notifying them at their California offices will suffice. I'll send them to both their business offices and their home addresses, certified. I'm sure that Mavis Dunning, at least, has been on the receiving end of c and d letters, from her impressive track record of bullying.

"Even though the letter itself is not legally binding, it has been clearly and carefully worded so as to leave no doubt that, in the event it is ignored, they will both be named in the resulting lawsuit. I'd love to be able to also threaten them with restraining orders but, unfortunately, conditions are hard to meet for that.

"Although, the fact that you are a celebrity and Mavis Dunning and Morris Trent are exhibiting repeated unwanted attempts to contact you, knowing that you have no wish to speak with them, could possibly fall into the guidelines of stalking, and then we'd be able to revisit the notion of restraining orders and at least have a judge weigh in on it."

He looked over the rims of his glasses at her.

"Your friend with the coffee shop actually helped in that regard, when she sent you the photo and those warning texts. And then there's William Cullen, who sat down to warn you that they were looking for you. It all begins to gel.

"Cheryl Jamison is not necessarily unrelated to their agenda, but let's save her for later. She's a big fish."

Hazel raised her brows at that, but made no comment as her lawyer sat a moment, silently mulling all this over. "I'll give a friend of mine a call, who's a judge in Orange County, and get his opinion."

Vince took his glasses off and peered at Hazel curiously.

"Speaking of William Cullen, I was seriously surprised not to find his name or his wife's name on your list."

"William had nothing to do with any of it," Hazel told him, not blaming him for looking a bit skeptical. "He's been especially considerate after Barry's death. I wish I could say the same about Louise, but I can't."

Vince lifted his papers in one hand and held up his other empty palm in an unspoken question.

"Louise is the one who contacted Mavis Dunning and got this whole thing started, but I can't make myself go after her. She's already circling the drain and William has more than enough to deal with."

Hazel rested her chin on one hand and sat studying the floor with a solemn expression. "Her drinking is out of control and short of physically restraining her or locking her up, I don't know how William will be able to stop her from hurting herself or somebody else. He did take her keys, though, so she has to call a cab to leave the house."

She lifted her sad eyes to her attorney's surprised face. "Recently, she showed up here. Out there."

She motioned toward the church yard. "It was like two in the morning when Grant called me and asked me to call William to come get her. All she had on was a robe and she was yelling about Barry, but I couldn't make out what she was saying, just his name."

She shook her head and let out a sigh. "Vince, I wish you could have seen William's face when he drove up and found his wife, drunk and disorderly, with hardly anything on, and had to get her back into the car and take her home.

"He was so grateful that no one called the police. The last thing he needs is for me to name Louise in a lawsuit. I can't do that to him."

"Well, from what you're telling me about her drinking, it wouldn't be worth pursuing. Unfortunately, that would make her defense attorney's job fairly easy. Let's leave it then, since you're not onboard with it."

He removed his glasses and rested his hand on his files and regarded his client intently.

"Now. Cheryl Jamison. First, let me congratulate you on obtaining the services of one of the most respected and honest business managers out there."

Hazel smiled at that. "Charles is wonderful."

"And sharp as a needle. You can thank him, in fact, for shifting funds into savings, the way he did. Charles was smart enough to set the savings account up in both your names, as a joint account, but the statements went only to Charles, as you agreed, so only the two of you knew about it, and there was no conflict of interest when money was safely moved from one of Barry's accounts, that we have since learned Cheryl had access to, into the savings account that also had Barry's name on it, but that she was completely unaware of.

"It was a simple, legal transaction on Charles Finley's part that saved a world of hurt, especially when Barry began exhibiting the irresponsible behavior that was cause for alarm.

"Cheryl Jamison had access to all of his earnings and would have drained that account, along with all Barry's other accounts she had illegally linked to. Client Trust Accounts are normally aboveboard, and attorneys like myself use them to hold money for their clients. The one she set up was presented as that sort of account, but it was a trap that Barry ignorantly walked right into.

"Once Charles found that Barry's personal accounts had been linked to Cheryl Jamison's account, he quietly moved his earnings from her account back over to Barry's and then unlinked them, notifying William, as Barry's durable Power of Attorney, and having his full consent and cooperation. Barry's account numbers were changed and she was essentially shut down, which is why she's hanging around now, I'm sure.

"As soon as Charles was notified of Barry's death, he then moved all of Barry's funds into the savings account, so that only you could access them."

Hazel wasn't necessarily surprised to hear any of this, but she did wonder why William wasn't going after Cheryl Jamison. Vince seemed to read her mind.

"Don't worry. Between Charles Finley and William Cullen, they've collected what amounts to strong evidence. As a result, Cheryl's own bank has been notified, which is the reason for her claims that her CTA is inaccessible. The bank has locked her out, pending their investigation.

"All that to say, her noose is tightening, and she poses no threat at all to you. She won't be suing anyone."

Hazel was clearly relieved. "You're a one-man posse, Vince. All these people are like something I stepped in, that I can't get off my shoe."

"Well, as far as having to clean anything off your shoe, you'll soon be able to own as many shoe stores as you want, so you can afford to just toss one, instead of having to clean it," he replied matter-of-factly.

"What does that mean? I saw the accounts just after Barry's funeral. I was relieved to see that I was going to be okay, but we're not talking about that kind of money."

"I'm not done," Vince replied.

She continued to stare at him blankly, not having a clue where he was going with all this.

"You're obviously unaware that you were listed as the beneficiary on Barry's life insurance."

"Me?" She was stunned. "Why would he do that? It wasn't even a real marriage, Vince! Why wouldn't he have made one or both of his parents the beneficiaries, or Brandy Hillstead, since they were planning a future together?"

"Whatever his reasons, you are listed, it is clearly his notarized signature, and his insurance company is paying out to you. Believe me, you are well provided for."

"But I can't take it," she protested. "He had to have been drinking when he did that."

"Maybe it was his way of thanking you for going along with that crazy scheme of a marriage, since it obviously vaulted his career." Vince replied, with a shrug. "Be that as it may, it is not being contested."

"How much was the policy for?"

"I've always wanted to do this," her attorney said with a grin of personal satisfaction.

He scribbled down a number and pushed the paper over to her in the dramatic manner of some movie character.

Hazel looked down at it and became perfectly still, hardly understanding what it was she was staring at.

"If you're looking for the decimal, don't bother," he laughed, leaning back in his chair.

Hazel raised her eyes to her attorney's smiling face and her mind refused to work anymore.

"Can we take a break?" she finally asked, clearing her throat and looking around, feeling disoriented.

"Absolutely. Get something to drink, walk around. I see I have a couple of calls to return."

He waved a hand and she got up and moved out into the hall almost mechanically.

Hazel stood outside the door of the pastor's office and lifted her hands to her hot cheeks, recognizing that she was flushed with color. Suddenly, she had to find Grant.

She could tell by the voices down the hall where he might be, and walked in that direction to look around the edge of the library door.

Grant was casually killing time, sitting in on a meeting that centered around the church's Thanksgiving activities, and glanced up when he noticed Hazel.

He excused himself and came out into the hall, reaching a hand to cradle her elbow and looking down at her with concern for her agitated state.

"What's wrong?"

Her eyes threatened to spill tears any minute, so Grant led her down to the end of the hall and out the back door to a small group of benches. He brushed some leaves out of the way so they could sit down.

"Talk to me," he said softly, taking her hand in his.

She gazed up at him, her beautiful face filled with all sorts of conflicting emotions. She was clearly troubled.

"I don't know where to start," she whispered.

"Take your time."

Grant laced his fingers into hers and sat quietly, letting her work through what she needed to tell him.

"Barry named me as his life insurance beneficiary, and I don't want it!" she finally blurted out, opening the dam that had been holding her tears back.

Grant switched hands and lifted his arm to put it around her and give her a hug.

"Okay. Why do you not want it?"

"Because it will change things between us, Grant."

She lifted her eyes to his and let him read her.

"Why do you think that?" he asked, after a bit.

"It's a lot," she whispered.

He knew why that was distressing to her. Years ago, when he asked her to marry him, he let her know that the life of a pastor was a modest one, and that money might be tight.

Grant knew that he and Hazel were beginning to discover that their years apart had failed to destroy what had kindled love between them in the first place, and that they were gravitating toward each other as naturally now, as they ever had.

He also knew that her fear was that he would pull back from any sort of commitment, if he felt she would be financially supporting him. He drew in a breath and tightened the muscles around his mouth, as he forced himself to admit that it was a valid fear.

On the other hand, he didn't feel he could ask Hazel to give up her career and her affluence and live the rest of her life having to be concerned about finances, just to be with him.

She was looking anxiously at him, knowing his thoughts and dreading where they might lead him.

"Grant?"

He pulled his gaze away from whatever it was he had absently been focusing on and met her eyes. He could see the intensity of what she was feeling.

"How do you want this story to end, Hazie?" he finally asked gently.

"I want to be with you," she breathed.

"I can't ask you to choose between me and that kind of wealth, Hay. I could never give you that kind of life, and you know that."

"I don't want it," she insisted, and began crying softly, leaning against him and hiding her face in his chest.

Grant reached his hand to stroke her hair and spoke soft, soothing words to calm her.

Finally, he lifted her chin in a way that made her look up at him. "Is it the kind of money that will fund your efforts to restore the theater?"

"Easily. With too much left over," she added miserably.

"Let me ask you this." Grant moved back slightly from her so that he could watch her face and determine for himself what she was thinking.

"What were you hoping for, when all this is over? The Christmas play, restoring the theater? What were your plans?"

"I was hoping you'd let me stay," she admitted, dropping her head and looking down.

Grant refused to let himself be affected by her words.

"What about your career, Hay? It's a very successful one and you're still winning awards. Are you telling me that you can just walk away from all that?"

She looked into his eyes in a way that made him feel she was pleading with him.

"You don't want me to stay?" she finally asked, in a broken voice.

"I want you to make your decision based on what you want. I have no right to tell you what I want."

"But what *do* you want, Grant? I'm asking you!" The tears kept coming and she was being wrecked by them.

Grant pulled her to him and held her tightly, closing his eyes and resting his face against her hair.

"Let's stop," he murmured. "You know how we are, when we try to resolve things too quickly. Let's breathe and take a minute. There's a solution to this, sweet girl. We just need to get quiet and spend some time praying about it."

That seemed to comfort Hazel and she slowly gained control over her emotions and began to feel some peace.

After a few minutes, Grant glanced down at her and gave her nose a light tap.

"We'll work it out," he said, causing her to look up at him with so much hope in her eyes that it made his pulse skip.

He gave her a soft smile and she reached a finger to stroke his brow.

"Promise?"

"I do promise."

He made himself stand and brought her to her feet, moving her back toward the door. He knew that people were waiting for both of them.

"We'll figure it out," he said, pausing to tease her with his eyes. "We might even kiss."

Chapter Twenty

William Cullen hadn't known who else to call. When he raised his eyes and saw Hazel and Grant standing in front of him, he seemed startled that they had really come.

Hazel knelt down in front of him and took his hand, watching him with compassion and concern.

"Has there been any change?" she asked quietly.

He shook his head then looked down at her hand on his, and finally tried to speak.

"I don't know. They told me to wait here and the doctor would be out as soon as he could."

He took in a deep breath and let it out in a way that caused his shoulders to slump and his head to bow.

"Our caretaker's wife found her. She called 911 and then he called me. I rushed back to the house, but they had already put her in the ambulance to bring her here."

Grant came around to rest a hand on the man's shoulder.

"Is there anyone you'd like us to call, William?"

He seemed surprised, but shook his head. "I can't think of anyone, right now. But thank you."

He patted Hazel's hand absently, looking around but not really focusing. "There wasn't supposed to be any alcohol in the house. I made sure, myself. I don't know where she could have gotten it."

Hazel looked up at Grant with a worried frown before giving William's hand a slight pressure.

"Are the caretakers there all the time, William? I don't remember seeing them after Barry's service. Do they actually live on the premises?"

"They live in the bungalow at the back of the property," he answered softly. "Whenever I have to be gone, I ask them to go check on Louise."

"I know you haven't had a chance to ask them many questions," she ventured. "So, I guess you don't know if she had any visitors or if she had any deliveries made to the house."

William looked up at her quickly, realizing that it hadn't occurred to him to wonder about the possibility of anyone bringing alcohol to Louise. Things had happened so quickly and as soon as he'd reached the house and was told that the ambulance had left, he jumped back into his car to rush straight to the hospital.

"I don't know. Our security cameras would have caught anyone at the door, though." He stared off down the hallway, vacantly. "I just don't know," he repeated.

Grant reached to lay his hand on Hazel's shoulder and get her to stand, when he realized that William was reacting to someone coming toward him. They both stepped back and let the doctor come and sit down beside him.

He glanced up at Grant and Hazel, visibly relieved to see that someone was there with William Cullen.

"Mr. Cullen, I'm sorry. Your wife failed to respond to any efforts to save her." He paused to watch the man silently process this before continuing. "Do you want to know details, or would you rather wait?"

He clenched his jaw tightly. "Go ahead, please."

"Your wife's blood alcohol content was extremely high, and it appears that she must have consumed a great amount in a very short period of time. She was in a coma when paramedics arrived with her, and never showed any signs of reviving, or made any effort to breathe.

"We moved quickly to try to save her, but she was too far gone. We did everything we could, but it wasn't enough. I'm so sorry." The physician reached his hand to rest it on William's shoulder and waited.

"Do you have any questions, Mr. Cullen?"

Grant stood listening to this while the conversation he'd had with Mark Wynn began to play over in his mind. It seemed ages ago now, but not so long that he didn't remember the funeral director's anger at the Cullens.

He suddenly felt the need to speak to Mark and urge him to move past his earlier dispute with William Cullen.

He waited until the emergency room doctor took his leave, then laid his hand on the bewildered man's shoulder.

"William, why don't you let me be the one to call for transport? That's the next thing that needs to happen, and I'd be glad to handle it for you."

He looked up at Grant, almost in a daze, before realizing what he had just offered to do. He slowly nodded.

"I would appreciate that, Pastor. Thank you."

"Absolutely. I'll go take care of it."

Grant whispered his request for Hazel to stay with William and she came over to sit beside him while Grant headed out the sliding glass doors to give Mark Wynn a call.

Grant seemed to be driving on autopilot. Hazel glanced over at him, watching him deal with his thoughts and not wanting to intrude, but after a while, she touched his arm.

"You have to let it go," she said softly.

He glanced down at her hand and then back up at the road with a faint smile.

"Not always, Hazie. Sometimes, God requires me to work through it."

"Is that what's happening right now?"

She waited quietly, feeling that she already knew the answer to her question.

"I expect so."

Grant pulled his truck into the gates of the Cullen property and drove around to park near the front entrance.

He turned off the engine and sat studying the door, silently praying that it wasn't too late to be a witness to William.

After a moment, he looked over at Hazel with another little smile. "Let's check on him."

They made their way to the door and rang the bell. Mrs. Copeland, the caretaker's wife, answered and moved back to let them come in.

"Mr. Cullen is just through there," she said quietly, pointing toward the adjoining den.

Hazel led the way into the large room and over to where William Cullen sat staring into the large fireplace. She laid a gentle hand on his shoulder and he looked up at her, making a sad effort to smile.

Grant stepped around and reached for his hand. "We wanted to make sure you're okay," he simply said.

William accepted his handshake and gave him a nod.

"I think so, for the most part."

Hazel immediately noticed a newly arrived large arrangement of exquisite flowers. "These are beautiful, William."

"There's a card," he replied, continuing to look into the blue and orange flames that cheerfully illuminated and warmed the room, in spite of the somberness of the day.

Hazel opened the card and looked at William with the surprise he expected.

"They're from Irving," she said, in hushed tones.

"Who would have expected that?" he mused, almost to himself.

Hazel handed the card to Grant and came around to sit by William and determine how he was really coping.

They sat silently for a bit before she heard William speak, almost apologetically.

"It's not that I didn't love her. It's just that I couldn't help her." He blinked rapidly. "I couldn't help her, and it made me angry. I was always angry."

"Maybe it was more about feeling helpless, than about being angry, William," Hazel offered, watching him with concern in her soft, brown eyes.

He smiled ironically into the flames. "There's that, too."

After a moment, he commented, almost lightly. "It was a nice service, wasn't it? I was worried that it might not be, but everything seemed to go well, don't you think?"

His words didn't seem to be directed at anyone in particular.

Grant laid Irving's card back on the table and sat down to look at William Cullen with both regret and kindness.

"William, I'm not sure if this is the right time, but I want to apologize to you. What I said at your son's service was spoken in the heat of anger. I stand by the theological soundness of it, but I want to repent for the spirit in which I said it. That was wrong, and I hope you can forgive me."

He nodded slightly, then let his gaze drift from the fireplace down to the floor for a moment, before raising his eyes to look at Grant.

"Do you think Louise is in hell, Pastor?"

He asked the question in a dull, weary manner and Grant's heart went out to him.

"I can only say with certainty that everyone must be reconciled to God, in order to be with Him in eternity, and that can only be done by receiving His Son as the only way to the Father. I hope, William, that somewhere between the moment Louise began drinking and the moment where she became incapacitated, that she called out for Jesus to save her."

"She must not have then, because she died," he said, in a faint, defeated voice.

"On the other hand, it may be that once her salvation was assured, God simply rescued her and took her home. Only He is outside of time and knows what her future on earth would have been, if she had recovered. Maybe it was mercy."

William sat pondering Grant's words, seeming to accept them without resistance.

"Mercy," he echoed, with a sigh. "Maybe it was. She certainly lived in her own hell on earth, I know that."

He fell silent and returned to staring blankly ahead.

"William, don't wait until your final moment to pray that prayer," Grant softly pleaded.

"You're not guaranteed that moment, and the scriptures tell us that today is the day of salvation and to seek the Lord while He may be found."

"You may have to pray that prayer for me, Pastor," he replied, with a rueful smile. "I wouldn't know the first thing about how to do it."

Grant looked over at Hazel and held out his hand. She moved from her chair to come and kneel in front of William, taking both their hands in hers and bowing her head.

Grant quietly and reverently had William pray with him, and Hazel, who knew the man well, heard the sincerity in his words and realized that he was really asking to become a child of God and to be born again.

When the prayer was done, she straightened up higher on her knees and gave William a tight hug, then settled back on her heels to wipe happy tears away.

"I'm not sure how I'm supposed to feel," he admitted, sounding a little embarrassed.

"If you do feel something positive, that's great, but you may not feel anything at all, and that's fine, too," Grant assured him. "It's by faith. That's how you're saved, by faith, not by feelings, or by doing anything on your own."

He stood to reach over for the Bible he'd brought in with him and held it out to William. "I'd like for you to have this, William. There are some bookmarks in it, and some verses highlighted that will help you."

He took the Bible and held it in both hands, blinking back surprising emotions. "Thank you," he simply offered.

After a moment, he looked up at Hazel, who had returned to sit near him.

"I think, Hazel, that I need to return to California at some point, and pack up Barry's things. I don't have a key to the house. I'm not exactly looking forward to it, but if you don't have any objections to my entering the house, and wouldn't mind getting me a key, I'd appreciate it."

She glanced over at him thoughtfully.

216

"William, since I want to also pack up my things, why don't I just take care of it for you?" she offered. "The house really needs to be put on the market. It's not doing anyone any good just sitting there."

"Are you sure? Were you really planning to go back out there, or are you just being kind?" He gave her a little smile.

"I'm sure. I think you've had enough sadness in your life, in such a short amount of time. If you feel it's okay to wait until after the Christmas play, then let me take care of it. I'm happy to do it."

"Thank you, Hazel. That's wonderful," he said quietly. He pressed his fingertips together and drew in a breath.

"I've been thinking of what to do with myself. This is such a massive place for one man to rattle around in." He paused and gave Hazel a searching look.

"Would you think I'm crazy, if I confess that I've been thinking of turning this place into a school of drama?"

Hazel lifted a hand to her throat, and stared at him. He wasn't sure if she was happy or upset.

"William!" She was filled with enthusiasm. "I think that would be amazing! What inspired that thought?"

"A little rumor I heard," he confessed, with a real smile. "The mayor tells me that you are the new owner of The Boards. When he first told me, I wasn't sure if you were still in possession of your faculties, but he assured me that you've got a solid plan and the ability to restore it."

"It's true," Hazel insisted, with a light in her eyes, since she was still excited about it.

"Well, that's what inspired me," William said. "What would be more fitting than to have not only a beautiful theater in this town, but to also have a school of drama? This place is certainly large enough and individual rooms can be reinvented for classes and specific needs. It would good for this town.

"Of course, it couldn't be as impressive as Tisch or Yale, but perhaps that might actually give it an air of exclusivity."

Hazel's eyes were dancing with excitement.

217

"I think this place is perfect for that! You have all your credentials, including your doctorate!"

She stopped and laughed. "Can you tell I like the idea?"

He laughed with her. "If you're happy now, wait until I tell you who I have in mind for chancellor."

She moved to sit on the edge of her seat and held her breath, knowing the name she was hoping he would say. When he did, she jumped to her feet and hugged him.

"Irving Lancaster is the perfect choice," she declared. "Talk about credentials! Have you told him?"

"You and the Pastor are the only two who know anything at all," William replied, feeling suddenly very good about what he had begun to think might be silly.

"William..." Hazel hesitated with what she wanted to say, but gave him a steady look and leaned toward him.

"My attorney told me that you were always aware of my being named as the beneficiary on Barry's policy."

He smiled faintly, but made no comment.

"I've earmarked some of that money to restore the theater, but there's still quite a lot left, after that's done. I really don't want to keep any for myself. I know you would tell me to," she added quickly, lifting her hand to keep him from doing that. "But for my own personal reasons, I don't want to. Would you please allow me to help with any structural changes to this building and designate the rest as an endowment to the school and also possibly create some scholarships? It would mean a lot to me, and this is something I would be honored to help with."

William's face was a study. He was deeply moved that Hazel would want to do something so generous for him. He hadn't been especially kind to Hazel when Barry was alive, and it was because she had allowed herself to be pushed into that marriage with his son.

He wasn't surprised to learn of Barry's cooperation with the whole thing, and so he wasn't necessarily disappointed, but when he found out that Hazel went along with it, he was not only taken aback but felt deflated, somehow.

He'd formed a higher opinion of her, and was let down, but instead of ever saying this to her, he had been gruff and abrupt, causing her to believe that he simply didn't like her.

He had insisted that his son name Hazel as his beneficiary, especially since he was going through girlfriends so frequently, that he couldn't always remember their names. Of course, he had never expected that his son's policy would be paid out so soon, certainly not in his own lifetime.

He studied Hazel with a trace of affection and smiled. "If this is something you're sure you want to do, then I accept, but only if you help me name the school. Thank you so much."

Hazel looked at Grant with the face of a child at Christmas. She was glowing and he was glad for her decision to use the money in a way that would make so many people happy, and would benefit their little town.

Still, he'd felt a sense of foreboding when she offered to go to California for William. He didn't know what triggered his misgivings. He knew that she would certainly want to pack her own things, but he still felt a bit of uneasiness.

For now, he simply gave her the smile she was hoping for and watched her happily encouraging a newly rescued and hopeful William Cullen to look forward to a bright future.

Chapter Twenty-One

Hazel struggled with the turkey she was packaging up to be included in the Thanksgiving dinner bundle.

Every year, Grace Chapel provided very complete cartons of groceries, so that families who needed a little help in order to celebrate the holiday, could prepare their own meals and fill their homes with the aromas and excitement of the day.

These were scheduled to be delivered two days before Thanksgiving to every home whose families had allowed their names to be added to the list. Meals were also to be delivered to some homes where the families were too shy or embarrassed to ask, but whose names had been added by a friend or neighbor who knew that they were in need.

There wasn't a large homeless population, due to the small town being somewhat isolated and rural, but the local soup kitchen also received donations of food from the church, in order to be able to serve those who would come by.

Hazel's particular turkey was just heavy enough and slippery enough to want to find its way to the floor, but she was determined not to let that happen, although when the bird did succeed in actually escaping, only to be caught very impressively by Hazel's last minute underhanded dive, she let out a shriek and an excited laugh that caused all the ladies in the church's kitchen to turn and stare, and then begin laughing, themselves.

Hazel had landed on her stomach, with the turkey resting innocently in her outstretched hands. Rather than try to get up right away, she laid on the floor giggling until she was breathless.

Grant looked over from his job of building boxes and lids from the huge stack of cardboard flats that were donated by the local paper company.

"Miss Todd, if you're trying to make a pet out of that turkey, you've left it a bit late."

He grinned and came over to take it from her, so that she could get up. "I don't know how to tell you this, but your bird is dead," he said in a loud whisper.

"Then why won't it be still?" she demanded, pushing herself up off the floor.

Grant laughed and waved away her attempt to reclaim it. "You need to keep your hands washed and dried. That's part of the problem, they're as slick as this bird is."

"Ladies! Everyone make sure you wash your hands after packing up each individual turkey! You don't want to contribute to mass corruption!"

"I think you mean cross contamination, Geraldine," Ivy Parker corrected patiently.

"Cross contamination! So, wash your hands!"

This command had been sternly issued by Geraldine Fowler and Grant moved closer to Hazel, with a quiet laugh.

"Did you ever think you'd be scolded in a house of God for contributing to mass corruption?"

Hazel couldn't hold back another scream of laughter and Grant hastily put on the innocent face of a choir boy when he felt Geraldine Fowler's disapproving frown aimed at them.

"You better not get me in trouble with that woman," he muttered to Hazel, as she dutifully scrubbed her hands and wiped them on paper towels.

"Who, her? You can take her," Hazel challenged, her brown eyes daring him.

Grant grinned and leaned over to murmur into her ear. "Behave yourself."

He headed back to resume building cartons and Hazel reached for the rest of the items that were meant to complete the box, before starting on the next one and tackling another turkey, all the while wearing a little Mona Lisa smile that had found its way to her face.

They had started a little after eight that morning and by the time it was late afternoon, everything was packed and ready to be delivered.

They formed a line and steadily passed the cartons from one person to the next, out through the kitchen's exit and into the waiting hands of the members who had volunteered to load the trucks and make the deliveries.

Once that was finished, and the food was on the way to waiting families, Grant met Hazel over at the sink to join her in hand washing one more time.

"My hands are gonna stink like raw turkey for a week," Hazel informed him with a scowl.

"Then stay away from me," he teased lightly, after glancing around to make sure no one was listening. "Because whenever you're near me, you can't keep your hands off me."

She looked up at him and twisted her lips into a smirk. "You wish."

"Upon a star!" He tossed a paper towel into the nearby trash can and tapped her nose with his fingertip.

"What are you doing with the rest of your day?" he asked, leaning his back against the countertop and folding his arms to wait for her to finish.

"We're not doing anything play-related until after Thanksgiving, so I seem to have a couple of free days. Unless you want me to pluck some chickens. Then, I'm busy."

Grant laughed. "Let's go do something."

"What'd you have in mind?"

"Let go out," he said simply.

"Out? Like a date, out?" She tilted her head and studied him. "Do we still remember how to even do that?"

"I bet we can figure it out," he assured her. "Let's go grab an early dinner somewhere, and we can decide from there, what we want to do."

She passed her wrist under his nose. "How do I smell?"

"I'm not gonna lie," he laughed, and she punched him lightly and made a face.

"Tell you what... let me run back to the apartment and shower and I'll meet you somewhere."

"No way, Hay. I'll come get you."

They exchanged a steady look before Hazel gave him a slow smile.

"Are we gonna flirt?"

"We might." He smiled down at her.   "Go get ready."

"Oh, I'm ready. Watch this."

Hazel slowly winked her right eye at him, and then winked her left eye, then simply blinked both eyes.

Grant gave her a confused look. "What was that?"

"Flirting. Flirting right, then flirting left was me panning you, big guy."

"What was that last thing?"

"Stereo."

He laughed at her, wanting so badly to wrap her up in a big hug, but some of the ladies were intent on hanging around to clean up, so he simply gave her chin a soft touch.

"Go clean up, then text me. I wanna get out of here."

She held her thumb up and then flipped it down, then rested it in the halfway position, waiting for him to choose.

Grant smiled to think that she remembered their little game and raised her thumb up, to let her know that it was dress up, rather than dress down, or casual.

She grinned and fished her car keys out of her jeans pocket, jingling them at him in a little wave on her way out.

Grant watched her go before leaving the ladies to wipe down the kitchen surfaces. He stopped by his office to check for messages, and then headed over to the parsonage.

He wasted no time grabbing a shower himself, and stood letting the hot water beat on his shoulders while he tried to think of a restaurant Hazel might enjoy.

He finally decided on a place he liked in the neighboring county that was a bit of a drive, but would give them a better chance to talk without everyone recognizing him and wondering what was going on with the pastor and the actress.

Grant turned off the taps and stepped out of the shower to dry off and get dressed, taking his time so that Hazel wouldn't feel rushed. He recognized that he was impatient to see her and actually felt a rush of adrenaline.

Finally, he got a text that she was "squeaky clean and smelled like flowers" and grinned to himself, before letting her know that he was on his way.

When she opened the door to her apartment, Grant drew in his breath and his eyes told her how beautiful she was.

His reaction made her a little self-conscious and she reached her hand down to smooth her periwinkle sweater dress with long, fitted sleeves that hugged her slim form only enough to be complimentary but not so tightly as to be immodest.

"In honor of my favorite crayon," she said with a nervous little laugh.

"I remember," Grant murmured, taking her coat from her after she had removed it from the rack by the door, and holding it out for her to slip into.

"You're beautiful, Hazie," he said simply, catching her hand in his to walk her out to his truck. Hazel had let him know early on that she loved his "pretty, pretty truck", so he brushed aside any concerns about her having to ride in it.

He brought her around to the passenger side and she paused when he waited for her to get in, and studied him closely.

Even though Hazel was considered tall enough to be a model, and even in her black heels, Grant was still taller than her, and she looked up at him with a little charge in her pulse, deciding that he cleaned up very well.

"You don't look like a pastor," she said, tilting her head and smiling at him.

"What do I look like?" he wondered, narrowing his eyes and waiting.

"You look like you belong on Wall Street," she decided. "Or modeling in a gentleman's magazine."

He laughed and held her arm as she stepped up and slid onto the seat in one fluid movement.

225

The drive to the restaurant seemed to take no time at all, because Grant and Hazel had found that familiar place with each other where there were no awkward silences, or efforts to have to keep a conversation alive. They could just sit and think their thoughts and be happy.

Grant pulled his truck into the parking area of a rustic, log lodge that would have suggested that the two of them might be overdressed, were it not for the ambience inside.

Hazel hadn't expected anything this elegant in the immediate area and gazed around with a pleased expression.

"This is lovely," she said softly, looking up at Grant with what he had always called her "sweet eyes".

He smiled down at her and took her hand when the host indicated a table was available.

After they were seated and had given their drink orders, they took a minute to study the menu.

"I expect you could cook anything on this menu with your eyes closed, Hazel, but hopefully the chef will come up with something you enjoy."

She smiled up at him and glanced back down before finding what she wanted and tapping the menu.

"Am I boring, if I order chicken Alfredo?"

Grant laughed at her. "Why is that boring? Actually, if it's as good as the photo makes it look, we can make it two."

She closed her menu. "Focaccia bread?"

"They make very good focaccia bread here actually, so that's a yes for me. Parmesan and rosemary."

"Nice!"

They were ready when their server returned and gave him their orders, then settled back to relax.

Grant rested his eyes on her with an amused look in them, and she wrinkled her brow.

"Why are you looking at me like that?"

"I'm just reliving that moment when I turned around today, and saw you lying on the kitchen floor with a huge turkey in your hands," he replied.

226

"And nobody even complimented me on my nice save," she grumbled, with a frown.

"Oh, it was big league stuff," he assured her.

"There, that's all I wanted. Was that so hard?"

Grant smiled and reached to toy with her fingers. "Do you have Thanksgiving plans, Hazie?"

"About that," she began, wondering what he was going to think of her plans.

"I kind of expected that your family would either come here to spend it with you or that you would go there, so I told William that I would cook there, and we invited Irving to come." She waited, trying to read his face. "I really want you to be with us, but I understand that it's really a family holiday."

"My folks know that Thanksgiving is a busy time for the church, so that's not a holiday we try to get together for," he explained. "And I won't be traveling there this Christmas either, not with the play happening."

"Oh, but Grant, I never meant for you to miss being with your family this Christmas. It's okay, if you want to spend it with them. I'll be so busy with the play, that I expect I'll hit a wall on Christmas day and slide down it."

"Well, let's focus on one holiday at a time," he suggested. "Back to Thanksgiving. Katie and Fred are going to her parent's house, which means I will be at the mercy of the church ladies. Please rescue me from that, and invite me to come eat your cooking. I'll be your sous-chef, and I'll even set the table."

"Will you come over to the apartment the night before and help me get a really huge turkey into a big container full of maple brine to sit in the fridge all night?"

"I swear it will be done," he committed solemnly.

She hooked his pinkie with hers.

"I pinkie swear it will be done," he amended.

She was happy and it was in her eyes.

"Good," she simply said.

She sat looking around at the restaurant's decor, and Grant studied her closely, until she became aware of his scrutiny and glanced back at him, pressing her lips together.

227

"Hazel, there's a chance that my family will come to see the play, this Christmas. I don't want you to dread that. You told me that you went back home looking for me, and that they were mad at you."

He took her hand in his. "I actually spoke to my mother about that, not too long ago, and she admitted that they were upset when they saw you.

"But she also said that they later felt badly about it and that they realized that God hadn't been pleased with the way they treated you. If you're willing to let them, I know they'd like to apologize to you."

She rested her eyes on him for a moment. "You didn't ask them to apologize?"

"I did not," he said. "This is all them."

A few tears rushed to collect on her lashes, which was no surprise to either of them.

She took a quick swipe at her cheek. "I'd love to see them, Grant. It would mean a lot."

He gave her a searching look. "You've hardly mentioned your mother at all, since we've begun spending time together, Hazel. Why is that?"

She looked away and shrugged. "Mom has just gotten more and more..." She seemed to be searching for the right word. "She's just in her own world. There's some kind of weird disconnect going on. When I went back home to find you, she was already different and I hadn't been gone very long."

Grant drew his brows in concern. "You're not thinking any kind of dementia, are you?"

"Not really. She's been changing ever since Dad died, so I thought it was that at first, but I don't know."

Hazel's father had died when she was seventeen and Hazel had drawn even closer to Grant during that time. He thought about it now, and there was a sober cast on his handsome face, as he looked down at their hands and let out a sigh. She watched him, then gave his hand a squeeze.

"Let's talk turkey," she suggested, and he laughed softly.

"Let's do that."

Their meal arrived and it was if the chef sensed that someone with high standards was dining. The chicken Alfredo was the best Hazel had eaten in years and she sent that compliment back to him, before they left.

Grant drove them around to look at Christmas lights and they seemed to stir something deep and peaceful in Hazel. Whenever Grant rolled the truck to a stop, so that they could take in something especially stunning, he could see her eyes reflecting what she was looking at.

"You're magic," she informed him, turning to look at him with a happy smile, while they sat parked at a turnout that allowed them to see a particularly beautiful village off in the distance. It looked like a scene from a Christmas card.

Grant loved seeing Hazel's childlike delight. She had always been someone who didn't seem to need things as much as experiences and she was enjoying this one.

They rode back in a comfortable silence, with their hands clasped loosely, and only the occasional remark.

Grant walked Hazel to her door and she tugged his hand to coax him to come in.

He allowed himself to be persuaded. "Just for a minute. I've got an early start tomorrow, and you've had a long day."

Grant stepped inside and held her coat, while she slipped it off, then hung it on the rack for her.

They stood, just looking at each other, before he smiled at her and pulled her close for a hug.

"I've been wanting to hold you all day," he confessed, in a low murmur.

She closed her eyes and rested her head against his chest. "I've been wanting you to hold me all day, so there."

She lifted her face to look up at him. "Why is it that you have a policy not to be alone with women at church, but you can be alone with me?"

"Because this is a date. I can't date a woman and not be alone with her. That's just hanging out, and I can do that with Fred, at the gym."

"Do you go on many dates?" she wondered.

229

"None."

She looked a little skeptical.

"None? But not the whole twelve years, right?"

"None."

"Not even once?"

"Should I spell the word for you?" He smiled at her.

Hazel drew in a breath and thought about that, but asked no more questions and closed her eyes, relaxing against him.

They stood quietly, just being together for a long moment, before Grant reluctantly pulled back and looked into her eyes, touching her chin softly.

"I know," she said, with a sigh. "We can't kiss."

"It's not that I don't want to kiss you, Hazie," he whispered. "It's just that once I do, it will become all I think about, and that would be trouble for someone like me."

"Fred and Katie kissed," she protested quietly.

"Yes, but Fred's not a pastor, who's expected to spend his time thinking about spiritual things and searching the scriptures for what to say to his congregation.

"I can't let myself begin to fantasize about how you make me feel, Hay, and that's what would happen. In fact, I'm already struggling with that. You make it hard for me to fall asleep at night, without reflecting on the way you looked at me, or the way your hand felt in mine.

"Can you imagine what it would be like for me to have to deal with what it felt like when we kissed? I'd probably never sleep again."

He watched her attempt to understand that, although a frown around her lips revealed her difficulty.

"I live in a fishbowl here, Hazel. I expect I do over think this sort of thing, and I know that makes it hard for you. For one thing, I'm sending you mixed messages. I realize that I shouldn't be reaching for you one moment and then telling you that we can't kiss, the next. You're right to be upset with me."

"You used to kiss me, when we were engaged," she pointed out cautiously, not wanting to argue with him.

230

"You're right, I did. I knew that I was called to become a minister then, but I wasn't yet a minister. I hadn't yet walked in that calling. But I'm a different man, now. I accepted that call and people have certain expectations of their pastor."

"Are you saying that we'll never kiss?"

"I'm saying that if you were able to rock my world the way you did back then, just by kissing me, I can't imagine what you would do to me, now that we're adults."

"You think I'll *wreck* your world?" she teased.

Grant rested his eyes on hers and she could see that he was trying to be both honest and tender with her.

She was unable to hide her disappointment, but she offered him a little smile, then touched her cheek.

Grant leaned down and laid a soft kiss there, then whispered next to her ear.

"I need you to know something."

He reached his fingers to stroke her hair and then rested his forehead against hers.

"If you were any other woman, I could probably give you a kiss goodnight and go on about my business, without a second thought. It would just be a kiss, and it wouldn't mean anything or haunt me later.

"Kissing you is dangerous for me, Hazel. With you, a kiss is not just a kiss, and a sigh is not just a sigh, because I'm in love with you."

She caught her breath and gazed up at him with beautiful eyes that were shining.

"Do you mean it?"

"So much."

She threw her arms around his neck and hugged him tightly and he held onto her.

"I'm in love with you, Grant. I never stopped loving you and I never will."

They shared a silent exchange with their eyes.

"Are you willing to think about a future with me then, or is this all there is?"

Her face reflected her bewilderment. "What does that mean, is this all there is?"

"You have a career," he reminded her.

"No, I already did that, and it cost me being with you. It wasn't worth it. I wish now that I had walked down that aisle. I wish it every day of my life," she said, with a little frown. "I wish I could have a do-over."

She stopped and looked into his eyes.

"Wait, does a do-over come with kissing?"

"I would think so."

"I want a do-over!"

Grant laughed and wrapped her up in a tight squeeze.

"Let's just get through the holidays first, and then see if you still feel that way."

Chapter Twenty-Two

Thanksgiving day had come and gone and even though William Cullen hadn't been sure of how it would feel to observe the holidays without any family, he had to admit to himself that it had been surprisingly enjoyable.

For one thing, once Barry left for New York, he had never been around for holidays and William and Louise hadn't made any effort to celebrate, mainly because she wasn't interested in any holiday that didn't involve drinking.

This year, Hazel and Pastor Sellars had joined him at his home. Irving Lancaster accepted his invitation as well, which was something that William hadn't really expected.

Hazel had spent most of her time in the kitchen and she held Grant to his promise to be her sous-chef, leaving time for William and Irving to sit and make awkward attempts at conversation at first, before finally letting down their guards and making some real strides to move forward and away from past grievances.

William had deliberately waited to tell Irving about his plans to establish a school of drama until he could do so in person and Irving responded with genuine enthusiasm, once he had gotten over his astonishment.

He was even more amazed to learn that William was offering the position of chancellor to him, and confided to him that it was his intention to remain in his hometown for the duration of his life and that he considered a chancellorship to be more in keeping with his advanced years, than continuing to put in long hours striding about onstage.

When Hazel had presented the Thanksgiving turkey, after informing Grant that it was the same one that had tried to escape from her at church, and the table was ready, William asked Grant to give thanks. The conversation began to gradually center around both the restoration of The Boards and the naming of the school of drama.

William told Hazel that he had already suggested Lancaster Conservatory but that it had been declined by Irving. When Hazel responded by suggesting Cullen Conservatory, he candidly reminded her that the name Cullen generated negative impressions, both locally and in their industry.

William finally suggested the Boards Academy of Drama and Hazel immediately declared that she wanted the first BAD sweatshirt, which caused some laughter around the table, but the name seemed to be the one that they all kept returning to. William said he would look into registering the name and starting things in motion as soon as he could.

He had drawn up some preliminary sketches of renovations that would allow some of the upstairs floors to be used as housing and was particularly excited about turning what was once considered to be a ballroom into a small staged area with limited seating for the purposes of presenting sketches and scripts as part of the curriculum.

These were presented after their dinner, and the more suggestions, the more animated the conversation became. There was an air of excitement and both Irving and William seemed to have a renewed sense of purpose.

Hazel sat at her table in Katie's shop now, thinking about that day with a little smile, while she rested her hands around her coffee and tried to focus on the fact that tonight was the first onstage play rehearsal. The scene was going to be difficult to direct, on a stage as small as the one at the senior center.

One of Henry Wadsworth Longfellow's heartbreaking tragedies came when his wife, Fanny, died after sustaining severe burns when her dress caught fire. Longfellow suffered acute, painful burns on his face and body, trying in vain to save her.

Henry had loved his wife deeply. She was buried on the day of their eighteenth wedding anniversary and he was so badly burned, that he was unable to even attend her funeral.

It was this intense grief and the fact that Longfellow's injuries resulted in unspeakable pain, requiring him to use laudanum and ether to ease his suffering, that caused him to cease from his writings and lapse into a deep depression.

Longfellow could no longer shave after this, because of how intensely it hurt his face. He grew out his iconic beard, quickly aging him.

Because of this, the role of the younger Longfellow was performed by Fred, until the scene of Fanny's death, before Irving Lancaster claimed it as the old man, to deliver some of the best work of his career, in Hazel's opinion.

Katie came over and pulled out a chair, then gave Hazel a knowing look. "You're fretting."

"Not fretting, exactly, but I'm going to have to make some changes to your scene with Fred that I hadn't wanted to make. The dialog is the same," she hurried to add, seeing Katie's faint look of terror. "Your lines don't change. But I don't have the room or the proper effects to depict Fanny's dress catching fire and Henry's attempts to save her.

"When I wrote the adaptation, I assumed it would be performed in California or New York, on one of the bigger stages. Not the senior center." Hazel smiled down at the script in front of her. "Stage plays are not the movies."

She sat mulling it over, before looking over at Katie and reaching to touch her hand. "In case you're wondering, I'm not really going to allow my best friend to be set on fire. You do realize that, right?"

Katie flashed her a big grin and laid her hand over her heart. "Wait, are you serious? Am I really your best friend? I think I'm gonna cry!"

Hazel shook her head with a little laugh. "It's not that great of a honor, Katie. It doesn't come with a trophy."

They both giggled and Katie hopped up to get to the counter when the door chimed.

Hazel continued to sit and study her predicament with her lips pursed and her coffee getting cold.

She glanced up when a woman stopped by her table, not realizing that her expression was still vacant.

"Miss Todd? We've not met, but I'm Shelby Fields. I'm one of the drama teachers at the high school."

"Oh, I've actually been meaning to reach out to you," Hazel exclaimed, standing and offering her hand. "It's so nice to meet you."

"I just couldn't resist coming over to tell you how very much I love what you do on stage. You're such a natural, gifted actress and no matter what role you take on, you always make me believe you."

The teacher looked a little embarrassed, hoping she wasn't gushing but Hazel received her kind words by simply thanking her and graciously indicating a chair.

Shelby Fields sat down and glanced over at the script with an air of excitement.

"When I found out that Grace Chapel was *not* doing 'A Christmas Carol' again this year, I almost broke into song!" she declared, causing Hazel to laugh.

"And then," she continued, "when I was told that you had written an adaptation of Longfellow's penning of 'Christmas Bells', I was almost afraid to hope it was true."

Hazel patted the papers in front of her. "Well, I suppose it is, although I'm having to come up with some unique blocking to accommodate the venue, due to the small stage."

"I know, and that's always been something sorely lacking in this town," Shelby sympathized. "A decent venue for plays, I mean. It's a shame that the old theater was closed down."

"You've not been hearing the rumors, then?" Hazel asked with a mysterious smile.

The drama teacher drew her brows in polite confusion and waited.

"Actually, the word 'rumor' suggests that it's not true, but in this case, it is. The Boards is being restored."

Shelby Fields laid a hand on her throat and opened her eyes wide in surprised delight. "You mean, the city isn't going to tear it down, after all?"

"They sold it to me," Hazel said, glancing around as if she hadn't meant to say that out loud. She was still experiencing that feeling of waiting for the other shoe to drop. This was the first time she'd said the words in public to anyone who wasn't a part of her immediate circle.

Shelby lifted both hands to cover her mouth and looked as if she was about to cry from sheer relief.

"That's the most wonderful thing I've ever heard!" she declared.

"Maybe not. I may be able to top that."

"How could you?" Shelby was holding her breath.

"By telling you that William Cullen is establishing a school of drama, right here in town," Hazel confided, only because William had finally told her that it was fine for her to mention it. "That large, three-story mansion he lives in, is being renovated with space for living quarters, classrooms, and a stage. The Boards Academy of Drama."

Hazel waited to see how she would receive the news and this time, Shelby really did begin to blink back tears.

"I don't know what to say," she said in a hushed whisper. "It's always been a pain in my heart to know what kind of talent hides in this small town, and to have to accept that once a student graduates, there's no one to nurture it. It's so hard to watch young talent have to leave home and travel off somewhere else in order to continue their education."

"They'll be able to obtain their degrees right here," Hazel assured her with a smile.

Shelby Fields looked as if she had just learned that Santa was real and she had been good.

Hazel couldn't resist laughing quietly at the joy on the drama teacher's face. "If you ever decide to teach anywhere else besides the high school, I know who's hiring," she teased, and Shelby laughed with her.

"Don't tempt me, I may just apply!"

She hesitated a moment, before continuing with her reason for coming over to speak to Hazel.

"I don't mean to be presumptuous, but I wanted to ask if you needed any sort of help at all with the play? A stagehand, or anything at all?

Hazel raised her brows. "Seriously? Yes, right now, in fact." She moved the script over toward Shelby and presented her issue with portraying Fanny's dress catching fire and her husband's attempt to save her, and Shelby could certainly see how that would be challenging to depict onstage, especially on a small stage, such as the one at the senior center.

"This is what I was thinking, and I'd love for you to weigh in," Hazel said. "I thought of having Fanny's accident happen offstage so that you can hear her distress and even have the effects of flames slightly visibly through a door, and have Henry rush offstage to try to save her."

"And then cut to a scene change!" Shelby was onboard with the idea. "I think that's the only way you could do it justice, considering you aren't going to actually set your actress's dress on fire. That's brilliant!"

Hazel was obviously relieved. "Thank you, Shelby! This was going to keep me up all night. But that's the way to go."

Grant waited to let his eyes grow accustomed to the dark, then slipped into the seat next to Hazel. He managed to find her in spite of only the stage lights being on, because of the way the book light that was clipped to her notebook lit up her face. He gave her shoulder a light bump, then watched Fred flirt with his wife onstage, per the script.

"Is this a love story?" he asked Hazel, leaning closer, but keeping his eyes on Fred. "I never knew Henry Wadsworth Longfellow was such an effusive romantic."

"Where do you think all that poetry came from?" she asked quietly, looking over at him with a little smile. "Hello."

"Hello." They held each other's gaze for a moment before Hazel tried her flirty wink panning and Grant laughed, trying not to be too loud, since the actors onstage were running through their blocking with Shelby Fields, who was Hazel's assistant for the play.

"Goof," he pronounced, looking back at the stage.

He watched intently, seeming to enjoy seeing people that he knew become other people.

"Are you happy with the way things are going?" he asked, glancing over at the director.

"I am," she replied. "So far, so good. Of course, when Irving takes the stage, I'll be delirious."

"I'm looking forward to that, myself," Grant admitted.

They sat quietly, simply watching the process and Hazel would occasionally jot down a note for herself, but resisted interrupting the flow.

Suddenly, she leaned forward and focused on Katie's delivery, before raising her pen in the air.

"Miss Katie?"

She looked out toward Hazel's voice. "I can't see you with the lights off out there."

"I know, sweetie. I just need you to hear me."

"Then we're good," she answered. "Yes, ma'am?"

"That last line... were you improvising?"

Katie looked down at her script, trying to find her place. After a moment, she looked back up with a guilty grin.

"It's my fault," Fred said, laughing at Katie's flush of color. "We were sort of messing around with the lines at home, and I guess Katie must have memorized the wrong one."

"Messing around with the lines," Hazel repeated flatly. "Yeah, don't be doing that."

Fred bowed solemnly and Katie stifled a giggle.

Hazel waved a script to one of the drama students who ran to retrieve it and carry it up to Shelby Fields.

"Take it from there," Hazel instructed, looking down to follow along.

"You're scary," Grant breathed.

239

She looked over at him to see if he was kidding.

"How am I scary?"

"Maybe scary is the wrong word," Grant admitted. "Maybe you're just all business."

"It's important to say the right lines."

He raised a brow but made no reply.

Hazel realized that she couldn't concentrate now. She looked at Grant steadily until he felt her eyes on him and glanced over at her.

"I'm sorry," she said so faintly, he almost didn't hear.

He rested his eyes on hers, then leaned over to whisper into her ear.

"We're good." He left a little kiss on her ear lobe and she smiled happily, taking in a deep cleansing breath and looking back up to watch her cast.

Grant grinned in the dark and settled back to try to follow the storyline.

Fred and Katie progressed to Fred's last appearance onstage, as they prepared to block the scene of Fanny's dress catching fire and of Henry's efforts to save her.

Hazel stood up and looked around to get the attention of the stage crew. "Where are my lights?"

The house lights came up and Grant folded his arms and remained seated, watching Hazel's method and seeing a facet of her professionalism that was impressive.

"Cast, take five, and I need my crew front and center."

She started to move toward the stage then turned and looked back at Grant. "I'll be right back. Stay close."

He smiled and lifted the back of his fingers to wave her toward the people who were waiting for her and continued to study her, in her element, a soberness beginning to rest on his countenance.

"Where is Travis?" Hazel called out, approaching the stage and looking around. "Where's my tech?"

"Right here!"

A member of the high school's drama class came out of the right wing, and downstage to sit on the edge, so that Hazel could see him.

"This set change has been bugging me for days," Grant heard Hazel confiding to the lighting tech. "I really don't want to fade to black, I don't like that. Or blue either, really. Let's try using scrims for the set change, but be really sure to light from the front only. I want it opaque, because that's when Irving will be upstage left, ready to take the role in the next scene. When he does, that's when you'll want to light him fully from behind, and kill the front lights.

"The fact that Longfellow's face is burned helps us tremendously with that transition, because he'll go from clean shaven to bandaged and then to his iconic beard, as the play progresses."

She continued to tell the tech the purpose for her choices and instructed him and the rest of the stage crew on the best way to represent the tragic fire and the sounds of panic and pain, just off stage right.

Grant noted the way they listened intently and nodded, seeming to realize that they were working with a stage veteran and wanting to do a good job for her.

He began to question Hazel's firm assurance that she had already "done" her career and that she wanted to focus on the two of them. She was as called to what she was doing, right now, as he was called to the ministry. That was obvious.

He took in a deep breath, tempted to slip out and take a walk or go home, but he knew that if Hazel returned and found him gone, she would become so concerned about his leaving, that she wouldn't want to continue with what so urgently needed to be done.

Grant stayed seated, and breathed silent prayers for God to show him how to surrender to His will regarding the woman that he had, once again, fallen in love with.

Chapter Twenty-Three

Fred stopped his own workout to watch Grant using the lat pulldown machine and raised his brows in surprise.

"How many reps?"

"Twelve, three sets." Grant answered him abruptly through clenched teeth.

"How much you got on there?"

"Two Ten."

Fred let out a low whistle. "Not bad, Grant. What are you... like, one seventy?"

Grant grunted some sort of response but Fred decided not to ask him to repeat it. Instead, he straddled the weight bench and grabbed his water bottle, waiting for Grant to finish his set, so that he could find out what sort of mindset he was in.

When he ended his pulldowns, Grant stopped to wipe down the machine, still wearing a frown of concentration and not hearing Fred's question.

"Grant?"

He looked up at him and waited.

"I asked if you're going to the play tonight. I know you've already been, but this is closing night and Katie says William Cullen is having all the cast and crew at his place for a sort of celebration and 'afterglow', whatever that means."

Grant slung his towel over one shoulder and glanced over at his buddy with a little smile. "I'm neither cast nor crew," he reminded him, heading off to the lockers.

Fred wrinkled his brows and followed him, trying to figure out why he answered him in that cool manner.

"Well, neither is William Cullen," he replied, looking around for him and spotting him at the sink.

Grant finished splashing some cold water in his face and used the end of his towel to pat it dry around his eyes, before looking at Fred with another one of his ghosts of a smile.

"He's the president of the new academy of drama, and it's his house, Fred. I think he rates."

Fred put his hands on his hips and looked at Grant in confusion.

"What's changed?"

Grant shrugged and fished his gym bag out of the locker, feeling around in it for his keys.

"Can't think of anything," he said lightly.

"Hold up, buddy," Fred said quickly, coming over to look closely at him, trying to read his expression. "It's me. Talk to me. Did you and Hazel have an argument?"

"We've never gotten along better," Grant replied, looking down at his phone to check the time.

Fred stood quietly, looking at his friend steadily, with a solemn expression. "Grant, you're not really thinking of not going to closing night, are you? I mean, sure, you were sort of drafted, but you're the one who asked Hazel to do this, in the first place. Now, you're giving off a vibe like you're entertaining the thought of not going and that would be a little mean, wouldn't it?"

"Mean?" Grant narrowed his eyes and paused before he headed out to his truck. "How is that mean?"

"It's closing night! She's your girl! You're not only supposed to be there for her when she takes her bow, you're supposed to give her roses and tell her how beautiful she is! That's just how it works, Grant!

"I know, having my first and only role in a play doesn't actually make me an actor, but I do know that closing night is special, particularly when the director is also the writer, and the producer and one of the top actresses on stage!

"You're not seriously expecting me to believe that you don't know how much you're being there will mean to Hazel? Or how much you're skipping out on closing night will hurt her? Come on, Grant, even I know that much!"

"Fred, you're getting all worked up over nothing," Grant returned evenly. "I never said I wasn't going. You came up with that all on your own."

"Maybe you didn't say it, but I've known you long enough to hear what you don't say, as well as what you do say. If you really have no intention of going, Grant, that just bites!"

Grant pressed his lips together tightly and breathed in deeply through his nose, before letting it out slowly.

"I'm not deliberately setting out to hurt Hazel. I expect if she looks around for me, she'll see me, but I don't plan to be part of an afterglow. I'll probably call it an early night."

"But you'll be at the play?"

"That's what I said."

Grant gave him a brief wave and headed out the glass doors to his truck, not waiting around for Fred to catch up, just to keep dogging him about his potential for being a jerk.

He pulled out of the parking lot and headed straight for his house and a hot shower, to try to work through whatever it was going on with him that Fred apparently had a better idea of than he did.

He pulled into his driveway and got out of his truck, intent on getting into the house, but stopped when Lucy Walker called to him from across the street.

He closed his eyes and blew out a breath, then turned around to find out what she wanted. She motioned for him to come over, something she never did. Grant's curiosity got the better of him and he dropped his gym bag on the ground by his truck and made his way over to her fence.

"Pastor Sellars, do you think animals go to Heaven?" she asked and it was then that Grant could see that she had been crying. He looked around her yard and realized that Buck was nowhere to be seen.

"Lucy, what happened?"

"I'm not sure," she said, reaching into her pocket and pulling out a well-worn tissue. "He was fine this morning, when I let him out, but when I came out this afternoon to feed him, he was lying down under the azaleas. I thought he was asleep."

245

She stopped to wipe her eyes. "But he wouldn't wake up. I can't understand what happened."

"I'm so sorry, Lucy," he said sincerely. Lucy Walker was a bit of a gossip and always seemed to want to talk to him at the most inopportune times, but she was a nice enough lady and her old dog, Buck wasn't exactly a menace to the neighborhood.

He looked around again. "Lucy, what did you do with him? Is he still here?"

"Yes." She was really crying, now. "He's a big dog, and I can't move him by myself."

"Let me help you," Grant said. "Do you have anywhere special you'd like for his grave to be?"

She stared up at the young pastor, hardly able to believe that he was actually willing to stop whatever he was doing and help her, especially when she didn't even attend his church.

"There's a nice flat area in the shade that's not too rocky," she offered faintly. "Are you sure, Pastor?"

"I'm sure."

Grant let himself in her yard and asked for a shovel, then waited for her to bring it out of the shed. She showed him where Buck was lying next to the azalea bush, looking for all the world to Grant as if the old dog was simply having his nap.

He reached and touched his stiff body and shook his head. "Goodbye, ol' boy," he breathed.

Grant stood up and began to dig where Lucy showed him, finding it relatively easy to break ground. When he had the grave large and deep enough, he looked up to see Lucy coming out of the house with a faded blanket and a ragged old stuffed bunny that had apparently belonged to Buck.

"I know I'm being silly," she said with a sad smile. "But I just wanted to leave him with a couple of things I knew he'd like. I guess that's dumb."

"It's very sweet, Lucy," Grant told her, with a little smile.

Lucy spread the blanket out next to her old dog's body and Grant lifted him onto it, before they folded it over him. Grant lowered Buck into his resting place and Lucy knelt down to lay his bunny beside him.

"Thank you, God, for Buck," Grant prayed, and Lucy bowed her head and began softly weeping over the loss of her faithful friend. "It's been nice always seeing him looking out for the neighborhood and keeping a watch over Lucy.

"Only You know the answer to the question about what happens to the animals we love, when it comes to whether there are animals in Heaven, Lord, but we do know that Buck is in no pain, and is not anxious, or lonely, or hungry, or afraid.

"Lucy gave him a wonderful home for many years, and I pray that You will bless her for her kindness to him, and that someday, when she feels it's right, that You will bring her another sweet animal, created by You, for her to love."

Grant placed a comforting hand on Lucy's shoulder, then began to cover Buck's grave, making sure that it was tightly packed and bringing over some of the pavers from Lucy's backyard to lay over the top, to keep other animals from becoming curious and attempting to dig up the dirt.

Lucy picked some of the azaleas from the bush and brought them over to place on the ground and stood up to smile at Pastor Sellars.

"Thank you so much, Pastor. I didn't know what I was going to do and I just prayed that God would send someone to help me and that's when you came home. It was like God sent you. It sure is a comfort having you next door."

"I'm so glad I could help," he said with a little smile. He gave her the shovel and told her to be sure to call him if she needed anything else, then headed back over to the parsonage to get cleaned up.

He stepped into his shower and just stood with his head bowed, with all sorts of emotions and thoughts moving around in his head, but feeling much more like a pastor in this moment than he had in some time.

Grant finally made himself turn off the water and grab his towel, then quietly proceeded to get dressed before heading into town to pick up the flowers that he'd already ordered weeks ago for Hazel's closing night.

He had no idea which direction his life would take after tonight, but for now, he would bring her flowers, put them in her arms and find a way to tell her how beautiful she was.

Irving Lancaster skillfully, and with heartbreaking realism, stirred from behind the opaque gauze shielding his presence and, as the lighting shifted from the foreground to backlight the set and bring transparency to what was hidden, a faint reaction moved through the audience as Henry Wadsworth Longfellow attempted to rise from his bed of suffering, weeping over the shocking loss of his beloved wife.

Women throughout the auditorium allowed themselves to dab at tears when he spoke in hushed tones and bemoaned the fact that the great love of his life was being laid to rest today, on the eighteenth anniversary of their marriage and shook with grateful sobs to learn that her beautiful face had remained unmarred by the flames that took her away from him, and that a circlet of orange blossoms had been placed in her hair, just as she had worn them on their wedding day.

Hazel watched breathlessly from the front row, having given Shelby Fields the responsibilities of a stage manager, and allowed herself to be caught up in what she considered to be the greatest moments of Irving Lancaster's stage career.

She hadn't yet been able to see Grant, although Katie told her that he was in the auditorium. She was visibly relieved to hear this, because she had been sensing a sort of detachment in his manner the past few days, and wasn't sure at all if he would even attend closing night. She couldn't cite any specific reason for it, but Grant had recently seemed to be more polite than warm, which troubled her.

Once she learned that he was there, she was able to make herself relax and be drawn in to the performance of her adaptation and watch her dear friend become the personification of the aging, bereft American poet.

248

His narrative continued to take the audience captive, unfolding the years marred by death, war, and devastation, until that poignant moment when the Christmas bells heralded the arrival of the day, despite the anguished, grieving man's unwillingness to acknowledge it.

"I heard the bells on Christmas day," he muttered in agitation, forcibly setting his pen to paper, as if he hoped doing so would silence them, as he grudgingly chronicled their tidings.

The bells tolled on. He frantically and angrily resisted, raising his voice in thunderous opposition to defeat them.

"And in despair, I bowed my head.
There is no peace on earth, I said;
For hate is strong,
And mocks the song
Of peace on earth, goodwill to men!"

The bells would have their say. Wearily surrendering to their persistent truth tempered the words of the poet, as he gave voice to their reply.

"Then pealed the bells more loud and deep:
God is not dead, nor doth He sleep;
The Wrong shall fail,
The Right prevail,
With peace on earth, goodwill to men."

The accomplished actor quelled his ardent, furious response to the ringing of the bells as suddenly as he had given vent to it, and now stood to look out his snow-trimmed window and speak softly to himself obscure words, that had flowed from Longfellow's pen many years long before the writing of this Christmas poem, but that now resonated within him.

"The dawn is not distant,
Nor is the night starless;
Love is eternal!
God is still God, and
His faith shall not fail us;
Christ is eternal!"

As the old man laid a hand on his chest and lifted his eyes to the night sky, the scene faded away.

Hazel stood to her feet to begin the applause that rapidly resounded throughout the auditorium.

Tears freely coursed down her cheeks while she slipped across the front of the auditorium and into the wings to watch Shelby send out the bit players together to acknowledge the applause, as the curtain call began.

They gestured to the crew and management before supporting actors took the stage and Fred and Katie bowed and smiled as the applause grew more fervent and animated.

Hazel's heart began to pound as Irving Lancaster stepped to the center of downstage and the audience stood as one, enthusiastically and emotionally paying homage to the caliber of a performance none of them could remember ever witnessing.

Irving held out his hand to beckon Hazel, his smile telling her that he would not leave the stage until she joined him. This was all the people needed to renew their energetic response.

The curtain slowly fell and the house lights came up as the song "I Heard The Bells On Christmas Day" began to be heard softly throughout the auditorium and people started to mill about, preparing to leave. Grace Chapel's annual Christmas play had wrapped.

Hazel stood behind the curtain emotionally embracing Irving Lancaster, then reaching out for Katie and Fred, chiding herself for joyful tears that she couldn't seem to stop.

There were collective congratulations among the cast and crew before William Cullen appeared with a pleased, happy look on his face, and invited them all to join him at the future Boards Academy of Drama for a celebration in their honor.

As the group dispelled and Hazel assured William that she would be there, she peeked beyond the curtain's edge to see if Grant was still in the auditorium. When she didn't find him, she felt disappointment wash over her and turned to go backstage to get her things.

He stood waiting for her and her face immediately revealed her heart as she came to him, almost shyly, although she didn't understand the reason for that.

Grant simply laid an exquisite bouquet of long stemmed peach and blush roses into her arms.

She looked down at them with a little catch in her breath when she realized that they were adorned with sprigs of fragrant orange blossoms.

"Grant," she whispered, looking up at him with a soft light in her beautiful eyes. "I've never seen flowers as beautiful as these." She gazed back down at them, not seeing him reach into his lapel pocket and bring out a small gift.

When she looked back up, he opened the box for her so that she could see the beautiful necklace with the round, crystal framed words of Henry Wadsworth Longfellow.

She read them in a whisper. *"When she had passed, it seemed like the ceasing of exquisite music."*

Hazel reached a finger to touch it reverently, only able to draw in a shallow breath as Grant stood behind her to place it around her slender neck.

She stared up at him in complete and utter disbelief before she carefully laid her flowers on a table and turned back to lift her arms to him and pull him close.

"Thank you so much," she whispered.

Grant made no reply, but pressed her to him and she let herself breathe in his scent and lose herself in the gladness of just being alone with him.

Chapter Twenty-Four

"Wait, are you telling me there was an actual reviewer in the audience?" Katie demanded. "If I had known that, I wouldn't have even come!"

"Which is why I didn't tell you," Hazel replied with a little grin, sliding the newspaper over to her friend.

Katie leaned over the counter and read the review, her eyes darting back and forth and her expression becoming more and more pleased.

"It's a rave!" she declared, holding up a high five for Hazel to hit.

Hazel laughed and folded the paper back up. "Well, it's gratifying to know that at least the guy didn't completely pan my adaptation."

"That's the part he raved about," Katie pointed out. "Oh, and Irving Lancaster's performance, but that was a given. I think he's just about the most interesting man I've ever met."

"Me? Why thank you, sweetie," Fred said, making the door chime with his entry, just in time to hear Katie's claim.

"Irving Lancaster, but you're a close second," his wife comforted.

"Fame has changed you," he observed sadly, causing her to break into giggles.

He stopped and looked around. "I thought Grant might be here. Usually, if he's not home, or in his office, or at the gym, I can find him here." He shrugged. "Maybe he's in the park."

Hazel looked up. "Did you try calling him?"

"Yeah. Voicemail," Fred said glumly, having a day off and no one to bum around with, since Katie was working.

Hazel frowned and looked at her phone. It had been a few days since they had spoken, although she had tried. She left two messages just the day before and one today, but there were no missed calls or texts showing that Grant had tried to respond.

"I wouldn't worry about it," Fred said, downplaying his original concern. "I guess, when you're a pastor, all kinds of things can come up that cause you to have to take off, or silence your phone. Like when he's counseling. He always turns his phone off for that."

Hazel nodded slowly, unconvinced that he wasn't simply just not answering his phone.

"So, you went to all those places looking for him, Fred?"

He noted her sober expression and waved his hand through the air. "That doesn't mean anything. Grant's one of those guys who just has to be by himself sometimes. He's been like that as long as I've known him."

"I guess," Hazel said softly, looking back down at the newspaper, but not really seeing it.

Katie reached for it and pushed it to her husband in order to change the subject.

"Did you know there was a reviewer in the audience on closing night, Fred?"

"Yeah?" He came around the counter to let her flip through the paper until she found it, and stood reading it, while Hazel got up and reached for her coat.

"Just hang onto that, Kate," she said. "I'll be back."

"She's going to the park," Katie said, when the door closed behind her. "Something's going on."

"Why do you say that? Grant came to closing night and Hazel told you about the flowers and the necklace. That sounds like things being okay, to me."

Katie peered out the window and watched Hazel walking down the sidewalk to the end of the street, toward the park. "Something's going on," she repeated.

Fred came around and looked over her shoulder. "Maybe she just wonders if he's okay."

254

"Oh, I'm sure she does, but not in the way you mean," she said quietly. "Something's going on."

Hazel was stopped several times between Katie's shop and the park entrance by people who had seen the play and just wanted to tell her much they enjoyed it. She tried to be gracious and smile, but she felt that if one more person stopped her, she was going to scream.

She had once speculated about which way Grant likely chose when he entered the park, simply because of the direction he'd be going whenever they'd run into each other, so she went the opposite way, hoping for that same result.

She tried wracking her brain to remember if she had done or said anything to upset him, but reminded herself that Grant was not the sort of man who suffered in silence and that if she had ticked him off, he would definitely let her know.

This caused her to wonder if he was reevaluating their current status and this, in turn, gave her a sense of misgiving. As sweet as Grant had been to her when he met her backstage, he still had been quiet and a little less free with his affection. She had already been thinking that he was distancing himself.

A lump rose in Hazel's throat, always a signal that she was about to cry, and she hastily reproved herself and tried to actually notice the things around her and enjoy her walk.

There had been a light dusting of snow the night before and it was just enough to coat everything like confectioner's sugar. She had been hoping for a white Christmas, but the snow had held off until the next evening.

Hazel suddenly thought about the fact that Grant's parents hadn't come for Christmas, as he thought they might. She wondered if there was something going on there, that he was dealing with.

She drew in her breath, wondering if she was the problem and if his parents had perhaps said something to him that indicated their displeasure at the thought of the two of them reconnecting. Just because they regretted the way they had treated her before, didn't mean that they were suddenly okay with her being back in their son's life.

This caused Hazel to feel an overwhelming sense of sadness but at the same time, she reasoned that Grant was a grown man and if he really loved her, surely he wouldn't take the cowardly way out and begin avoiding her, just because of what his parents might think.

The very thought of him doing something like that so disturbed her that when Grant saw her from a distance, she was staring fixedly at the ground and walking so slowly that she was barely moving forward.

He stopped and waited, knowing she had been trying in vain to reach him and supposing that this was what she was deep in thought about, apparently unaware of anything around her.

She had almost reached him before she sensed someone on the trail and looked up at him with a vacancy in her demeanor, instead of her normally joyful reaction when seeing him. Now, she simply examined him with a cool reserve.

"You're not taking my calls."

"No."

"I see," she said in a voice like ice, deciding that if space was what he wanted, space was what he would get.

She moved past him. Grant recognized her intent to continue on her way, and turned to watch her as she steadily walked away from him.

"Hazel, stop."

She did stop, but she didn't turn around. She just stood, looking around at the trees with her hands in her pockets, waiting for him to either come or go. It was up to him.

He moved toward her, then hesitated, wondering if it might be better for both of them, if he just let her keep walking.

Hazel focused her eyes on the snowy ground for a moment then muttered, "This is stupid. I don't deserve this."

She took a few more steps away from him, then spun around in her tracks and raised her voice to yell at him.

"Do you hear me, Grant Sellars? I don't deserve this! You may be a man of God, but you're also a jerk!"

"Possibly."

Hazel narrowed her eyes and fixed him with a heated glare, unaware of how beautiful she was, as color rushed to her face and her brown eyes began to smolder.

His sarcastic comment caused a slow anger to ignite inside her. She drew in a sharp breath then suddenly charged at him, punching him in the chest with her hands.

"You said you forgave me! You liar!"

He reached to stop her from continuing to hit him, in order to keep things from escalating, and she shook off his hand.

"What am I, your stalker, now? Trust me, you don't have to screen your calls, anymore! When your phone doesn't ring, that'll be me, not calling you!"

Grant seized her roughly when she tried to walk away and pulled her back. He crushed her up against himself and kissed her, and the anger he felt because of his lack of restraint only served to heighten the strength of his intention to claim her mouth with his.

Hazel completely surrendered to his kiss and leaned into him, returning every one he gave her, until whatever the provocation was that had forced this showdown between the two of them, began to recede to a less turbulent state.

"You said you forgave me," she repeated in a whisper, tears crowding her eyes.

"Stop it," he scolded, folding her into his arms and burying his face in her neck, holding her in a way he never had before. "You know I have, Hazie. You know that."

She weaved her fingers into his hair and closed her eyes, sensing some sort of desperation coming from him and feeling helpless to know how to reassure him.

She pulled back and cradled his handsome face in her hands and looked closely at him.

"Then, please tell me what it is. Please."

He raised his eyes to hers and she was shaken to see tears in them.

"Grant, I love you," she said softly. "Please tell me."

He looked beyond her, blinking rapidly and tightening the muscles in his jaw, clearly struggling. Finally, he lowered his eyes to hers and took in a deep breath.

"Someone called the church, looking for you. He left a message and I found it a couple of mornings ago, when I stopped by the office. I'm sorry I didn't give it to you then."

She frowned in confusion. "Was it that guy who wrote the review that's in the paper?"

He shook his head. "Some producer who read the review, apparently. I guess the reviewer mentioned the name of the church and he got the number and called, asking if someone could have you contact him. It's a California area code."

"What's his name, Grant?"

"Preston Geller."

Hazel knew the name and stared at him. "Was that all, just have me contact him? Nothing else?"

"He just began his message by introducing himself as a producer and said that he needed to reach you."

Grant's eyes were troubled as he waited for her response. She touched his face with soft fingers.

"Why is this upsetting you, Grant?"

He slipped his hands into his coat pockets and looked around, wondering if she really couldn't understand why it would. Finally, he brought his gaze back to hers.

"I guess, if you don't want to call him back, you can always just meet with him, when you get to California."

"When I get... well, yes, I'm going back to pack my things and I told William I'd pack Barry's. I'm going to have the house put on the market."

"Then that would be the perfect time for you to talk to the producer, I would think."

"Talk to him about what? He didn't even say why he was calling."

"Well, he wasn't calling to talk about the weather, Hay."

Hazel suddenly realized what it was that Grant wasn't letting himself ask her.

He was wondering if she was going to return to the stage and even if she didn't live in California, if she would travel back and forth, staying weeks and months at a time, until a particular play wrapped. He was wondering if nothing had really changed.

"If I tell you that I have no intention of staying in California, or anywhere else other than here, and that I have no desire to return to the stage, you're not going to believe me, are you, Grant?"

"It's not right for me to expect you to just give it all up," he said quietly.

"You haven't asked me to. I want to."

He shook his head and glanced down as her hand slipped into his coat pocket and found his fingers.

"I want a do-over," she reminded him softly.

"Have you asked yourself why you want a do-over?" He studied her carefully, not surprised at her confused expression.

"What does that mean?"

"It means that a do-over isn't some sort of magic eraser, Hazel, that makes something as if it never happened. It did happen, and it's not a matter of me not forgiving you. It's a matter of the both of us understanding why it happened. You left me for a reason. Maybe that reason still exists."

"But it doesn't."

"That phone call suggests something different. So does that review. So does the overwhelming ovation you rightfully earned on closing night.

"I just need for you to know completely, Hazie, without any influence from me, whether or not that reason still exists. Because if you were to learn later on that it's alive and well, and you left me again, that would be the end of me."

He looked away from her, obviously wrestling with very strong emotions.

"Why would I be restoring the theater, and helping William establish the school, if I was just going to go back to acting, Grant? The things I'm involving myself in here, in this town, have roots. That's what I want."

She pulled his coat open and slipped her arms around his waist, pressing into him, while he brought his arms up to shelter her against a sharp winter wind that suddenly rushed at them.

Hazel raised her face to his. "Do you love me?"

"You know I love you," he whispered. "If I didn't love you, I never would have let you get close to me again."

"Grant, if you're worried about me going to California, then just come with me."

He laughed quietly. "I hardly think that would be spiritually appropriate, Hazel."

"Marry me," she breathed, not missing his reaction.

"Marry you."

"Yes."

"Just like that."

"Yes."

He let out a sigh, unsure if she was teasing or actually proposing to him.

"Ask Pastor Morgan what he thinks," Hazel said, resting her eyes on his lips and thinking about his kiss that almost made her faint, wondering if she would ever be kissed like that again.

"As tempting as that is, Hay, I owe my congregation better than to just up and get married and not even tell them."

"Why would they care?"

"It's not my getting married they would mind; in fact a lot of the women in the church would be relieved. It's the way I go about it. They would want to be a part of it. They'd want to celebrate it, not be told, 'Oh, by the way, guess what.' That's the part that would be upsetting to them."

"I guess I don't have to go to California," Hazel said slowly, trying to think of whether she would want to saddle her assistant with such a big job.

"No, you need to do what you need to do. I need to grow up, apparently."

She twisted her lips and gave him a teasing look. "I wasn't gonna say..."

"No, you were too busy calling me a jerk."

"But you're my jerk and you're such a handsome one, if that helps at all," she laughed.

She continued to look up at him for a quiet moment, musing to herself about something.

"What is it?"

"You said you couldn't kiss me, but you did."

"I was angry."

"You're ugly, and your mother dresses you funny."

Grant laughed and kissed his fingertip, then laid it on her lips. "Nice try."

She imitated him by kissing her own finger and resting it on his lips, then stood asking him a silent question.

"If you ask me again when you're back from California, then we'll see," he answered, looking down at her with his love for her resting in his eyes. "If you don't, then..."

"You'll ask me?" she finished, hopefully.

"No, not this time, sweet girl," he warned. "This time, it's all on you."

Chapter Twenty-Five

Marshall Portmann spread out the blueprints that his brother had brought by the theater before heading off to check on another job, and looked through his bifocals to be able to answer a question Grant Sellars had for him.

"Well, 'The Boards' was built on a continuous pile, column foundation, and very well anchored, which is really good news." He moved his index finger across his prints. "It was elevated and actually, that was more for a grandiose appearance than it was for flood protection, but it was a good decision and one that ended up literally saving this building.

"We didn't come across any sign of collapse or lateral movement, and we didn't expect to. It was a slow rising flood, as a result of the river cresting, so damage has been more along the lines of floor boards and interior walls, rather than anything structural. Even the interior support is in good shape. All the load bearing walls are solid and there's no sagging."

Grant leaned over to study the area of the blueprints that the man was showing him, with a look of relief.

"I guess that's why the water didn't seem to be as high up on the walls of the theater, as it was in some of the pictures of other buildings that you showed us, from the flood."

"Oh, most of those buildings were flattened as soon as the waters went down. I never could understand codes allowing anyone to build this close to a river without insisting on raised foundations, but you wouldn't believe how many of those businesses just had simple slabs. Codes are a lot more restrictive now than they were back in the day, though."

"What about mold?" Grant wondered. "We could smell it when we came by the first time to see the building."

"It's there," Marshall Portmann admitted. "Not in any of the ceilings and not way up in the walls, but all the first level floors have to come out and new ones installed, and all the first level interior walls as well, because mold tends to spread.

"Miss Todd was very insistent to get professionals in here to get rid of it. Normally, we go ahead and remove all the damaged materials and then have them come in to check for mold, before we start any new installation. That's just how Larry and I work. So the first floor is essentially a gut."

"Are you needing to finish any current projects before you can start on it?" Grant looked at him hopefully, wanting to be able to tell Hazel that the restoration was underway.

"We're good to go, or I am, and Larry will be joining me as soon as the inspector passes what he's been working on."

"That's great news," Grant declared, happily.

"Well, I tell ya, Pastor, we're pretty enthusiastic about this job. It's always upset us whenever the council started talking about demolishing the theater because Larry and I both knew that it has good bones and that it could really be something special, if the right person got involved. I guess Miss Todd is the right person."

"I'll have to agree with that," he laughed.

Grant let Marshall Portmann get back to focusing on site prep, and hopped into his truck to drive around to the square to grab some coffee and give Hazel a call.

He remembered the time difference, and decided to wait to call her, but the thought of coffee had reminded him that he hadn't had any at all, this morning.

Katie looked up as he made his way into the shop and then over at Fred, when he started laughing.

"How do you do that?" she demanded.

Grant looked puzzled as Fred continued to laugh.

Grant just raised his brows and shook his head, and let their little private joke belong to them.

"Got any house brew left in the pot?"

264

"It's your lucky day," she said, proving it by pouring him a fresh cup.

"Why are you up and out on Monday?" Fred demanded. "That's your day off, or so you're always telling me."

"What did you want me to be doing?" Grant asked with an amused look, coming over to his friend's table and settling down, knowing he was expected to.

"Sleeping in!" Katie declared, deciding to join them.

"Grant's an early riser, honey."

She wrinkled her brows and gave their friend an odd look. "That's disgusting!"

The two men laughed at her, and Grant set his coffee down and folded his arms, getting comfortable.

"Well, I had to meet the contractor at the theater this morning to find out where we are in the whole restoration. I promised Hazel I'd stay on top of it while she's in California."

"When is she coming back?" Katie wondered. "I miss her, plus Ed Crockett has been asking about quiche and I don't know if Hazel just made that up in her head, or if she has an actual recipe."

"Most of what she cooks is just what she's worked out on her own, until she's happy with it, but I honestly don't know if she's ever taken the time to write anything down."

"I wish she would, but not a cookbook. Just for me, so people have to come here and buy stuff, and not make it themselves. I'm cunning, that way," Katie informed him.

Grant laughed at her. "I'm sure Hazel's happy to share."

"Seriously, though, when's she coming back?" her friend persisted. "Has she said?"

Grant shook his head. "Her assistant met her over at her house and packed up William's son's things, while Hazel packed her own, and I think that ended up taking a couple of days.

"She's having it trucked out here, once she flies back. William's gonna take care of Barry's things and she'll rent storage for hers. So the house is empty, and she's listed it with an agent. I don't know what's keeping her, but I'm sure she'll bring me up to speed when we talk."

"I wouldn't be surprised if word leaks out that she's back in California and offers start pouring in, after her play got such a great review," Fred speculated.

Katie flashed him a warning look and he glanced over at Grant. "Not that she'd be interested," he added quickly.

Grant lifted his fingers up from the tabletop and shook his head. "If she is, then she is. That's how we left things. She's not supposed to base her decision on me."

"But, why?" Katie looked upset. "It should matter to her how you feel about it, and I happen to know it does matter."

"Have you ever seen Hazel onstage, Katie?" Grant glanced up from staring down at his coffee, and looked at her. "Not directing, but as an actress?"

She shook her head slowly.

"I watched a few clips of her online. You can find them fairly easily, they're scattered all over the Internet. You wouldn't believe how gifted she really is.

"I watched her closely, when she was directing the Christmas play, and I began to think that she's actually called to be part of that world. And, if she's called to do what she's doing, then I can't act as if my calling outranks hers."

"Yeah, but why do I get the feeling that you think each of you doing what you're called to do means that you can't be together? Fred and I do two completely different things, but it works. I just don't get it."

"Success in the world of stage performance almost always requires the artist locating to either the West Coast or the East Coast." Grant shrugged, trying to appear nonchalant, but he was still struggling with the issue.

"But that's not a hard and fast rule, buddy," Fred pointed out. "It seems to me, that with the theater coming back to life and the school of drama opening, this could become a niche for the arts. I admit, it's not my field, but the ingredients are there."

"Well, time will tell, I guess," Grant said quietly, with a touch of resignation.

He stood up and stretched, then prepared to do battle with Katie over the ticket. He always won and forced money on her, so he reminded her of that fact and did, once again.

"I'm still undefeated," he grinned over at Fred. "Your wife's a pansy."

Katie made a face at him and they watched him leave, before they let their smiles fade.

"Do you really believe what you said to Grant, Fred? About this place becoming a niche for theater?"

Katie came around behind his chair and bent over for him to look up at her. He signaled for a kiss and she gave him one, then came around to rest on his lap.

"I don't see why it couldn't, sweetie," he replied. You've got three of the biggest names in that industry right here, and with the resurrection of The Boards and the opening of the academy, I wouldn't be surprised if things took off."

She sighed and looked toward the door that Grant had just walked out of.

"I sure hope you're right."

Hazel flopped down on the sofa in her hotel suite and kicked her shoes off with an exaggerated wide-eyed expression.

Her assistant smiled perceptively at her and joined her in relaxing. It had been a full day and they deserved a break.

Hazel looked around searchingly. "Where's my phone, Maddie?" She dumped her purse out on the couch in vain.

Maddie joined her in glancing around to see if it was within view, then picked up her own phone to call the number and listen for it.

They both strained to hear if Hazel's phone was responding but neither one of them heard it.

Hazel jumped to her feet and began frantically searching around the suite. "Call it again, please."

Maddie tried the number again, with the same results.

Hazel blew out a breath and tried to remain calm.

"When did I have it last? Think, Maddie. I need help remembering. I had it here, and did I have it at Preston's office? Do you remember?"

"Yes, because you pulled up your calendar on it."

"I did! I wonder if it's in his office?"

"If it is, and he hears it ringing, why wouldn't he just answer it? He should figure out that we'd be trying to call it," her assistant reasoned.

"Can you call him, Maddie? Do you have him in your phone?" Hazel continued to look around for her own phone, although she was beginning to realize that she hadn't come into the room with it.

"I have to leave a voicemail." Maddie waited a few seconds. "Mr. Geller, this is Madison, Hazel Todd's assistant. Hazel thinks she may have left her cell phone in your office. If you see it, please call this number and let us know."

She recited her number in case it hadn't appeared on his screen and hung up.

"Do you want us to grab a cab and head back over there, Hazel?" she asked, seeing how flushed and upset the actress was becoming about losing her phone.

"Yes, but first, Maddie, call the cab company and ask them if the driver might have found the phone in the cab."

Her assistant called the company and gave them the information for their previous ride, and the pick up and drop off addresses, then waited on hold, impatiently tolerating some sort of weird music with a xylophone in it.

After a minute, she was reconnected. "Yes, I'm here."

Her face fell, and Hazel knew that no one had found the phone. She came over and sank down beside Maddie. "Can you go ahead and ask them to send a cab, since you're already on the phone with them?"

Maddie nodded and put in the request for a cab, and the two women left the suite and went down to the lobby to wait for the doorman to notify them when their cab arrived.

Hazel's beautiful eyes had tears puddling in them, and Maddie reached over and touched her arm, with concern.

"Were you expecting an important call, Hazel? I can see how upset you are."

She nodded but didn't offer to explain. She just pulled a tissue from a dispenser on the large, ornate coffee table and dabbed at the corners of her eyes.

"All of your contacts and important things are on your phone," Maddie realized. "You wouldn't want any of that getting into the wrong hands."

"I care more about missing a call than I do about any of that," Hazel said in a dull voice.

She seemed to be thinking deeply. "Maddie, I need to borrow your phone."

Her assistant handed it over and Hazel closed her eyes a minute, trying hard to remember Grant's phone number. Once he put it into her phone and she saved it, she had always just hit the speed dial to call him.

Finally, she called the coffee shop instead, and waited for Katie to answer. When she did, Hazel was flooded with relief.

"Kate? Katie, it's Hazel!"

"Did you get a new number?" she asked curiously. "I mean, hello! But yeah, this isn't your number."

"No. Listen, Katie, will you please get in touch with Grant and give him a message? It's really important."

"Sure, sweetie! Go ahead."

"Tell him I've lost my phone. My assistant and I are looking everywhere for it. We're heading back to the last place I remember having it. If I can't find it, I'll get a burner phone."

She looked around desperately. "Katie, what's Grant's number?" She signaled for a pen and paper to Maddie. "It's in my phone and I don't remember the actual number."

"Oh, I know how that is. Let me dig my cell out and look. Hang on, honey."

Hazel seemed so relieved just to be talking with someone who could get a message to Grant that her whole countenance suddenly became lighter.

Katie came back on the line and rattled off Grant's number and Hazel smiled and let out a big cleansing breath.

"Oh, thank you, honey! If you don't mind, please do give him my message but I'll also try to call him. I'll talk to you soon. I love you, Kate."

"Love you too!"

Hazel hung up and immediately tried to call Grant's number, but after several rings, it went to voicemail.

"Grant?" She sounded jittery. "Grant, it's Hazel. I lost my phone, and we're out looking for it."

Hazel didn't realize it, but she had begun crying, while trying to explain to Grant about her phone. She was all but sobbing, and her voice was husky, as she left her message. "This is my assistant's phone. So call me at this number, okay? Maddie will answer, she's my assistant.

"I'm so sorry, Grant! I know you must be trying to reach me. I'm so sorry, but I'll keep trying to find my phone. If I can't find it, then I'll get a burner phone and get the number to you."

The more Hazel spoke, the more emotional she became, and her assistance's face was filled with concern.

"I love you, Grant," Hazel finally said, in a watery voice. "Call me, okay?"

When Maddie heard Hazel tell Grant that she loved him, she suddenly understood why she was crying, and Maddie even wiped a few tears of her own away.

The doorman had approached to alert them that the cab was waiting and Maddie touched Hazel's arm to let her know. Hazel hopped up and practically ran to get into the cab.

As they headed to Preston Geller's office, Maddie sat marveling over the fact that Hazel Todd, who was known for her stoic, apathetic personality that only changed when she was in character onstage, was obviously hopelessly in love. She never would have thought it was possible.

"It'll be okay, Hazel," she soothed, giving her hand a little pat of reassurance. "Now that you and your friend have both reached out to tell him what's going on, you can breathe. It'll be okay, now."

Hazel pressed her lips together and nodded, but more tears continued to fall as she realized that she just needed to get home to Grant.

Even as the thought occurred to her, she realized that she had just thought of it as "home". That's because Grant was there. She knew it with all her heart and suddenly she couldn't get out of California fast enough.

Preston Geller's secretary took them into his office. He had left for the day, and had said nothing to her about finding Hazel's phone, but she helped them look anyway, and Maddie tried calling the number again. It simply didn't respond, or even vibrate and Maddie hung up, disappointed.

Hazel thanked the woman and then left with Maddie in the cab that had waited to take them back to the hotel.

As soon as they got back, she began throwing all her things into her bags. Maddie didn't need to ask. Whoever Grant was, that's who Hazel was determined to get to.

Maddie called the airlines and got Hazel booked on the next flight out, then helped her get all her things together. Once again, she arranged for a taxi and rode with her to the airport.

After a bit of pacing and checking the time every few minutes, Hazel was finally allowed to board into first class. She gave Maddie a tight hug, then looked down in surprise as her assistant placed a phone in her hands.

"Did you know you can now buy smart phones here in this airport?" she asked with a grin. "It's not a throw away phone, but still... it's a phone."

Maddie tore a piece of paper out of her notepad, and put it in Hazel's carry on.

"That's the number, carrier info, and everything else you need. Let me know when you get there, Hazel, and whoever Grant is, give him my best."

Hazel hugged her again and made her way onto the plane, trembling and anxious to just get back as quickly as she could. She looked down at the phone and the piece of paper.

Maddie had written Grant's number on the paper, so she tried it again, but there was still no answer.

271

Hazel forced herself to calm down and breathe and sent up a silent prayer, asking God to put an end to whatever confusion was trying to come between herself and Grant and to let her get back to him safely.

Grant had stopped trying to call Hazel. Every attempt immediately ended up going to voicemail. He'd left enough messages for her to know that he'd been trying to reach her.

He'd finally tossed his phone into his gym bag and headed off in that direction to either hit something hard, or press something heavy. He'd know when he got there.

He deliberately didn't tell Fred he was going, because he just wanted to be alone to think and he didn't need Fred trying to give him Katie's viewpoint on what he needed to do where Hazel was concerned.

He'd seen that Katie had called, probably asking him yet again when Hazel was coming home. He decided not to call her back until he actually knew. He'd also noticed a strange California number on his recent calls, but figured that was someone else calling to reach Hazel.

This was the day Geraldine Fowler and Beatrice Gandy cleaned the church and whenever they were around, and the church phone rang, Geraldine had the irritating habit of not only answering the phone when she'd been asked not to, but then giving the caller Grant's private cell phone number, as if she were doing him a favor.

He'd tried asking her to please stop doing that, but it was like talking to old Buck, next door. Grant admitted to himself that this was an unnecessarily morbid thought and managed to feel bad about it. He decided that the California call was more than likely the producer again, and he wasn't the guy's personal assistant or his messenger.

He headed into the gym's locker room and tossed his bag inside his locker, then put the key around his neck and went in to see what machines were freed up.

He took a moment to remember what day this was, for his routine, and then started with the chest press, moving through his reps without really feeling them, since his mind was so tuned into wondering what was keeping Hazel in California, although he thought he might know.

He did try to turn his thoughts into prayers but then he had to deal with whether or not his prayers were selfish. He finally forced himself to count reps and sets and began moving through his workout as if he were in training.

Some scantily clad blonde decided to stand around and watch him, so he got up with a scowl and headed to the locker to just get his bag and go running, instead. Usually, when Grant and Fred met at the gym, there were very few, if any, women around so he hadn't expected to run into any.

"That'll teach me to come without Fred," he muttered to himself, as he hopped in his truck and headed off to the park.

He hit the trail with a vengeance and ran the perimeter of the park over and over, as if he were deliberately trying to exhaust himself.

He passed by a few places where he had run into Hazel before and again wondered where she was and what she was doing and why she hadn't called him back.

Finally he'd had enough and headed back home to go stand in his shower until all the hot water was gone.

Chapter Twenty-Six

Hazel let herself into the apartment and left her bags by the door, weary from her flight, and despondent over the fact that Grant had still not called her. He was supposed to have met her at the airport, but that didn't happen either, although she'd left him plenty of messages telling him what time she'd be in. She'd ended up just getting a taxi to bring her home.

She told herself that she should go to bed, but she was still feeling the pacific time zone and knew she would just lie there and stare at the ceiling. She thought about going for a drive, but Katie's shop had already long been closed for the night and it was clear that Grant wasn't waiting to hear from her.

She stood with her arms folded and stared around the apartment, with no direction, no plan, no purpose.

She'd discovered that the airlines had lost one of her bags, and had to wait around for a while before it was finally located and now, the more she thought about the day she'd had, the more tired and irritated she began to feel.

Once again, Grant was screening his calls and didn't want to talk to her. Fine. She certainly wasn't going to go knock down his door and demand that he explain himself.

Hazel drew her brow into a grim, forbidding line and asked herself exactly why it was, that she wasn't going to go knock down his door and demand that he explain himself.

She got up and grabbed her keys and pulled her apartment door to with a loud slam, heading off to her car with a frown on her face and warning flecks of anger in her eyes.

She started to drive straight to the parsonage but she recognized that she was too angry.

She wouldn't be able to string two words together, and when she confronted Grant, she didn't want to just yell insults at him and call him a jerk again. She wanted her words to count, so she drove aimlessly around the square, even though all the storefronts were dark and the traffic lights had all begun blinking yellow. It must be after eleven then, she realized.

She drove over a couple of streets and stopped her car in front of the theater, then saw the big sign that advertised that the coming renovation was another Portmann Brothers project. Despite her wanting to find Grant and tell him to go sleep in the river, she felt a rush of pleasure seeing that work had already begun at the site.

She grimaced, remembering that Grant was supposed to have met with the Portmanns and call her with a report of what was happening. True, he might have. Until she could find her phone, she had no idea who had called her. But she had called him herself, plenty of times, with nothing from him at all. He had her number.

"I've got yours too, big boy," she muttered, putting her car into gear and heading for the parsonage, regardless of her original intent to dial herself down.

When she drove up, of course all the houses were dark, including Grant's. She stood on his porch, debating how loudly she could knock without having a repeat of the night that Louise Cullen had appeared in this neighborhood.

The last thing she wanted was for the lady across the street to turn on all her lights and stare out the window at her. In fact, she had actually parked her car at the church and walked back over, just to draw less attention to herself.

Hazel had never been inside the parsonage before, so she didn't know the layout of it. If she had, she would have just gone around to Grant's bedroom window and thrown rocks at it. "Boulders," she silently amended.

She took a deep breath and decided to just get it over with and lifted her hand to knock, when a set of headlights flashed across the porch and swept across the churchyard before going out.

Grant shut his truck door quietly and stepped up onto his porch, staring at Hazel as if she had just materialized out of thin air. He looked around for a car, then saw it parked over in front of the church.

Neither of them said anything. Grant unlocked the door and caught Hazel firmly by the wrist, pulling her inside and shutting the door, not even stopping to turn on a light.

"What are you doing here?" he demanded roughly.

"Hello to you, too, jerk!" she offered in a tight, hostile tone, trying to free her hand.

"Hazel, what are you doing here?"

"I'll tell you what I'm *not* doing here! I'm *not* proposing!"

Grant still had a grip on her wrist and hadn't yet bothered to turn on any lights. The only illumination filtered in through the blinds from the streetlight, and the longer they stood there in the dark, the more they became accustomed to it and could begin to see each other.

"You were supposed to call me to let me know when you were coming back," he said, in a low voice.

"You have got to be freakin' kidding me!" Hazel stared at him in disbelief. "How many times was I supposed to call, Grant? Were you waiting for the magic number, or were you just gonna call when you felt like it? Are you sick? Have you been ill? Because, apparently, you never felt like it. Stupid jerk!"

"What are you talking about? Maybe if you use words that actually make sense and dispense with the third grade name calling, I could crack your code!"

She could tell that he was glaring at her, every bit as angry as she was.

"Do you want me to use adult words, Grant? Because I know some! Wanna hear?"

Grant grabbed her by the shoulders and placed her firmly up against the door, standing only inches from her.

"I want you to explain whatever this nonsense is you're spewing about calling me. I didn't have one message on my phone from you!"

"Is that right? How about you just get your phone out, and let's see, Pastor! Go ahead, I'll wait."

Grant breathed in and clenched his jaw. "It's in my gym bag, out in the truck."

"How convenient."

"How about shutting up?" He flashed her a hot look. "Cut the crap, Hay, and tell me what you mean by saying you called me. When did you call me?"

She raised herself up on her toes and put her face right up to his, meeting his eyes defiantly and answering him in slow, measured tones, as if she were dumbing it down for him.

"All. Day. Long."

"You did not!" He wanted to shake her and she wanted to punch him.

"Grant Sellars, are you calling me a liar?" she demanded, in a seething voice.

"I'm saying that I looked at my phone constantly and your number is nowhere in my recent calls list."

She grew silent and studied him, hints of anger still in her eyes but beginning to fade, as she suddenly realized how tired and worn out she really was. Her head was beginning to hurt.

"Of course my number wasn't in your recent calls list, Grant. That's what happens when you lose your phone and have to borrow someone else's, and then have to buy one at the airport just so you can keep trying to call some stupid guy you love, but who obviously doesn't love you, because he's not even worried enough about you to answer his dumb phone! Katie answered *her* phone. I bet she tried to call you to tell you what happened and you passed on her, too. That just figures!"

Grant had been taking in shallow breaths, feeling his blood pressure begin to rise but now he forced himself to slow his breathing and stood hovering over her, as she remained up against the door, continuing to scowl up at him.

"I did see a call from Katie," he admitted, in a less aggressive tone. "She had been asking me over and over when you were coming home, so I figured that's all it was. I decided that I'd just tell her when I actually knew."

"So, you're an equal opportunity heel," she muttered. "It wasn't just me you were ignoring."

"I saw a couple of California area codes," he continued, as if he hadn't heard her last dig. "Beatrice has been giving out my number again, and I thought one of those was just that Geller guy, and I didn't want to talk to him."

"So you're saying that you never heard even one of my messages?" Hazel asked, not even trying to mask her skepticism.

"How many did you leave?" He narrowed his eyes and waited, not wanting to accept what she was telling him.

"Nine! Nine pitiful, pathetic, sobbing, crying messages that you can listen to after I leave, and feel really good about yourself. I guess you showed me!"

Her last remark stung him. Even in the dim cast of light that streamed in through the windows, Hazel could see the hurt on his face.

"I wouldn't have ignored your calls," he said softly.

She didn't know how to respond to that, so she simply stared up at him, trying to believe him.

"But you did," she finally answered, as tears of both fatigue and disappointment were highlighted by the streetlight. "Just like last time, after the play."

Once Grant had brought Hazel into his house and pressed her up against the door, he had never moved away from her, during their entire confrontation. Now, he lowered his head to hers and lifted her chin with his fingers.

"I didn't mean to," he whispered. "I'm so sorry."

Hazel began to cry softly. "All I could think about was coming home to you, Grant. It hurt so much when I thought you had changed your mind and didn't want me."

He pulled her away from the door and into his arms, and wrapped her up protectively.

"I am so sorry, baby. I'm just so sorry."

She slid her hands up to caress his back and closed her eyes. "I'm sorry, too," she whispered. "You're not a jerk, and I'm sorry for calling you that. I should have waited first, to find out what happened.

"I just thought it was like last time, when I saw you in the park and you said you weren't taking my calls."

He laid a kiss on her forehead. "That will never happen again, Hazie. I can promise you that."

She shook from too much emotion but finally looked up at him. "Would you do something for me?"

"I would do anything for you, sweet girl."

She smiled faintly. "Would you follow me home? I'm running out of steam, I guess. I'm not sure I can even find it."

"I'll take you home and we can sort the vehicles out in the morning."

Grant guided her away from the door and opened it so that they could step out onto the porch. He caught her hand and walked her to his truck, helping her inside and belting her in, since she was too tired to think about it.

When he started the engine, he eased the truck slowly forward, using the street lights to see with until he got to the end of the road, before turning on his headlights and driving in the direction of Hazel's apartment.

"Do you think we woke anyone up?" Hazel worried.

"I think we're good," he assured her, looking over at her with a wink.

When they arrived at her apartment, Grant took her to her door and only stepped inside to stroke her face and give her a gentle smile.

"Go get in bed, Hay. When the number on my phone that called nine times calls me again in the morning, I promise I'll answer."

He laid a soft kiss on her lips, then stopped before letting himself out, to make sure she was alright.

"I love you, sweet girl."

"I love you." She was still a little weepy.

Grant couldn't resist kissing her again, and pulling her close for another hug, before they said goodnight. It was becoming harder for him to let her go and Hazel seemed to want to cling to him, but he finally convinced her to go to her room.

He locked her door before closing it and drove back to the parsonage with a grim, worried look on his face, as he recalled the way she had looked up at him with so much hurt and disappointment in her beautiful eyes.

When he got home, he reached for his gym bag and let himself in, tossing it onto the couch and digging his phone out of it. He went into his room and undressed, putting on his pajama bottoms and climbing into bed.

He made himself play every one of Hazel's voicemails, and his own eyes clouded up with tears, as he heard the emotion and the longing for him in her voice. He didn't have to try hard to put himself in her place and recognize how distressed and frantic she had been, fearing that he was once again not taking her calls. Why wouldn't she? He had done that to her, before.

Finally, he put the phone away and stared at the ceiling.

He didn't know how in the world he could undo that kind of hurt, but he was going to do everything he could to try.

He was in love with that girl, and he was going to make sure she knew it.

Hazel opened the box the courier had delivered just as she was leaving the apartment. She had waited until she and Grant had arrived at "Oh, It's Coffee!" to open it, because she had already received a call from Maddie the night before, letting her know to expect her phone to be delivered.

Maddie told her that even though the cab driver who took them from Preston Geller's office back to the hotel hadn't found her phone when dispatch asked him to check, his relief driver did.

It had somehow fallen between the back door and the right side of the seat and had continued to slide its way underneath, out of sight. Hazel had silenced it after arriving at Preston Geller's office, so it had remained undetected until the relief driver finally thought about where he had found things before, and felt around under the back seat until he located it.

The cab company had called Maddie, who rushed over to pick up the phone and send it on its way to a very relieved and grateful Hazel.

She lifted it out of the box now, and held it up to Grant with a mischievous grin.

"We shall see what we shall see."

"Oh, we shall," he agreed, returning her gaze in a way that caused Katie and Fred to raise their brows at each other.

Hazel turned on the phone and pulled up her call list, then lifted her eyes to rest them on Grant with a sweet smile, before laying it down and leaning forward to capture his face in her hands.

"Fourteen," she whispered. "But who's counting?"

"You are," he laughed softly. "And I win."

The two of them continued to exchange looks that began to make Katie and Fred a little self-conscious.

"Okay, break it up," Fred commanded, coming over and spreading his arms apart like a referee in the boxing ring.

They leaned back with little smiles still hovering in their eyes and Hazel checked the side of her phone to turn the ringer back on before slipping it into her jacket pocket.

"So, did Preston Geller beat my record and call you fifteen times?" Grant asked her, his eyes toying with hers.

"You were so ready to punch his lights out, and all the poor man wanted was to ask me if the production he's working on could be the first one to play at The Boards." Hazel gave him one of his own patented little taps on the nose and he caught her finger and kissed the tip of it.

"Taste this!"

Hazel leaned back quickly and looked up at Katie, who was prepared to shove a bite of quiche into her mouth.

Hazel took the fork herself to avoid injury and tasted it, before opening her eyes wide. "You nailed it, sweetie!"

Katie did her customary jumping in place and clapped her hands in excitement.

"She wouldn't believe me," Fred grumbled, pulling up a chair at their table. "She had to hear it from the renowned Hazel Todd, star of stage and stove."

"I nailed it, I nailed it," Katie sang, dancing her way back to the kitchen. "Come see what else I nailed," she called back to the star of stage and stove.

Hazel laid her hand on the top of Grant's shoulder and gave it a little squeeze, as she moved past him to go see what Katie was so happy about in the kitchen.

Grant watched her go with a tender look then leaned over to Fred once she was out of hearing.

"We need a good excuse to be gone for a few hours, Fred. You have to help me come up with something."

"Scheming! I'm so good at this," he declared, rubbing his hands together and lifting his brows.

He stopped and regarded Grant guardedly. "Of course, you do realize that I may have to resort to lying."

"That's between you and God," his pastor assured him, "but I'm willing to overlook it."

Fred didn't have to fake his surprised stare. "This is big!"

Grant leaned back to peer around toward the kitchen, then fixed him with a steady look.

"Big," he simply said.

Fred drew in his breath and did some rapid-fire musing as the two women were returning to the dining area and pushed up from the table.

"Honey, I told Grant I'd run with him to pick up what Jarvis lent to the play and get it back to him. We'll probably do the restocking for him too, since Jarvis can't lift the heavy things, anymore, and then we're gonna go see if we can find out why my truck is making that vibrating sound. We might be gone a while, if you ladies think you can survive without our strong male essence for a few hours."

"How many hours is a few?" Katie asked, pulling a napkin from the table dispenser and wiping off her fingers. "Hazel said I nailed the scones, too!"

"You're going to be famous." Her husband gave her a little kiss. "I'm not sure, it depends on what we find out about the truck, but I'll call you."

Katie waved him away, but Hazel stood looking at Grant with a query in her eyes.

"That came out of nowhere," she commented quietly, as he moved his chair back and came around to rest his hand lightly on her waist.

"You know Fred," he grinned.

She raised up to whisper in his ear. "You'll notice that Fred gave Katie a kiss. I'm just pointing that out."

"Like this?" Grant surprised her by being willing to kiss her in front of their friends.

"Look at you, all brave," she breathed, running her finger softly across his brow. "Frieda Gathright doesn't know what she's missing."

"You better behave," he growled, making her laugh. "Come on, Fred, let's get a move on."

The two grabbed their coats and headed off to their fabricated obligations, while Katie came around to stand beside Hazel and join her in looking thoughtfully at the door that closed behind them.

Chapter Twenty-Seven

"Talk about out in the sticks!"

Fred looked around at the little town that finally appeared, as Grant drove his truck over the railroad tracks, taking a sharp right turn to enter onto a street that featured what few businesses there were.

"You grew up here?" He continued to be amazed.

"I did," Grant confirmed. "Both Hazel and I did. Of course, I was born here. Hazel's family didn't move here until she was starting third grade."

"Why?"

Grant looked over at him oddly. "Why, what?"

"Why did her family move here, of all places? For the booming commerce?"

"Nothing wrong with rural America, Fred. It suited us just fine. Or, it did, until Hazel graduated high school. She'd had enough of it. I guess I understand that, now."

"Your folks are still here?"

"They are." Grant's expression took on a bit of unrest. "I don't like the idea of coming all the way here and not even letting them know I'm in town, but I need to keep moving. I may just have to call them."

He stopped the truck in front of a red bricked building and glanced over at Fred. "Do you want to just hang here? I'm hoping it won't take too long."

"Sure, I'll sit and people-watch. Well, I mean, as soon as some people show up."

"Stop it," Grant laughed. "It's not a ghost town."

Fred fixed him with a bland expression. "Says you."

Grant got out of his truck and gave his friend a little wave, then disappeared into the building. Fred could see him through the large plate glass window as he approached the counter and began a conversation with the woman who apparently had asked what she could help him with.

He reached for his phone and grinned when he saw the caller ID. "Katie Buckley's husband, how may I help you?"

Katie stifled a little giggle. "This is Katie Buckley."

Fred gasped loudly. "Oh, Mrs. Buckley, what an honor! I have every scone you've ever made! No one is going to believe me when I tell them about this phone call!"

Katie had to laugh, in spite of herself. Fred never had any trouble at all making his wife laugh.

"Get off the stage, Fred, the play's over. Anyway, I have a question."

"You? No way!"

"Stop, Fred, I'm being serious."

"Am I on speakerphone?" he suddenly asked.

"Why, does it sound like it?" Mrs. Katie Buckley hedged.

"Just answer the question, Mrs. Buckley, and let me remind you that God and I are really tight. He'll tell me if you're lying." He winced at his own hypocrisy, but asked again. "Am I on speakerphone?"

Katie and Hazel gave up.

"Hi, Fred," Hazel offered in surrender.

"Oh, wow, two celebrities for the price of one. I'm all about the luck!"

"So, Fred, if Hazel and I were to drive over to see Jarvis at his store, would we find you and Grant there?"

"You would not," he answered truthfully. "That hasn't happened, yet." He craned his neck to look around him.

"Right now, I'm looking at a gas station with a guy who looks as if he could build my truck from the ground up with one hand, and chug a case of beer with the other. Why do you ask, dear ladies?"

"No reason," Katie said nonchalantly. "Just missing your male essence, I guess."

"And who could blame you?"

He spotted Grant coming back out of the building with a pleased smile on his face and an envelope in his hand.

"So, Hazel, should I put you on speakerphone too, so you can tell Grant that you miss his male essence?"

"I'll tell him later," she laughed. "Bye, boys!"

"Bye, girls!" Fred hung up and smiled broadly at Grant, who had just returned to the truck.

"What was all that?" he asked, looking bewildered.

"That was my wife and your..."

He stopped to think of what Hazel's title actually was.

"Anyway, they were checking up on us. I guess my story wasn't as convincing to them as it was to me."

"Well, we're about to head back that way, anyway," Grant told him, putting his truck into gear and backing out onto the street.

Fred just looked at him. "Wait, what? We drove two hours to get here, just so you could go into that little building and now we're driving two hours straight back?"

"I told you that I need to keep moving," Grant reminded him, looking both ways before turning left to drive back over the railroad tracks.

"I thought that was metaphorical," his friend replied. "Where to, now?"

"To see a friend of mine."

"Around here?"

"No, back home."

Fred let out a loud sigh. "Okay, I think it's about time you told me what's going on, buddy. I mean, I lied for you and the women are already checking up on us, which means I'll probably have to double down on the whole lying thing."

"You're right," Grant said, with a little grin. "But Fred, I don't care how close you and Katie are, and I don't want to hear the whole 'and the two shall become one' thing. If you breathe a word of this to your wife, then she better become your gym buddy too, because I'm done."

"Seriously, you're threatening me?" Fred exclaimed.

"Yes, Frederick," Grant assured him, looking over at him to let him know he was serious. "Sometimes things are too important to mess around with. This is one of those things. If you can't keep from telling Katie, then just say so, and we're good. But I can't tell you what's going on, in that case. So you'll have to stop asking me."

"No, I mean, I may not like keeping things from Katie, but if this falls into that category, I get it. Is this something she'll eventually find out, anyway?"

"Absolutely."

"Oh, well why didn't you say so?" Fred laughed. "Sure, I can sit on it. Your secret's safe with me."

Grant reached over and gave his buddy a light frog on his arm. "My man!"

They drove on in silence for a bit until Fred couldn't take it anymore.

"Okay, so when are you gonna fill me in? 'Cause I'm right here." He waved.

Grant laughed. "Soon, buddy."

After a while, they arrived back in town and Grant stopped his truck. Fred looked at him strangely.

"Okay, we're at old Pastor Morgan's house. Do I come in or wait here?"

"Come with," Grant invited.

Fred grinned and slapped his hands together, hopping out of the truck to follow his friend to the door.

Ellen Abbott asked them in and Pastor Morgan stood up from the chair he'd been sitting in to welcome them.

"Now you're just showing off," Grant said, when he demonstrated his ability to sit and stand without assistance.

The pastor laughed. "If you've got it, flaunt it!"

He rested his eyes on Fred. "Young Mr. Buckley, it's good to see you! Have a seat, both of you."

Ellen left them to visit, using this opportunity to go take care of a few things while her brother was unlikely to get up and try to walk around on his own.

"Well then, Pastor Sellars, what brings you men to my door? I can sense a purpose to your visit, although you're always welcome to drop by for no reason at all."

Grant reached his hand into the inside pocket of his jacket and brought out the envelope Fred had seen him with, when he came out of the brick building at his home town.

Pastor Morgan reached around to locate his glasses and put them on before taking the envelope in his hands and removing the paper inside.

He looked at it curiously while a slow smile traveled across his face and into his eyes.

"Oh, my!" He continued to read through it again, just to make sure, then folded it up and returned it to the envelope before giving it to Grant. "Sooner rather than later?"

"Yes, please."

"I'd be honored," he said, with a little laugh. "How about Saturday and that way, I can also help out with Sunday morning, if that's also needed?"

"Are you up to it?" Grant asked, not wanting to put too much on his friend during his recuperation.

"I am, indeed!"

Fred sat through this exchange about to burst. Finally, he couldn't stand it any longer.

"Can I at least see what's in the envelope?"

"Oh, he doesn't know?" Pastor Morgan thought that was funny, and his eyes crinkled with his laughter.

Grant looked over at him with a little smile before giving Fred a more serious look.

"You promised, right?"

"I promised!"

He handed the envelope to Fred and both he and Pastor Morgan waited for his reaction.

"Wait... is this real?"

He looked up at Pastor Morgan, who nodded with pleased delight.

"Oh, it's very real. One of this state's unique rulings."

Fred looked at Grant in stunned surprise.

289

"Are you kidding me right now?"

"I'm very serious," he assured him, with a grin.

"Wait, Saturday? As in this Saturday? As in three days from today?" Fred was incredulous.

"Why not, if Pastor Sellars is agreed?"

"Pastor Sellars is agreed!" Grant declared, enjoying Fred's comical struggle to believe his own eyes.

"That's... the logistics of this are crazily improbable!"

"I agree," Grant said, standing up and retrieving the source of Fred's astonishment to put back into his pocket. "But not impossible. So, I need to keep moving."

"It's not that I mind," Hazel sighed, standing to one side while Katie nervously fumbled with the keys Grant had given her. "But I don't really know Tracie Holloway, so I'm not sure why she's expecting me to be here."

"It's not Tracie, it's Grant," Katie replied, almost ready to throw the keys into the bushes when they wouldn't work. "He needs a plus one."

Hazel calmly took the keys from Katie's frustrated fingers and unlocked the back door of the church with no problem, then handed them back to her friend.

"Why didn't that work for me?" she demanded.

"Because you're all flustered, for some reason," Hazel observed. "I just don't know why, though. You and Tracie aren't that close, for you to be all worked up about this."

"I know, but it's all so last minute," she said, opening the door slightly and peeking into the hall before she pushed it wide enough to admit them. "I'm supposed to help with the dress."

"I think it's in here," Katie decided, opening an interior door just to their right.

"This is it!" she announced, and they entered the room where all of Tracie's things were apparently ready for her.

"Wow, her dress is beautiful," Hazel breathed. "Where in the world would she have found something like that?"

"I don't know, but I wish I'd seen it before *my* wedding."

Hazel simply nodded mutely, and approached the dress to finger the material and inspect its lines and adornment.

"But yours was beautiful, too, Kate," she hurried to add.

"Not like this, come on! Who are we kidding?" Katie joined her in admiring the elegant creation.

"I would think she'd already be in here, getting ready. She sure is leaving it until the last minute."

Hazel crossed her arms and walked slowly around the room, taking in the lovely shoes and the makeup cart and vanity table that someone had set up.

She saw the box for the bouquet and glanced around to make sure it was safe to peek, then lifted the lid.

Her face registered shock and she looked up at Katie with a trace of sadness around her eyes. "She must have come to the play, I guess."

"Why do you say that, sweetie?" Katie came over to look into the box.

"Her bouquet. These are orange blossoms."

Tears sprang into Hazel's eyes. "I was going to have orange blossoms," she whispered.

"You still are," Katie said softly, smiling with her own tears when Hazel looked at her in confusion.

Katie crossed back over to the breathtaking wedding dress and caught the skirt to lift it up. "You'd better hurry, Hazel. Grant's not exactly the most patient man I've ever met."

She sank down slowly onto the nearest chair and laid a hand on her throat, finding it hard to breathe.

"He said he wouldn't ask me. He said it was all on me."

"Well, honey, he did ask you, twelve years ago. He's still waiting." Katie came over to her and knelt down, bringing a tissue with her that she seemed to have known Hazel would need. "And he's hoping and praying with all his heart that when the music starts and the doors open, his beloved Hazie will come to him. He'll be the handsome one waiting at the altar, with his heart in his eyes."

Hazel had moved beyond dabbing at tears and was now openly weeping. "But how? How can we even do this?"

"Under the auspices of the great state of Mississippi, where a marriage license never expires, whether it's used or not."

Hazel continued to be stunned.

"But I've been married since then," she protested.

"And widowed," Katie reminded her. "The original license is still valid. Trust me, honey, this has all been verified and Grant drove four hours just to hear it in person and have the license handed directly to him."

Hazel hung her head and began to shake.

Katie stood up and took her hand.

"Let's stop those tears, sweetie. As beautiful as you are, this is gonna turn into ugly crying, real quick, if we don't plug you up, right now."

She reached down and caught Hazel's other hand and held them both tightly, looking carefully into her friend's face.

"Hazel... when the music starts and the doors open... you *will* be there, right?"

She couldn't speak, but she nodded and burst into more tears, as her dear Katie began to lovingly fuss over her and attempt to tidy her up.

Chapter Twenty-Eight

There was the gentlest of knocks on the door and Katie came over to cautiously open it. She grinned with delight and stepped back to admit a perfectly attired Irving Lancaster, who returned her welcome with an impressive bow.

"I do love a happy ending," he informed her.

He trained his blue eyes on the vision before him, and stretched a hand toward Hazel with a pleased smile.

"Come, my dear. It would appear that we have a wedding commencing much too quickly for me to indulge in the proper amount of time to pay homage to your beauty. You must simply know that you are a walking poem."

Hazel rewarded his gracious appreciation of her by offering him her hand, which he tucked into the bend of his arm, and placing a light kiss on his cheek.

Katie quickly lifted the bouquet from its box and placed it into Hazel's keeping, drawing another look of glad approval from the archetype of Henry Wadsworth Longfellow.

"Your groom has certainly thought of everything," he assured her, with a gesture toward the door.

Katie picked up her matron of honor flowers and stepped out into the hallway in order to precede Hazel, feeling her own small rush of excitement, as she wondered how Fred would look at her, from his position next to the groom, when he saw her come through the doors.

It was hard to believe that this wedding had only been three days in the making. In spite of the unexpected and swift nature of the occasion, the church was practically filled with happy guests in the sanctuary and busy ladies in the kitchen.

Grant's mother had lightly scolded him when she learned that he had come to their town, and hadn't stopped by. She and Grant's father had only been shocked by how quickly their son was hurrying to marry his Hazel, but not at all by the wedding, itself. Once they'd heard that Hazel was living in his town, they knew that it was only a matter of time, since Grant had never loved anyone but the Todd girl down the street, and they had long ago realized that he never would.

They immediately dropped all their plans to attend and offered to have Hazel's mother come with them, but she seemed to be more disappointed to learn that Hazel was retiring from acting and settling down with a minister than she was happy for her daughter, so when she declined, the Sellars didn't persist.

Of course, the wedding had been pulled together so rapidly, that there was no time for Hazel's agent or Maddie to attend, but their apologies had to be made through Katie, since they realized that Hazel was being surprised.

Clayton Ballard simply asked Katie to give Hazel his best, and Maddie asked her to remember to tell Hazel that as soon as she took care of last minute details, she would be ready to relocate to their little Mississippi town in order to work closely alongside her employer in preparation for the grand opening of The Boards, especially since Hazel was considering taking a teaching position at the academy.

Mayor Pollard and his wife were thrilled to have been invited and were eager to see Hazel make her appearance. The mayor had arranged for the local paper to cover the wedding.

William Cullen had been shown to a seat near the front left of the sanctuary, and escorted Shelby Fields on his arm as his plus one. The two had discovered so much in common, as they discussed the opening of the academy, that they seemed to find more and more social events to attend together.

Lucy Walker had been asked personally by her neighbor to attend his wedding and she had been astonished and emotionally grateful to be included.

She had asked him to wait at the fence and ran into her house, then immediately came rushing back out with Mister, her black and tan, ten-week-old German Shepherd puppy.

Grant was so glad that she hadn't opted for a silly little lap dog or, as he and Fred put it, a "yapper", that he showed great enthusiasm for Mister and solidly approved of his name.

Lucy sat now holding a picture of Mister, surrounded by every dog toy he could ever want. She was ready to show it to the young pastor after his wedding, at the gathering that the church ladies were fiercely in the middle of putting together.

Ivy Parker wasted no time commissioning a team of women to undertake their biggest challenge yet, in the form of a an emergency wedding reception.

Mrs. Payne was still taking pictures of the beautiful cake she had created and women were bustling about arranging tables and chairs and moving swiftly down the list Geraldine Fowler had passed out to each of them.

Someone had thought to run into a neighboring town to a large party goods store and had returned with generic, but beautiful napkins, table coverings, plates and punch glasses, and anything else that could be thought of to make things nice.

These were all being placed strategically around what the women decided would be one long central serving station, with the wedding cake front and center. Guests would be able to choose their own seating and serve themselves glasses of punch and hors d'oeuvres.

When the ladies felt that things were as ready as they could make them, they slipped away to be able to see their handsome, young, single pastor become a happily married one; something they had all hoped and prayed for, for years.

They had all decided that their lives were about to become much less stressful, now that Pastor Sellars would have a woman in his house and a ring on his finger.

They each rushed to seats that they had saved, excited to find that the wedding music had not yet started and began fishing around in their purses for tissues.

They whispered and pointed to their handsome pastor, as he stood at the altar with his best man, Fred, whose job seemed to be to quietly reassure him that all was going well.

Pastor James Morgan stood happily in front of his walker, with his Bible resting on a portable stand in front of him, simply waiting for the church's pianist to begin.

When she lightly rolled her first chords, an expectant hush fell over the sanctuary, and Grant's heart suddenly began to beat in his throat, as the moment felt all too familiar.

"Steady," Fred whispered. "God's got this one, Grant. He didn't have the other one; you had that one. This one's His."

Grant drew in a steady breath and nodded, but tears had already begun to form in his eyes.

"I checked, myself," Fred offered in the faintest voice. "I'm told she's here, she's ready, and she's beautiful. In the words of that bastion of truth and wisdom, Bullwinkle J. Moose, 'This time, for sure!' So, there ya go."

Grant went from beginning to cry, to shaking with silent laughter. No one did a better impression of Bullwinkle J. Moose than Fred Buckley, and he had never appreciated it more than he did right now.

He was still trying not to laugh when the official music began and it was time for Katie to present the bride, by paving the way for her entrance.

When the moment came, Fred's lingering, tender smile told her how much he loved her and she blushed, as if it were their wedding and returned his sentiment, before taking her place in order to assist the bride, who was about to enter.

The music changed to an old hymn that Grant and Hazel had both always loved and the ushers at the back opened the double doors.

The prophecy of Bullwinkle J. Moose was fulfilled, as the most beautiful woman Grant Sellars had ever seen approached him so gracefully, that she appeared to float down the aisle on the arm of her much-loved, distinguished friend, who managed to silently will her to measure her steps, rather than dash, full speed ahead, to get to her groom.

Gasps and murmurs of appreciation rippled through the church as Hazel made her stately way, locking eyes with the man she loved and giving him a flirty panning left and right wink.

"Is she having a stroke?" Fred whispered, causing Grant to have to struggle not to laugh again, but he maintained control and gave her his own soft wink.

Irving Lancaster stood perfectly straight by her side, as they stopped, and gave his old friend, James Morgan a quiet nod.

When asked, he simply informed the minister that he was giving this woman to be wed, and fused her hand with Grant's before making his genteel way to his reserved seat.

"Hello," Grant whispered to his sweetheart.

"Hello." She then gave him the stereo flirt and when he failed to control that burst of laughter, the guests all began to laugh with him, although none of them knew why.

Pastor Morgan signaled for guests to be seated, then made his opening remarks, greeting all those who had come to share in the celebration of love and commitment between the two who stood before him now, ready at last to make their vows to each other.

Before he prayed, the old pastor simply took a moment to smile at Grant in a poignant way that seemed to highlight all the conversations the two of them had shared. Grant suddenly saw him, not as he had long thought of him, the strange old bachelor preacher that nobody really knew that much about, but as a man who had once stood in his place and pledged his love and commitment to his beloved Marty and who, in the wake of tragic loss, steadfastly declared the trustworthiness of God.

The emergence of this revelation surprised Grant with an unexpected rush of emotion, and the smile he gave back was filled with gratitude that this old servant of God had poured so much of himself into the life of a bitter, unforgiving, cynical young minister. In that moment, Grant knew that he loved old Pastor James Morgan dearly.

Pastor Morgan offered up his simple prayer and then spoke only briefly about the kind of love that sustained injury yet somehow endured.

He observed that time had intended to fade that love from memory, as an attempt to lessen the sting of it, but instead, it deepened and enriched it.

He talked of a love that, when facing challenges such as betrayal, loss, or misunderstanding, was healed and strengthened through the willingness to forgive and to understand, and that it had grown into a love that would withstand the ravages of time.

Before leading Grant and Hazel to speak their vows, he looked down at Hazel with a kindness in his manner that touched her heart.

"Hazel, your groom has a three day advantage over you, in that he knew that today was your wedding day. That being the case, he has been able to prepare what he wishes to say to you, today. You, however..."

A ripple of suppressed laugher swept through the sanctuary and the minister paused and grinned at the irony.

"You, however, have known that today was your wedding day for approximately..." he glanced over at Katie with a question in his eyes, then turned back to Hazel, after he heard her response and had to laugh softly to himself.

"You, however, have known that today was your wedding day for approximately forty minutes."

The laughter became obvious and Hazel gave Grant a look that promised she'd get even. He squeezed her hand and seemed to welcome the prospect.

"As that is the case, you are not expected to suddenly and spontaneously burst forth in effusive, poetic words, but if you do wish to say anything at all to your groom, you may certainly take that opportunity. That is, as long as it can be said in a church," the old man of God added with a chuckle, stirring another round of amusement.

Hazel accepted the challenge and handed her beautiful bouquet of orange blossoms to her matron of honor before reaching for both of Grant's hands and resting her eyes on his, with her love for him on display.

"Our love sustained injury but it has somehow endured."

She smiled over at Pastor Morgan before continuing.

"Our love was damaged by my selfishness, my fear, my panic, and my foolishness. A dozen years passed and the light all but went out in my eyes and in my heart. Love was too fine a thing to be touched again by me. I had broken it, before.

"You could have thrown away all the pieces of it, swept them aside and committed yourself to forgetting they had ever been. But you kept them, in spite of the pain they caused you.

"You told me that I was forgiven and in that moment, I felt the movement of all those pieces as they began to be reformed and put back together. You healed me. And the love that has been allowed to thrive and live and that will now withstand the ravages of time comes from your willingness to perhaps not trust in me, but to trust in God, in me."

Her words caused Grant's heart to pound, as the memory of what he had learned about trust from his dear old friend began to awaken in him.

Hazel glanced down then raised her eyes again to his.

"Entreat me not to leave you or to return from following you; for where you go I will go, and where you lodge I will lodge; your people shall be my people, and your God my God; where you die I will die, and there will I be buried."

Tears ran freely down Hazel's beautiful face and Grant lifted his hand to touch them tenderly before reaching for her hands again and holding her gaze with his own.

"You speak of your selfishness, your fear, your panic, and your foolishness and yet, had you not taken the path in life that you chose, you would not be the woman standing here before me today; the woman I love with all that is within me.

"Had you remained in that place where we grew up, and simply resigned yourself to your fate, yes, you would be as beautiful, but would you be as wise? Would beautiful words have remained a confusing mystery to you, or would they be as heavy with meaning as they are for you, now?

"Would you be impatient with those who struggle around you or would you be able to empathize with others simply because you have learned how to become that person through your profound gift and calling of interpretation and portrayal?

299

"I am not the man to effectively quote the poet, but thinking of the years that separated us has caused me, from time to time, to consider the words of Robert Frost when he said, 'Two roads diverged in a wood. I took the one less traveled by, and that has made all the difference.'

"How can I behold the woman you are today, Hazel, and not recognize that the road you took was certainly the one less traveled?

"Back then, we all made the expected choices. We all traveled the well-worn road that our peers had taken. There was little risk, but there also little reward. But you chose differently.

"For whatever reason, God allowed our choices and, as He stands outside of time, knew that our paths would meet again, regardless of the roads we chose. And now, here we are.

"Yes, I have forgiven you, but you have also forgiven me. And yes, Hazel, I do trust God in you, and I pray that you will trust God in me.

"I promise to always protect your heart and to love you without measure."

He stopped and grinned boyishly at her.

"I promise to help you down from trees and tall ladders."

Grant's parents began to shake with silent laughter, with too many memories rushing at them of their son having to coax little Hazel Todd down by calmly saying, "One and done, Hay. Come on, I've got you. One and done."

"I promise to learn how to do that little flirty panning wink thing." This time it was Hazel who was laughing.

Grant leaned forward and touched his forehead to hers. "I promise to always take your calls."

She smiled up at him and gave him the same soft stroke across his brow with her fingertip that she had always given him in moments when she was feeling especially tender toward him, then drew in her breath when she heard Pastor Morgan whisper his confirmation to Fred to present the ring.

Hazel looked quickly over at Katie with a small bit of alarm, but saw that her best friend had already anticipated this moment and held a ring in her hand.

She flashed her a grateful smile before returning her attention to Grant who had taken her left hand in preparation for placing his ring on her finger.

He simply repeated the words that Pastor Morgan led him to say and when he slipped the beautifully elegant diamond on her finger, he blinked back tears at the realization that the woman he adored was wearing his ring.

Hazel took the beautiful band from Katie and softly said the words to him that he had said to her, never taking her eyes from his as she placed the symbol of their union on his finger.

Everyone except Hazel and Grant heard Pastor Morgan say that by the power vested in him, he now pronounced them man and wife. They were standing there lost in each other, and by the time the minister advised Grant that he could kiss his bride, he was already very much involved in doing so, to the shock and embarrassment of quite a few church ladies.

Fred finally stepped in with his patented referee stance and ordered them to break it up, then gestured to a laughing Pastor Morgan that he was free to introduce them to the congregation now.

He happily declared, "Ladies and gentlemen, I present to you Pastor and Mrs. Grant Sellars!"

The pianist immediately began to play a spirited and energetic recessional as the newlyweds made their way down the aisle and around the side of the building, so that Grant could finish kissing his bride before Fred and Katie found them.

This happened fairly quickly, and he whispered to her to remind him where he left off.

They were at the mercy of others telling them where to stand for pictures and when to appear at the reception and how to cut the cake and all sorts of things that the two of them tried to patiently endure, but would just as soon be done with.

Finally, they did make their way into the reception area, to the delight of family and friends and church members, and performed the conventional traditions that were expected, especially since it was clear that the ladies of the congregation had worked harder on this reception than anything in memory.

Each woman, in turn, was pleasantly shocked when her pastor actually hugged her as he gave her his sincere thanks, and went about her tasks for the rest of the day with a happy smile on her face, none more so than Ivy Parker.

William Cullen approached Hazel with a content little smile, and rested a hand fondly on her shoulder.

"Well, Hazel, Shakespeare once said, 'Our indiscretions sometimes serve us well when our deep plots do pall.' It looks like you're getting a do-over."

Hazel widened her eyes and looked up at Grant with a happy laugh before reaching to give her one-time father-in-law an affectionate hug.

"I think we all are, William," she said, nodding toward Shelby, who was listening to an animated Katie Buckley giving her the details of how they managed to pull this wedding off without Hazel finding out.

"You might be right," he conceded. "Congratulations to the both of you." He gave the groom his hand before making his way over to continue to escort his plus one.

Tracie Holloway and her fiancé spotted the couple and smiled and waved from their chairs, completely unaware that their own future wedding had been the basis for the subterfuge the schemers had chosen, in order to keep Hazel from discovering what they were up to.

Ellen Abbott had helped her brother enter the reception area with the help of a couple of the church's ushers, and he was seated comfortably with his friend Irving Lancaster beside him, as they gladly spent some time reminiscing and speculating about the future of their small town.

Grant noted them with a grin and caught his wife's hand to cross over to them.

"Well, young Pastor Sellars, I began to fear that you and your new wife were going to preach tomorrow's sermon during the ceremony," Pastor Morgan said with a chuckle. "But, I may give it a go anyway, and see if I can steal some of your material without your congregation noticing."

"No, you get the credit for anything I said of any value," Grant reassured him. "I just appreciate your always being willing to spend the time sharing what you've learned over the years with someone still wet behind the ears."

"Loaves and fishes, I'm afraid," the old man laughed. "But I expect our Lord still does His miracles."

"I've never understood these strange, connubial rituals," Irving Lancaster admitted, beholding the happy couple with a knowing look, "which demand that a freshly elated groom and his blushing and euphoric bride stand patiently in a room filled with smiling, chattering people, and old men who have not yet begun to fully describe the aching in their various limbs, and pretend that they have nowhere to go and nothing to do."

He noted the flush of color on his beautiful friend's face as she and her groom exchanged their own knowing looks.

"Perhaps, someday, you will enlighten me and explain this bizarre custom... when you do, in fact, have nowhere to go and nothing to do."

"I see that wisdom is contagious," Grant laughed, as the two elderly men seemed to enjoy their awkward restraint. "And your observation is a valid one."

He glanced down at Hazel and she simply nodded.

"Thank you both, so much," Grant said, as he and Hazel prepared to abandon what the seasoned thespian referred to as a strange, connubial ritual, and leave the chattering to their guests.

Katie tugged at Fred's hand, when she saw Hazel looking around for them, and they excused themselves to meet their friends near the doorway.

"Do I travel in this, Katie, or is it okay to change back?"

"I raided your closet," she confessed, with a laugh. "That's what you get for not demanding my key back. I brought something for you."

Hazel gave her a tight hug and then followed her down the hallway, while Grant and Fred headed over to where they had dressed for the ceremony, in order to toss a few more things into a suitcase and allow Grant to exchange his tuxedo for jeans.

"Okay, so the monkey suit is not due back until Monday. I'll take care of that, and Katie and I will meet you guys back at your truck with the luggage," Fred said, looking around for anything they were forgetting. "Kate's still got your keys, right?"

"I sure hope so," Grant answered, also checking for what they might be leaving.

"Better scoot, before Ivy Parker realizes you're gone."

Grant laughed at that and willingly followed his friend around to his truck, where Katie and Hazel were already waiting.

"Fred, we can't just leave, though, and not say goodbye," Grant reminded him, although it was very tempting to just take off. "For one thing, my parents would be steamed."

"I guess so. Tell you what, follow us to the door, and we'll just let everyone know it's time."

"Fred." Grant laid his hand on his best friend's arm and gave him a watery smile. "I love you, buddy."

"Right backatcha," he said gruffly, unexpectedly placing him in a harmless headlock and roughing up his hair.

"I take it back," Grant laughed.

Hazel reached for Katie, wanting to say her goodbye privately, before the guests spilled out of the church's fellowship area to see them leave.

"You really are my very best friend, Kate, and I love you," she whispered, already needing to wipe her cheeks. "God gave you to me, the minute I walked into your shop, and you're all the sister I will ever need."

Katie stared at her in astonishment, knowing that Hazel, who was an established celebrity, and known all over the country, could claim any number of friends. She began to cry her own tears, and pulled her close for a hug.

"I love you, too!" she declared. "And as soon as you're back, I'm going to make you some braised short ribs."

"I thought you said you loved her," Fred unwisely said, earning him a punch on the arm.

He laughed and motioned for them to wait by the door, then called loudly to announce that the bride and groom were ready to leave.

A rush toward the entrance caused him to step back and yell, "Watch out!" to the newlyweds.

Grant's parents managed to get to him and Mrs. Sellars pulled her new daughter-in-law close for an embrace.

"Welcome to the family, sweetheart," she breathed.

Hazel looked up at her with a glad smile, and Mrs. Sellars got her first close look at her in many years.

"My goodness, Hazel! You were a cute little girl, but who would have expected you to grow up to be such a beauty? No wonder Grant has carried a torch for you all these years. I expect we'll have gorgeous grandbabies!"

"Mom," Grant reproved with an attempt at a frown that he couldn't quite manage.

"I'm just saying!" she laughed, reaching for her son next.

Grant and Hazel continued to move toward what Fred told them was their escape pod, and finally called out their last goodbyes before they were safely inside and ready to launch.

Fred and Katie watched them leave with happy tears and big grins, before high-fiving each other and heading off to gather up wedding garments and flowers and tend to all the things that needed their attention.

The guests wandered back into the church, talking among themselves, laughing, revisiting the punch bowl, and just enjoying the day.

Grant stopped his truck for a red light, and looked over at his bride with a soft smile, catching her hand and giving it a slight tug.

"My pretty, pretty truck comes equipped with middle seat belts," he bragged modestly.

"I'm sure you're very proud," she returned, pretending to look around casually at their little town.

"Get over here!" he fussed, dispensing with subtle hints.

Hazel laughed and scooted over, discovering the middle seatbelts for herself.

She looked up at her husband as they waited for the traffic light to change.

"William said I got a do-over."

"I heard that," Grant admitted, continuing to monitor the light and still pay attention to her.

"You said a do-over comes with kissing."

"I remember that," he confessed.

"When?"

He looked over at her and raised his brows in question.

"When does the do-over come with kissing?"

"I gave you your do-over kiss, at the altar."

Hazel tilted her head and looked at him with narrowed eyes, twisting her lips into a scowl.

"Is that it, then?"

He laughed quietly. "I'm driving."

She surprised him by suddenly throwing her arms around his neck and kissing him in a way that was intended to lead to many more kisses. It would have, if the light hadn't changed and annoyed drivers hadn't begun blowing their horns at the couple in the truck, who apparently didn't have anything better to do with their time, than to hold up traffic with all their kissing.

Grant obliged their loud requests by pulling his truck forward and whipping it over to the side of the road, before turning off the engine and giving his bride a slow smile.

"Thank you for meeting me at the altar."

"Thank you for still being at the altar."

She raised herself up to lay a little peck on his cheek.

He wiped it off, giving her a dissatisfied look.

"What was that? I want a do-over."

Also by Rhonda Hanson

The Father Series

Father's Choice
Father's Wings
Father's Song

A linked novel

Father's Friend

The Master Of Hawthorn Manor

Buying The Farm

The Adventures of Pahwoo and Her Friends

Grace Under Pressure Publishing
P.O. Box 337
Bell Buckle, TN 37020

graceunderpressure.com